Constance Maude Neville

Behind the Arras

Constance Maude Neville

Behind the Arras

ISBN/EAN: 9783337024031

Printed in Europe, USA, Canada, Australia, Japan

Cover: Foto ©Andreas Hilbeck / pixelio.de

More available books at **www.hansebooks.com**

A Novel.

BY

CONSTANCE MAUDE NEVILLE.

Behind the arras I'll convey myself,
To hear the process.
— Hamlet: Act III, Scene 3.

SAN FRANCISCO:

A. L. BANCROFT AND COMPANY,

721 MARKET STREET,

1877.

TO

THE MANY FRIENDS

WHO HAVE

ENCOURAGED ITS PUBLICATION,

THIS BOOK

IS

GRATEFULLY INSCRIBED.

BEHIND THE ARRAS.

BEHIND THE ARRAS.

BOOK FIRST.

CHAPTER I.

My business in this state
Made me a looker-on.
— Measure for Measure: Act V, Scene 1.

SCENE: The grounds of Bratton Hall, ——shire. A gently undulating surface, with here and there little knolls clothed with the greenest of grass and crowned with groups of stately oaks and majestic elms. Charmingly cool arbors covered with creeping vines whose flowers, peeping within through the interstices of the lattice work, seem to invite one with their delicious odors for a lounge on a warm day, are scattered in the little valleys formed by these hillocks. A murmur of waters is heard as a winding stream feeds a miniature lake, whose placid surface is screened from view by the weeping willows that fringe its banks. Shrubbery is in abundance everywhere, furnishing homes for multitudes of birds, and luxuriant shade for less sweet voiced mortals. Nor are flowers wanting in all their varied hues; but so artistically are they arranged that the brightest colors blend harmoniously, and nothing glaring meets the eye. This seemingly enchanted spot is surrounded by towering poplars which give character by their stiff beauty to the whole scene, and form the boundary line beyond which stretch far away on every side long vistas of rolling park land and verdant meadow.

The *dramatis personæ* are three: One, a man, tall and *distingué* in appearance as he approaches in the distance; by his side, the slight, graceful figure of a young girl who moves silently along with bent head, listening, it seems, to her companion. The two are Alva Ingolsby, a friend and visitor at Bratton Hall, and Lucy Egerton, the adopted daugher of Sir Griffith Egerton, Bart., its master. As they turn down one of the rose-bordered paths that lead to the lake before reaching the arbor in which, I, Julia Lifford, the third, am enjoying the cool of the afternoon and beguiling an hour before the dressing-bell sounds for dinner, with thoughts of days now long past and gone, let me, by way of prologue, say a few words gleaned from the recollections that have been uppermost in my mind—a prologue which I hope, unlike prologues in general, will not be totally without interest to you, my dear reader: the audience.

I am an old maid now; that is, if six-and-thirty years can make one; but long ago—when I was a blooming, and I may without vanity say, a pretty girl, having by this time lost all youth and freshness, and seeming a totally different person to myself—Griffith Egerton, a distant relative, but next in succession to the baronetcy and estate of my step-father, Sir Ralph Egerton, had come here to Bratton with his wife and only child, Guy, a boy of eleven years, for a week's visit during the shooting season. A dear old place was Bratton Hall then, with its mazy passages and antique nooks, and where, as a child, I loved to play, and was often lost in old, almost forgotten rooms. But of all my youthful days, the happiest were those when I could escape from the old house, and wander through these grounds with Louis Dunraven, my betrothed. They were happy days, too happy to last, for a moment's work shattered them for ever. One morning Louis went out for his favorite sport, taking young Guy Egerton with him. The two started together after breakfast, Guy, as I remember him, a handsome, impetuous boy, with a head full of wild tales of adventure, and with a boy's love for the marvelous. They were both in high spirits, laughing and talking as they walked down the avenue, their merry voices borne back to me as I watched them out of sight and hearing. They were gone all day, an unusual occurrence, and even when dinner time came, had not returned. We delayed the meal some time, and then lingered over it, but still they came not. Later we were all standing on the terrace, thinking they must indeed have found good sport and wandered far, when a group of men appeared in the avenue bearing some heavy burden between them.

Nature robed in the calm and gentle beauty of early evening was little in harmony—as how often many aching hearts can testify—with the sensation of dismal foreboding and horror that then crept slowly over me, paralyzing every nerve. Such a feeling can only be understood by one who has parted cheerily from a loved one in the morning, to see him brought home at night as was mine, for that heavy burden was my own, my darling Louis, dead; mortally wounded by a shot through the lungs. What was hardest to bear, and is most trying to remember even now, was that we had no last words—no parting.

The terrible shock was more than my strength could withstand, and for years after my mind was not my own. When, at last, reason returned, it was only by degrees that memory came back to me. I was alone in the world, my step-father dead and gone, and Sir Griffith Egerton installed as master of Bratton Hall. My step-father, whom I loved as an own parent, was a widower and childless, and to Sir Griffith he had left all his private fortune in trust for me, requesting him to care for me as his own. Right well has Sir Griffith followed the provisions of the will, and has allowed me to remain here in my old home. But no one could ever fill the vacant place in my heart. Never have my affections been given to other than Louis Dunraven, for with Moore do I believe that,

"Those who have truly loved, never forget."

Close upon that fearful event, his tragical death, followed the inquest. The evidence clearly and circumstantially established the fact that he had been murdered, and pointed to young Guy Egerton as the perpetrator of the crime, his sudden flight and continued absence after the commission of the act, for since that fatal day he had never re-appeared, satisfying the coroner's jury—though a motive for the deed was sought for in vain—that the shooting was not accidental, and by their verdict they charged him with willful murder. None know except himself, if he still be living, what were the true causes of the tragedy enacted in the lonely wood—whether he be really guilty or innocent; and though the mention of his name is forbidden in our household, and all that could bring to mind the fact that he ever existed has long since been banished from the place by order of his father, in short, though his guilt is regarded as an accepted fact by all, still, I have ever believed the poor boy innocent of the terrible offense laid to him by the jury.

Shortly after the loss of their son, Sir Griffith and Lady Egerton adopted a child, a little, fair-haired imp of a girl, self-willed and passionate. But, lo! suddenly a change came o'er the spirit of her dream, and behold in yonder gentle creature, again approaching with her companion, the subject of a wonderful metamorphosis. She still retains the beautiful hair of her childhood, which some people, when anger or envy curls their lip, would sneeringly call red; but by no means is it that ordinary shade associated in our minds, as often in reality, with freckles. It most resembles burnished gold, shaded by the faintest tinge of red, and is now brought back in waves from the low, broad white forehead, and caught in a Grecian knot behind the ears. Beneath dark eyebrows, and long dark lashes, shine bright black eyes that can sparkle with merriment or

flash forth brief signals of the willful spirit within; but quite natural to them is the rarer, more soft and warmer light that now
lingers under the drooping lids, whispering of a sweet and gentle
disposition. The determined mouth and chin denote strength of
will, and it may be a trifle of obstinacy. Altogether it is a striking
rather than a strictly pretty face, but a pleasing and a fascinating
one for all that—one that is apt to send you off into wondering spec-
ulations as to the effect which worldly trials may have upon the combined strength and sweetness of her nature.

To describe her companion is a not less pleasing task. He has
reached that time of life when a man's character is formed; and,
looking back with a smile upon the follies of boyhood, he can yet
feel that there are years of an appreciative and still youthful enjoyment of life before him. His well-knit frame is above the middle
height, and there is a certain dignified ease and frank courteousness
in his manner that rarely proceeds from high-breeding alone; or,
when it does, is not so perfect and whole-souled as when culture
acts merely as a guide through the channels of refinement, for impulses of the heart naturally good. He has a handsome face, well-
cut features, and in repose a thoughtful, pre-occupied expression.
Hair, whiskers, and mustache are a dark brown. The eyebrows,
though not heavy, yet seem to cast a shadow on the changeable
eyes beneath, which vary in color from the lightest shade of violet
to a darker and warmer tint of gray—changeable in expression as
in color, sometimes laughing, sometimes grave, often sad;—but for
that indescribable shadow, one might read his very soul in their
otherwise clear depths. And his smile—how quickly it chases the
gloom from his eyes, and lights his entire countenance in a but too
fleeting joyousness.

As they come within hearing of my place of concealment—I say
concealment, because I can both see and hear, though unseen myself—he, in a full voice, deep without gruffness, says to her: "Let
us rest on the bench outside this arbor, Miss Egerton. You must
feel fatigued with our long ramble, and I fear it was very selfish in
me to lead you on and on simply because I enjoyed your conversation."

"You alone cannot plead selfishness, Mr. Ingolsby, for I became
so interested in the subject we were talking about that I quite forgot I was keeping you from your afternoon ride, and it is too late
now. But tell me: Do you really leave us so soon as next week?"

"Yes. I have some business of importance to attend to in town,
and I have been playing the idler here a long time; but now Mam-
mon calls me peremptorily from Paradise."

A pause while they seat themselves on the bench which runs around the outside of my arbor; then the softer voice says, while its owner's fingers slowly pull a rose to pieces:

"You have spoken of a change in me since your first visit two years ago—would you like to know the cause?"

"I should, indeed," Ingolsby replies, twirling his hat in his hands as he leans forward with his elbows on his knees. "Do you know, Miss Egerton, that I have actually been upon the point of asking you the cause several times, but fearing you might think my inquisitiveness bordered on impertinence."

"Yes? How very absurd. I'll tell you, then; but you mustn't think me egotistical, for you are the only one to whom I would speak on the subject of my uninteresting self. Do you remember that day two years ago when you gave me a lecture on temper?"

"I do recollect something of the sort; yes. What did I say? But I shouldn't expect you to remember my words, when I can't do it myself. Of course you forgot what I said the very next minute."

"On the contrary, so great an impression did they make on my mind, for I got very angry"—

"I remember that, distinctly."

"Don't interrupt me, please," with a gentle tap with the point of her parasol. "I say, so great an impression did they make on my mind that I can repeat your very words. Listen and judge for yourself if I had not reason for anger. 'Miss Egerton' you began in a solemn tone; 'let me have a few words with you on a rather painful, but to me, most interesting subject, and believe me I do not wish to hurt or wound your feelings, for I speak from motives of pure kindness to yourself—ahem!'"

"Not a bad sort of a prelude that, barring the 'ahem!' I don't think I was quite guilty of that."

"I'll not be positive that you cleared your throat at that point of your remarks. But let me go on, please. 'My dear child'—

"Oh, come now; I never called you that."

"Yes, indeed, you did—but it was two years ago; you mustn't forget that. But I shall never get through if you keep on in this way. I sha'n't tell you another word until you promise not to interrupt me again."

"I promise," in a solemn voice, as he holds up his right hand.

"'My dear child, you must be conscious of possessing, to speak candidly, a most ungovernable temper, and *brusque*, unpleasing manners.' Not a word, remember your promise. I listened with pretended indifference, but your words stung me to the quick. My blood was boiling with anger while you calmly went on: 'Why cultivate and foster these disagreeable traits which make yourself and all about you unhappy and miserable? With your strength of character, at present perverted into obstinacy, you might make yourself what you should wish to be. A great man noted for his good humor once said: "It matters little that you have the worst possible temper by nature if you have the best possible control over it by philosophy;" and he was a living example of his own theory.' You were continuing in the same strain, when I with some saucy words broke away from you, and you left next day thinking your kind words wasted—Hush! yes, they were kind words, though I thought them not so then—and that you had made the perverse girl hate you. Was it not so?" and she glanced at him archly. "Candidly, and without nonsense, was it not so?"

A shade of seriousness comes over Ingolsby's face at her words, and he answers in a low tone, not entirely free from embarrassment: "To deal candidly with you, Miss Egerton, and eschew all badinage—yes, I will confess that I left with a heavy heart, expecting and fearing that your worst traits would grow with your growth and strengthen with your strength. But it has become lighter as I have since remarked the gradual change for the better in you. Now I reproach myself that I did not see more clearly and leave those unlucky words unspoken; for I cannot be vain enough to imagine that they could have had any influence with you—those unlucky words that seem only to have been treasured up against me."

"No, no, Mr. Ingolsby, don't—please don't say that. It was those words that worked the change. I tried at first not to remember them, but they would come unbidden to my mind again and again, and the wish to try the philosophical experiment grew upon me. Then I thought of the abominable disposition with which I was born, and with which philosophy would have to contend single-handed, and despair seized upon me. Still I could not banish the idea, and on the impulse of the moment I made the effort, and the battle began in real earnest. The struggle in my mind was continual, and often was I tempted to give up the fight; but my pride was roused; you were right, I had a will, and would not yield. When angry words rose to my lips, I bit my tongue and substituted kind ones, although it nearly choked me at times to think that people might imagine I was growing amiable. But at last the reward came: life seemed happier and brighter; every one seemed to love me better, and it was such exquisite pleasure to feel that I deserved their love. I imagined I had conquered, till you came this time, and I thought of telling you all—of the victory your kindly-spoken words had enabled me to achieve; and then the war I had to wage against the thought that the avowal **would** flatter you too much, showed that the fortress was not yet won. But you see that I **have, at least, gained another** outwork by telling you this."

There is silence for a minute, she looking undecided whether to stay or run away, but quite decided as to the wish that she had left all unspoken; he, looking down at the bent head beside him with pleasure and admiration in his eyes, is the first to speak. Taking her hand, which she yields passively, he says:

" Will you answer me one little question?" There is no answer, and he continues: " Was it simply the wish to test your strength and the hope of conquering yourself unaided and alone that led to this marvelous change? Or, was there," and his voice sinks so low as to be almost inaudible to me, " any trifling thought of pleasing another? Tell me, truly—Lucy," and he bows his head low to catch her answer.

Lucy evidently understands him, for the blood rushes to her face as she turns it from him towards the latticed walls of the arbor, and her eyes are soft and gentle; but as she lets them rest for an instant upon the twining climatis a bright willful look comes into them, and still holding her head away from him, she replies: " The thought of succeeding was so absorbing and overpowering that it has chased all recollection of a motive from my mind."

Ingolsby's lips close tightly with a pained expression, but open again to speak, when, in spite of my efforts to control it, an unlucky sneeze warns them of my presence.

As Lucy's head appears around the door-post, I start with well feigned surprise; ask how long she has been there, and, yawning, say: I must have slept some time.

I am no heroine, and do not hesitate to say that I have no foolish horror of what is commonly called "eaves-dropping;" at least, I am honest enough, I hope, to confess a belief shared, but sedulously concealed, by nine-tenths of mankind. If one's purpose is a good one, or even a harmless one, where it pleases yourself and hurts no one, bribing servants, or making use of a key-hole for other purposes than locking a door, or any little trifle of that sort, is to my mind, quite allowable.

Curl not your lip in scorn, O reader, but only if you belong to the other one-tenth will your sneer be genuine; for were I never to feign ignorance where I know or suspect much, and were some others as well as myself to have practiced, so far as the habit of eaves-dropping is concerned, as it is thought popular to preach, the knowledge that has enabled me to construct this little tale had never been mine.

I am rewarded, in the present instance, by a kiss from a pair of soft lips, and by a smile from Ingolsby; whereas, had I not practiced the harmless little deception, all would have felt uncomfortably embarrassed; or, had I discovered my whereabouts at first, Alva Ingolsby might never have heard what has caused the happy smile that has now returned to his face. But the warning bell clangs out on the soft evening air, and silently we leave the arbor, and wend our way back to the house to dress for dinner.

CHAPTER II.

Draw the curtain close.
We shall hear more anon.
— Henry VIII: Act V, Scene 2.

A FEW minute's walk beneath overhanging boughs brings us to an opening in the trees where involuntarily we pause as the house comes full in view with the rays of the setting sun falling upon its turrets and gables, enlivening the clinging ivy, and casting intense light and shade upon the old gray stones.

"The beauty of a serene and dignified old age," remarks Alva Ingolsby in a low tone, with a look of reverence in his eyes.

"It must have been massive and mighty once," says Lucy; "but papa has thrown out wings in every direction, until, like a spoilt child, its worst features have increased with age, and little good is perceptible except to the eye of a fond doting parent. I mean no disrespect to papa's taste, for to me it is beautiful with all its defects, but strange eyes can only see an incongruous and decidedly ugly building. Look at that broad balcony across the southern wing. It is better suited to a cottage than to this castle-like structure."

No word from Ingolsby; but the shadow darkens in his eyes, and we again move onward.

I cannot gainsay the justice of Lucy's criticism, although the place is so dear to me. It *is* a queer-looking structure. Of no particular shape now, whatever it may have been originally, wings jut out in every direction, no two of them being exactly alike. Some are low and rambling; some tower above the main building, while others reach to the principal roof only. Windows of every conceivable size and shape puncture the walls, and a few peep out from spots where it seems impossible that a room can be within. From numerous doors, narrow winding stairs lead into the grounds beneath. The grand entrance is reached by a flight of massive stone steps, low, broad and easy of ascent. And here one sees an odd whim of the owner, for they are guarded like the approach to the Ming Tombs of China, by animals in bronze. At each end of every step stands a dog, life size and natural. You first encounter a pair of fierce watch dogs that almost frighten you into retreating, dumb inanimate figures though they be. Provided you have courage to pass the two foremost, you are gazed at in your ascent by mastiffs, greyhounds, and Newfoundlands, and are finally ushered into the house by a pair of the dearest little poodles, that look flossy enough for petting and fondling. In fact it is a house or castle (I hardly know which to call it) that seems to have been thrown together utterly without plan, or formed from the discarded odds and ends of numerous designs: a place where one can feel supremely happy, or thoroughly miserable; in the seventh heaven or the depths of purgatory, according to one's disposition. 'Twould drive a neat housewife wild to keep its holes and corners in anything like order; it would kill a lazy man, with its innumerable steep winding stairs; delight young people with its mazes; please a student with the silence and solitude of its remote rooms; and surely, would it break the neck of every careless person, with its three steps up, and five steps down, in the darkest, most obscure passages. This is Bratton Hall, the place where I was born and reared.

Two minutes and a half, and we have ascended the winding pathway across the lawn, choosing it in preference to the broad, dusty avenue. And now, we pass through the ranks of watchful canines, and enter the large square hall, adorned with carvings in oak. Here we part till dinner time. Lucy, with a burst of song, springs up the stairs to her room; Alva saunters away to the library; and I, more slowly and staidly, as becomes my years, cross the inlaid floor and proceed to my apartments, thinking of the confession so recently heard from Lucy's lips.

Now I know why the careless, passionate girl changed so marvelously into a thoughtful woman. Formerly, none dare thwart her slightest wish from fear of the storm that would be raised about their ears, and the dread of some practical joke in retaliation. Now, no one could be more considerate of the feelings and wishes of others than she. Truly sweet tempered has she become—not with the mawkish docility of one who is too phlegmatic or without sufficient depth of feeling to be otherwise, but with the sweetness of a strong nature, when all the sourness of uncharitableness is cast out, as if by force, and only that which is good retained, solely because it is good. A great change, verily! But the cause; is it love? *Qui vivra verra.*

Naturally gifted with a gentle and loving disposition, sympathetic and highly sensitive, Lucy, in her childhood, had been allowed to spring up with little or no training to guide and strengthen her good qualities. Taken by the Egertons from a father who implored their charity for his motherless child, at a time when they were in deep sorrow for the loss of their son, no definite plans were formed for her future. A young child, scarcely more than a baby, coming into the midst of a lonely household, she soon became a pet with her odd little ways, which even then showed themselves; and neither the eccentric Sir Griffith nor his trouble-shunning wife being competent trainers of a female child—I, at the time, was incapacitated by illness from lending my aid—she grew up in fact quite as she pleased; now petted and praised; again, scolded and blamed. When she arrived at length at an age when some course in regard to education and her future life could no longer be postponed, the odd whim seized Sir Griffith of adopting the child as his own, and, overcoming his wife's scruples in that respect, he did so; straightway installed a governess in the house, and forbade that Miss Egerton, as in fact he had long since given orders that she should be called, should be told that she ever had another name. Never from the first moment of her arrival at Bratton Hall, allowed to hear anything of her past life, whatever dim recollections of it she may have had, of course, at her early age, soon faded from her memory, and at this present moment Lucy has not the very faintest suspicion of her origin, but looks upon herself as the true and lawful daughter of Sir Griffith and Lady Egerton. Miss Biggerstaff, the governess, though read in all the book lore, and versed in all the arts and graces, a knowledge of which polite society deems essential to the well-being of every young lady, was yet, unfortunately for her pupil, a very weak woman. Lucy's mind, though thoroughly educated and accomplished, was not disciplined. I say everything when I say her training lacked

"A mother's eye—a mother's fostering care."

Sensitive to the smallest kindness, and shrinking from harsh words, yet ashamed to acknowledge what was soft and womanly in her nature, she assumed a brusqueness that was at war with her true feelings; and an impatience of obstacles in her path soon developed into temper. Altogether, the girl was not lovable to those who had not discovered sterling good qualities, when two years ago Alva Ingolsby came to stay at Bratton Hall. At first he and Lucy were good friends; but without warning, and, as we all thought, without cause, she declared war against him, refusing even to bid him good-bye on the evening which ended his last visit here. From that time there was a marked change in her manner: at first becoming irritable and shunning companionship, her demeanor soon settled into a pleasing gentleness broken only on rare occasions by outbursts of her old temper; and when Miss Biggerstaff left us a few months ago, she was with reason proud of her pupil.

How much time I have wasted in thought! Only ten minutes left to dress, and then down to the drawing room. I am the first to enter, and I take my place at an open window beneath the heavy damask curtains, from where, not being in the mood for conversation, I can watch the others come in, and, perchance, keep dinner waiting a little beyond the usual time, before I make my appearance. Not a very amiable proceeding, perhaps; but one, in its results, exceedingly amusing, if Sir Griffith, according to custom, becomes restless and stamps about, and his wife throws imploring glances alternately at him and at the door, as though that poor piece of wooden usefulness could aid her.

Ah! here comes Lucy. She glances around, sees no one, and seating herself at the piano, rattles off a brilliant prelude. Strange that it can be the same fingers which immediately after draw forth soft, pathetic sounds. What a pretty picture she makes, sitting there in a muslin dress of a delicate shade of green, the open sleeves showing her rounded arms, and the color contrasting with the pure whiteness of her skin.

A ray of sunshine, beaming through a western window, falls on the golden hair, lighting it up and bringing out the auburn tint to perfection. The entrance of Alva Ingolsby is unnoticed as he comes in, looking better than when last seen, for to him, as to most men, full-dress is becoming. He also gives a swift glance around, and, perhaps, a morsel of my dress peeps from under the curtains, or it may only be instinct that causes him to lift it and discover to view my old faded self. A smile, and he drops the curtain into place again without a word, turns toward another window, and regards the scene without. Lucy stops, turns, sees him, and then recommences her music. But now her touch is weak and less decided, and perhaps the air is not pleasing to that dark figure in the window, for it draws him not towards it. A moment, and then it changes to tones sharp, quick, and defiant—a sort of *noli me tangere* air. All is but dumb pantomime, yet how expressive!

Now appears on the scene, gliding into the room in a most ladylike manner, my Lady Egerton, who takes a mirror-studied pose on one of the sofas. As she reclines there, dressed in black velvet and diamonds, the former falling in soft, graceful folds, she looks a very handsome woman, and knows that she does. Of medium height, well-formed, but decidedly inclined to *embonpoint;* with skin smooth and unwrinkled; eyes and hair black; teeth white and even, she seems no more than forty, though in reality some years older. Of a phlegmatic disposition, she has glided through life, as she now glides through a room, always ladylike, always placid, allowing nothing to enter her mind that may ruffle that brow or whiten those locks.

The perfect antithesis of herself is her husband, who comes bustling into the room with a little, trotting step. A small, wiry man is he, quick and energetic, with a frequent motion of the head—bird-like in its briskness of movement. His hair, though snowy white, still strangely retains its stiffness, having none of that soft look so beautiful in grey hair, but being cropped close to the head, stands bristling forth in all directions, covering every inch of scalp, and leaving not one bald spot, in spite of his sixty-five years. His thick, overhanging, and grizzled eyebrows, which seem originally to have run at each other defiantly, are now locked in a close embrace, leaving no space between, and almost hiding a pair of small, piercing, blue eyes.

With his negligent style of dress, he looks just what he is—an eccentric old gentleman; unfortunately one who has plenty of means to carry out his odd whims and fancies. Were he a poor man, much superfluous energy would be carried off in that grandly sublime work of most men's lives—money-making.

As it is he is nothing but a busy idler, always perfectly happy when working over something that amounts to nothing in the end. To-day, he has been overseeing the erection of a sty, built "with all the modern conveniences," for his favorite Berkshires; and, occasionally, in his impatience to have it completed, lending a hand himself, as he now informs the company, to my Lady's great disgust—disgust, shown by a most energetic (for her) curl of the lip, and tapping of one pretty foot. In such glowing terms does the old gentleman speak of his latest hobby, that one can almost imagine him describing some modern villa or Castle of the Graces. How much more acceptable would the pearl be to a poor family of the village! Interesting as the subject is, yet the thought of dinner is still more so after his afternoon's labor, and now he starts up, pulling out his watch much in the style of Mr. Weller, Senior, and announces in quick sharp tones:

"After seven, and that child not here yet!" (Well grown "child" think I in my corner.) "Think I'll advise her to begin dressing in time—before breakfast might do—might give her enough time," and he walks with a fretful air to the fireplace. "Or, I'll give her some work to do that will furnish her with an appetite when dinner time comes," falling with a thump into an arm-chair. "Suppose you give her a blowing up, old lady," as he jumps up again, and takes a few quick turns.

I, in my hiding-place, fancy Lady Egerton blowing one up; Alva looks whimsical and whispers to Lucy who laughs and glances towards the curtain that conceals me.

"You appear to be jolly, young lady," says her papa, "when you are my age, your good humour will depend more on a good dinner, than it does now. Agnes, you must really lecture Miss Julia Lifford, for you women know best how to apply that lash—the tongue. In a quarrel, your sly little under-cuts are much more effective than our strong rough language," and he rushes to one of the windows.

Should he come to mine! I tremble and wish myself well out of this scrape.

A few more brisk turns, and he stands in the centre of the room, with hands in pockets, eyes bent on the carpet, and quotes in a low tone:

> "The lords of Creation, men we call,
> And they think they rule the whole;
> But they're much mistaken, after all,
> For they're under woman's control."

and with another drawing forth of the watch, makes directly for my place of concealment.

A moment he stands, like Nemesis, with arm raised upholding the curtain; with brow puckered and lips pursed; then just as dinner is announced, with a sort of dive he stoops for my hand, and tucking it under his arm without a word, strides to the door, crosses the broad hall to the dining-room, and dropping me by my seat, takes his place at the foot of the table, leaving the others to follow at their leisure.

CHAPTER III.

Let it serve for table-talk.

— Merchant of Venice: Act III. Scene 5.

"OUR last day of quiet;" remarks Lady Egerton, breaking a long silence, as the soup is removed. "To-morrow our first guests of the season will arrive. You know we do not look upon you as a guest, Mr. Ingolsby, but quite as one of the family."

"Thanks. But I am afraid your ladyship thinks that I have made myself so much at home, as to have become a most unpleasant member of your family."

"No, she doesn't, Ingolsby!" cries Sir Griffith. "She told me in confidence the other day, that you were the only man she ever saw, who did not require more waiting upon than any two women. That wife of mine is so fond of quiet, that I often wonder how she ever—"

"Married you, Griffith? It *is* strange, is it not? Perhaps I hoped to smooth out the wrinkles in your character, not suspecting that they were too deep to be effaced. I don't know what will become of the county, now, that that other oddity, Jolliffe Tufnell, has returned to the neighborhood."

"He is a most unprepossessing man to me," says Lucy; "and yet he's quite a privileged character, I believe; invited everywhere, just because he has courage to set the world at defiance, and do as he pleases. I suppose people look on him as a sort of fascinating horror."

"Do you know the story of his life, Miss Egerton?" asks Ingolsby. "I have often heard it hinted at, but no more."

"Oh, yes, I heard it long before I knew him. When he was a young man of about twenty, he was very wild and unruly, but of an exceedingly generous disposition; and being the cause of a friend's becoming involved in a quarrel with some professional gambler, a noted shot, took the whole affair upon his own shoulders. The friend, I forget his name, was weak and unmanly enough to allow this, and the two met. Jolliffe Tufnell was slightly wounded in the cheek, and still bears the scar; but the other was killed on the spot. It has always been a wonder to me how men of sense can call these meetings 'affairs of *honor*.' Is murder *honorable?*"

"Don't talk of what you don't understand, my child," interrupted Sir Griffith; "no woman can comprehend a man's feelings where his honor is involved."

"Perhaps not, papa; but I at least understand this much: Murder is always in the intent to kill, and what man with a human nature can stand up before his antagonist's pistol, and not have the wish pass through his mind, though he may not acknowledge it to himself, that he may not be the one to fall, but, necessarily, his adversary. In my mind, it requires more courage to brave public opinion, and refuse to fight a duel, than to stand up as a target to be fired at."

"If the world was arranged by such as you, Lucy," he replies, "there would be no crime, and peace would reign as it should nowhere but in Paradise. This, unfortunately, is *not* Paradise; therefore, live in hopes of entering it some day, and take things as they are for the present. Have you anything more to say of Mr. Jolliffe Tufnell?"

"A very little more," she says, looking a trifle abashed, and yet, with the air of one unconvinced, and firm in her own opinion. "He became gloomy and peculiar from that time, and deserting his gay companions, has led a wandering, lonely life, until quite lately, when he surprised every one by settling down on his estate. One cause of the great change in him was the loss of his affianced bride, who refused to marry him after the duel—and who can blame her— for oh, the horror of being united to one with the stain of blood upon his soul!"

A pause; for Lucy's remarks have brought painful memories to some of us. I glance up presently from my plate, and catch a glimpse of a dusky flush dying out of Ingolsby's face, leaving it very, very pale. Can it be that he was ever a party to one of these affairs? It is possible; for nothing is known of him beyond the facts that he is an Englishman who lived many years in America, from whence he brought letters of introduction from lawyers of eminence to his own countrymen, standing high in the same profession. He shows no desire to break the silence, and after a short interval, Sir Griffith asks, in a constrained tone:

"Is Squire Strong coming, Agnes?"

"Oh, of course," Lady Egerton answers. "We expect Lady Caroline Hamilton, you know, and what pleasure for her would there be without her rough admirer with his eight thousand a year?"

"And we are to have the German heiress, Miss Van Praet," exclaims Sir Griffith. "Set your cap for her, Ingolsby, and live in idleness the rest of your life."

"I'm too much afraid of her guardian, with his scowling brows and aggressive features," is the response. "Nothing but a title will do for him."

"'Sits the wind in that corner?'" quotes Sir Griffith. "Well, the charming heiress will find plenty here to exercise her powers of fascination upon. Let me see. There will be Lord Eversley, with his eternal lisp, and Lord Mortland, Sir Henry Beresford, and Lord Lennox, all quite willing to barter their freedom for a check-book."

"Why don't you give him a list of the ladies, papa?" Lucy asks, "and let him judge what chance of pleasure there is in store for himself."

"Because, my dear, when I mention a lady's name, I begin to think of the charming owner, and forget the rest of the story."

"Then it is to be hoped you will place your wife at the head of all lists of fair ones," I remark, laughingly. "You tell us, Lucy, what ladies are coming."

"Oh, the greatest number," she replies, checking them off on her fingers. "Lady Fullerton, and her daughter Jessie; such a pert little thing, but good-hearted in the extreme; Lady Fortescue and her three daughters—"

"Such beauties, Ingolsby!" interrupts Sir Griffith; "tall and gracefully slender as lily stalks, with loveliest shade of amber complexions, and blooming noses."

"For shame, papa! They cannot help their appearance, poor things. Then there are Emily Wilbraham and Ruth Ferrers—"

"Dashing, gentlemanly young women," comments Sir Griffith.

"And Lady Juno Althorp—"

"On the look-out for a third—take care, Alva."

"Lady Lyndhurst—"

"And *her* daughters," croaks Sir Griffith.

"Maud, Mabel, and Mildred," continues Lucy.

"Rather pretty girls," adds Sir Griffith, in a 'faint-praise' tone; "but most exasperatingly alike, in appearance, character and dress. No man would care to marry one of them, and feel that two other fellows were as lucky as himself. One likes to think that one has carried off the prize, and not left *fac similes* for other less-deserving mortals. Eh, Ingolsby? But go on with your list, Lucy, and banish that deprecating look."

With a smile struggling on her lips, she proceeds:

"Mrs. Archibald Smythe, Miss Wilhelmina Smythe, Miss Andromica Smythe, Miss Lavinia Smythe and Miss Araminta Smythe."

"'Ye gods and little fishes,' what an array! All vitality and character crushed out of them by the weight of their very names, poor things. What induced you to ask such namby-pamby creatures, Agnes? To form the necessary background, I suppose, to show off the other young ladies to advantage—useful in their way, anyhow.

But where are you going to put them all? They will be frightened out of their wits at some of our ghostly old rooms." Then a twinkle comes into his eyes, and he asks rather abruptly: "Do you believe in ghosts, Alva, my boy?"

"Well—really—Sir Griffith," is the hesitating answer, as astonishment takes the place of amusement on Ingolsby's face, "the question is so unexpected, I hardly know—"

"'Know thyself,' says Shakspeare," from Sir Griffith. "So—you don't know on the instant what you believe, eh? And you want time to remember what your opinion is, before you say black is black, eh? Why, you must have your thoughts as firmly packed away as those of Mr. Toots."

"Don't be so hard on him as all that, papa," says Lucy; "they are only a little rusty for want of use down here in our stupid old place."

"And pray, who is most unkind and hard in their remarks now, Miss Egerton," asks Ingolsby. "Sir Griffith, now that I have had time to dive into the depths of my mental luggage-room, I find the belief in ghosts quite snugly stowed away."

"Oh, horrible!" shudders Lady Egerton: "What could have induced you to bring up such a dismal subject, my dear?"

"Something that I chanced to hear to-day; a rumor; just a little trifle about a wandering spirit, who clanks her chain at the witching time of night. That is, I don't quite remember the sex, but it must be a female, for they say it is troublesome and noisy," answers Sir Griffith, and continues: "Julia, did you ever hear of any tradition or legend connected with—a—any portion of our mansion?"

"What, papa?" exclaims Lucy, "a legend—this house? Oh, do tell us all about it, please."

I, rather puzzled and a little alarmed, answer: "No, Sir Griffith, I don't remember to have heard of any legend in our family. In fact I have always been rather sorry that we had no romantically haunted chamber, or anything of that sort. But why do you ask?"

"Perhaps you will feel rather sorry for another reason before long, my dear," he says, with a slight twinkle in his eye. "But Ingolsby, you say that you believe in spirits; let us hear your reasons."

"I have none worth giving, I assure you, sir. I never saw a ghost. I never knew anybody who ever saw one, and yet I cannot but believe in them. In this way: I do not believe that they are able to speak to mortals either with words or rappings; but that the image of a person who is dead can be seen by the living, I do believe. Whether the so-called spirit is the departed soul or a nameless something conjured up by the brain, and only perceptible to the one mind, of course no one can tell. My theory is this: The mind when excited, sometimes unconsciously falls into a sudden sleep or stupor, and then the form of a loved or hated one who is gone appears as in a dream, when one sees people life-like yet unnatural. Only that we know when we have dreamed, but in this case of the stupor of the brain we are not aware of having lost consciousness for a moment, but the ghost is said to 'vanish' when it is simply the mind recovering itself."

" A very good theory, my dear fellow," approvingly remarks Sir Griffith; " but one that would not at all suit the Spiritualists, eh ?"

" How can you call a theory 'good' on such a subject, Griffith ?" says his wife. " Though I must confess that I consider Mr. Ingolsby's idea far superior to the vulgar superstitions about those nasty cold, clammy, noiseless creatures, who have not the manners to remain outside of a locked door."

" Why it is a perfect theory, mamma," says Lucy, with animation; "just what has been in my mind this long time, only I could not find words to express it."

" A good reason for its perfection, pet, its having been in your sensible little head," rejoins her mother.

A pout and a toss of the sensible little head, is the only answer.

"But good folks all," say I, " you seem to have forgotten the cause of this discussion. Tell us, cousin Griffith, of what you were thinking when you frightened us all with your dreadfully mysterious question: ' Do you believe in ghosts ?' "

" Oh, nothing, nothing," answers he, rising from the table, the cloth by this time having been removed; "that is, nothing of any consequence, only—I don't care to smoke just now, Ingolsby, so you can accompany the ladies to the drawing-room, if you have no taste for a solitary weed." He is at the door now, and turning towards me with a sly look, says: "Only, Julia, I thought it but right to warn you in case that you should hear any uncommon noises in the wing to the left of your rooms"—and he pauses.

We all sit with mingled feelings of curiosity and horror, expecting to hear something that will make our blood run cold; I wondering why a goblin should choose my neighborhood of all others, when he opens the door and goes out, but before closing it, puts in his head and continues, "I have given orders for some alterations to be made there, and the men will soon be at work."

His peculiar chuckling laugh is heard as he passes the open window, while we simultaneously burst into a chorus of hearty laughter—all but Lady Egerton who smiles blandly—and I know full well that I have received my punishment for that shocking behavior before dinner.

CHAPTER IV.

—— Fate is above us all;
We struggle, but what matters our endeavor?
Our doom is gone beyond our own recall;
May we deny or mitigate it? Never!
—L. E. L.

LATER in the evening, when Sir Griffith has returned from his twilight ramble, looking as innocent as possible of ever having done an unkind action; and while Lucy and Ingolsby are deeply engaged at the piano over snatches of pretty music, his rich baritone and her highly cultivated *mezzo* soprano occasionally blending in a duet, the question is mooted between the other three members of our party of five: In what manner shall Lucy Egerton's coming *fête*-day be celebrated?

"Let us have a good old fashioned dance on the lawn," proposes Sir Griffith, "with tables set in the grounds for the peasantry. On such an occasion they should have as much enjoyment as their betters."

"That is all very well in theory, Griffith," returns his wife, as she reclines on a sofa, and fans herself languidly, "but you fail to take into consideration that it is more than likely to rain, and then, how are we to entertain our guests in this gloomy old house on a wet day? And even if it prove fine weather, still, remaining in the open air with thin dresses, which, of course, would have to be worn, we should all catch cold."

"Like Dundreary's ' birds of *a* feather,' eh? Well, Agnes, suppose you think of something better suited to you birds of gay but airy plumage."

"If you try to remain quiet for a moment, Griffith, I'll tell you what has been in my mind all along. Do sit *in* the chair, not on the edge. You look like Sampson Brass sliding off one of Quilp's uncomfortable seats."

"Much obliged, my dear," gathering himself up and sinking into the depths of a large arm chair, which almost conceals his small frame. "Now, I suppose, you will say I resemble old grandfather Smallweed."

"You do very much, dear. However, it doesn't matter, for you never could appear in a comfortable attitude. This is my idea, and it will be so much less trouble than anything else. Have a large dinner party, and in the evening let the young people dance."

"And who the deuce cares for trouble, or anything of the kind, on an occasion like this, eh?" is the excited answer, as he struggles from the depths of his chair, and stamps about like a caged lion. "I'm sure I don't, old lady; and I don't propose to have any humdrum old fogy dinner party on my child's birthday, you may be sure. If you can't think of anything better than that, why, I'll make a bargain to pay the doctor's bill for every one who catches cold, and just see if it won't be a success."

"How very unrest you are," is the cool remark from his wife. "Allow me to assume your prerogative of quoting, my dear husband, and remark that this scheme of yours is 'the insane root that takes the reason prisoner.'"

"Madam!" pausing before her, "permit me to reply in the same manner, 'though this be madness, yet there's method in it.'"

"May I make a suggestion, Sir Griffith?" I inquire, anxious to stop the discussion.

"Oh, you can make as many as you please, but I won't promise to conform to them," is the *brusque* answer as he resumes his walk. "Do you know, sir, I should rather like your plan, if it were not for Lady Egerton's sensible ——"

"Fiddlesticks!" finishes he.

I continue: "I have always thought that in this rambling old place a masquerade ——"

"The—very—thing!" interrupts he, emphasizing each word with a resounding clap of the hands, that makes his wife wince, and causes the two singers to turn from their music.

"What's the matter, papa?" Lucy asks.

"Only a little discussion brought to a strangely happy conclusion, my dear. But you go on with your thrumming, and send that young man over here; we want his opinion on a matter of importance. Don't look so doleful; I'll return him safe and unhurt in half a minute."

"Why, you naughty papa," she says, with cheeks flushing; "how can you have a secret from your own child," and turns away to her "thrumming."

Alva joins us in our corner, and stands awaiting the pleasure of his host.

"What may the knotty question be that I'm to have the honor of deciding?" he asks.

"Hear, hear!" cries Sir Griffith. "Lucy, this young man is making dreadfully bad puns on your words."

"How could he do otherwise with such poor material?" she replies, glancing over her shoulder.

"Miss Egerton means that her words are so perfect as to be unsusceptible of improvement, and that is why my pun, unpremeditated I assure you, was so lacking in merit," explains Alva.

"That's right, always pay a compliment when you have a chance, my boy," says Sir Griffith, "flatter in the right way, at the right time, and in large doses, and you'll be a favorite with the women."

"Very true," adds Lady Egerton, "but the great difficulty is to hit the right time and way. A flattering remark had better be left unsaid than spoken in a bungling fashion."

Were it not for her ladyship's good humoured smile, one might imagine a sly hit at Ingolsby's *calembour*, and accompanying compliment.

"Right again," returns her husband. "However, it is not the art of pleasing we wish to discuss, but a question less abstruse. Now, Ingolsby," lowering his voice, "we want to celebrate Lucy's birthday in a suitable style. My proposition of a *fête champêtre* is denounced by my old woman here, with remarks on the uncertainty of the weather, and the certainty of our all catching colds. She has no more romance in her composition than a modern young lady, but wishes to have a stiff, formal dinner party, forsooth. Why, the very thought of one makes my hair more on end than ever," running his fingers with a whimsical look through his bristling locks. "This sensible creature here," patting my head, "suggests a masquerade which strikes my fancy; and yours too, Agnes, I'm sure. For if you don't want trouble, what is easier than to bid your guests, and don the skin of some unlucky ancient who can be murdered for the occasion without weapons or blood-spilling. What say you, Alva; or can you think of anything better yourself?"

"Nothing could be better, sir, and it is sure to give pleasure to the young lady herself. But by-the-by, I heard her express a liking for private theatricals the other day, and why not let the most interested person choose for herself?"

"But my dear fellow, we wish to give her a surprise. Let me see though," pondering, with his forefinger on his nose. "Yes, she shall decide!" He winks, takes out his pocket-book, and after scribbling a few words, tears the leaf into strips, which he places in a small Japanese cup from an *étagère*, and going over to Lucy, says: "Here child, draw your *fête*. Ha-ha! but for your life don't read it."

"My fate! Why papa, what's all this about? You surely don't wish me to tempt Fate without learning its edict? That's hardly fair, is it, Mr. Ingolsby?"

"Ingolsby will tell you that 'all's fair in love and war,' and—don't blush, my dear—this is a case of great show of love on my part towards an ungrateful little baggage."

"But papa dear, I'd rather not draw. I don't like chances of any kind; not even one so simple as this."

"Nonsense, Lucy, don't be foolish. I bid you draw, and you are simply to carry out the order of 'children, obey your parents,' which is to be found in some good book, and 'when found,' *et cetera, et cetera.*"

"Please, papa, don't ask me. I have a prejudice against anything of this sort, and believe it has more influence on one's life than is imagined. It might perhaps have an effect on mine—an unlucky effect."

"Don't be ridiculous, child. Of course it will have an effect. Be the cause of spoiling your dress, perhaps—which I shall have to replace—and in the new one you captivate some fine cavalier who falls in love at first sight. So romantic, you know—not a bit unlucky—for I'm not an old tyrant, and will not carry out the plot by forcing you to marry him against your will. Don't waste time—" this a trifle sternly.

"No, no, papa, I had rather not. I made up my mind once never to tempt fate to do me an ugly turn, and I never will."

She turns to the music stand to find a sheet of music, and Sir Griffith still holds forth the cup, an obstinate, angry look about his mouth.

"Are you gone daft, child?"

"Not that I am aware of, papa. Only we all have our little prejudices, and this is one of mine."

"I'm sure Ingolsby here would much prefer witnessing the real thing, than this little parody of Shakspeare. 'Much ado,' indeed, and 'nothing' with a vengeance."

"I am afraid I shall lose in your estimation, Sir Griffith, when I say that I have actually never seen the play," says Ingolsby, as he turns over the music upon the piano, with evident disrelish for this discussion. "In truth," he adds, laughingly, "Shakspeare is not much of a favorite with me."

"Your want of appreciation is nothing to boast of, young man. Come now, Lucy, stop fussing over that music, and do as you're bid. I will take all the responsibility of your broken vow upon my own shoulders." She looks up hesitatingly. "No more nonsense, girl, I command you," he says, sternly, and Sir Griffith can look very stern when he pleases. A quick flush spreads over Lucy's face. She bites her lip and throws back her head. Pride does not relish a command even from a parent. But he is her father and she must obey, so reluctantly she puts forth her hand and draws from the cup a slip of paper, which he takes from her before she can see what is written upon it.

"Remember then, papa, it was by your order I did this, not from any wish of my own. On your head rest the consequences."

"As solemnly spoken as though you were invoking a curse for some foul crime. Pretty thanks for all my trouble."

"Don't be angry, papa dear," she pleads, throwing her arms round his neck and kissing him. "I am nervous this evening," and she returns to the piano and runs her hands over the keys as she looks up at Ingolsby with a smile, and asks him if he is tired of music.

Sir Griffith rubbing his fingers on his cheek, and looking at them, mutters: "Tears, by Jove! and not mine either;" and as his hand opens in the act of raising it to his face, the chosen slip flutters to the floor, and as it lies there face upwards, I read the single word—Masquerade.

CHAPTER V.

—— Motley's the only wear.
— As You Like It: Act II, Scene 7.

THE twenty-fifth day of September, and Lucy Egerton's nineteenth birthday. Two weeks of preparation have passed since that evening on which her *fête*, or, as she persists in calling it her *fate*, was decided upon, and to-night the masquerade takes place. A busy, busy fortnight has it been to me, for the issuing of invitations to all the halls, lodges, parks, courts and granges in the neighborhood; and the preparation of my own and Lucy's costumes, without her knowledge, has been my share of work. We all have endeavored to keep her in ignorance of the style of entertainment, but it seems impossible that she cannot have guessed something of the truth; for, as she says, at her approach, "dark figures scuttle away like mice in the wainscot, leaving scraps of silk and ribbon to mark their passage, and the whole house wears an air of most uncomfortable mystery, while every one seems fully occupied with their own devices." Perhaps that is the reason why she has not been her own equably bright self, but has alternately moped about with drooping head and listless manner, or has been restless and brimming over with fun and mischief. Poor Ingolsby has been the patient subject of all her pranks, for he, having postponed his return to town until after the ball, and not being a woman, and therefore having the making of no dress for the occasion to superintend, has been left to the tender mercies of the capricious girl. They have quarreled perpetually; that is, she would take offense at some remark, while he would argue it out for the mere sake of argument, not because he thought himself in the right, and she would go off in high dudgeon, leaving him to wonder at her strange irritability. Here is a scrap of one of their many discussions, as I heard it through the open windows of the library, while enjoying the fresh air on the balcony without:

"May I ask what you have been reading, Miss Egerton?" as the noise is heard of a book sliding into the case.

"This is only a book I found on the table," is the answer. "Papa always feels uncomfortable when one is out of its place, for he says it spoils the look of the shelves. Did you ever hear such an idea? I have been reading ' Paradise Lost '—a work that I don't admire."

"Why? It is one of the most beautiful poems in the English language."

"Yes, I acknowledge that portions of it are surpassingly beautiful, and many passages ennobling in their tendencies. But I think that Milton was exceedingly wrong, if not a little blasphemous, to write words of his own imagining as being spoken by the Deity."

"He was a courageous man to do it, I admit, but not blasphemous, for they breathe forth a pure spirit of piety. Would you be willing to lose such a work from English literature for a few such squeamish scruples?"

"Indeed, I don't consider myself squeamish, in the least. Were those objectionable parts omitted, the poem would contain nothing to offend a Christian, and it would, to my mind, be perfect. I do not think that religion should, as a rule, be meddled with in either poetry or romance. It should be confined to books of theology."

"Were I a novelist," he says, "I should not think it a crime to inculcate religious doctrines between lighter subjects at every opportunity."

"You don't understand me," she replies, "or rather, I have not expressed myself properly. I mean that by way of instructing their readers, authors should not put down in black and white all the conflicting doubts on questions of religion they may see fit to make arise in the minds of their characters; doubts, which by being read, are impressed on the mind of the reader, and are not generally removed or counteracted by sufficiently good and sound reasons. They cannot but have a bad effect on all but very well-balanced minds, and do much harm by suggesting thoughts, which might never otherwise occur to us."

"Very well; I shall remember to give hints to all my literary friends, that the young ladies of the present day do not approve of moral instruction in novels, but think that all characters should be most unnaturally good, without any religious thoughts whatever, disturbing the even tenor—" and the sentence is cut short by a sound very much like the sharp closing of a door, and is finished by a low laugh instead of words.

However, it is the ball of which I wish to speak. When I bring Lucy's dress to her early in the evening, she puts on a pretty little look of surprise, very becoming, but not quite natural, I fear. Her horror at my costume is extreme. A ragged black dress, mantle and hood, and the wrinkles on my face, arms and neck, made with paint, form a Witch of Endor, which she says will be a horrible success. Fortunately she is pleased with the choice of the character I have made for her: that of Queen Cybele. One of the class of flower-girls, I knew she never would adopt, and selected this for its digni-fied simplicity of style. The dress is a long-trained, plain robe of white cashmere, embroidered around the top of the waist and bot-tom of the skirt, with a Greek pattern in gold. Around the cen-ter twines a myrtle wreath, also in gold embroidery. A band of gold encircling the waist is engraved with lions, a symbol of Cybele; and the open sleeves are looped with golden fibula. A blue scarf is fastened on the left shoulder, after the antique; its color con-trasted by a broad band of gold embroidery in that Greek pattern, which is supposed to have been suggested by the waves of the sea. On the head, above the coronet of shining hair, rests a crown of golden towers, and a sceptre and key to be carried in the hand, are also emblems of Cybele. She looks the stately character, and the dress is decidedly becoming.

Having adjusted her mask and thrown on a white domino, she as-sists me to don my black one, and we descend to the garden by a stairway leading from her *suite* of rooms.

It is a beautiful night; the moon in her soft bright glory eclipsing nearly every star, and rendering the lights in the avenue almost use-less. We make a circuit through the grounds without fear of colds, that dread of Lady Egerton's life, find our carriage waiting accord-ing to orders, in a side path near the avenue, and like invited guests, are driven beneath arches of lanterns, up to the grand entrance. It is a lively, pretty scene, as the carriages deposit their muffled treas-ures, and wheel off in an opposite direction, leaving room for a seemingly endless stream to follow. We are ushered up stairs to the dressing-rooms, as though we had not a moment ago left the ad-joining apartments, and thence descend to the reception-rooms, where we are received with a few words of welcome by the host and hostess, neither of whom suspect our identity. They are, of course, unmasked. Lady Egerton is queenly as Cleopatra; and her pearl ornaments would be worthy mates to that gem so famous in history. Her dress is white merino, Egyptian, of course, the upper dress loose and belted in, cut low, showing her beautiful neck and arms, and the skirt, with a long, sweeping train, both richly ornamented with seed pearls and jewels. A robe of white tissue, thickly studded with stars, is fastened on the shoulders, falling in graceful folds to the floor; and a tiara of pearls adorns her black hair. A pair of dainty white and gold sandals, complete the custume. As one beholds the welcoming smile bestowed upon each new arrival, one can almost believe that "age cannot wither" *her*.

Antony — Sir Griffith Egerton — is, of course, close at hand receiving the guests with less grace, certainly, but in a far heartier manner. His buff shirt, robe, and fleshings are gorgeous; his gray hair is hidden in a yellow wig; his brows bound with a white ribbon, and his feet encased in sandals. My idea of Antony has always been a perfect Apollo, not such—but no disparaging remarks on my host.

Lucy does not remain with me long, for she is led off by a black domino for the first quadrille, and I am left to my own devices. No Saul is here to seek me out, so I take my place alone in a recess near the door, to watch the scene and see the people as they enter.

The entire floor of this wing is thrown open for the dancers, and the long vistas formed by the open doorways are dazzling with light and splendor.

Jewels are flashing, and so are bright eyes beneath envious masks that hide the pretty faces from view. Of course, there is the usual incongruous crowd of a masquerade. Spurs of cavaliers catching in the gauzy robes of sylphs and fairies; monks walking with girls of the period; angels and devils meeting unconcernedly; pages of the time of *Louis Quatorze*, and pages in "buttons;" flower-girls and "Nights" circulating by the dozen, with numbers of dominoes—men too lazy to act a part for amusement, though ready enough to do it through life for a good stake.

But it seems that I am not to enjoy myself in loneliness, for here comes Alva Ingolsby, to whom I confided the secret of what I should wear. He, as he told me he would be, is the Man in the Iron Mask; his dress a black velvet "shape," with glazed calico mask.

"Do you know who that Cybele is?" he asks; "she is attracting universal attention."

"Yes, I know most of the people here," I answer, "but I am not at liberty to tell their names."

"Why not, if you have found them out for yourself?"

"Oh, I am not quick enough for that; and besides, I don't know many of their little peculiarities."

"Then how do you come to recognize them, pray?"

"Simply because they told me themselves what they would wear," I reply: "By mutual consent, and under vows of strict secresy, many confided in me that I might warn them if any two chose the same character—a plan that I proposed in order that we might avoid *contretemps* and insure variety. You surely would not have me break confidence?"

"Certainly not," he answers; "but at least tell me who they are meant to represent. I am either very stupid, or else that man is so badly dressed that I cannot make out whether he thinks himself a Michael Feeney or a Uriah Heep."

"He is not one of my confidants, and the characters are so much alike that it is hard to determine; but, judging from the hand so often on the chin, I should say he was the very 'umble,' and very clammy Uriah Heep."

"There is another of Dickens' characters," says Ingolsby, "a Dolly Varden. I wonder why none of the ladies try a Miss Miggs or Sairy Gamp?" and the last word is brought out with a jerk; for an immense umbrella hooking into his arm almost pulls him over.

"Beg parding, sir," says a gruff voice. "For as I says to Mrs. Harris, says I, one does not feel dispoaged"—and the old nurse moves on talking to herself.

"A gentle hint to be careful how one speaks without knowing who are one's neighbors. That was not a woman's voice. All the ladies want to look as lovely as that dear creature over yonder in the short white skirt and the muslin kerchief tied under the arms. See— that one in the full crowned white cap."

"She is Charlotte Corday," I remark.

"And looks exceedingly like a milk-maid," he replies.

"Well," say I, "if she is too simple, here is a gorgeous one just passing. The yellow-flowered silk bunched up with crimson satin bows over the crimson satin petticoat. That high-pointed felt hat, and that stick in the hand, look uncommonly like Old Mother Hubbard's. I wonder who that tall man is, with wig askew, in the old-fashioned darned coat and blue serge trousers?"

"If you once heard him yell 'pro-dig-eous!' in your ear as he did in mine, I don't think you would long remain in doubt."

"What! Old Dominie Sampson? And to think that I did not recognize so old a friend! Doctor Primrose in his black suit, white cravat, black stockings, shoes, buckles and three-cornered hat, looks something like him, does he not?"

3

"Yes," he answers, with an absent air. "But tell me, Miss Lifford, is not that Miss Egerton in the white and black dress?"

"That is one of the prettiest costumes in the room," I say without noticing his question, "and deserving of a better description than yours. It is white lawn, striped and dotted with black, and covered with little bells that discourse the sweet 'Music' it is meant to represent."

"I see you will not give me even a clue to Miss Egerton, and I am not ingenious enough to discover her unaided."

"Then I fear you will have to wait till the unmasking. Do you see that robe of white tissue with the deep point lace flounce?"

"Yes," he replies, "I have been trying to make out the pattern of the lace; it is quite odd, is it not?"

"She is Marie Laczinska, wife of *Louis Quinze*. The pattern of the flounce represents the principal events of his reign, and it cost a fabulous sum of money," I tell him.

"Then she should pin on a card explaining it, for it might be the procession from the Ark, for all an uninitiated person could tell."

"Pretty work to be at, comparing people as they pass to wild animals leaving the Ark!" exclaims a voice behind us; and we turn to find a little *vivandiere*, who overheard Ingolsby's last words. "You are not in your element," she says, "talking to such an old fright. Come and walk with me;" and linking her arm into his, she leads him off, while I breathe threats of vengeance against the young minx, to be carried into effect when I find her out. I should not wonder if it was that saucy little Jessie Fullerton.

CHAPTER VI.

Done to death by slanderous tongues.
—Much Ado About Nothing: Act V, Scene 3.

LEAVING my place, I wander off among the crowd, avoided by all on account of my unprepossessing appearance, but overhearing scraps of most interesting conversation. Two old dowagers are in a corner by themselves, and tiring of my aimless wanderings, I get as near to them as possible, to be amused with whatever choice bits of scandal are told loudly enough to be overheard.

As I steal quietly up I perceive another listener like myself, a pensive figure in a plain brown dress, white apron and jaunty cap. The first words that reach my ears are about an unfortunate member of the sterner sex.

"He puts on more airs than enough," says the fatter of the two.

"And who is he, anyhow?" asks the friend.

"Oh, an adventurer, I'll be bound. Some pick-up of Sir Griffith's."

"Oh, oh!" think I; "here is something worth listening to."

"One of your exemplary young men who are never worth a farthing," continues Number One. "The old man wants to get the girl off his hands before her birth becomes generally known, I shouldn't wonder, and thinks it will be an easy matter to palm her off as a genuine article on this unfortunate young man." Her sympathy for the "picked-up adventurer" is truly quite refreshing.

"Your Matilda was very much taken with him last season, wasn't she?" inquires Number Two.

"Oh, no; no, indeed. He was very attentive, but she could not endure him; in fact, she always discouraged his attentions after that evening when your dear Emily showed so plainly—innocent girl!—that his attentions to my Matilda were making her miserable."

Cut for cut; stab for stab.

"But what do you mean about the girl's birth being known?" asks Number Two, as she smothers her anger.

"Simply that she is not their own child," is the answer, in a chuckling tone of keen enjoyment. "Everybody knows it; *I* have always known it, but passed it over. Now, however, circumstances have changed."

"Strange that I should never have heard it! Are you quite sure, Mrs. Grampus, that you are rightly informed?"

"Humph!" (a sniff of confident superiority) "I never speak without good authority for what I say, Mrs. Talons, let me tell you that—never. If you care to listen, I will tell you the story."

"By all means; dear, dear, I am dying with curiosity."

"Don't you remember a long, long time ago—sixteen or seventeen years it must be—what a commotion there was when a fearful murder was committed here near Bratton by quite a youth? The boy, you know, was Guy Egerton, the son of Sir Griffith. He killed the husband of that old thing (who still clings to her maiden name, dear knows why; and who, in consequence, Sir Griffith has been obliged to support ever since), and was spirited away in some mysterious fashion, to save his neck from the gallows. Just about that time there was a low drunken fellow in the neighborhood, a man of very low birth, and worse character, if possible—a common laborer, or something of that sort, and after his wife had died from the effects of a beating he had given her, he also disappeared, and would you believe it, Mrs. Grampus, left his only child with Sir

Griffith. The man, it was strongly hinted at that time, knew more of the son's whereabouts, and his manner of getting out of the country, than Sir Griffith would care to have made public, so he took the little brat to keep the man's tongue quiet, and pretended to take a fancy to it. My sister wrote me the whole story at the time, but as the Egertons afterwards adopted the child, and have chosen to regard her in the light of their own daughter ever since, of course, as such, I could not refuse to allow my daughter to visit her. Now, however, I hear the man, Miss Egerton's father, ha, ha, and whose name is Sullivan, or some vulgar name of that sort, is making a fortune in America, and is going to try to get his child back again. Just fancy, my dear, this grand entertainment being given to commemorate the birthday of a navvy's daughter—a navvy who beat his wife to death. Don't you think Miss Egerton has good cause to give herself airs? ha, ha!"

"How dreadful!" croaks Mrs. Talons. "You quite take my breath away, Mrs. Grampus. But as you are so sure of this being true, I wonder at your letting your daughters visit here."

"I could not deny my dear girls the pleasure of coming to-night, my dear; but rest assured, it is the last of their acquaintance with the future Miss Sullivan."

A movement on the part of the listening figure in brown, and it stands before them.

"You vile scandal-mongers! Have you no regards for the rules of hospitality, that you cannot refrain from maligning people under their very roof? For shame! you basest of the base!" and as the indignant words leave her lips, she turns and vanishes in the passing crowd.

Is it Lucy? But no, it cannot be. She is Queen Cybele, and happily heard not this story, in many of its features but too true— only too true, poor girl!

Without a glance at the discomfited old dowagers, I move away, anxious to get out of the crowd and on to the balcony, anywhere to think.

Yes, the balcony is deserted; and there is one gloomy corner where I can think what is best to be done—what can be done to prevent the circulation of their vile slander. To speak of it to Sir Griffith, or to wait? But wait for what? Little good ever came from delay, and the first evil had better be faced at once than allowed to grow and increase with time. What trouble is caused in this world by meddlesome people! Words spoken lightly, or from a pure love of mischief, how often do they cause misery and sorrow far beyond the intent of those who gave them utterance. Poor

Lucy! how will her proud spirit bear this if it gets abroad, even though it is not so bad as those women made it out to be? Her mother was a lady, idle and sickly, who had married beneath her station. The child was shamefully neglected, and taken to be educated for a governess, but she so grew into and filled the lonely hearts of Sir Griffith and Lady Egerton, that when her mother died of a rapid decline—not from a blow—and her father, a man of shady antecedents—nothing worse— left the country, they determined that she should always be to them as their own child, and should never go into the world alone to fight her way through life. What is that? A moan; and from the brown figure which leans against the railing within two yards of where I sit; but with a now unmasked face turned from me and towards the moon.

My lips open to speak, when another figure appears, coming towards us. It comes closer, and I see it is Ingolsby. With both hands extended he advances towards the shrinking figure, saying: "Ah, Lucy, I have found you at last in this simple costume, after following every grand stately character in the room, hoping each might be you. But why try to leave me? I must speak a few words, for to-morrow parts us. I cannot leave here with my future undecided; it is in your hands and you must form it, Lucy, my darling. Will you be my wife and make all the future happy? Will you give me permission to prepare a home for you to fill and make bright? Will you return with me to that home when I come for you? Tears! sobs! what is this, Lucy?"

Bitter, bitter tears are they which fall on his shoulder for a moment; then she breaks from him, and standing upright in the moonlight, with little hands clenched, gives the answer in a firm voice, almost cold in its suppression of emotion.

"Mr. Ingolsby, I can never be your wife. Circumstances have come to light which will prevent my ever becoming the wife of any gentleman. Don't blame me; don't think badly of me," and the firm voice trembles; "for those circumstances are not of my making, are no fault of mine, and were never known to me until to-night. God forgive those who have kept this secret from me! In that station of life in which I was born, I would have been happy; might have loved an equal. But now—Oh Alva, I fear I have given you reason to hope for what I knew not then can never be. Forgive me; forgive me! I knew not what I did; I hardly know now what I say!"

"Indeed, Lucy, I don't think you do know what you say. Be calm, my darling, and tell me what has happened; what is the meaning of this raving about birth? Or else, cast it all from your mind and think only of this: I love you?—Do you love me in return?" and he once more takes her hands in his.

"Do I?" and there must be assurance in those ambiguous words. Yes, and in that upward glance; for stooping, he imprints a kiss on the soft pink cheek.

A low cry, the words, "But I can never, *never* be yours!" and she has freed her hands from his grasp, darted past him and is gone. He turns to follow her, when I start from my seat where amazement has held me spellbound, and catch his arm, thinking it best that he should be told all now, rather than it should come first to his ears, tortured and twisted as it has been to-night.

"Mr. Ingolsby! Alva! Let the girl go, give her time to think and grow calm. I can explain this, and I want your advice. The poor child must have changed her costume or she never should have overheard what she did, while I had power to prevent it;" and I proceed to tell him my own sad history; hers; that of the unfortunate Guy Egerton, and how to-night it all became known to her, after being carefully concealed for seventeen long years. He listens to my tale in perfect silence; his eyes, now dark with emotion, looking far, far away, even beyond the sky it seems, where it is fringed by the poplars in the grounds below. When I have finished, his eyes lose that absent look, and with a deep sigh, he moves for the first time as though awakening from a trance. Turning slowly, he walks with bent head away from me, along the balcony, down the steps and disappears in the shrubbery.

How the ball ends, I know not. I have eyes only for Lucy as she goes about among the guests after the unmasking, in her resumed dress of Cybele, with a light word for all, and receiving their congratulations and good wishes of the day. None but I guess the storm that is pent up beneath that gay exterior, to burst forth in all its fury when the compress is removed.

Once in passing me she whispers: "Is this true? Am I adopted?"

And thoughtlessly I utter the words that are ready on my tongue: "Too true, Lucy!—only too true!"

CHAPTER VII.

Flies an eagle flight, bold, and forth on,
Leaving no tract behind.
— Timon of Athens: Act I, Scene 1.

MORNING comes at last after a sleepless night; comes, as it always does, neither delayed nor hastened by the human emotions of joy or sorrow, hope or fear.

The breakfast hour arrives and the guests string along one after another to the informal meal. The first to come down stairs, after myself, are the rollicking Squire Strong and Sir Griffith, arm-in-arm, laughing and talking of last night's revel.

"And you didn't know who was in old Dominie Sampson's skin?" laughs the Squire; "how unconcernedly people moved into my neighborhood, and fled with hands to their ears and expressionless faces when I shouted 'pro-dig-eous!'" and he again tries the strength of his lungs, and nearly upsets Lady Egerton by the mere force of the sound as she enters behind him.

"'As you are Strong be merciful!'" she exclaims; "I am so fatigued after last night's exertions that the least noise is trying to my nerves;" and she takes her place behind the tea-urn.

"Why you look as fresh as a daisy," answers Squire Strong. "A perfect Cleopatra still!"

"Do you know the reason of that?" asks Sir Griffith, standing before the fire with his hands in his pockets. "She was so worn out by the exertion of watching the energetic people about her, that she has not yet felt equal to the effort of throwing off the assumed character—Eh, my dear Agnes?"

"Well, Griffith, if I am behind time in one way, you are also in another; for you are but just *beginning* to resemble the witty Antony."

"Ha, ha!" roars the Squire. "She has you there, Egerton. Good, my lady—'Pro-dig-eously' good!"

"What, still keeping up the jokes of last-night?" asks the *fainéante* Lady Caroline Hamilton, who, entering at the moment, catches the last words, and languidly takes her place at the table. "I never could understand your energy, Mr. Strong, though I confess to admiring it," with a sweet glance from her sleepy-looking eyes.

"Cherry ripe, ripe, ripe, I cry,
Full and fair ones,—come and buy!"

Gaily sings pretty, romping little Jessie Fullerton, skipping into the room. "Good morning to you all! Do you know I've been listening at the door, and I've found out who it was who roared in my ear, and then softened into a whisper, and said all those absurd things in the other ear, that luckily escaped being deafened. Oh, Squire, Squire, I've a great mind to repeat it all? Shall I, Caroline?"

"Egerton, don't you think its high time we paid that visit to your Berkshires?" demurely asks the Squire.

"Ah, coward, coward!" cries the little tease. "Come here, my lud!" to Lord Eversley, who just appears, "and console me for the good fun I'm about to lose. Why don't you go before I begin, Squire? I'm afraid you know how good natured I am, and don't fear me as you should. Never mind, Carrie and I will talk it all over by-and-by, and find a way to punish you;" and she glances slyly from him to Lady Caroline, and back again.

A bevy of ladies now enter: Old Lady Lindhurst and her three meek little daughters; Lady Fortescue, Emily Wilbraham, Ruth Ferrers and Miss Van Praet. After them come a number of gentlemen: Alva Ingolsby, Horace Gilford, the promising young politician; Arthur Alresford, a rising barrister; Julian Thalberg, the young painter; Sidney Carleton and Reginald Percy, of the Queen's Bays, who are quartered at the neighboring barracks; Sir Henry Beresford, Lord George Mortland and the Honorable Charles Melton, gentlemen of leisure. There follows such an incessant clatter of tongues that one can catch but scraps of conversation, which strangely dove-tail themselves into a most ridiculous incongruity.

Lady Egerton : "James, muffins for his lordship."

Lady Fortescue : "I assure you, it created quite a sensation in London, last season—"

Horace Gilford : "The fastest horse on the—"

Lady Caroline : "Piano is my favorite."

Lady Fortescue : "You were away at the time, I believe. I was her particular friend, and—"

Squire Strong : "I'll trouble you for some more omelette, your ladyship."

Lord Eversley : "Aw-yeth; blue eyeth-a-a-my weakneth, you know, and—"

Miss Van Praet : "Long ears also, and the most fearful ——"

Lady Fortescue : "Case of infatuation; went on the stage under the assumed name of ——"

Honorable Reginald Percy : "Chatterbox won the Derby that year."

Sidney Carleton : "Let me recommend these muffins ——"

Jessie Fullerton : "So stale, you know, and ——"

Sir Henry Beresford : " Not in the least dry; the speech was racy and full of ——"

Ruth Ferrers : Berkshire pigs, Sir Griffith."

Lady Caroline : " Quite the thing now, and one might as well be out of the world as ——"

" *Squire Strong :* "Stowed away in the hold of his ship, and mashed out of ——"

Arthur Alresford : " Potatoes never spelled without the *e* ——"

Horace Gilford : "The traces broke; the horses started forward, and amid wild screams and crashing of glass, we were precipitated over the edge of ——"

Lady Egerton : A pigeon pie, Sir Henry—allow me."

Emily Wilbraham : "The most exquisite shade of blue silk, trimmed with pearls."

Horace Gilford : "Dragged through the mire ——"

Honorable Charles Melton : "By Miss Fullerton, I believe, and such a pity ——"

Lord Eversley : "The nithetht little pair of ——"

Sir Griffith : "Caterpillars, my Lord—nothing but caterpillars; they eat ——"

Lord George Mortland : "Like Lady Caroline about the eyes ——"

Sir Griffith : "Gentlemen, would you like to walk down to the stables?"

Jessie Fullerton : " Now, your Lordship, I won't let you off that game of croquet."

Lady Lyndhurst : " I want to see your fernary, Lady Egerton, if it will not trouble you too much."

Miss Van Praet : "Lord Mortland, you must really come to our archery practice on the lawn."

And those who have breakfasted saunter off, laughing and talking, to the croquet-ground, conservatories and stables. They have been so full of themselves, that none but Ingolsby and I notice the absence of one.

" Is Miss Egerton not well this morning ?" he asks me.

" I have not seen her yet, but will go to her room," and I go up stairs and knock at her door. No answer. Again I knock, and still silence. The handle yields to my touch, and I look into Lucy's neat dressing-room. I glance at Cybele's dress folded on a chair; at two little sandals side by side in front of the bureau; at Cybele's crown in its box on the dressing-table, and my eyes light on the open window through which the fresh morning air pours into the apartment between the gracefully-looped blue and white curtains. But I see no Lucy. She has been up some time, and at work with her usual neatness, I think. A few steps take me to the door leading into the sleeping chamber. There are the same evidences of a tidy hand, but still—no Lucy. She must have risen before any of us and gone out for an early walk, I am now sure. So I tell Ingolsby, whom I find in the morning room making himself useful, holding the old ladies' worsted, and picking up stray balls that *will* roll into holes and corners from the many laps.

Presently the other guests begin to return to the house, and the previous hum swells into a perfect Babel of tongues. Sir Griffith comes in to ask a question of his wife, and, as he is passing out again, Alva touches his arm, and whispers:

" May I speak to you a moment, Sir Griffith, on a matter of great importance?"

" This is rather an inopportune time, my dear fellow; but come to the library and I will spare you a few minutes before taking Miss Ferrers to see my ' Lady May;' " and they go off together, and I hear the door close behind them.

Three or four young ladies now gather round me asking for Lucy, and chattering away like magpies; but I hardly hear them, my thoughts are so intent on what is passing behind that closed door. There is no denying the fact that I am gifted with the curiosity peculiar—it is said—to my sex. If I could but hear them! And I will; for a closet with a door at either end leads like a passage-way from the library into the adjoining breakfast-room, and through that door one can easily hear what passes beyond.

So, in about twenty minutes after they enter the library, I am close to them with but a thin partition between us. Ingolsby is speaking:

" Doubtless, the tale she heard last night was most galling to her pride. However, if you call her now, her mind can be at once relieved!"

" Ay, ay! her mind can be relieved, but mine! After all these years of care and protection, my Lucy is to be taken from me, and will soon forget the old fellow who had no claim upon her;" and there is an affecting sob in the old man's voice. " Ah, my boy, you have never been a father, or you would not think altogether of the girl."

" Forgive me, my dear sir," and sharp pain is expressed in his tones; " I see for the first time how thoughtless I have been. I should have prepared you for this, but I only thought of what the the poor girl's suffering would be after what she had overheard, never remembering that another might love her as well, if not better, than myself. I cannot forgive myself for this unpardonable want of consideration."

"Never mind, my boy, never mind. I *won't* be selfish!" and the stamp of his foot shakes the door against which I lean. "Here, Butters! Watkins! James! *somebody!*" shouting in the hall; "see if Miss Egerton has returned, and send her here immediately!"

The steps of the two now silent men are heard beyond, pacing up and down, and I am on the *qui vive* to hear in what manner her mind is to be relieved. But no one answers to the call. Stealing quietly from my hiding-place, I go to inquire if she has returned. No; she has not been seen. Perhaps she has come in unperceived, and I go up stairs and through her rooms once more, but without finding her. Pausing in thought before the bureau, something catches my eye which escaped me before; something which makes me feel strangely uncomfortable. 'Tis only a bit of paper pinned to the cushion, but the sight of it seems to stagnate the blood in my veins. Under certain circumstances, this is the place where a letter is always found. Can it be? Trembling with apprehension, I take it up and read the words: "*I have gone ; search will be useless.*"

I am stunned for the moment, but quickly recovering energy, I fly from the room, run rapidly down the stairs, knock, and hand in the paper at the library door. Then I am sorry for what I have done, and have not the heart to return and listen to the conversation, but instead, go to my room and lock myself in from the impending storm.

CHAPTER VIII.

Ay, an you had any eye behind you, you might **see more** detraction at your heels, than fortunes before you.
— Twelfth Night, Act II, Scene 5.

ERY soon the storms breaks. The murmur of many tongues, the tramp of many feet re-echo through the house, and rush and rumble and grumble through halls and corridors like a fierce winter's wind forcing its way between the ruins of some old building. Presently the clamor subsides—wears itself out; and all that can be heard is the occasional slamming of a door, or the rapid movement of a pair of feet.

How I hope and pray that the search for the foolish, impulsive girl will prove successful; but I have my doubts. She is strong-willed, she is clever, and having fled from what she thought disgrace, is not likely to leave a clue which might lead to her discovery. Fortunately for myself, I can look upon her absence more calmly than the others, for I have much of the fatalist in my nature.

I do not think that when misfortunes come, we should sit idly down, and, folding our hands, sigh forth " It is my fate! " No; we should fight the battle bravely for success; but, whichever way the combat ends, then say, with a heart relieved by the consciousness of having done all that human power could do, " *Kismet!* It was to be— and I am resigned ! "

> Who can shun inevitable fate?
> The doom was written; the decree was passed
> Ere the foundations of the world were cast.

A step approaches my door, and I open it to ask what news.

" Wilson, where are Sir Griffith and—every one ? "

" Oh, Miss, they are all off to the town, looking for our Miss Lucy. Just to think, mum, that a young lady like she should go and run away from her happy home an' her good father! "

" It may appear strange, Wilson, but of course she had good reasons," I say, to keep up appearances with the servants; " and it is just one of Sir Griffith's whims to make such a fuss about nothing; for, without doubt, we shall hear from her before long."

" Very likely, Miss," (and her tone of voice means: " Not much, Miss, I'm no fool.") " But I really do pity poor Mr. Ingolsby, Miss; he must be dreadful fond of her—if you will excuse my saying it— for he seemed all struck of a heap like, an' the color of his face was more like a piece of white cloth nor sound flesh an' blood. An' oh, Miss Lifford! The awful look in them big eyes o' his! They looked as if they were lookin' right straight into the next world."

" I am not in the least surprised at his seeming anxious, even if he did not feel so, out of politeness to his host;" and I say the words with the same good purpose as before, but with as little suc-cess. For though the woman's eyelids drop over that tell-tale fea-ture, the eyes, she can't control the muscles which elevate her upper lip into an incredulous curl.

" But where is your mistress, Wilson? She surely has not gone into the town ? "

" Oh, no, indeed, mum; my lady is in her room tryin' to keep quiet, for she says the confusion is very tryin' to her nerves—an' all the nerves *she* has!" in a lower tone not exactly meant for my ears.

" What's that you say, Wilson ? " very sternly.

" Nothing, Miss—I mean, my Lady sent me to ask you if you would not go down and see the ladies who is all alone by theirselves in the drawing-room."

In obedience to this disguised command, I go down stairs and find the ladies with their heads together whispering away at a great rate. They do not perceive me at first as I pause in the doorway, and old Lady Fortescue, unconsciously raising her voice, informs the others that she never *could* like the girl. To her there was something ill-bred and vulgar about her.

"I shouldn't wonder if she had run off with one of the footmen!" cries Mabel Lyndhurst.

"Very likely, my dear, if she has not gone with one of the grooms!" comes from Miss Ferrers, in a yet louder tone. "Indeed I always observed that she had a taste for low company. Only the other day I met her in a lane, walking with a most disreputable looking character."

Chorus: "Dear—dear! You don't tell me so?"

"Indeed, yes," the young lady proceeds. "He was dressed in a seedy old suit of gray, with a slouched hat; and he had red hair, and green eyes, and the most villainous expression of face, and was smoking a nasty pipe!"

"For my part, I always guessed from her red-head, what kind of stock she had sprung from," exclaims Lady Fullerton.

"Now, mamma," expostulates her daughter Jessie, "you know very well that you are only jealous because I have not the same lovely shade of hair. There never lived a sweeter, prettier girl; and as to the ruffian Miss Ferrers has so vividly described, it was no other than the eccentric Jolliffe Tufnell, who has recently returned to his estate in the neighborhood."

After this the silence of discomfiture falls on the entire party, till Lady Fullerton suddenly turns and sees me.

"Ahem! My dear Miss Lifford, we have all been expressing our sorrow for this sad occurrence, and, believe me, you have my sincerest sympathy in this, your hour of trouble. It seems an age already since I saw our pretty Lucy's face!"

And they all crowd around me and condole, and chatter, and hum, and buzz, till I am almost distracted, and but little consoled after the recent specimen of their good-will and charity.

A couple of hours pass slowly by, lagging as hours have seldom done before, and then the tramping of horses' hoofs is heard on the gravel without.

Sir Griffith enters first and goes directly to his study, without giving us a word. Alva does not appear, but the other gentlemen come in and join us and report that no trace of her can be found.

"Ith the queervetht thing—gone! Vanithed! And no one thaw her in the protheth," is Lord Eversley's comment.

"Don't be down-hearted," says Squire Strong, "it was but a passing freak of the girl's, and she will return of her own accord as soon as she discovers the difference between a home and the wide world. It will do her good to experience a few of the ills that flesh is heir to, and make her contented for the rest of her life with the lot that *she* is heir to."

"Miss Lifford, I am going up to town by the 4.20 train, and if there is anything you should like done in the way of prosecuting a search for Miss Egerton, I am quite at your service."

"Thank you, Mr. Arlesford, but I could not think of troubling you."

"I am at your service also, Miss Lifford, as I must return to-night," says Horace Gilford.

"And pray command me," from Sir Henry Beresford.

And thus many of them, both ladies and gentlemen, equally divided between consideration for us and themselves, leave by the 4.20 express; and the few who remain pack their trunks in secret, preparatory to an early departure.

Just before dinner hour, Wilson, her ladyship's maid, knocks at my door.

"Please, Miss, my lady says, would you kindly excuse her to the company, for she is not able to appear."

So, I am to have the not very cheerful task of taking the post shunned by Lady Egerton, at the head of her table!

When Sir Griffith passes on his way down, I join him.

"You have had no success?" I ask.

"None so far," he says, sadly; "none at all. From what the station-master said, we judge that she cannot have left the place by rail, for he saw every passenger from here by the early train to town; and according to an account of one of the servants, her room was empty before six o'clock this morning."

"Could she be hiding in the town, do you think?"

"We shall soon know, Julia, for proper inquiries have been set on foot; and should they fail, to-morrow I will send for my legal adviser. Nice trouble I am taking for another man's benefit."

"Why, you surely don't intend to give the girl up to that man, her—her father?"

"Of course," he answers, sharply, "what else can I do? But let the subject drop for the sake of our guests, and Ingolsby."

"And for yours too, poor fellow," I reply, pityingly.

"Never mind me!" he snaps back, "I am old enough, and ugly enough too, I should think, to take care of myself;" and he makes a sadly failing attempt to assume his natural tone.

A sad evening it is altogether; for Alva, when he comes, is not a lively addition to our party, and many subjects of conversation are started which, as if by mutual consent, are unsustained, and fall to the ground.

We separate early, all no doubt glad to be from under the restraint of each other's society; some, perhaps, anxious to resume their interrupted gossip. It would be amusing, under different circumstances, to watch the white figures that flit about the halls well into the wee small hours, going from room to room with an ever increasing budget of scandal.

The next day the search through the neighborhood is renewed with unabated energy. About noon a telegram is sent to the family lawyer in London to come down without delay. The entire town of Bratton is in a state of intense excitement, people coming to the house ostensibly with offers of assistance, but no doubt anxious to learn the true version of all the rumors afloat. Horsemen gallop unceasingly to and fro, sometimes with word that a clue has been discovered; again, to say it has failed.

Several times during the day the rumor spreads that Lucy has been found, and when our joyful expectation has reached its height, the report is proved to be false, and our hopes dashed to the ground.

Sir Griffith seems to be everywhere at the same moment, but confused, and incapable of giving instructions. Ingolsby, the mainspring of action, is calm and collected, taking upon himself the responsibility of giving directions, the wisdom of which becomes at once apparent, although it had before entered no other head that such-and-such a thing was unmistakably the one to be done.

Toward evening a telegram arrives that Sir Griffith's legal adviser cannot leave London until the following afternoon. The household is in utter confusion; servants demoralized, and guests departing in twos and threes by every train.

Some leave with the time-worn excuse of "unexpected letters," (which appear to arrive in the very nick of time,) calling them away much against their wish. Some go without excuse at all, considering it a natural consequence of what has occurred; and a few—a very few—with unfeigned good wishes, and the promise to complete their interrupted visit under happier auspices. .

CHAPTER IX.

Grim reader! did you ever see a ghost?
— Byron: "Don Juan."

THE last guest has gone, and confusion reigns supreme, when Lady Egerton comes to me in greater tribulation than she has yet shown.

"What shall I do, Julia?" she exclaims. "At this time of all others, to think of her behaving badly, and she who has always been so well treated too!"

"Who is behaving badly, Agnes—what is the matter?" I inquire anxiously.

"Who'd believe she would act like this, and I always so kind to her!" she proceeds, paying no heed to my question. "I know I can never go through all this trouble; it will kill me, I'm sure it will!" with an effort at tears. But they won't be forced, and she sinks down on the sofa, a picture of unappreciated benevolence.

"Unless you tell me what is your trouble, I cannot help you, Agnes."

"Oh, will you help me? Will you take this burden off my shoulders? How good you are, Julia!" suddenly reviving. "Just ring that bell, my dear, for Wilson, and reason her out of this freak. It's nothing but a freak, and you have such a persuading way with you, my love, that you will soon convince her, I have no doubt."

Snatching thus at the first hint of relief from annoyance, she lies back languidly waiting for Wilson, and for me to settle a matter of which I as yet know nothing whatsoever.

"Suppose you tell me what I am to say to Wilson when she comes," I quietly remark.

"Oh, you know best, my dear. You are always better at talking to these people than I; and you can reason her out of this freak,"

"But you have not told me *what* this freak *is*, Agnes."

"Why, don't you know?" elevating her eyebrows, (as though thinking "how stupid you are!") "Well, Julia, she has actually had the assurance, after all these years in my service, she who has always appeared so faithful, to give warning. And not only she, but half the other servants as well. Come in! Wilson, I have been telling Miss Lifford how shocked I am at your behavior."

The woman curtsys, and then I ask her:

"What is the reason of this sudden notion of yours, Wilson? Do you not think that there is worry enough in the house now, without your giving us more? I am surprised—very much surprised."

"Well, Miss, I'm sure I'm very sorry, but indeed, indeed Miss, it's no freak as my Lady calls it at-all-at-all; and I wouldn't add to your trouble for worlds, but—but—" and she stammers, and pauses, visibly embarrassed.

"But—what, Wilson? Have you anything to complain of?"

"No, indeed, Miss; its right sorry I am to leave, and Watkins says he never was better treated anywhere; but—but—well, to be honest, Miss, me and Watkins, and James, the groom, an' Sarah, the 'ousemaid, feels as we dare not stay no longer in this 'ouse, mum."

"Did you ever hear anything to equal that!" exclaims Lady Egerton. "Just get her to tell you some of the foolish stories, to which I hadn't patience to listen."

"Explain your meaning, Wilson, in not *daring* to remain."

"Well, Miss, I'm sure its right sorry I am to be obliged to say such things; but mum, we all believes," and she looks fearfully behind her, and opens her eyes very wide, and lowers her voice to a whisper, "we believe, mum, that the 'ouse is 'aunted! Yes, 'aunted by poor dear Miss Lucy! An' we 'as good reason, and so we 'as, mum, for our suppogicians," she hurries on, "for each of us four 'as seen her. The very mornin' after she disappeared—yesterday morning, it was—I was up betimes to go to early mass, mum, an' as I was a passin' along the 'all to leave a clean-washed combin'-wrapper in my Lady's dressin'-room, I sees a figure with one 'and all blazin' with fire, a glidin' along, an' it went through the baize door, without openin' it, an' the light vanished, and there I stands all in a tremble, I could not even 'oller, I was that scared. But I didn't say nothin', Miss, for there wasn't no need to scare the rest of 'em; but at breakfas,' Watkins he said as 'ow his pantry was all hupside down, an' things a lyin' round as if the witches 'ad been there. An' this mornin' he was awful white, an' told us as 'ow the night before he was a goin' with a message to Sir Griffith to the library, an' what did he see but the spirit o' Miss Lucy a standin' guard at the door, an' all of a suddint it glides off an' vanishes. An' then James, the groom, he speaks hup an' says, very late at night he hears the black mare as Sir Griffith bought last week, very huneasy, an' as he goes to see what's the matter, he notices a light in the dinnin'-room, and thinkin' as 'ow it might be robbers, he steals up an' looks in, an' what does he see but a figure just like Miss Lucy, on'y brown, an' not white, like ghosts is, a walkin' about, an' all of a suddint a light, as he could not tell where it come from, goes out, an' he runs away scared. An' then, Miss, this mornin', Sarah, the 'ousemaid, goes to the luggage-room to look for a chair as my Lady

4

says we might 'ave in our room, mum, an' when she hopens the door, there stands the same figure as James had spoke of; and so she turns round and runs away, a thinkin' the old boy (savin' your presence, my Lady), was a'coming after 'er. An' James, he 'as seed lights a movin' habout in Miss Lucy's room, Miss, late o' nights, when you all was asleep; an' so, mum, we've hall made hup our minds as 'ow we'd better go."

While she has been speaking, I have determined on a course, the only one to pursue with superstitious people, and though it involves a little sacrifice of truth, 'tis the only way to restore harmony to our distracted household. When she has finished, therefore, I burst out laughing.

"How can a woman of your sense, Wilson, be so ridiculous?" I ask. "Who ever heard of a brown ghost, or of one wandering about in the day-time, or of one pillaging a pantry!" Then I become very stern, and continue: "You might go away from here, and set false reports flying, and believe all your life that you had once lived in a haunted house. So it is that legends are founded. It fortunately happens that I can give you a satisfactory explanation of all this; and in future be cautious how you allow your imagination to fly away with your reason. The morning you supposed you saw—a ghost, forsooth!—I, becoming restless, had been to Miss Lucy's room, and was returning with a candle in my hand, which I extinguished on reaching the baize door. I had on my brown dressing-gown, and in that same garment I went to the library door in the evening, intending to write some letters, but hearing Sir Griffith within, came away without entering. It was probably as I stood, hesitating a moment, that Watkins passed through the hall, and saw me; and, being excited like the rest of us, mistook me for a ghost."

I pause to give my words time to become impressed on the mind of the woman, who stands open-mouthed looking at me.

"That same night," I proceed, "sitting up late, I remembered having left something in the dining-room, and went in search of it, taking no candle, but lighting matches as I went. This morning I was looking over some old trunks in the triangular room, when I heard the door slam, and hurrying to it, saw Sarah speeding away in the distance. There are Sarah's and James's ghosts, and yours and Watkins's. As to the lights in Miss Lucy's room, why I have been there frequently, as you know. Now, I hope your fancies are laid quietly at rest; and if you please, you will repeat in the servant's hall what I have said, and then, if any should not be satisfied, send them to me. You may go now, Wilson."

Utterly dumbfounded, she mutters something unintelligible, curtsys again, and leaves the room. Then Lady Egerton exclaims: "Just see what trouble you came near getting us into, Julia, by your night-wanderings!"

"Do you mean to say that my story imposed upon you also? Ha, ha! Why, not one word of it was the truth."

Her ladyship looks scarcely less astonished than did the woman, and forgetful of the good effect my words have had, begins a lecture on my shocking habit of want of veracity.

"Shall I ring, and tell them it was all false?" with my hand on the bell-rope.

"No, no!" she cries; "let it be now, as the evil is done."

And that is the last of her ladyship's lecture; and also, the last that is heard of ghosts or warnings from the servants. I even learn sometime after from one of the housemaids, that Wilson was dreadfully "high and mighty," as she expressed it, in the servant's hall, assuming an air of superiority over the unfortunates who had confided to her their fears; and spoke with such irony of "imagination flying away with their reason," and of "brown ghosts," that none durst venture to again give expression to their superstitious imaginings.

But although I succeed so well in convincing others of the absurdity of their notions, many painful doubts and fears are raised in my own mind, by Wilson's strange recital. For what reason is there for disbelieving that the four servants really beheld something supernatural?

CHAPTER X.

———Methought what pain it was to drown!
What dreadful noise of water in mine ears!
What sights of ugly death within mine eyes!
—Richard III: Act I, Scene 4.

UNDER-SIZED, shrivelled and pugnacious, Mr. Jedediah Strutt, of Lincoln's Inn, Solicitor, arrives from London. His rule is contrary to the precept, "Be not wise in your own conceits," for no man ever thought more highly of his own opinions, or took less pains to conceal the fact. No matter how he may be worsted in argument, he still holds to it, that he was "right, perfectly right, from the stand he took, and the way in which he looked at the subject." By what process of logic he arrives at this conclusion, is something unknown to all but himself, and, perhaps, beyond the comprehension of lesser minds than his own.

The train which brings him to Bratton arrives very late, giving him but a few minutes to make his preparations for dinner, and leaving no time for any discussion of the subject which requires his presence. At the table, all allusion to Lucy is avoided in deference to the apparent wish of Sir Griffith. The conversation, chiefly of politics and questions of law, frequently flags, and all but Mr. Strutt appear to talk without exhibiting the slightest interest in what they or anyone else may be saying. He, however, rattles away with his usual loquacity, ready to enter the lists for a tilt at words with anybody upon any subject whatever; but unfortunately there is no one willing to take up the gauntlet.

When, at length, Lady Egerton and I leave the gentlemen to their wine, we know well what will be the subject of their talk; and it is long before they seem to resolve upon a proper course to pursue.

The sole occupants of the large drawing-room, Lady Egerton and I, settle with our books before the fire—a welcome luxury on this chilly evening. As I glance slyly from the open pages that I do not care to read, I can guess by her ladyship's fixed look, that she has, like myself, taken up the book for the mere purpose of avoiding conversation. Presently the volume slips from her fingers and her eyes rest upon the blazing logs; and then, by degrees, the lids close and she is in the land of dreams, where there are to her no disturbing emotions, but a peaceful life where domestic machinery moves easily and smoothly upon wheels lubricated with the oil of tranquillity. Or else, perhaps, where, with their worst faults magnified, untold Lucys, and discontented servants, and argumentative Mr. Strutts, and eccentric Sir Griffiths abound to a tantalizing degree, giving her even less chance of a calm life than she has here upon earth.

How silent is the house! So still and quiet, in fact, that I begin to have a wild fancy that I must have become deaf; that surely a great clamor is going on around, although I cannot hear it; and that should a cannon be fired off in the room it would have no effect upon my ears. But just as the fancy reaches its climax, a sound, mysterious by its distance, breaks the death-like silence, and my delusion quickly vanishes. Yet again and again it returns, each time more impressive, and each time dispelled by some far-off sound —a human voice—the sigh of the trees without—the faint echo of a distant bugle at the cavalry barracks, as watch is set for the night— or the shrill whistle of the night-express, passing through the town two miles away.

How lonely it seems! I wish Agnes would wake up and be companionable; for what if—and I look nervously over my shoulder—

what if a brown figure should be moving about the room, and should come and lay its cold hand upon me! And I almost feel the touch, and give an involuntary start. Or, what if a supernatural guard should be looking upon us from the door-way! or some ghostly eye peering in through that crack in the shutter to the right! Can that be a stealthy step upon the stairs? These idle fancies crowd upon my mind till the silence becomes unbearable, and I poke the fire vigorously and noisily, arousing Lady Egerton from her nap.

"Haven't they come in yet to their tea?" she asks with the slightest tinge of peevishness in her tone—the farthest limit she ever allows herself; and I am now sure that her dreams have been of magnified evils—not tranquillity.

"No, indeed, they haven't, Agnes; and it's quite eleven o'clock. Hark! There is the dining-door opening, and I hear their voices."

In another minute Sir Griffith enters alone.

"I don't know what I should do without Ingolsby," he says placing a chair for himself before the fire. "He insists upon neglecting his own business and attending to mine. As it is best that I should remain here to superintend matters, he goes up to London to-morrow, and he and Strutt have now gone to the library to make arrangements about employing detectives, and advertising and all that. They may want me, so I think you had both better go off to bed, my dears."

"I shall be only too glad, Griffith; but don't you come up at two or three in the morning, as you have lately been doing. It disturbs me dreadfully. You can't bring the girl back in that way, and such late hours will only injure your own health."

The baronet gives a long look into his wife's placid face; sighs sadly, and taking it between his hands, kisses her with a visible tenderness unusual for him, and then, as though ashamed of the weakness, abruptly rushes from the room.

Agnes raises her eye-brows at me.

"Don't you think this trouble is having an effect on his mind?"

"If anything affects his mind to-night, it is you, my dear. But come, let us take his advice and go to our beds;" and I move toward the door, and her ladyship follows."

We find Sir Griffith in the hall, lighting our bed-room candles, and there we separate for the night.

*   *   *   *   *   *   *   *

Early the next morning Alva goes up to town, promising to telegraph the first good tidings. He is gone several days, but writes only of failure in the search.

On the evening of the third of October, one week from the date of Lucy's flight, he returns; and a glance at his sad weary face, with dark circles beneath the eyes, tells the ill-success of his journey.

After the most uncomfortable of many comfortless dinners, he, Sir Griffith and Mr. Jedediah Strutt meet in conclave in the library; and I, deserting Lady Egerton, betake myself to my former post at the closet-door, in the hope of learning what has been done. As I take my position, I hear the squeaking voice of Mr. Strutt:

"I am sorry to inform you, Mr. Ingolsby, that we cannot find the faintest trace of the missing young lady. It is very strange indeed, for, according to my opinion, she started at once for London, and I cannot understand how she managed to pass through the town where she is well known, without being seen or recognized by a solitary person. Our only hope now, is in tracing her from the London railway station. Here, my men give the absurd report that she cannot have left by foot, rail or private conveyance. Now, admitting, for the sake of argument, that such be the case, how can we account——"

"Never mind that, just now, Strutt," impatiently interrupts Sir Griffith; "but let Ingolsby tell us the result of his trip. Proceed, my boy!"

"I followed your instructions, Mr. Strutt," says Ingolsby in a spiritless tone, "and employed the detectives you recommended. They took much interest in the case, and appeared to be greatly mortified at the final report they were obliged to render of their investigations. No such person as the one described could be traced from Euston Square, the terminus of the Bratton trains, and no clue discovered of her whereabouts. Dismissing them, I played the only other card in our hand. I advertised in the *Times,* and it was with great repugnance to my feelings that I did so, for I felt sure she would dislike the publicity."

"She brought it on herself," mutters Sir Griffith, as Alva continues:

"Should this fail to bring her back, there is only one conclusion at which we can arrive, and that——"

His voice breaks.

"'Tis a very pretty case, Mr. Ingolsby, and, if I may venture to say it, you did wrong in dismissing the police; for a young, inexperienced girl like her, could not hide herself long from their lynx eyes.

"With your permission, Sir Griffith, I shall write at once to have the search renewed."

"Do what you think best, my friend; only get her back; get her back, that is all I ask."

"Most assuredly I shall, Sir Griffith. If she be living, you will have her with you in a few days," replies the lawyer; and in a moment the scratching of a pen is heard.

"Ah! *If* she be living," sighs Alva.

"And who the deuce would kill a pretty, helpless creature like her," is the sharp retort from Sir Griffith. "I beg your pardon, my dear fellow, but something happened yesterday which has quite unhinged me. Do you remember once saying, that you believed in ghosts, though you had never seen one? What would you say, if I, who do not believe in them, were to tell you," and his voice lowers, "I was almost sure I saw one yesterday morning? Either a ghost, or our Lucy! I was wandering about the eastern wing, looking for an old book, in one of the unoccupied rooms, and trying to keep my mind off the girl, when a sensation that there was another presence near me, made me turn, and there, gliding off in the distance, was a figure I ought to know, in a water-stained brown dress. Suddenly it paused, the head turned, and, as I stand on this spot, I saw Lucy's face, though persistent search through the rooms found nothing! Why, man, what's the matter? Here, drink this water." And then there is silence for an instant in the room beyond.

"How do you feel, now, Mr. Ingolsby?" queries Mr. Strutt. "Ah, the color is coming to your face. The excitement of the past few days has—"

"No, not that," interposes Ingolsby, "not that, but this recital of Sir Griffith; it has strengthened, almost confirmed a suspicion to which I have never given words, of which I have barely allowed myself to think, 'tis so terrible. Sir Griffith, Mr. Strutt, I have not told you of something which occurred on that evening of the masquerade, which has preyed upon my mind ever since, giving me no rest night or day. During the evening, I chanced to find Miss Egerton on the balcony. She spoke strangely, even wildly, and fled from me. Miss Lifford, who happened to come out at the moment, told me how Lucy had overheard that unlucky conversation, which seems remarkably to have influenced her fate."

"Ingolsby," hoarsely asks Sir Griffith, "do you ever think of her reluctance to choose the slip of paper?"

"I thought of it then, sir, as I wandered off through the grounds, my mind disturbed by painful memories. But do not let that distress you; it is but one of those strange coincidences which serve as a foundation for foolish superstitions. I was about to say, that in my ramble I unexpectedly found myself in the neighborhood of the lake, just by the boat-house. As I leaned against one of the trees in the shadow, the water, rippling in the moonlight, had a soothing effect upon me. It could not have been more than a few minutes before there was a rustling in the bushes, and rapid footsteps on the gravel. I turned my head, and there stood Lucy gazing up at the moon, its light falling on her white face. My first impulse was to speak to her; but, on second thoughts, I determined not to pain her by the knowledge of my presence, and remained silently where I was, in the shade of the trees. She moved quickly to the water's edge, and stepping into one of the boats, rowed herself to the middle of the lake. There she dropped the oars, and I could dimly see her standing in the boat, with arms stretched upward. A sudden movement, a low cry, a splash, and she was in the water! I was scarcely conscious of having moved, before I found myself in the lake supporting her. I carried her to the shore. I don't think she had lost consciousness; but lying there in my arms, she was speechless, frightened, stunned. I took her to the house, up a private staircase, to her room, and left her with her maid. Then I went to my own room to change my wet clothes, but did not rejoin the revelers.

"When her absence was discovered the next day, I told her maid not to speak of what had occurred; and perhaps I was wrong in doing so, but my purpose was to save others from the anxiety I suffered myself.

"The last time I saw Lucy, she was lying on her sofa, a brown dress clinging to her as the water dripped from its folds on to the carpet; her eyes following me to the door, dumbly imploring. This seems almost like a breach of confidence."

He pauses, but nothing is said by the other two.

"While we have been searching for her," he presently continues, "each day bringing nothing but disappointment, the thought has formed and grown in my mind, was that fall in the water accidental? Is it possible that she can have— But no, no; I will not allow such thoughts to sully her pure memory. I should not have told you this!"

"Compose yourself, my dear sir," says the lawyer. "You have done right to speak. Your only error has been in not informing us of this sooner, that a different kind of investigation might be adopted than that hitherto pursued. The lake must be dragged at once."

"Come, cheer up, my boy!" says Sir Griffith with forced cheerfulness. "Don't give way to despondency. Just imagine yourself a Mahometan and look upon all this as having been written in the Book of Fate long before we or our forefathers were born to our inheritance of mingled joys and sorrows. Remember, that all your worrying will not alter the past. Think what the state of my mind would be, did I permit myself to believe that I am the cause of all that has occurred from having forced the girl into acting against her wish. I simply believe that I have been the cat's paw of circumstances, and that all was foreknown to a Power above, long before it happened. Mercy on us, how late it is! After twelve; and into what an abstruse subject I have been led. If you'll excuse me, Strutt, I'll leave you here to write your letters in peace. And Ingolsby, let you and I go to bed."

Good-nights are exchanged, and as their footsteps die away in the distance, I steal off to my room.

When half way up the stairs, I catch their voices returning, and fly back to the dark hall below. Twice or thrice I think they have gone to their rooms, but their footfalls sound again as they pace to-and-fro, now near, and now far. At last, I hear the words, "Good-night, my boy." "Good-night, sir." and then I go up stairs once more. As I reach the last step, a shadow—a dark *something*—moves quickly past and is lost in the gloom. What is it? Frightened and trembling, I reach my room, hurriedly strike a light and glance around. Nothing unusual is to be seen, and I think it an idle fancy, conjured up by my over-excited brain, and go off to bed, but only to dream of Lucy's body found floating in the lake. Once during the night, I imagine she is beside me with one hand on my pillow, the other, glowing as a ball of fire. Starting up wide awake, I light my candle, but see nothing, hear nothing, but the mice in the wainscot. Everything remains as I had left it, and I lie back fully convinced that it was only a dream, but, nevertheless, keep the candle burning beside me till dawn.

CHAPTER XI.

I summon up remembrance of things past.
—**Shakspeare: Sonnet XXX.**

I SIT alone at my window, looking out on the snow-covered ground, and trees red with berries, contrasting with the white mantle of mother earth, and reminding one forcibly of the happy day so lately passed—the anniversary of that event which brought redemption to the world with

"Peace, good-will, towards men."

My thoughts are of that blessed occasion, as I gaze on the lonely scene without—the snow, chaste and bright, beneath the cold though brilliant rays of the winter sun, as they glance from icicles which droop and sparkle on leafless trees and evergreens, forming a fringe of hues rivaling the varied tints of rarest gems; and my occupation, that of writing up my diary, is forgotten, and the book lies neglected in my lap.

At length, turning from the view which has so many attractions in my eyes, I re-open the leaves that contain the history of my own life, and events in the lives of many others. For the first time since it was written, I glance over the account of the disappearance of Lucy, and the fruitless search that followed. A little over four months has she been gone, and it seems an age to me, left alone here in this desolate old place which all now fully believe to be haunted by the poor girl's spirit. The holidays have gone by uncelebrated for the first time in the eighteen years since that other disappearance of the son of the house.

Unfortunate family! to lose two children in the same mysterious fashion.

The snow was already deep on the ground, and the pretty little robin red-breasts hopping about, when Sir Griffith was ordered to a milder climate for the benefit of his health, which, after all hope of recovering his lost darling was past, had begun perceptibly to fail in spite of his energetic attempts to hide the fact from us, and appear himself in the face of this second sorrow of his life. But his malady refused to obey his will, the disease would not be thwarted, and by the command of his physicians, he, accompanied by Lady Egerton, went to pass the winter on the continent, much to the satisfaction of her ladyship who took the astounding event of Lucy's flight quite philosophically and with wonderful composure even for one of her phlegmatic temperament.

Mr. Jedediah Strutt's confident prediction of Lucy's speedy return to her friends remains unfulfilled, notwithstanding his re-employment of the police, and the advent upon the scene of some of the most expert detectives of Scotland-yard. They carefully explored the house, discovering several out of the way passages and secret doors that none of us knew existed, and dragged the lake, but all to no purpose; the only trace of the missing girl to be found, the brown merino dress in which she played the housemaid, discovered hidden away in one of many unused rooms, being a clue that ended where it began. Of course, gossip was not idle in the neighborhood at these strange doings, and the old story of Guy Egerton, and his mysterious spiriting away, was revived, and in everybody's mouth.

Poor Ingolsby! Few would have guessed from his calm, almost cheerful demeanor, all that he suffered; though, to a keen observer, lines of sorrow were perceptible about the firm mouth and beneath the sad grey eyes. He **was** young; yet, his face showed that this was not the first time sorrow had been met and conquered.

When the others left, he accompanied **them** to the south of France, to recuperate his somewhat shattered health, **and shortly returns** to England to renew the search. He would never give over, he said, till some efficient clue was found. The last words of Sir Griffith on leaving home were to the assembled household:

"On my return," said he, "if it ever takes place, let me never hear the sound of her name; let every reminder of her be removed from sight; let her be as one who has never existed. She may be living or she may be dead; and, in either case, she has acted a most ungrateful, shameful part, and no longer has she any hold upon my heart. I say this openly, and without hesitation to you all. Remember it!"

And he was gone; so feeble, yet so stern, and having spoken each word clearly and decidedly in spite of his wife's imploring gestures; for though she loved Lucy less deeply, yet her woman's heart would have spared the poor girl's memory this bitter humiliation. How cruel, and yet—I cannot help saying it—how just these words of his seem, as I read them over! But to erase them from my mind, I turn the leaves in search of others, more kind and loving, that I have taken down in happier times.

But what is this that I find between the leaves? A letter directed to Miss Lifford, which, surely, I never saw before, and never placed in that position. With fingers trembling from excitement, for I recognize the handwriting, I tear it open, and it drops to the floor as, turning to the end, I see Lucy's name! It must be from the spirit-world, I think, and I would cast it into the fire, only my curiosity—that bane of my life—tempts me to read. Thrice I stoop for the letter, and thrice it drops from my fingers to the floor. At last it remains in my faltering hand, my foolish fears are dispelled, and my fingers grasp it firmly, as I begin to read:

"O Julia, Julia! I am going to leave you—to leave my home, every one, everything—and my heart is breaking. Would that I had courage to brave the humiliation of remaining and being claimed by that man! But I have not. Am I very, very wicked, Julia, not to have any filial feeling toward my father? O, the misery of finding, after all these years proudly imagining myself the daughter of that good old man I love so well, that I have been cruelly deceived by those I loved and trusted most on earth, and that I am nothing but a lowly-born village maiden! Why was I taken from my rightful station and given thoughts and tastes that did not of right belong to me? Why did they cultivate a mind into being ashamed of its possessor's true position in life? It was all cruelly mistaken kindness; and now, I have to pay the penalty, by going out into the world and earning my living in that sphere for which my past life has unfitted me; for to return to my father, and sink from a highbred lady into a village lass in the place where I was born and have lived so many happy years, is more than I could endure. I cannot —I will not do it! *He* has never known a daughter's love and he will not miss it. Sir Griffith will move heaven and earth to find me, I know; and (were I but to speak the words) would sacrifice all he possesses to keep me with him; but that I will not have. If I do not take my true position in life, I will not occupy a false one. He must not find me—he shall not. I will never consent to live as I did, and I could not exist as *his* child—*his!* I have laid my plans well, and they can never find me. Besides, I have good reasons for knowing that they will all think me dead. It is far better that they should imagine I am out of this sad world, than living, they know not where or how. There will be a stain on my memory—but what of that? Who will care after a very short time? Even Alva, to whom I was at first tempted to write as I am doing to you, even *he* will soon recover from the blow; for he knows of something which will confirm the general suspicion, and will help to erase the memory of one he must think so wicked from his mind. Oh, Julia, 'tis the unkindest cut in my poor heart to think that he believes me capable of the base wickedness and cowardice of taking the life which belongs to my Maker. But it is better so—better, far better; and he will forget me sooner, and take one more worthy, though not more loving, to his heart. Ah, never, never will he find one *more loving!* Good-bye, Julia, dear; you have always been good to me, and do not change now, by telling the secret of my existence, a secret which a wise girl would have kept to herself, but my full heart would have burst, had I not poured it forth to some one. If you knew my plans for flight, which, of course I dare not tell, you would see how utterly futile will be all attempts at recovery. I leave it to your honor to keep my secret, and close these many lines with tears wrung from me for the first time in all these unhappy hours by thoughts of the step I am compelled to take. O Fate—Fate!— why so cruel to poor Lucy."

She is alive! is the first thought that passes through my mind. And she will soon be found! Then I remember the months that have gone by without the occurrence of any such event, and I am filled with grief that this letter, which would have been such a spur to our exertions, should not have been sooner found. It would, at least, have saved much heart-burning and many regrets, if nothing more. But how came it here? 'Tis surely very strange. She could not have placed it here herself that night, for I was in my room when the ball broke up, and she remained down stairs until the last. The next morning she had gone before I was awake. Had she a *confidante* amongst the servants? We never thought of that, and yet, it must have been so; for now I recollect how anxious was

Jane Wilson to leave her place as soon as her young mistress was found to be missing.

This news should be sent to Mr. Strutt at once; and I immediately sit down and write to him, enclosing a copy of Lucy's letter. It seems unkind to disregard her wish for secrecy after the confidence she has placed in me, but I cannot allow her to wreck her happiness by any of her foolish whims. The letter must go, and having sent it off to do its work of assisting in the recovery of our pet, I return to my window, and there watching the softly-falling snow, dream of a re-united and happy family.

CHAPTER XII.

Oft expectation fails, and most oft there
Where most it promises.
— All's Well that Ends Well: Act II, Scene 2.

WITH paper before me, I am about to write to the Egertons when the post comes in, bringing me a characteristic epistle from Sir Griffith:

"BASLE, February 4th.

"MY DEAR JULIA: 'The Campbells are coming.' My wife desires me to say: Have the town-house in readiness for our return, which, being interpreted, means, immediately proceed to open all the doors and windows, and having thus formed a thorough draught, drench the entire place with soap-suds, to make it moist as well as airy; shroud the furniture, and turn everything topsy-turvy, upside down; then, having got all things into beautiful confusion, perform the laborious task of setting them to rights again; and I give you three weeks in which to accomplish it all. I won't stand this beastly place any longer. I've had quite enough of balmy, humbug, fiddlestick climates, and am determined to return 'hame, hame, hame to my ain countree,' if it kills me. Better die a violent death at home than be *ennuyé* into one's grave in a place like this. Agnes enjoys it immensely—doesn't wish to return, and would stay behind were it not for appearances. We leave here this afternoon for Paris, where my lady intends to replenish her wardrobe, and we will start for home in time to reach London on the twenty-eighth.

"We have been constantly on the move since Ingolsby left us for Italy, two months ago; and consequently, have heard from him but once. Agnes wishes you to make a *few* purchases in town. She intends re-furnishing her own *suite* of rooms, and I inclose a list of articles which begins its expensive career by costing me triple postage.

"In the name of all the furies, manage to forget the most of them, or you'll leave me beggared in my old age.

"Agnes forgets to send her love in the excitement of *watching* her trunks packed, but I send it for her.

"Expect us in London on the twenty-eighth, remember.

"I am,

"Yours,

"GRIFFITH EGERTON."

"P. S. Close the hall, and bring all the servants to town. It is doubtful when I shall return to Bratton."

Little use in writing now, and I will keep the good news of Lucy's letter for a welcome home. But how unfortunate that they are to arrive so soon, leaving me such short space in which to complete necessary arrangements. It is just like Sir Griffith, however, to suppose that others require as little time as himself to form and execute resolves. I only hope that the change of climate at this early season may not be injurious to him.

Nothing is to be done but to obey orders, and after several days spent in the performance of many duties attendant on shutting up an establishment like this for an indefinite period, I start for London.

The house in Park-Lane is a dismal old place with, at present, but few habitable rooms kept in readiness for flying visits. The rest of the house having remained closed since the end of last season, all the carpets are rolled up and put away, the furniture is covered closely, and dusty windows are screened by dustier shutters. In the few habitable rooms I take up my abode, and at once set the domestic machinery in motion. Windows are thrown open and the sunlight let in, showing everything thickly covered with a dust that is soon seen stirring in the sunbeams; gloom is chased away by light and air, and the place is beginning to assume an orderly, cheerful aspect, when I start out to execute my numerous commissions, not daring to follow Sir Griffith's hint, and forget them. Even Lady Egerton would be ruffled at that.

One afternoon, while I am at Jackson & Grahams, the upholsterer's in Oxford street, giving orders about some violet satin hangings for her ladyship's boudoir, a lady enters the shop and accidentally upsets a cornice, which, falling towards me, just grazes my shoulder.

"A thousand pardons!" she exclaims; "I hope my awkwardness has not harmed you."

"Not in the least, I assure you," is my reply, although the shoulder *is* a little painful. My excuse for the fib is the beautiful face looking with unfeigned kindliness into mine; a face so fascinating that I cannot forbear glancing at it rather oftener than good **form** permits, while she stands at a little distance. I may be ordering purple curtains lined with blue, for aught that I know, my attention is so fully occupied with the dignified, yet graceful figure. A window at the back of the shop throws its light on a countenance expressive of all that is womanly in the highest sense of the word—amiability, gentleness, love, and tenderness toward all mankind—all the soft and winning qualities of woman, mingled with a firmness and courage unmistakable; and from the eyes beam that best and rarest gift to human nature, true heartfelt sympathy—a fund of it never to be exhausted. The color of the eyes is dark liquid brown, lustrous as a young girl's, beneath the smooth bands of simply parted white hair, which proves the advanced age of an otherwise young-looking face. Her ungloved hand, with its taper fingers and delicate nails, shows high breeding, as does her whole air, and I am quite enchanted by the most beautiful old lady I have ever seen.

On passing out she smiles and nods another excuse for the accident, and my eyes follow her into a coroneted carriage at the door.

As the equipage turns slowly in front of the shop, my glance is caught by a small, ungloved hand very like the one I have been admiring, that rests upon the door. A quick flash in the sunshine, and as the horses step out more briskly, something glittering falls, apparently unnoticed, from that hand, and rolls into the street close beside the pavement. With a bound to the door, following a sudden impulse of curiosity, I dash into the street, to the astonishment of the shopman, who has already regarded me with wondering eyes, and in I plunge amongst the throng of passing vehicles. A policeman is by my side instantly, and idle passers-by stand and gaze. For a moment I am at a loss what to do or to say. Then I tell him I have lost a ring, for I think it the most probable article to drop from a lady's hand, and he, requesting me to step on to the pavement, searches for that glittering something. Ah, there it lies! He sees it as quickly as I, and rescues it from the mud. I have one fortunate glimpse of it as he brushes it free of dirt, and, thanks to my clear sight, I recognize it instantly, oh, wonder of wonders, as a ring that I have seen before.

It is a carbuncle in a peculiar, old-fashioned setting; a setting that is strangely familiar, and, with my heart throbbing from excitement, I stretch out my hand to receive it. But the man, with professional caution, holds it back, and asks me how he shall know that it is mine?

A curious crowd is gathering around us. I run a great risk in claiming and attempting to identify this ring, but I am sure that I recognized it. I could not mistake what was my own property for years before I gave it as a birthday present to Lucy Egerton.

"It is a carbuncle ring," I say boldly with I hope no outward sign of inward tumult; "and inside it are engraved the initials, ' L. E. from J. L.,' the date, ' September 25, 18–.'"

The man holds the ring up to the light. Am I right? I stand holding my breath as he screws up one eye and peers into it. The crowd is increasing, and people press upon and stare at me most unpleasantly, and make uncomplimentary remarks. Some of them evidently take me for a shop-lifter, caught with stolen goods in my possession.

"'S., S. F.' (how I tremble!) "No, 'L. E.'". (Ah!) "'from I., J. L.' Yes, mum; it's all quite right, mum," and touching his hat respectfully, the policeman hands me the ring, and bids the crowd move on. Very unwillingly it does so, considering itself defrauded of its rights, no doubt, in that there has been neither row nor arrest to entertain it.

Clutching my prize tightly, I rush back into the upholsterers. There I have time to examine it, for the clerks are busy with other customers. What a marvelous incident is this. The ring given by me to Lucy Egerton, falling from the window of a private carriage and coming directly back into my hands. What a mystery it would have been to me but for Lucy's recently-found letter; but now of one thing I am convinced, this ring and the woman who occupied that carriage will be clues to the girl's whereabouts. Either she herself was the occupant, or the occupant knows something of her. That is logic.

Prompted by a sudden thought, I seek out the head man of the establishment, the man who waited upon the lady who upset the cornice. From him I demand her name.

"I don't know her name, ma'am," is the aggravating answer, uttered in an indifferent tone by the upholsterer.

"Don't know it! Why, did she leave you no address?"

"No ma'am, she is not a customer. Only came in to make some inquiries."

Greatly disappointed, and with throbbing heart and puzzled mind, I leave the shop. Thinking that I ought to impart my discovery at once to Mr. Strutt, I drive directly to his office. 'Tis but a few streets to Lincoln's Inn Fields, and a long flight of stairs takes me up to his chambers, where I find his little wizened confidential clerk who might be a relation of the solicitor himself, from the likeness between them.

"Good morning, Miss Lifford, take a chair, Miss; a very pleasant day. Take this chair, Miss; you'll find it more comfortable."

"Thanks, Mr. Wiggins, the one I have is very comfortable. Is n't Mr. Strutt in?"

"Well, now, Miss Lifford, isn't it unfortunate that you should have all the trouble of coming this long way, and Mr. Strutt not here," rubbing his chin with the feathered end of his quill-pen. "You see, Miss, he was called away suddenly to draw the will of an old gentleman who is supposed to be dying down in Suffolk, and they sent for Mr. S., post-haste."

"Oh, dear, I'm so sorry! Nothing could be more unfortunate! When do you expect him back?"

"I can't say when he'll return, Miss, for the old gent may live a week or two, and he's a reg'lar cranky old curmudgeon, who may insist on having half a dozen or more different wills drawn up before he gets one to suit him. He has given the alarm of dying often before now, Miss, and kept Mr. S. there, day after day hard at work, and when, at last, he had a document to please him all published, signed and witnessed, why Miss, he'd get well again and tear it up."

"I wonder that Mr. Strutt will dance attendance on such a crazy old man."

"Well, you see Miss," he replies, using his knife vigorously on the pen, "he gets well paid for it—very well paid; for the old gent isn't a miser, Miss, but only wants to leave his money to the best advantage, and he thinks he can use it better himself than any one else, and is afraid to keep a satisfactory will executed when he gets one, imagining as somebody mentioned would be tempted to kill him to get the money at once. For he's very queer—a reg'lar old curmudgeon, Miss," and he gives an emphatic nib to the pen.

"When did Mr. Strutt leave town?" I ask, little interested in the whims of this odd creature.

"On the fifth, Miss; and there is a letter here for him from you, Miss. I didn't forward it, as he told me not to send him all his letters, not knowing exactly how long he'd be away, but to open them myself and only send to him anything of great importance. I didn't think it would make much difference, if this matter you wrote about was not attended to at once, as so much time has already been lost since the young lady's disappearance; but if you consider it necessary, I will write at once."

"*If* I consider it necessary! I should think I did consider it necessary," I answer angrily. "One would suppose that so much time having been lost already, was the very reason that none should be wasted now. How do we know that she is not at this moment in abject misery—starving, perhaps—and too proud to ask for help?" (As he has been so negligent I choose not to tell him of my adven-

5

ture at the upholsterers' shop-door.) " Your conduct has been most strange, Mr. Wiggins, and I cannot understand your motives. You will oblige me by writing immediately to Mr. Strutt, and telling him **there is** work of more importance awaiting him here in town, than **pandering to the whims of that** old will-making dotard," and I sweep from the room, followed to the stair-head by the cringing clerk offering apologies and excuses innumerable. A nice person **for** Mr. Jedediah Strutt to leave as a judge of the importance of matters in his business!

I return home in such a bad humor that I feel tempted to wish that the " old curmudgeon " may this time be obliged to make his *last* will and testament. **If Sir Griffith or Ingolsby were only here!** But they are miles away, and I must trust to my own resources. A whole night I pass in forming schemes for tracing Lucy, but discard them again as unsatisfactory, with even greater rapidity than that old wretch in Suffolk destroys his wills.

When morning comes, **I have** determined that for **the present I** can do nothing—absolutely nothing—but wait and **keep** my eyes **open and** look about me for the reappearance of that coroneted carriage. Having met it once, 'tis more than likely to cross my path **again.**

CHAPTER XIII.

Yet when an equal poise of hope and fear
Does arbitrate the event, my nature is
That I incline to hope rather than fear.
— COMUS.

UNCTUALLY on the twenty-eighth the Egertons arrive. Sir Griffith but little improved by his trip, poor man; Lady Egerton as calmly benignant as ever, retiring at once to her room, with a few cold words of praise at the general appearance of order in the house. Sir Griffith is more cordial in his manner.

"Ha, Julia," he says, " how nicely **you have arranged things.** Wonderful, considering the short time you had! And just see here," opening his library door and going in; " everything placed to my hand as you know I like it, **and** all the little trifles I forgot. **You** are quite a treasure, Julia, really," looking at me kindly. Then his eyes wander round the room again, and starting slightly, he exclaims, " But not this, Julia; this must not be here!" He points with a trembling finger and frowning face at the wall where hangs a **portrait of** Lucy when a child.

"Oh, Sir Griffith, I have something to tell you about her," I say, with a slight feeling of diffidence.

"No, no," he replies, nervously fingering some papers on the table; "I will hear nothing, Julia. And you will please to remember my parting instructions."

"But, Sir Griffith," I boldly hurry on; "she is alive! and she wrote—"

"Saying where she was, and with whom?" he interrupts, with a shade of relenting in his voice, as his face brightens.

"The letter was written at the time of her flight, but I only received it a short time ago. Since then I have heard nothing further; only ——"

"That will do," raising his hand, and his face growing sterner. "If she prefers the society of strangers to that of her benefactors, let her have her own way. I will not be cajoled into speaking of the girl; and I lay my positive commands upon you never again to mention her name in my presence," and he motions me to leave the room.

With what harshness Sir Griffith judges her conduct! But I have little doubt his feelings would soon change, were he to read her pathetic letter to me; and I still have hopes of a reconciliation, if I can only prevail upon him to listen to me. I can but wait and trust that time may soften him. In the meantime the girl must be found, and the next afternoon I start out to inquire if Mr. Strutt has yet returned from Suffolk.

As I am leaving the house, Lady Egerton's maid hurries down stairs with the request from her ladyship that I will call for a lace flounce at Hayward's in Oxford street. It provokes me not a little to be compelled to go so far out of my way, but the event proves that, for once in her life, her ladyship has been the means to a good end; for when I drive up to the shop, there is that same coroneted carriage before the door!

The sole occupant is just stepping out, and to my great disappointment, 'tis neither Lucy nor the old lady, but a *petite* young girl. We reach the shop-door together, and she pushes her way past me somewhat rudely, with a haughty sweep of her skirts. Her little head, with its straw-colored hair and watery-blue eyes, is carried very high, and a face that might otherwise be pretty is marred by an expression of scornful contempt for everything beneath her. While looking in vain for the eyebrows and lashes, that have either forsaken their position, or are so light in color as to be imperceptible to my old eyes, I feel that I would not trust that girl with the life of a dumb animal. I take an intense dislike to her on the spot

—very absurd, no doubt, but as uncontrollable as is love at first sight. However, she possesses an interest for me, and having lingered over silks, and satins, and laces till she has completed her purchases, I give orders to the coachman to follow her carriage from place to place.

A long and rather exciting chase it is, for often do we get entangled in the block of vehicles. Straight on through Oxford street the coroneted carriage drives without stopping again, and we lose sight of it as it turns into Regent street, but catch up again near the Quadrant; thence on up Piccadilly and past Green Park it goes, once more nearly giving us the slip in the crowd at Hyde Park Corner, and I wonder to myself as we toil slowly through the jam, whether it will turn down Grosvenor place, or keep on out Knightsbridge way to Brompton. The former it does, and at last draws up before a handsome house in Eaton Square, and the blonde young lady, dismissing the carriage, enters the house and the door closes on her small figure.

Shall I get out and make inquiries for Lucy? Inclination answers, yes; judgment says, no. For if she still wishes to remain undiscovered, a glimpse of me may send her off again like a startled fawn. So, with the feeling of a detective who has successfully run his game to earth, and endeavoring to emulate one in the wariness of my conduct, I forbear from making any demonstration whatever. Taking out my tablets, I carefully note down the number of the house, and then drive off with my information to Mr. Jedediah Strutt. He receives me with many apologies for his apparent neglect, saying he had just arrived in town, and my letter with many others had been awaiting his return.

"As the young lady's letter does not afford any clue to her whereabouts, I don't see that we stand any better than formerly," he says.

"Pardon me, Mr. Strutt, we stand very much better, for I have at last discovered traces of her."

Then I tell him circumstantially of my finding of the ring, and he laughs over my description of its recovery. My recital, however, evidently makes no change in his opinion, for as he takes up the ring that I have placed upon his desk, and scrutinizes it carefully, he says in a low, unexcited tone:

"I think, Miss Lifford, that you are much mistaken in supposing"—

"Mistaken! mistaken in a ring that was mine for years; that is remarkable for its setting? The letters engraved upon it might possibly be a coincidence, but to think that the setting, combined with the letters, is also a coincidence would be, to say the very least, unreasonable."

"Be patient, madam, and hear me out. I do not doubt the identity of the ring" (how very kind, think I, and no doubt express the thought in my face); "but as to its being a clue to the young lady, you are mistaken, lamentably mistaken."

"But my dear sir, I saw it drop from the carriage not ten yards from where I stood, and it must naturally have fallen from Lucy's own finger or from the finger of some one who has met the original owner."

"Not necessarily, Miss Lifford, not by any means necessarily," slipping the ring on to his little finger—his nasty, crooked little finger—and holding it up before him. Then he looks at me over his spectacles and says slowly and impressively: "Have you ever heard of pawnbrokers, Miss Lifford? Be patient," holding up his hand, feeling proud of its unusual adornment doubtless, "and I will explain to you my ideas upon this subject. Let me demonstrate. Miss Egerton—we will call her Miss Egerton for convenience—left her home under the impression that she was the daughter of the man Sullivan. None but a clever girl could have escaped as she did, eluding the most skillful detectives. If she be alive, her motive for having fled must be as strong as ever, or she would have returned; and, under the influence of that motive she has talent enough to keep herself well concealed, and wisdom enough not to go about as you suppose probable, to be seen and recognized by any former acquaintance. But Miss Lifford, I do not believe she is alive—she may be found yet, but not among the living."

"Not alive, Mr. Strutt!" I echo. "You cannot have read the copy that I sent you of her letter to me."

"Yes, madam, I have read it. Read it carefully, and studied it."

"Then you must have forgotten it again—forgotten that she said 'the unkindest cut in her poor heart was that she could be thought capable of the base wickedness of taking her own life.'"

"Yes, madam, I remember that perfectly; and here is the copy to remind me, had I forgotten."

"What under the sun then, do you mean?" I demand, losing all patience. "If you doubt the authenticity of that paper, I will produce the original. I have often heard of the distrust of lawyers, but I did not expect to be insulted by you, who, if you doubt my veracity in general, at least must surely know that I could have no motive for making false statements in this matter."

"You misconstrue my meaning altogether, Miss Lifford. Had I any doubts, your word would be quite sufficient to remove them," he replies, trying to smooth my ruffled feathers with oily words. "I feel firmly convinced that every line of this letter was written by Miss Egerton, apart from any assurance of yours."

"You seem to have forgotten your logic, Mr. Strutt; for if she wrote that letter, and if she meant what she wrote—ah!" with suspicion coming quickly, "can that be your reading of it?—that she wrote, not meaning what she said?"

"I am an old man," he answered, "and I know something of the world. I have read letters pathetic and soul-stirring, that have been written from the head, not from the heart. As such things have been done before, analogy teaches that they can be repeated. I liked the young lady, and admired her talents, and I think that in this instance, she has used them cleverly."

"Mr. Strutt!" and I rise indignantly, "I, too, am old and worldly-wise, and I flatter myself know something of human nature also. Besides, I am a woman, and better able to judge of her woman's nature than you, and I would be willing to take oath, that every word of that paper now before you, came from the very depths of her heart. Lucy descend to such subterfuge? Never! You cannot make me believe it! Your experience, I should judge, has been derived from intercourse with people, not of noble natures, such as her's."

"Well, well, my dear madame, do not get so excited; for my saying it does not make it so. I am seldom wrong in my opinions, though," he pompously adds, "and I don't think I am in this instance. But I shall at any rate do all in my power; and if you will furnish me with the number of the house in—in Eaton Square, I think you said it was—I shall let you know in a few days the result of my inquiries." He takes out his note-book and I give him the number.

"This transaction must be strictly *entre nous*," I say with regained composure; "for Sir Griffith is still incensed at her for leaving her friends so abruptly and without a word of farewell."

"I am very sorry to hear that. Believe me, whatever my opinions may be, you have my sincere good wishes for a happy ending to this strange affair. For the ring, it may have been lost, pawned or stolen; sold and resold; for its curious workmanship, bought by the present possessor—owner I should say—for really, Miss Lifford, *you* have no right or title to it."

CHAPTER XIV.

Poins. Nothing but papers, my lord.
Prince Henry. Let's see what they are: read them.
— Henry IV: Act III, Scene 1.

"AS usual, late for breakfast!" is Sir Griffith's greeting to me, when I enter the breakfast-room, as he finishes his second cup of coffee. "You'll never catch the worm, Julia."

"Hot rolls, Watkins!" ordered Lady Egerton, languidly sipping her chocolate.

"It has always been my opinion, Sir Griffith," I say, as I seat myself at the table, "that the birds would gain but little by leaving their snug nests, if the worm itself were not an early riser."

"Perhaps the worm is of a dissipated turn, and stops out all night," chuckles Sir Griffith. "How then? Fancy a worm singing 'We won't go home till morning!'—Eh?"

"Well," I proceed, "suppose some winged fowl should mistake me, as would be most probable, for a worm, and snap me up? I prefer waiting until their maws are filled, and picking up whatever stray morsels may be left after their feast."

"Had that sentiment come from Agnes, it would not have surprised me," he remarks, busily plying knife and fork. "But from you, who are forever worming out secrets and bits of scandal, and varied information, it sounds very strange—'passing strange.'"

"You cannot accuse me of ever having wriggled into your confidence," I retort.

"'That's wormwood.'"

"What nobleman, I wonder, has his seat in Avington?" says Lady Egerton, glancing up questioningly from the *Morning Post*, which she has just begun to read.

"Where?" queries Sir Griffith, as he pauses in the act of raising his cup to his lips.

"Avington," repeats her Ladyship. "Here's a long paragraph, headed 'Romance in High Life'—'Sweets for the British Public,' it should be—devoted entirely to the private affairs of a certain Earl of A——. Some public man, I should judge," running her eye again over the article. "Can it be Lord Acreman, I wonder? But no; his two places are Pontfort Court, Moncton, and—and—"

"The other place is in Ireland, isn't it," I ask. "County Meath, I think."

"Yes; somewhere in Ireland. Remind me, Julia, after breakfast, to look through the A's in the Peerage; or, you might do it for me, if you will. Such execrable taste, isn't it, Griffith, to publish one's family affairs in the public newspapers?"

"A public man can't always help himself, my dear," he replies, in a voice that makes me glance quickly at him. As he holds out the cup for more coffee, his hand trembles visibly, but his countenance is imperturbable, and his voice again steady, as he continues: "When a man tries to serve the people, they think he belongs to them, and take the right of ferreting out his private affairs, in spite of any resistance he may choose to make. But let's hear this article, Agnes. What is it all about?"

Lady Egerton reads aloud:

(From the *Avington News* of March 3.)

ROMANCE IN HIGH LIFE.—We take great pleasure in announcing to our readers the extreme good fortune that has lately befallen the well known and popular Earl of A——. It has been a constant source of regret to us that this universally beloved Earl and his beautiful Countess, upon whose head rest the benedictions of the suffering poor, have had no heir to endow with the rich inheritance of their own good qualities, and to be to a future generation—if possible—what Lord A—— is to this. Though we can never cease to deplore that there is no direct inheritor of the title, yet our regret is much lessened by the fact that a richly deserved blessing has been bestowed upon Lord and Lady A——, in the recent recovery of a long-lost and lovely daughter. Many years ago, this child was stolen from her parents, and bravely did they bear the great and irremediable loss, passing a lonely, childless life, with the milk of human kindness unsoured, and with a keener sympathy for the sufferings of others.

By a marvelous chance, unequaled in the pages of romance, but as yet imperfectly explained to us—has this child been returned to them in all the loveliness of early womanhood. Beautiful and accomplished, may she be to them the blessing that they themselves have been to many; and may the good wishes of the townsfolk of Avington for her own happiness be amply fulfilled.

"Newspaper hyperbole," laughs Lady Egerton. "Beautiful she may be as regards personal appearance, but where would a stolen child acquire the education, refinement and polish necessary to fit her to fill the position of a daughter of a peer of the realm? They have my sympathy, and well for them if they are not obliged to close their eyes to the pity likely to be hidden under the congratulations of the world. I must say I consider myself more fortunate in our loss than they are in their gain."

Without comment, Sir Griffith gathers up the letters that lie beside his plate and slowly reads the addresses. One letter he selects from the others and puts in his pocket unread; another he tosses across the table unopened, saying:

"Here, Agnes, this is for you, not for me. Butters is getting careless." The rest he opens but merely skims them over, before he jumps up from his seat and leaves the room, his face puckered by some annoyance. Then I remember my *one* letter, hitherto neglected, and opening it, read:

"19 Lincoln's Inn Fields, W. C., Monday, March 4, 18—.

"Miss Lifford—Dear Madame:

"If you have no engagement for next Friday, I shall do myself the honor of waiting upon you at an early hour on a matter of importance. Friday is the nearest day I can name, being the only one this week from which I can spare a few hours.

"I have the honor to be, dear Madame,

"Your obedient servant.

"Jedediah Strutt."

"Do you want to read this, Julia?" and Lady Egerton, handing me the letter thrown to her by Sir Griffith, rises and glides gracefully from the room.

"Travelers' Club, March 4.

"My Dear Lady Egerton:

"I called at your house this afternoon, and was greatly disappointed to find no one at home. Only two days in town, engagements of importance have unfortunately kept me from paying my respects sooner, and not having heard from you in nearly two months, I am most anxious to learn the state of Sir Griffith's health, and also what news there may be of the missing one. I have been in Italy, as you know, for some time past, and was buoyed up from day to day by the hope of good tidings that never reached me. Although so anxious, I almost dread to meet you, not knowing what there may be to tell, that you had not the heart to write. However, so soon as I can again 'screw my courage to the sticking-place,' I shall do myself the honor of calling in Park Lane.

"With kind regards to Sir Griffith and Miss Lifford, believe me,

"Yours very sincerely,

"Alva Ingolsby."

CHAPTER XV.

Reproachful speech from either side
The want of argument supplied;
They rail'd, revil'd—as often ends
The contests of disputing friends.
— Gay's Fables.

N Friday morning, long before the hour for fashionable calls, I am waiting impatiently in the drawing-room for the arrival of Mr. Jedediah Strutt.

He showed a great ignorance of womankind, for all his vaunted knowledge, in sending his note so long before; for what woman could wait patiently three whole days to hear a matter of importance—under such circumstances, especially? Or, perhaps, he merely wished to annoy me; in which case I have amply revenged myself by making him answer my three notes a day ever since; though in all his replies, the wily old creature never so much as gave me a hint of what his matter of importance was, but was still curt and secretive.

I am busily knitting away, when the servant announces, not Mr. Strutt, but—

"Mr. Ingolsby!"

The first glance at his face as he enters, shows it to be radiant, fairly beaming with some happy emotion, not in character with his recently received note. I confess to a feeling of disappointment, for I had pictured to myself the dark cloud I should lift from his handsome brow, with the news *I* believe to be true, and my greeting is, therefore, somewhat cold.

"My dear Miss Lifford!" he exclaims, his eyes sparkling as he takes both my hands; "pray accept my warmest congratulations on this happy *denouement*."

"I am at a loss to understand your meaning, Mr. Ingolsby," I reply, coldly. "Will you kindly explain yourself, and say for what I am to accept such enthusiastic congratulations?"

"Now don't put on that grandiloquent air—it doesn't suit you," he says, sitting down beside me and playing with my ball of worsted, "and it makes me uncomfortable. If Florence were but here now to take the starch out of your manner."

"And pray allow me to ask who Florence may be?—a *fiancée*, no doubt."

"Yes," he answers, nodding and laughing with an arch look; and with indignation, I say—

"I don't see why *I* should be congratulated on such an occasion.

You are doubtless confused by great joy, and on entering spoke the words you expected to hear from my lips."

"I most assuredly imagined I should hear them echoed," he replies, somewhat reproachfully. "Such a happy event demands something of the kind."

"I confess to being so obtuse as not to see how 'the event' can affect any one but yourself, Mr. Ingolsby. As to congratulations, it would be to the young lady I should offer them, for her conquest of such a paragon of consistency and constancy as yourself."

"Thanks, Miss Lifford," he says quite good humoredly, not appearing to notice the sarcasm in my tone. "It's all one—or soon will be, I hope sincerely—to whom you offer them; and I'm glad to see you fully appreciate me."

His assurance in talking so coolly and shamelessly quite takes my breath away, and there is silence for a moment as he unravels my knitting."

"You have a good memory," I at last remark.

"I flatter myself I have; and I don't intend to forget your cruel conduct in not letting me know the good news. I am indebted to an accident for my enlightenment, and no thanks to you, Miss Lifford."

"Indeed; I am very happy to hear it," I reply, thinking he must refer to Lucy's letter, about which he has probably heard from Mr. Strutt, yet wondering angrily how he dare allude to it in the same breath with the announcement which he has just made, and feeling too indignant to gratify him by speaking of it. "But it strikes me you must have learned the art of exaggeration from your *fiancée*, for nothing but very trifling good news has it been my good luck to hear lately."

"Now what is the use of keeping up that air of ignorance, when I am in the secret? You are awfully bitter this morning about something. I was never so thoroughly and completely sat upon in my life. I really wish she were here to soften you a little."

"If I am bitter, Mr. Ingolsby, you are vague and incoherent; and I am utterly at a loss to comprehend what secret you allude to."

"Oh, very well. Keep up the jest if it pleases you. I suppose you will go so far as to pretend not to know her, when she and her mother come to call?"

Thoroughly roused, I tell him: "The young woman and her mother will be wise not to try the experiment of calling. Of course they can't though, for Lady Egerton will never consent to call upon them."

"Indeed!" and it is his turn to look dignified and to speak with compressed lips. "Pray, why not?" I am too angry to answer, and he goes on: "Your knowledge of good breeding seems to be on the decrease. I cannot accuse *you*, Miss Lifford, of possessing a good memory, and I have my doubts of your being troubled with a heart."

"I beg to inform you, sir, that my heart is here in its proper place—not flying around at the beck and call of every one who may ask for it, as is that of a certain person of my acquaintance."

"As is mine of course. I must really return thanks and observe that I am not aware of having given any signs of fickleness. Whereas your remarks in regard to Florence——"

"How dare you mention that name in the same breath that you deny the charge of fickleness!" and I jump up, no longer able to suppress my anger. "You should be ashamed of yourself, but I don't believe you know the meaning of the word. Do you wish to insult me by speaking in this manner when you are aware of how much I know of your pretended love in the past? You will please excuse me, Mr. Ingolsby, I have an engagement which calls me away from your very pleasant society;" and I am about to leave the room when he places his hand on the door-handle, barring my passage out.

"Wait one moment, Miss Lifford. It cannot be possible that you are really ignorant of the facts of the case, and that we have been playing at cross-purposes? I thought at first that we were only having a mock passage-at-arms, but—do you mean to tell me you haven't heard the story of Flo——"

"I mean to tell you, young man, that I don't wish to hear that name again; and you will have the goodness to let me pass."

At this moment the handle is turned from without, Alva moves away, and Mr. Strutt, bearer of important news, is announced.

BOOK SECOND.

CHAPTER I.

> I have heard,
> And from men learned, that before the touch
> (The common coarser touch) of good or ill,
> That oftentimes a subtle sense informs
> Some spirits of the approach of things to be!
> -- Proctor.

TO Lucy Egerton Sir Griffith's project of a masquerade for the celebration of her birthday, did not long remain a secret. By her own penetration, by catching occasional inadvertently dropped words, she could not, although without any particular desire to do so, but discover what was the intended surprise that Sir Griffith had planned for her. Then she in her turn began to plot and scheme, and in the retirement of her own rooms prepared a disguise for herself, not being sure that one to her taste had been chosen for her, and determined, in any event, to glean an extra share of the evening's amusement by puzzling those who would expect to see her in another character.

The costume she formed was not, by any means, complex—only the simple dress of a housemaid. With keen anticipation of pleasure, she gave odd moments to the altering of a brown merino, so that it might not be recognized as hers, and busied herself with making the necessary muslin apron and little white cap of the order; yet the approach of the eventful evening brought a strange and increasing sense of sadness. For days the jaunty cap and apron lay undisturbed in their box; the brown merino hung neglected in her clothes-press. It no longer gave her the pleasure it had done at first to take them out and admire her handiwork, while she mused on what she should say and do when she had put them on. During this time she might, at any opportune moment, reasonably expect a declaration from Ingolsby, yet, as girls will sometimes do at this greatest and most pleasant crisis of their lives, she avoided a *tête-a-tête* with him, and when they were unavoidably thrown together, took refuge in argument and in quarreling. These days should have been to her the brightest within her memory, and yet they were not. Why, she could not have told, unless it were that an occasional constraint in his manner, an oft repeated pause in his talk, as he hesitated over some soft nothing, were sufficient to make her doubtful of his earnestness, and so cause her unacknowledged distrust.

Whatever the reason might be, when the hour at last arrived for the great surprise—the grand climax—when Sir Griffith divulged his scheme for the evening's amusement, she was unusually low-spirited. Her beautiful dress of Cybele was brought to her, and she tried to fight against melancholy, accusing herself of ingratitude toward those who were seeking to give her pleasure.

Whatever one's real feelings may be, it is possible, when one makes the effort, to at least appear to be light-hearted and happy; and none would have guessed who heard Lucy's merry laugh, or could have seen the smiling face behind her mask, how heavy was the heart—heavy in an unreasonable, persistent, unintelligible way—with which she entered the ball-room, clad in the gay dress of Queen Cybele.

It sometimes happens on a winter's day that a broad belt of clouds, encircling the horizon, leaves a space of blue above, through which the mid-day sun shines down upon earth so brightly, that, if not chancing to glance upward, one would never guess the storm which brews so near. Thus it is that sorrows unseen crowd around us, ever ready to meet above, and come crushing down upon us with a weight of darkness.

Here stood this girl in all her pride of youth and beauty, and those who saw only the bright and gay surroundings, indicative of wealth and position, how little could they know of the lowering clouds that hung heavily upon her horizon, ready at the very moment to join together and shut out the sun of prosperity that now shed its rays upon her!

Not long could she sustain the character of Cybele. It soon became unendurable, and stealing away to her room, she assumed the simpler one she had herself prepared; and then, hidden in a corner unnoticed and unsought, hoping for pleasure as a mere spectator, she overheard the tale told by the two old gossiping dowagers.

It was the story of her origin that she heard, and she believed it; but it came upon her so suddenly, and unexpectedly, that at first she did not realize the full force of what was embodied in the narrative. But when she had fled from the gay scene, dazzling and confusing in the extreme, and had reached a portion of the balcony without, which had been deserted for the dance, the cool night air calmed her throbbing pulses, and for the first time it came upon her, in all its cruel reality, that she was not what she had always supposed herself to be. The thought was unendurable to one of her proud temperament, and never doubting the truth of what she had heard, her memory turned with bitterness toward those who had deceived her. What though they had lavished affection and wealth upon her, giving her everything that could be wished for and anticipating her every desire, they had deceived her in this! They had fostered a pride of birth—and what was she? Not only the child of a common village laborer, but one who had killed his wife—her mother!—in a drunken fury. Had they never educated her, never heaped these luxuries upon her, she would not now feel the weight of all this. Could she leave her station in society to join that man Sullivan? Never! Yet, though she could not, her sense of right forbade that she should occupy a false position; and as these thoughts passed through her mind, she determined on a course to pursue. Taking her fate into her own hands, she would flee—assume an humbler position in the social scale, where unknown she would not be pointed at as one who had enjoyed fine feathers till they had fallen from her. She would flee from real and false parents alike—from friends—from society—from *him!*—and he just then coming out, disturbed her meditations and told her of his love and asked her to be his wife. Then she found—unhappy girl!—that there was something which, though it strengthened her purpose, yet made the pain of this more poignant than it would otherwise have been. Loving him as she did, could she permit him to marry one against whom she knew not what scandal might be erected on the foundation of this one truth? Would he not have to fight with society for her sake? Would he not, perhaps, be ashamed of her?—and her blood tingled at the thought; and though she could not blame him, yet she felt it would be more than she could bear. And as she put her head down on his shoulder, she thought, "perhaps, if he knew what I know, he would not be speaking so. Shall I tell him all and try him?—and perchance, find him wanting? No, no!—let me carry away into the world the image of one noble and good, as I have always known him; and neither take away all light from my own future, nor, by my selfishness, ruin his."

Starting away, she told him, with a composure she had not thought a moment before she could have assumed, that his hopes were never to be fulfilled; and yet, unconsciously she let him know that she loved him, and with his kiss on her brow wandered off alone into the garden, self-communing, her mind busy weaving plans for a secret flight.

Unconsciously her wavering steps took her down over the sloping lawn; down to the lakeside, through the weeping willows, on to the bank—to the very water's edge. She gazed at the calm surface which seemed to her excited fancy to have a strange fascination in its cold rippling glitter. All was like a night-mare—her spirit would have fled from the spot, but the water held her as though by iron bands. Then it seemed as if a hidden power drew her forward—on, on towards the glitter and ripple of the water into the little boat that lay upon its bosom. With every nerve quivering, she took up the oars and rowed herself out over the silvery surface toward the one reflection of the round white-faced full moon. She looked at the pale orb as it seemed to lie in the water at her feet, and then glanced up at it overhead, and as her eyes rested there the almost painful silence was broken as a breeze swept gently by, sighing sadly through the poplars. A sudden burst of music came from the ball-room with the hum of laughing, happy voices; a little bird twittered and chirped in its nest near by; a frog croaked hoarsely from among the reeds; an owl hooted in its tree—nature seemed with one accord to arouse, and ask this girl what she was about to do. The spell that had bound her seemed to break as the silence was broken, and she put the question to herself. Shuddering, she rose hastily to her feet, forgetful of her insecure position, conscious alone of the horror of herself, and the great yearning for help and pity that swelled in her heart. Passionately she clasped her hands and raised them toward heaven as all her soul spoke in the sobbing prayer:

"From pride and temptation, oh Lord protect me!"

As the prayer was wafted upward, the soft breeze once more came floating by, and in its passage swayed the boat with sufficient force to make her lose her balance, as she stood upright. Tottering, she fell, and as she felt herself nearing the water that had but now appeared so attractive, she shrank from meeting that death which she had so recently longed to embrace.

Ah, human nature—human nature! is it not always thus? We crave, we strive for an object with all our heart, and when it is attained, our eyes are opened to its defects, and we would shun it; yet, not learning by sad experience, we still wish with a great desire for others, which in their turn prove as unsatisfactory as those that have gone before. And, alas! after all our wasted hopes and desires, how often will the unpleasing object—its charm lost as we grasp it —cling to us in spite of all efforts to cast it off. Fortunately it was not to be so for Lucy. Her hand had not yet closed upon that of death. By a lucky chance Ingolsby was near and saved her from the watery grave which he then thought she had sought of her own free will.

She had not lost consciousness in falling, and as she rose in the water she felt a strong arm thrown around her and knew that she was saved by one who was swimming with her to the bank. When, dripping and cold, she felt herself laid upon the grass while some one supported her head, she opened her eyes and looked, with no sensation of surprise, into Ingolsby's face. She knew that it was he before she saw him, as you do sometimes feel the presence of a loved one. Gladly would she have died there and then—pardon her, she was only a romantic girl—for the arms of him she loved were close around her, while his face was bent very near to hers, as he tried to see by the moonlight if she were conscious. When he smiled with relief at her wide-open eyes, and caught her up again hastily in his arms, striding away with her toward the house, she knew that his burden was very dear to him; for he laid his cheek tenderly against hers and called her endearing names. Yet her heart gave no responsive throb of joy. She knew that it was for the last time. If he could ever forget that she was not his equal in the eyes of the world, *she* could not—no, not even now as she lay in his arms.

She knew that she might trust him not to cause a scene; so she spoke no word, and he avoided as she wished the walks where guests might be loitering, and took her in by a private way through empty halls up to her own room, laid her upon a sofa and rang for her maid.

"Your mistress accidentally fell into the lake," he said. "Attend to her quietly and don't disturb any one."

He left her then, and her eyes followed him to the door with a grateful, yet—as he construed it—imploring glance, that influenced him long in keeping what he thought to be her secret.

Still her purpose remained unshaken. She would leave this house before her courage flagged, and to succeed she must avoid drawing attention to herself.

"Hodges," she said to her maid, who had dried her and put other clothes upon her, indulging the while in exclamations of wonder and sympathy; "Hodges, is my hair dry enough to be re-dressed?"

"Miss?"

"Is my hair dry enough to be re-dressed?"

"Why, miss, you don't surely mean—"

"I mean, Hodges," with determination, "that when my hair is sufficiently dry I wish it rearranged. I am going down stairs again."

"But Miss Lucy, mem; you'll be sick. I am sure my lady, mem—"

"Never mind 'my lady,' Hodges, but hurry. I want to be there

6

before supper, at the unmasking. If you don't help me I must
dress myself."

"That be somethin' the ladies I 'as served 'as never 'ad to do yet,
Miss," with offended dignity. "I knows my dooty an' I does it.
If I persumed over much in hattempting a word of hadvice, I beg
parding, I'm sure, Miss; and I shall remember, Miss, not to offend
again."

"You have not offended me," said Lucy, wearily, as she sat before her glass watching the rapid fingers that braided and arranged
her hair; "but I like to have my own way, Hodges, you know, and
I am too tired to argue about it."

"Humph!" said the woman to herself; "too tired to argy, but
not too tired to dance and caper, and laugh and chatter till daylight."

Because a brain fatigued does not necessarily include bodily exhaustion, but is sometimes best served by physical exertion, if you
but knew it, Hodges.

Returning to the ball-room with a vague sense of misery upon
her, and with a dull, heavy aching at her heart, she yet forced herself to laugh and talk, and the flightiness of her words and actions
was looked upon by all as being mere exuberance of spirits; but
when the festivities finally drew to a close, she fled gratefully to her
own apartments, which seemed, in their quiet, a perfect ark of refuge. Dismissing her sleepy maid, she sank, with a sense of relief,
despite the numbness and leaden heaviness of her heart, into a
chair before the fire. The bright firelight played with the golden
tint of her hair, as it swept loosely over the hands that pressed her
burning cheeks, and as a flame died out, leaving a dark shadow on
the falling tresses, another leaping forth, supplied its place, and
recalled the shade of gold. And so, minute after minute, the reflection of the flickering blaze played at hide-and-seek in the streaming
hair, and in the dark eyes that gazed into its glowing depths, review-
ing the happy past, and maturing plans for the future, which seemed
so dark and hopeless. The present she cast from her mind, until
receding further into the past, it could be looked upon more se-
renely from a distance.

The minutes passed and lengthened into hours, and the flames
forgot their game of hide-and-seek, and sank slowly and sleepily
back into their bed of glowing coals. Occasionally, one more lively
than the rest, would leap forth and try to rouse the others into renewed play; but at last even they sank into perfect rest, and drawing over them their coverlet of ashes, died away for ever in sleep.

Then the first light of dawn crept slowly into the room, but still the dark eyes looked steadily into the half-empty grate. Not a movement had there been, beyond the stirring of a hair, or the quiver of a muscle, in these long hours. The day brightened gradually, the sun rose above the horizon, and a stray beam stealing through the shutters, at last roused the musing girl into life and activity.

Wildly she started up, tossing back her falling hair. Was it too late for action? Had she wasted too many precious minutes in idle dreams? No, no! there was yet time for everything; and in a moment her busy hands were at work. What was done? A clothes-press was opened, a few plain dresses taken forth, and placed in a small, black, leather traveling-bag, with some books, writing materials, and a few trifles of no intrinsic value—only mementos of days gone by. When the bag was closed and locked, she turned to the window, threw up the sash and breathed in the fresh morning air, as one in a fever would drink cold water. The view was so peacefully beautiful, with a mist just rising from tree and hedge, discovering the deer trooping back from their morning draught at the lake's edge; but a glance at the sun showed it to be well up in the heavens, and with alarm, she sprang away from the window, hastily caught up the bag, and threw over her arm a brown dress, water-stained, green with crushed grass, and still damp from its recent immersion in the lake. Moving to the door, she cautiously opened it and looked without. No one was stirring; and drawing her dressing-gown around her, she stealthily crossed the hall, and passed into a long corridor that led past the doors of vacant rooms. A turn to the right, another to the left, up a flight of stairs to another long corridor, and a few steps down into a triangular room used as a repository for odds and ends of broken furniture, luggage and unused articles of all kinds.

Pushing her way through the labyrinth of lumber, she passed behind a pile of mildewed books, and with a readiness of hand that proved her perfect acquaintance with its secret, found and touched a hidden spring which slid back a panel in the wall, revealing a small room beyond.

It was one of her childhood's discoveries, which, with a reticence unusual in children, she had kept to herself, for no weightier reason than that she liked to have a secret, and it was a nice hiding-place and play-room. Many were the stolen minutes she had passed there, first with dolls, then with books; later it had been her favorite spot for meditation when she struggled for mastery over temper. This unruly spirit, a flaw in her character, she fondly thought was conquered; yet still it lived and lingered in her, latent, but ever

ready to break forth in some new, and, at first, unrecognized form,
and fiercely rage in all its fury, until, detected for what it was, she
crushed it down once more. Even now had it rushed forth with over-
whelming power; for call it what she might—pride, sensitiveness,
duty—it was the fiery, not yet thoroughly disciplined spirit which possessed her that now brought her with a fixed purpose to this wierd,
ghostly room. Ah, it was a ghostly looking room, one likely to strike
terror to a childish heart, and yet, whatever fear she had ever felt, had
been a sort of pleasure to her, and she had always loved the place.
The walls were hung with torn and musty tapestry; air, a dim light,
and occasionally a little rain, admitted through a broken, stained
glass skylight which cast fantastic shadows on the once polished floor.
In the far corner stood a high, old-fashioned carved oak bedstead
stripped of its ancient hangings; beside it a high-backed chair, with
treacherous-looking spindle-shanked legs, slender enough to be
suggestive of untimely weakness. To the right of the door hung a
mirror, the quicksilver all granulated and streaked, giving forth
reflections as dismal and contorted as those of any misguided mind.
Just beneath it in a tiny cradle, where it had rested peacefully for
seven long years, lay a one-legged, armless, noseless doll, neglected
and forgotten. Its appearance brought a faint, quickly-passing
smile to Lucy's lips as she paused an instant on the threshhold.
Then her glance passed on to the far end of the room, where, upon
the dusty wall hung a picture—it seemed to be a portrait—of a boy
with curly hair, and laughing, guileless eyes. Moving across the
floor, she clasped her hands and looked up at the innocent young
face.

"Poor boy! poor Guy!" she said, "Yes, you must be Guy, the
outcast from society; or why did I find you, pretty child, so many
years ago hidden away from sight. I little knew your story, or who
or what you were when I brought you here in secret, from fear that if
I spoke you would be taken from me. You have had a strange fascination for me, Guy, as child, as girl, and now as woman, for I am
a woman henceforth. And you, you are a man now, surely—but
what sort of a man, poor fellow! You are a comfort to me, Guy—a
sad sort of comfort; for your fate seems so much worse than mine,
that I can take heart and go about the work that is before me. I
am going away from you soon, Guy, to leave you hanging here,
perhaps never to be seen again by human eyes, till you are faded
out of all likeness to yourself. I wish I could take you with me, to
be always before me as young and innocent, not as the image my
mind will surely form of the murderer. Oh, that fearful word!
Forgive me, Guy, that I could have applied it to you, for you must

be my confidant and help me to pass the weary hours that I am here. But I must work. It is the best, the surest remedy for a heart-ache like mine."

She cast off her wrapper then, and put on the brown dress she had brought upon her arm. "If any one sees me by accident," she thought, "they will take me for the uneasy spirit of one who has drowned herself." The correctness of this conjecture was fully proved by the event. Then she sat down upon the dusty chair forgetful of her resolve, and said to herself how much harder to bear than was all else that *he* should believe her capable of the act. "Yet I was almost guilty when he took me from the lake—guilty in thought—and not knowing that I fell in accidentally, he will be the more ready to believe that I have made away with myself. Better for him, better for him, that it should be so. He will despise, and despising forget me, and love again as I can never do. Oh, I could bear anything, everything, if he but knew the truth; knew that I fled to save him from the bitter alternative of a miserable marriage or sullied honor!"

How selfish even the purest love will sometimes make one! She knew it would be best for him to think her dead and gone with a stain upon her name, yet she would have him know that she lived and was innocent. Are there not many who, without a pang of conscience, would shut up a loved one from the world to live only for them, while they lived for everyone, and enjoying all things themselves, without a thought of faithlessness, would yet wonder why the other should experience any feeling of jealousy? Yet they think they love unselfishly! Lucy's love was being purified of selfishness by self-abnegation.

"Hark!"

She started to her feet and stood listening intently as a door shut noisily in the distance, and the echo died slowly away.

"I thought they had discovered my absence already; but if they had there would be confusion and noise enough to reach my ears even here. The time has not come yet, and oh, how I wish it were over."

With a sigh she turned to the black leather traveling-bag, opened it and took out writing materials, and dusting the table laid them upon it. Then she wrote one line upon a bit of paper.

"The less I write, the less I shall reveal," she thought.

But how cold, how heartless the words looked, staring up at her from the paper.

I have gone. Search will be useless.

She hesitated. The Egertons would draw the desired conclusion from these abrupt sentences, and no others she could think of would serve her purpose so well; but rather than leave them this, she would write nothing. Ah, but they must be induced to begin the search at once so that it should soon be declared hopeless. These first three words would inform them of her flight, while the other four would prompt **them to seek** her, at **the same time** that it prepared them for failure. She closed her lips tightly and rose from the table.

"If I should be seen in the act of leaving this in my room, I can still return here during the day, though it would not suit my plans so well as that they should think I had had time to get far away before they discovered my absence. It was stupid to forget it, and perhaps I had better run no risks."

But still she moved across the floor and, opening the panel again, walked boldly forth into the larger room beyond. Passing cautiously through the piles of abandoned and broken furniture, she gained the long corridor, and stepping quickly and noiselessly along, reached her own door unperceived. A moment she paused on the threshold of this room she had left so lately never expecting to see again, and to re-enter which she knew would entail the taking of a second farewell of the familiar objects within; but while she stood hesitating, voices sounded in the hall beneath, and a footfall was heard on the broad staircase that ended just beside where she stood. To retreat without being seen was impossible; the only way of escape lay before her. Quickly turning the door-handle, she glided into her room, and closing the door softly behind her, walked straight to the dressing-table and pinned to the pincushion that scrap of paper with those few curt words: *I have gone—search will be useless.* At that instant a knock sounded on the door, and she sprang lightly away into the adjoining room, and stood there breathless, just within the doorway. Only an instant she stood, for that paper was there on the table, and if any one entering should chance to read it before coming in to where she was, what would become of her? Flight might then be impossible. She must recover it at any risk, and even were she seen, they would not see *it;* and back she darted and snatched it up. As her fingers closed upon the paper she heard the door-handle turn. To regain her former shelter unobserved was now out of the question; but a massive oaken clothes-press stood near at hand against the wall, and quick as thought she sprang into it. Scarcely had she drawn too its ponderous doors upon herself, when the room-door opened and Miss Julia Lifford (for it was my step and knock that had alarmed her) looked into an empty tenantless room, and after a hasty glance around, passed into the vacant one beyond. Then from Lucy's hiding-place a hand and arm was cautiously stretched forth, and the paper once more fastened to the pincushion on the dressing-table; and when Miss Lifford, returning, went up to the press and glanced in, nothing but dresses hung revealed to view, and it was on a trembling, frightened girl that she closed its heavy oaken doors, and turned the key.

CHAPTER II.

"'Tis strange how many unimagined charges
Can swarm upon a man, when once the lid
Of the Pandora box of contumely
Is open'd o'er his head."

WHAT must have been Lucy's sensations as she heard the ominous click of the lock! Was she to perish like Genevra in the chest; or must she call for aid, and thus ignominiously end her well formed plans? For the moment she felt more inclined to choose the former fate, and horrible thoughts of how in some far-off day her bones would be found there, were passing through her mind, when an exclamation from without her narrow prison broke the silence, and footsteps were heard hurrying from the room.

"She has found the paper!" and Lucy listened intently for the alarm which she knew would now be given. How long it seemed before the hum of far-off voices was borne to her ears! and presently horses' feet grated on the gravel without, and directions for the search came to her through the open window. When Ingolsby's voice rose above the rest, firm and commanding, how her heart beat and sank with a still greater weight upon it than before. 'Twas long ere the sounds surging through the house, now near, and now far, died away; and longer even to this girl, shut up here with but two alternatives before her, of death that she actually thought herself capable of enduring, or the home of that man Sullivan—the latter thought branching out into dismal pictures of Alva generously marrying her and being dragged down from his position in society, or proving false and wedding another before her eyes—longer to her seemed the hours of that long day than to those waiting in the drawing-rooms below, or even to those engaged in the search. And when they returned at last—how unsuccessful she well knew—she was distracted by the remembrance that she had left the panel of her ghostly room open, and then by the fear that they might come here to seek her.

Once during the day the room door opened and there came a

whispering as between two people. Then by degrees the voices sounded more distinctly, as if those who spoke were gaining confidence. One voice said:

"Such a pretty, pretty room! and really arranged with good taste. I wonder if it was her own taste or Lady Egerton's."

"Not her's you may be sure, Mabel," spoke the other; "how could one expect refinement from such a source."

"But, mamma, a home like this must have had a refining influence upon any nature."

"Such refinement, like gilding on brass, takes little to rub it off. My dear girl, while I think of it, I want to give you a piece of advice. While you are young, never publicly give an opinion such as you expressed a short time ago before every one down stairs. It passes for unamiability and has no weight whatever with any one. Wait till you are my age and such remarks will have greater force, passing then for a knowledge of the world—not for mere spitefulness."

"Oh, it is easy for you to talk like Chesterfield, mamma, but at my age I'm sure you never practiced such precepts."

"It would have been better for me if I had practiced them; but unfortunately, there was no one to teach me early in youth, and I only learned wisdom by sad experience."

"But now, mamma, don't you think what I said was correct: that she has run away with one of the footmen?"

"What you said, my dear, was a mistake in a double sense; it showed a want of tact, and it was improbable. It is far more likely that she has run away for the mere sake of being thought a heroine; and courting publicity for such an affair proves the possession of a vulgar nature. Had the girl brains, she would have endeavored to hush it up, and coaxed old Sir Griffith into buying the man off; but instead she runs away, fondly imagining and believing that she will be brought back and reinstated in her old position. Without a thought for the feelings of her friends, she enjoys the prospect of notoriety; but who ever yet 'made a silk purse,' you know, my dear?"

"Where do you think she has gone, mamma?"

"Not very far, Mabel: taken refuge with that Jolliffe Tufnell, perhaps, of whose society it appears she was so fond."

Oh, the pang of wounded pride that shot through poor Lucy's heart as she listened! To be so misjudged by a woman and by a girl like herself! 'Twas bitter, bitter, this awakening from her first delusion, that all the world would put the right construction on her conduct, understand her motives, and appreciate them; would feel with her, that she could not in honesty retain her position, and sympathize with her, that she could not remain in sight of her old home and become the object of their pity. Her first awakening from her first delusion, 'twas the more bitter, for, though she knew it not at the time, with this dream melted away many others she had cherished; the bright visions of perfect goodwill and loving kindness in the world, true charity and human sympathy. The iron entered into her soul, and formed the first opening for the entrance of unbelief in the unalloyed goodness of human nature; but her own nature was too pure, though she fancied herself very worldly-wise, to admit more than would serve as a shield against evil in going through life. With a heart that felt bleeding inwardly, she asked herself, if her parentage was so stamped upon her that none could believe good of her. Were she to die here she could not call to these people for aid; never could she return to the position she had left, to be sneered at by such as they. And the two women went out carelessly as they had entered, little knowing the sting they had left to rankle, and never be forgotten, though it might be forgiven, in one innocent heart.

Still no one came to seek for her. That one move was neglected which changed the future of her game of life; and she was left there to suffer undisturbed. So the day passed. The evening came and darkened into night, and still no one else had come to that room. All had been dark to her from the first, and the advance of time not marked by the changing light, but by the striking of the stable clock. After the unsuccessful searchers had returned, six, seven, eight, nine, ten, sounded from the great time-piece, and during those weary hours she tried in vain to quiet the confusion in her brain, and bring her mind to bear upon some plan of escape. But it would not obey her will, and kept wandering to all subjects but the all-important one of what she should do. Gradually it failed to grasp even these, and she thought of nothing but the horror of her situation, as she crouched down in a sort of daze, watching and waiting for the striking of the hours, and striving to keep back the growing sense of womanly weakness and fear. At last the silence and loneliness became unendurable. She felt as though she were dying in that corner, and again she shrank from death as she had done the night before. Was every night in her future life to be filled with ever-increasing horrors? Slowly and painfully she rose from her cramped position, and, with a faint, wailing cry, full of anguish, yet too low to be overheard, pushed againt the press-door with all her strength, dimly expecting and fearing a strong resistance. It was the strength of despair that she brought to bear, but the expected resistance was not met; the door yielded and swung back upon its hinges, for, oh, blessed chance! it had only been **closed,** not shut, and the bolt of the lock had shot harmlessly **forth** on the outside, leaving a long, narrow opening, through which had entered the air that had saved her from suffocation. With a dull, heavy sound, she fell to the floor, and lay there unconscious. The sudden relief had been too much for her already overtasked nerves.

CHAPTER III.

Alone she sate—alone! that worn-out word
So idly spoken and so coldly heard;
Yet all that poets sing and grief has known
Of hope laid waste, knells in that word—*Alone!*

—The New Timon.

MIDNIGHT was sounding from the great clock in the stable tower. The moon, riding high in the heavens, looked down from a cloudless sky; and, bathing all nature with a flood of silvery light, cast one pale beam through the open window of a dainty little boudoir upon the bent figure of a young girl rising from the floor. Slowly the figure rose to its feet, and gliding noiselessly to the door, stealthily opened it, looked out and listened. All was dark; not a sound to be heard, save the reverberation of the last stroke of the hour just dying away on the soft night air.

Presently a shadow, dark even in the gloom of the corridor, groped its way warily along, at times stumbling in the darkness, and then pausing with strained attention to catch the first and faintest sign of alarm. None came, however, and the shadow moved on. On, on it went, traversing the obscure corridors, mounting and descending the long, dark flights of stairs, and cautiously feeling its way in and out among the *debris* in the lumber-room—and so, at last, Lucy reached her place of refuge in safety, and closed the secret panel behind her. A weird light was in the little room, throwing strange shadows about her; for the moonbeams struggled in through the dusty skylight above, and in their dim light Lucy might well have passed for a ghost, as she wandered purposelessly about.

"I wonder why I am so timid now," she said aloud, with no fear of being overheard here. "Having gone so far successfully, why should I feel this fear and trembling? Are not my escapes of last night and to-night signs that I shall succeed in the end?" Yet a

chill of horror crept over her as she thought of the death from slow
suffocation that would have been hers had the press door but closed
more tightly, and her cries for assistance been unheard in the general excitement. "It must be want of food that makes me so faint-
hearted and undecided. I *will not* turn back now." And out into
the silent house she went once more. 'Twas no easy task to find
her way in the intense darkness, but a perfect knowledge of every
turn and stairway assisted her in reaching the butler's pantry at
last. She opened back the window-shutters, and by the light of
the now sinking moon, gathered together a supply of food sufficient
to keep her from starvation till she found another opportunity for
a like expedition. Then, from its nail in the corner, she took down
a dark-lantern, and lighting it, pictured to herself, with that keen
sense of the ludicrous in her nature which brought a smile to her
lips in times even of greatest sorrow and pain, for

> "Some things are of that nature as to make
> One's fancy chuckle while one's heart doth ache,"

the consternation of poor Watkins when he found his larder so
mysteriously devastated, and wondered, with a little compunction
of conscience, on whom the blame would fall. Closing the shutters,
and letting a mere thread of light stream from the lantern in her
hand, she went back up the broad, grand staircase, an incongruous
figure in her brown, stained dress, with the basket of food on her
arm, and munching a biscuit as she went; for let romantic ideas be
what they will, heroines, even in the midst of greatest trouble and
distress, feel the pangs of hunger like other human beings, and
practical and unpoetic as it may seem, must eat to sustain life.
On she went, up to that spot which now seemed all that was left to
her of home; and having deposited her basket upon the floor, came
out once again. After many trips to and from one of the vacant
rooms off the long corridor in the east wing, she succeeded in bringing a mattress and bed-clothing for the old-fashioned canopied bedstead in the corner.

Cautiously, tirelessly, and almost noiselessly, ever on the alert
for a surprise, yet with firmness and determination she toiled, and
it was not until the first grey streak of dawn appeared in the east
that her difficult task was completed. Then with a weary, weary
sigh, she lay down for a well earned rest; but long she tossed to
and fro before sleep closed her hot and aching eyes. A dreamless
sleep of utter exhaustion, bodily and mental, it was, that lasted
through the morning hours, and well into the afternoon. And the
search for her went eagerly and fruitlessly on—the search for this

girl who reposed peacefully and unconsciously within the very walls
from which her sorrowing friends went forth to seek her:

"So near, and yet so far."

that distance could not have erected a more effectual barrier between them.

When at last she awoke refreshed from her long sleep, it was with
renewed strength and energy she set about making her arrangements
for her final departure.

For six days longer she remained, going boldly about the house
in the dark, still hours of the night, sometimes even stealing up to
the library door to listen to the footsteps of Sir Griffith, as alone he
paced restlessly within (for Alva was gone up to town, and Lady
Egerton and I shut up in our rooms). Lucy's heart yearned toward the old man who had been to her all that she had ever known
of a father, and who was suffering now for her sake. But the
thought would come to her of how cruelly misjudged she had been
by others, and that he might misconstrue her motives as they had
done; and she felt that if she had but been told the truth from the
beginning, and had grown up with a proper humility of mind, this
could never have happened. And so, a barrier which a mere trifle
so often raises between two hearts that love, and would fain be
one, but for the invisible bulwark that separates them, kept these
two apart, and she remained steady to her purpose. Once she met
him face to face. Venturing forth one morning early into the lumber room, she was stooping over an old trunk in quest of some article
which she needed, and was so absorbed in the search that approaching footsteps were unheard. The door opened and Sir Griffith entered. A pile of trunks between them partially shielded her from
view, and he walked across the floor, without observing her, to an
old book-case in one corner, and reached for a dust covered tome
on the uppermost shelf. As he did so, an old glazed print on one
of the walls, swayed by the draught from the open door, broke
from its fastenings, and fell heavily to the floor. He, looking
round to see what it was, did not perceive the figure that started up
within a yard or two of where he stood. She, white and trembling,
stood for a moment unable to move; then darted quickly away like
a hunted deer to the open panel, and as she turned in the act of
closing it, beheld a face, white as her own, with eyes and mouth
wide open, gazing at her in blank dismay.

With hands tightly clasped and beating heart she stood behind
the thin partition, listening, as she heard the old man stamping about,
muttering to himself and overturning everything that stood in his

way, in his frantic endeavors to solve the mystery of her sudden disappearance. He came and beat upon all the panels of the wainscot
with his hands, and she felt sure that discovery was now inevitable.
But on he passed still searching, and thumping with his knuckles; and
again returned, and went away, and came again; but all his efforts
proved unavailing, for presently the noise ceased, and he was gone.
Then her color and courage, partially returned, but all that day and
night she spent in fear and trembling not daring to venture forth;
and afterwards her expeditions were fewer, farther between and
made with even more caution than before.

Nothing came of the adventure however, for poor Sir Griffith felt
convinced that 'twas naught of flesh and blood that he had seen, but
a veritable ghost. It was no wonder that all the household firmly
believed the house to be haunted.

Could any one have looked down through that dim skylight, the
strange sight beneath would have puzzled them. There sat Lucy
with clothes strewn about her on every side, a needle and thread in
her fingers, sewing, sewing, sewing; and the style and appearance
of the garments she thus formed would have been a stranger sight
still. But strangest of all would have been the figure that appeared
there one afternoon after the work was completed and the needle
laid aside. Where was Lucy? Gone! and in her stead was the
queerest, quaintest little old woman imaginable. A black dress,
short, skimpy and untrimmed; an enormous cloak; a white cap, and
over it a huge old-fashioned bonnet; a stick; a hobbling gait; a
wrinkled old face under a brown veil, and a pair of very, very
bright black eyes, made a most enchanting old lady indeed; and
when a pair of rosy lips were folded inward and something unintelligible was mumbled between them, who could look at her without
feelings of veneration and kindliness stirring in their bosoms. But
when, a few moments afterwards, there stepped from out those ancient garments a slight girlish figure with a halo of shining hair
about the still wrinkled face, these feelings would doubtless change
to admiration for the genius that had formed from the scanty means
within her reach so complete and baffling a disguise.

CHAPTER IV.

Vanished like dew drops from the spray
  Are moments which in beauty flew;
I cast life's brightest pearl away,
  And, false one, breathe my last adieu!

                  — G. W. Clark.

THE time had come when Lucy must go. Seven long and weary days had gone by, the search must now have been given up, she thought, and everything was in readiness for her flight. Now or never must the yearning, lingering fondness for all that was familiar and dear to her be crushed from her heart—every sacred tie which bound her affections to the dear old place be severed—perhaps forever. It was pain, intense pain, to part even with the lifeless objects about her; from the portrait of Guy Egerton, which seemed to her excited fancy to plead with beseeching eyes for her to remain; from the old mirror that appeared to give forth a more kindly and less distorted reflection of her own white face, and from the stiff-backed chair that looked comfortable and easy for the first time. The entire room all at once assumed a more enticing appearance in her eyes. And if it was pain to part from these, and to feel that old associations could never be renewed, how much more painful the thought of leaving those she loved without a word, without a glance of kind farewell! With a cry of anguish, and the first tears she had shed through all these bitter days, streaming from her eyes, she drew paper before her and poured out the agony of her soul in writing. Long she lingered over the pages that told so much of her secret, and had she obeyed the promptings of her heart, to *him* would they have been addressed; but in the hope that he might think her dead, she refrained. At last the task was done, and with bowed head on her folded arms, she lay and sobbed away the hours. And when the shadows of night had darkened the room, and the calm of exhausted nature hushed the passionate sobs, leaving naught but an occasional quiver to give sign of life to the quiet figure that had lain there so long, she raised her head and stretching forth her hand in the darkness for the letter, she rose quickly, lighted her lantern and passed from the room. Her purpose was to leave the letter in some spot where it was most certain to be discovered—yet not immediately—by her alone to whom its contents were addressed. To accomplish this, undetected, was a most hazardous step, she knew; but her life of late had been but a succession of risks and she had encountered them all so victoriously, that she did not hesitate now that she was required to subject herself to one more. Besides, there was a sort of excitement about these chances of detection which she took that seemed to buoy her up, and which she had grown to regard as almost necessary to her existence.

Pausing at one of the bedroom doors near the head of the grand staircase, she knocked sharply, listening intently for a response, and prepared upon the faintest sound from within to dart away under cover of the darkness. No sound came to her from the room, and then she knocked again, but with the same result. Yet a third time did she repeat her summons without a reply, before she felt satisfied it was safe to venture in. Opening the door softly, she cautiously looked in, and, sweeping the room with a stream of light from her lantern, saw no one. Then she entered and glanced around for some place to put her letter. Upon a small table beside an *escritoire* lay an open diary and between its leaves she inserted it.

"She will find it here," she said to herself, "the first time she writes, and no one else will be likely to open the book." That it was not till months afterwards it chanced to come to light the reader already knows.

As Lucy turned to leave the room she heard voices on the staircase. Hurriedly drawing the shade across the lens of her lantern she stood motionless, but listening with a beating heart. It was Sir Griffith's voice she heard and then an answer came from Ingolsby. "No danger of their coming here," she thought, and stealing to the door she closed it gently, leaving a slender chink through which she peeped out at the two figures coming slowly up the stairs. Arm in arm they came, and paced along the hall to and fro, the older man erect and firm in step, the younger with bowed head and eyes never raised from the carpet.

"True—true;" were the first intelligible words from Sir Griffith; "time passes and we find her not; but from that very fact I gather most hope. If she be alive we cannot but find her eventually, and if she had destroyed herself, long before this some tangible proof would have been discovered to confirm the suspicion. So you see that when I bid you hope, it is not without reason;" and they passed out of sight and hearing.

A wild desire to rush out, and falling in their arms, ask that this load of care might be taken from her, as her presence would take it from them, came to the listening girl with almost irresistible force. The two had turned in their walk and as they passed back again Sir Griffith was saying:

"Did right in telling me? Of course you did right; and honestly, my dear boy, you have always seemed a true son to me; and now more than ever do I feel the need of one. This is a sore trial at my time of life, for I love the girl dearly, and cannot bear to think that she is suffering. It makes me absolutely furious that people should have it in their power to gossip about her."

As they passed on, tears of something very like remorse streamed from Lucy's eyes, and faster they flowed and more and more she wavered in her purpose, as she caught his slowly-uttered words.

"The loss of my son was, until now, the one great sorrow of my life, and *it* almost crushed me. People call me eccentric, but I can say to you, my boy, what I have never before admitted to human being; my odd ways, like many anothers, have been but a mask put on to hide a sorrow which it would be unmanly to show."

The door moved on its hinges, and had their eyes turned that way as they went slowly by, they would have seen a dim figure hesitating in the doorway, checked in its mad impulse to fall at their feet by the words that now fell from Alva's lips.

"I could not marry Lucy now," he said. "Under existing circumstances, considering her position and mine, it would be out of the question—not to be thought of for an instant."

"In yourselves, you are equals, and love should remove all such obstacles," argued Sir Griffith.

"Not in these days," Ingolsby answered, with a sneer in his voice. "What is love weighed in the balance with wealth and pedigree, and spotless name? A chimera! the delusion of some poor, half-starved wretch in a garret!"

"Of course, of course," assented Sir Griffith. "I understand that perfectly; I don't blame you for the feeling. This affair has become so deucedly public that it will take at least an earl's coronet to make it be forgotten. To tell you the truth, my heart begins to harden toward the girl for all the unnecessary pain she has given those to whom she owes so much. She's an ungrateful hussy! To think that I have reared and educated another man's child for this! But go you to your bed now, and dream of happiness, if you cannot feel it. Good-night!"

"Good-night, sir." And then they separated and went off to their rooms, leaving a second arrow to rankle in the girl's soul.

Ah! quiver with pain, poor heart; shrink in agony, throb with each new pang, and bleed with every stab! Wounds from those we love are not so few but each must have his share; and if to thee comes more than is thy portion, remember this: It is a trial of thy goodness. Hardened wilt thou be into adamant; deadened to pain thyself, and to pain in others; or else, the better alternative, softened in like proportion, alive to sorrow, pain, and misery in other hearts, then will all poisoned arrows lose the power to do thee harm. Choose the better, nobler lot, poor heart, and soften, soften as thy wounds increase.

An instant Lucy lingered on the threshhold, and then, hearing another step upon the stairs, glided off into the friendly, sheltering darkness of the corridor—the gloom that told no tales to her who followed after.

All hope of happiness seemingly over for her in this world, her resolve, strengthened with each passing day and by every chance word, now irrevocably fixed, she entered the tapestried room for the last time. There was no sleep for her that night, neither was there any tumult in her mind. Her senses happily deadened by this last, heaviest blow of all—those cold, cruel words of Alva's that had sounded as the knell of dying hope—she lay upon the bed, motionless, numb in mind and body, and utterly incapable of thought, yet,

> "Over all things brooding slept
> The quiet sense of something lost."

The first faint light of early dawn was the signal for renewed working of her brain. Wearily she arose, and casting aside her own attire, dressed herself by the light of the lantern in the costume that had cost her so much time and labor to contrive. Deadening her complexion with a dye she had found in one of the old trunks, she make a few dark lines upon the forehead, about the eyes and mouth, and a dark spot upon each cheek; but still fearing the strong light of day, she threw an old-fashioned figured lace veil over her bonnet, so that no eye could detect aught beneath but what appeared to be the wrinkles of veritable old age. She had fifty pounds in notes, her birthday gift from Sir Griffith. For the future her money was to be of her own making, but this she must take to use until such time as she could earn enough to replace it, as, indeed, she felt she would like to do everything that had been lavished upon her. This sum, with a few articles of clothing she placed in the black leather traveling bag. Her mind was in a sad state of bitterness toward all mankind, poor girl, as she turned to go. It was not with the agony she had expected to feel, but with scarcely a pang that she found herself now about to leave this once happy home. Her last illusion had been dispelled; and leaving a heap of water-stained brown merino lying upon the floor—the last discarded relic of the old life—she turned coldly away, even from the portrait of the boy she so long had pitied, and went forth alone out into the wide, wide world.

7

CHAPTER V.

The frighted chase leaves her late abodes,
O'er plains remote she stretches far away—
Ah! never to return!

—The Chase.

IGHT o'clock of a bleak, gray morning, and the early London express, speeding noisily on its way up to the great metropolis, carried passengers, cold, gloomy and irritable from the effects of the weather; their minds destitute of gratitude for the blessings of steam, that saved them from greater hardship and inconvenience than an hour or two of a rapid, bustling trip on comfortably-cushioned seats.

Growl as ye may, ye British public, at what you are pleased to call the discomforts of your railway system; at the long stoppages and crawling pace of the accommodation and slow mail, on the one hand, and the lightning rattle, and no-such-thing-as-reading-in-it whiz of the express on the other; at (if you don't smoke) the vile odor of tobacco that always hangs about the cushions, or, (if you do) the utter impossibility of enjoying a quiet weed all to yourself, without having some grim-visaged female get into your compartment, of all others, at the next station; at the rudeness and "dressed in a little brief authority" swagger of the guards; at the squaling babies thrust in upon you just as you have closed your eyes for a nap; at the non-adoption (as yet) of the continental and trans-atlantic method of checking your luggage, and the consequent chances of some one else walking off with your trunk at some station where you don't remember to look out; at the horrors of solitary confinement in a box, or imprisoned companionship with a beetle-browed villian of chloroforming propensities; yet who is there among you who would willingly go back to the suffocation, and cramp, and horn-tooting of the old coaching days in exchange? Not one among you if it came to the point of sacrificing your present unacknowledged comforts.

This early train carried away from the town of Bratton a woman, aged and quaint in appearance. Not many hours before had this same person passed down a narrow flight of steps at Bratton Hall to the grounds beneath, and after a rapid flight across the lawn and a tedious trudge in a hobbling gait through the fields, where the harvesters were gathering to their labor, and from whom many a hallo and laughing inquiry as to "granny's" health and business greeted her ears unheeded, reached a turnstile set in the wall half a mile from the lodge gates, and passing out, gained the high road. On down the dusty road she kept, not stopping to rest until she reached the "Alnwick," a small inn in the town near the railway station. Here a story had to be coined for the landlady about a granddaughter lying dangerously ill in a distant town, and of how her son had driven her over from the neighboring village of Whitby, and left her at the station, as he was obliged to get back to his work; and she, finding she was nearly an hour too soon, as the London express was n't due till 7:49 (so the station-master told her), had wandered over here to "get summat to eat," as she was very hungry, having only taken a bite before she left home. Such deception was new to Lucy, and a sore trial to her frank and truthful nature which rebelled against using it even though absolutely necessary. But her tears were unfeigned, and though their genuineness somewhat endangered the condition of her disguised face, by their aid she succeeded in gaining the sympathy of the little household. So full, indeed, of pity and compassion for the "poor old soul" was the landlady that she would not leave her to eat her breakfast in solitude, and a sad quandary was the "poor old soul" in, not daring to expose her uncovered face to the other's keen eyes in the morning light. Perplexed and annoyed at the dilemma in which she found herself placed by the good woman's mistaken kindness, a happy thought came to her rescue, and in the high shrill voice she had assumed with her disguise, she cried out as she put her hand to her face:

"Ah, my poor old eyes! my poor old eyes! little sleep ha' they known o' late, an' now they be revengin' o' themsels, so they be, wi' smartin' pains an' waterin'. Just obleege me, good friend, and draw the curtain across yon window an' shut out the glarin' light. More, more, shut it out entirely; there, that'll do nicely, thank ye;" and then she raised her veil, and while the landlady's eyes blinked and strained in the unaccustomed gloom, ate and finished her meal long before the distant whistle of the train announced its near approach.

The usual din and confusion that succeeds the stoppage, and continues during the brief stay of an express, surrounded Lucy on her arrival at the station; the babel of tongues, the rushing of feet, the crying of babies, the hissing and panting of the impatient engine, the trundling of the luggage-barrows, the multitudinous "How d'ye do's?" of the comers, and "Good byes" of the goers, heartfelt and heartless, spoken and shouted; the howls of the struggling dogs being thrust into their long, narrow cells beneath the seats, and the barking and yelping of the others just let loose, the rush for tickets and scramble for window seats, the muttered growls at the "engaged" compartments with one occupant, the groans of the "baccy" chaps at the absence of a smoking-carriage, the dragging and grating and slamming of trunks, portmanteaux and boxes, the warning cries from the carriage windows to the old party at the book-stall, or the young one in the refreshment-room, the unchecked insolence of the flymen after unsuccessful extortion, the jostling, crowding, elbowing and shoving, and over and about all that peculiar odor of coal, smoke, steam and hot oil, without which a railway station would not be a railway station, nor a train a train. In the midst of the noise and tumult Lucy bought her ticket, and found a seat in a second-class carriage, unassisted. The bell for starting rang, the guard shouted:

"Any more going on?" the engine shrieked, and, with a tug, the train went whizzing on its way again.

And as it sped on through the green hedge rows and yellow fields of swaying grain, dashed over bridges, whisked under roadways, shrieked into tunnels and clattered past intermediate stations, Lucy sat in her corner by the window, looking out at the laborers busy in the fields, and the buxom lasses and ruddy-faced mothers, who stood in the cottage doorways, watching the train as it whirled swiftly by; and a ray of sunlight seemed to penetrate the cloud that enveloped her, as she thought how happy they appeared in their humble sphere; how much happier, indeed, than those in the one she was leaving. But—and the cloud grew dense once more—what tastes or feelings could she, brought up in luxury and refinement, have in common with these people who had no thought beyond their simple cottage homes? Yet they had a home and she had none.

Home! of which so much has been said and sung, but which no language can define as it is pictured to our mind at the mention of the one little word that stirs all the deepest and purest pulses of our being; alas! never more was there to be a home for her in this world, unless she made one for herself by the labor and toil of her own hands.

The sound of voices aroused her from her reverie, as two men, whom she had not before noticed at the other end of the compartment, got up and took their seats opposite to her. Small farmers they looked, in holiday attire.

After the first rude stare at the shabby old woman, they paid little heed to her, but went on with their talk about crops and cattle and different breeds of sheep; and the monotonous hum of their voices was gradually soothing her to sleep, when a name spoken by one of them awakened her with a start. With beating heart and strained attention she listened to what followed the mention of "Sir Griffith Egerton."

"Wot a fuss it ha' excoited, to be sure. Aw th' warlt knons o'it an tawks o'it; an' yo'd be sorprois'd at aw the stories they tell, fo' be me troath, lad, they be o' aw sorts an' soizes."

With a grandiloquent air, the other man answered:

"Theaw'd nah foind me makin' a toime abou' noa chilt o'moine. Hoo moight' a' dun what she loike an' she didna disgrace hoo feyther. An ey heert say t' lass wa' noa chilt o' he noather."

"Ay; so t' say."

"Boh wheer dun yoa think she be goane to?" asked the second speaker.

"Well, soame say she ha' made awoay wi' hursel, an' soame t' she be goane wi' a young chop; boh moast o' aw' say, an' me wi' 'um, beloike she be a hoidin' i' th' toawn o' Lonnon. An' t' p'leece be on t' loak owt fo' hur aw' owr Lonnon. Be t' mess, ey 'ope t' win catch t' lass; an' t'be a goade whoapin' ey'd gi' hoo wi' hoo freaks an' foncies. Whoy, a protty 'somple hoo be t' onest fooks gurls t' run auf an' scare 'm ef aw things dunna plees 'm a' whoam."

"Eh woander 'ow hoo win git hoo livin', Zacheriah, aw' bey hersel?"

"Eigh, Jem, she be able t' moind hursel, fo' ey ha' heert as how hoo tuk trunks an' boxes o' siller an' joawls an' money an' aw t' foine duds o' me lady wi' hur."

"Yo dunna sa' soa! Be th' hokey, lad, ey ha' got t' vary roate o' t'aw, noaw!" slapping his companion's knee and gesticulating gleefully into his face. "T'owd mon ha' got in t' trouble an' debt, an ha' sent hoo t' furren parts wi' aw he cud scrape an' gother, an' protty soan t' Hall win be shut, an' they win aw goa t' furren parts an' ha' ease an' cumfort fo' t' rest o' t' loives while t' croditers may whostle fo' 't pay. Eigh—eigh, mon?"

"Ey shud na wonder, Jem, boh theaw'd guest it. 'Twould be boh honest noaw t' gi information toa t' croditers, an' mayhap, Jem, t' moight gin us a trifle fo our trouble, eh, lad?"

"Hist! we be owerheert, Zacheriah," and they looked suspiciously at the old woman who was leaning forward, listening eagerly to their conversation.

"Whot ye be doain', oald woaman?" demanded one of them roughly; "lossnin' toa ower tawk, eh? Lossners nay hear goad o' thersels, soame toimes."

Without answer she shrank quickly back into her corner, thinking how apt was the proverb the man had so unwittingly quoted, and accusing herself, poor thing, of being the cause of all this indignity to Sir Griffith. She felt no resentment at what they had said of herself, for had she not overheard from the lips of those who knew her far more bitter words than any they had spoken, and why should these rough, uncultivated men understand her motives better, and interpret them more charitably, than those above them in refinement of feeling? Yet, as they continued their talk, in cautious whispers now, she felt hurt—grieved—that all classes—all people should be against her in their judgments. She might be called strong-willed —as no doubt she was, for it would take many an obstacle well nigh insurmountable to turn her from her purpose—but for all that, her heart yearned for one kindred soul to sympathize with her, one hand to help, one arm to lean upon.

"Alone, alone, all, all alone,"

She must fight the battle of life, with none to love and cherish her, none to love and live for in return. And what value has life with no one to live for but oneself? It is scarcely life—it is mere existence. Nor can it be a fit preparation for the world to come.

To mortals is given the capacity for loving, the desire for companionship, and the faculty to enter into one another's joys and sorrows, hopes and fears. But solitude and a selfish life in oneself must needs lessen the power of love and charity and human kindness, and deaden all the most sublime emotions of the heart, leaving one even more imperfect—more unfitted for the life hereafter. It is surely meant for none to live always for themselves alone; some one they must find to take an important place in their minds, and sooner or later, though she knew it not, could not have believed it at the time, some one must be found to be to Lucy a subject of interest and thought.

But a new difficulty had arisen in her path; detectives were on the watch for her in London, the men had said. It might not be true—perhaps as untrue as the rest of their story; yet it was possible, she thought, that some steps of the kind might have been taken by Sir Griffith; London, then, was no place for her. But it was too late to turn back, or get out at a by-station, for the last way stoppage had been made a half hour ago, and the train was already entering the suburbs of the great city. She must go on; but she would follow out the idea that had first come to her mind when she had determined on flight: she would cross the channel at once and go to some place on the continent where as a stranger none would question her, none pity her, and where, fewer being on the roll of necessity than in the monster London, a subsistence might be more easily obtained.

At last the train rolled in under cover at Euston Square, and stopped with a sudden jolt, and the two farmers left the carriage, and hurried away—to seek out Sir Griffith's imaginary creditors, no doubt, and impart to them their valuable information. Lucy stepped boldly out upon the broad platform, and though she knew not but that each man who looked at her might be an emissary from Scotland-yard, yet she felt safe in the disguise which had so successfully passed through the ordeal at the "Alnwick," and going out with the crowd, took the first cab that offered itself, and drove across the city to Charing Cross, fully resolved to go on to Folkestone, and cross to Boulogne without delay. But, as others have experienced before her, events do not always coincide with our designs, and she found that the Tidal Train was not to start for two hours. Two long, weary hours to wait! Slowly and tediously the time crept by, while trains arrived and departed, and the bustle and noise continued, now increasing, now subsiding, and throughout it all, in a dark corner of the ladies' waiting-room, passive and motionless, her mind a chaos of contending thoughts, sat the shabbily dressed old woman. People came in and looked at her curiously, and some even questioned her, but to all she paid no heed, gave no answer, for it was the easiest way to avoid conversation. At length people with foreign labels on their luggage began to swarm in, and, for the dozenth time since she sat there, the din of departure grew loud again; the porters ran round more briskly with their trucks; the guard came out and swaggered up and down the platform; the passengers clustered around the carriage doors, and the engine backed up and hooked on. Then the old woman, with her ticket clasped tightly in her hand, hobbled across the platform to an empty compartment, and got in. Hardly was she seated when she heard the clink of money, and a voice outside say:

"Remember, guard, no one else in here."

"Very good, sir."

Then a dark body scrambled in, and the guard slammed the door to, and locked it as the train began to move. And as the spasmodic *kugh! kugh! kugh!* of the engine grew of shorter interval, and the train emerged from the long dark terminus into the light of day, Lucy looked up, and, seated before her, beheld—Jolliffe Tufnell.

CHAPTER VI.

'Tis with our judgments as our watches, none
Go just alike, yet each believes his own.
— Essay on Criticism: Part I.

ES, there he sat, in a rough corduroy shooting-jacket and leather leggings, his hands on his knees, his Glengarry cap off, beside him on the seat, and his abundant crop of red hair exposed to view. Not golden, not auburn, but veritable red it was, so vivid in color as to give one the impression that his florid complexion was the result of its bright reflection. He was short, he was awkward; his hands and feet seemed too large to be disposed of comfortably, his ears were obstinately expansive; his eyes—ah! there was his one redeeming feature—

"Blue, darkly, deeply, beautifully blue,"

large and bright, in expression, sympathetic and benignant. But it was seldom that one could get a chance to look into their marvelous depths, for, as if ashamed of this one oasis of beauty in the desert of his ugliness, they were always covered by spectacles. They were not weak, as their clearness showed even through the glasses; they were not short-sighted according to his own confession, and he was certainly not old enough to require an optical assistant. And so, people wondered, and some even ventured to inquire, what induced him to assume this badge of age. His invariable answer was, that he thought them in keeping with his personal appearance. But this concealment of nature's gift was certainly not in keeping with his character, for one more frank, and more willing to disclose every thought and feeling, were they complimentary or derogatory to the person whom he might be addressing, it would be difficult to find.

The shipping in the Thames had scarce passed out of view, when leaning forward with his hands still upon his knees and his elbows bent outward at an acute angle, this redly-tinted creature addressed his companion:

"Candor compels me to say that this costume is not so becoming as the one you wore at the masquerade, Miss Egerton."

When she had first recognized him a vague dread had come upon her, but at this speech, worse in its import than anything she had feared, she forgot all prudence, her discretion deserted her, and clasping her hands imploringly, she sat upright.

"Oh, Mr. Tufnell! you are naturally kind-hearted, and I am sure—"

"Ah, I am not mistaken!" he broke in, leaning back with the pleased expression of an ogre who has discovered a delicate morsel, in the shape of a baby, for his breakfast. Then she saw the *faux pas* she had made, and paused, eagerly hoping against hope that she had not completely betrayed herself.

"Well, young lady, this is pretty behavior, isn't it?" he said, moving over beside her, and very quietly but firmly taking her hand from which he drew the old woolen glove. "Humph! this is confirmation, for no old lady ever possessed such a pretty, plump, white hand. No need to snatch it away so fiercely, my dear child; the harm's done. The secret's out, and no help for it, you see; so you may as well make the best of it. Would you like to return from the next station? that will be Croydon, I think; or go on all the way to Folkestone for the night? Now, that I think of it, perhaps we had better go on, as a whiff of sea air will do you good, and besides it will give me time to reason with you a bit." Taking out his watch, he looked at it, and went on: "Two hours and ten minutes more together. There's plenty of time for talk, and as you don't seem in the least disposed to sustain a conversation just now, let me tell you a pretty little story, to beguile the time it takes you to compose yourself.

"This morning at daylight I went out shooting. A most unseasonable, not to say heathenish, hour to go banging about one's preserves, I'll confess—not the correct thing nowadays, of course; but then I am given to doing things differently from the rest of mankind, I fear; so taking my gun and 'Fanny'—Fanny's a pointer, you know —off I started, see, just as I am now. But somehow, once I got out, for some reason or another, I didn't seem to care a straw about shooting, and let the birds get up and go whirring over my head untouched, while the poor old dog pointed till she must have been sick and tired. I suppose I must have had a premonition of the larger game I was to come across, which made the partridges look too uncommonly small to waste cartridges upon," and he gave a diabolical grin; "but I anticipate. Well, I kept wandering on and on in a sort of gloomy abstraction, for the morning was gray and dismal, and the first thing I knew I found myself at the confines of my land. I stopped, and— for the life of me I can't tell what made me do it—stood looking over the dividing hedge between Sir Griffith's land and mine. Suddenly I heard a rustling in the bushes on the other side. 'If this be the big game coming now,' thought I, 'I fear I shall be sadly tempted to play poacher for once in my life.' The rustling continued, and grew nearer, and I kept my eyes glued on the spot from whence the sound came, thinking it might be a hare, at least;

though I confess that I had my doubts as to that, for, beyond a slight elevation of Fan's ears, when she heard the noise, the old girl gave no sign. I hadn't long to wait to find these doubts were well founded, for the next minute there emerged from the thicket into the open, no hare, but—a queer, quaint-looking old woman who glided past and off with a most suspicious rapidity for one of her apparent age. Instantly it flashed across my mind what was up, and off I started in pursuit. Keeping you well in sight—for it was you, Miss Egerton—and thinking I should fall in with one of my gamekeepers as I went along, and give him the dog and gun, I followed your steps on my side of the hedge until you reached the road, and thence tracked you all the way to the 'Alnwick.' Not one of my men turned up, however, and a pretty figure I must have cut tramping along the dusty road at that time of day, with a gun under my arm and a dog at my heels, and looking for all the world like some itinerant poacher or gamekeeper out of place; though, perhaps, my spectacles saved me from such an appearance, for I don't think anybody ever saw a poacher or a gamekeeper with spectacles.

"When you came to the field where the harvesters were at work, and I saw your quick steps change to a hobble, I thought my suspicions were confirmed beyond a doubt, but when you boldly entered the inn, I confess I was staggered—nonplussed. If you were, as I suspected, Lucy Egerton—though I had no earthly reason for fancying anything so improbable from the first, beyond a sort of intuition—but if you were Lucy Egerton in disguise, how had you the courage to go into that public house and subject yourself to the close scrutiny of so many inquisitive eyes? It puzzled me immensely, I assure you, and I had half a mind to turn about and go home. Yet I waited loafing about the place till you came out again, and when I saw you go to the station and take the train for town, my suspicions were rekindled; and leaving my dog and gun to the tender mercies of one of the porters, I got into the train myself, determined to see the thing out. I was on the point of getting into the same compartment with you and trying the same experiment I have tried here, but I found those beastly farmers had got ahead of me. On our arrival in London, I followed you in a hansom from Euston Square to Charing Cross, as indeed I would have done from one end of the world to the other till I found an opportunity of speaking to you in private without chance of interruption. That I couldn't do as you sat in the waiting room, for the people never stopped coming in and out. And a nice tiresome two mortal hours I had of it, I can tell you. I couldn't leave the Terminus and go anywhere in town in the rig I was in, and besides I didn't want to lose sight of you. So I sat in the men's waiting room and read and re-read the sauce and cocoa and corn-flour posters until I got them all by heart, and then I got up and paraded the draughty platform, watching the trains come and go, and getting in everybody's way, until they must have thought I was an escaped lunatic with a pedestrianic mania. Luckily I had my short clay along, but a man can't smoke all the time, so I filled up the rest of the time eating sandwiches in the refreshment room. Positively I don't think I ever got away with so many sandwiches at one sitting before in my life. By-the-bye, I noticed that you took no refreshment, and so I bought these for you," and he drew a large parcel of sandwiches from a capacious pocket in his shooting-jacket, "thinking they would be acceptable to any old woman, even if said old woman did happen to be Miss Egerton. Allow me to offer you some." No answer beyond a shake of the head. "Nonsense; you must be hungry, and they are really very good. Do, now, take just one," still holding the tempting package toward her.

"I am *not* hungry," she said, visibly irritated.

"No? why how very odd. Notwithstanding the vast number I have already consumed, do you know that I actually still feel uncommonly peckish; so as you will not, with your permission, I will," and half a sandwich disappeared in his enormous mouth. "Come, now, won't you be tempted?" as after a moment's interval of vigorous munching, he held them out once more.

Very snappish, it must be confessed, was the "No" that escaped from Lucy's lips, but conclusive it was in its effect on her companion. He pressed her to eat no more. And as he sat and ate the sandwiches himself, alternately taking big bites and talking, her anger and vexation gradually gave way before the genuine good nature and odd kindliness of manner of this man who, with what would have been cool effrontery in another, took to himself the right of doing in his own peculiar way, what he thought was most for her good; and before he had ceased speaking, her thought, "This man is insufferable," changed to the conclusion, "He means it all for kindness."

"You don't know what you're missing, young lady," continued Tufnell, taking another bite; "they're good, remarkably good; in fact, no end goo—" His teeth closed on a sinewy piece of ham, and his laudations suddenly ceased. "I suppose, now, you have been wondering," he went on after a pause, which he devoted solely to the mastication of the sinew, and, with a more serious air, broaching the subject he most desired to talk to her upon, "why it was

that I wished to speak with you alone without fear of interruption,"
—munch, munch—"why, in short, I couldn't have said all I wanted
to say to you"—munch, munch—"in the waiting-room at the station. In the first place"—bite—"I knew we couldn't talk there"—
munch, munch—"without attracting attention, for it's against the
rules for men to invade the ladies' rooms, and that I imagined you
wanted to avoid. But setting that reason aside"—bite—"it would
not have suited my purpose"—munch, munch—"to speak to you
there, for to tell you the truth—I never could tell a lie"—munch,
munch—"I knew I was powerless to force you to return against
your will"—munch, munch—"so I determined to have a good long
talk with you, and by calm, dispassionate reasoning try to persuade
you to abandon this foolish freak of yours,"—bite, munch, muuch.
"There! the last sandwich is gone, and now I'll make a bargain
with you. We will take hold of this subject of your running away
from home, and argue it thoroughly. If I convince you that you
are in the wrong, you must promise to return with me to-morrow.
If you convince me that you are in the right, I promise to aid and
abet you to the very limit of my power. Will you consent, my
young friend?"

"I am no child, Mr. Tufnell," Lucy replied, still a trifle angry at
him; "I can see how much you keep in your own power. I am not
so simple but that I can tell that you would never own to being convinced; and that you merely want to extract my promise by means
of this farce."

"My dear Miss Egerton! I never dreamt of such a thing! I give
you my word of honor as a gentleman, that I will be a perfectly im-
partial umpire of the two sides, and give a fair and honest opinion.
To tell you the truth, I feel tempted to help you without further
argument, for I know well what it is to have all the world against
one when one is striving to find the right path of duty. But we
must go through with the form to satisfy my conscience; and, perhaps, we shall find that you are mistaken in the path you have
chosen, and I may help you to find a better. Come, say you agree
to the plan."

Not long before, she had been wishing for some one to confide in,
some one to talk to of her grief, and he came at the right moment;
for although Jolliffe Tufnell was not one whom she would have
chosen to fill such a position, yet her heart was so sore that even a
trifling act of kindness was sufficient to win her at once and forever.
At one time she had thought she rather disliked this man, but so
much did she feel the loss of all she held dear upon earth, her
home, her friends, her day-dreams of happiness, that his disinter-

ested kindness thawed her out of her dislike and distrust. She answered:

"Yes!" heartily, and gratefully.

"Very well, then," he said, smiling; "it is agreed."

"Agreed," she echoed.

"And shake hands on it."

CHAPTER VII.

Give sorrow words; the grief that does not speak
Whispers the o'er-fraught heart and bids it break.
—Macbeth: Act IV, Scene 3.

"IN the first place," said Mr. Jolliffe Tufnell, folding his arms and settling himself comfortably as though with a keen relish for the discussion about to begin, "I will briefly state the facts of the case as they are known to me, and you will kindly suggest any necessary correction. You, the young person beside me, have been brought up by the Egertons of Bratton as their own child, and from the first dawn of reason you have always looked upon yourself as Lucy, only daughter of Sir Griffith and Lady Egerton. For nineteen years—a very long time, young lady—no word, no hint was dropped that you were other than what you supposed. Last week a ball—a masquerade—was given to celebrate your nineteenth birthday, and at that ball two old ladies had, as is their custom all the world over, a quiet gossip about things that did not concern them. You played eavesdropper, a character of questionable propriety, and taking for gospel truth what you had every reason to believe to be a tale, manufactured, prepared, for the occasion, swallowed it, not *cum*, as you should have done, but *sine grano salis;* and putting aside the evidence of your senses for the past—we'll say seventeen years, for you can't very well remember further back than that—not pausing to consider that evidence, you took the other alone, consisting of a mere gossiping statement, unsupported by a single fact or circumstance, so far as you are aware, and which amounted to positively nothing, and fled. Phœbus! was there ever a more idiotic proceeding! for even admitting, for the sake of argument, that the old women's tale was true, in every particular, how could it possibly mend matters to fly away from the soft, snug nest fortune had found and feathered for you so lavishly, and wander out into the cold, heartless world?"

He paused, and his quiet attitude with arms calmly folded contrasted strangely with the energy of his language.

"All you have said, Mr. Tufnell, is quite true," Lucy answered, with visible emotion; "all true, with one exception. I did not rely solely upon the mere statement of those women. At first it was a great shock to me, and I believed it; but as the evening passed, doubts of its truth, suggested by what you have thought I did not consult— my recollections from infancy—entered my mind. After the un- masking I sought out Miss Lifford, who had also overheard what the women had said, and asked her if it was true. She answered, 'Too true, Lucy—only too true!' Those were her precise words."

"That woman's an idiot," he muttered, with a shake of the head.

"She told me all I wished to know," warmly; "and I can never be sufficiently grateful to her. But as though that was not enough proof, I overheard others speak on the same subject—even Sir Grif- fith and—and—some others, for I hid in the house a whole week."

"You don't say so!" he exclaimed. "They must be—uncom- monly—not to put it too strong—stupid, not to have discovered you."

"I was too well hidden for that, Mr. Tufnell; but let me go on. Every night after dark I wandered about the house, for my hiding place was so lonely," with a sigh, "and in that way I heard many talk and give their opinion of my disappearance. From scraps of the servants' talk I learned beyond a doubt that a large number of people knew of my having been adopted by Sir Griffith when I was a baby, and that at one time it had been the chief topic of conversa- tion in the neighborhood, though now in a measure forgotten. For that matter, something I overheard Sir Griffith say is proof positive of the fact."

"Yes?—and that?"

"Speaking of me, he said, 'think that I have reared and educated another man's child for this!' What doubt can I have after that? I am no Egerton, Mr. Tufnell, but a—Sullivan."

"Humph! Well then, I suppose we must admit as a fact, though on evidence not by any means the most satisfactory, that you are *not* Lucy Egerton but Lucy Sullivan."

For all that she had imagined that she had become accustomed to the name from her own mental repetitions of it, she winced as she heard it now pronounced from the lips of her companion; but the sensation of repugnance was scarcely felt, ere she thrust it aside with a powerful effort."

"Do not you, Mr. Tufnell, who were a young man and in the neighborhood at the time, *know* it to be a fact?"

"I did not think you could be so spiteful, my young friend, as to remind me of my forty odd years. I was as you say, a young man, then, but not in the neighborhood, although I had recently come into possession of Knocklofty Hall. I was a half-crazed wanderer at that time, and not till years afterward did I hear of the murder of my friend, Louis Dunraven, which occurred but a short time before your adoption by Sir Griffith. I went down there a year or two ago, when you were between sixteen and seventeen, to ask Sir Griffith for particulars of the murder. The subject was a painful one to him, but when I informed him of my reason for making the inquiries, that I had a certain object in view, he not only gave me all the information in his possession, but joined with me heartily in my efforts to gain a knowledge of all the facts connected with the crime. This, of course, has nothing to do with the present subject beyond the fact, that during one of our talks together, he told me that you were not his own child, but an adopted one. I asked him if it was generally known, and he said that it could not be otherwise, as he had taken you from the town of Bratton, but that people were aware that he did not wish you to know it, and strange to say, you were still ignorant of the truth. He also said, that his adoption of you as his daughter had caused great wonder, not so much at his whim as at his wife's consenting to it; he believed they had been censured, but all that had ceased when you turned out such a credit and ornament to the old name of Egerton. But what an idiot I am to tell you all this! It is my misfortune that I never can keep anything to myself." And as he stopped suddenly in his recital, he moved uneasily in his seat, but happily for his peace of mind, did not see the tears that streamed silently down his companion's face, making sad havoc with the wrinkles beneath the old lace veil. "Well, well, it's out now, and can't be helped," he went on; "but this is not by any means an end of our discussion. We have yet to prove whether you, as Lucy Sullivan, were right or wrong in flying away from home. What could have been your purpose?"

"To earn my living by the work of my own hands," was the answer, in a low, trembling voice.

"A girl brought up as you have been? Ridiculous nonsense! I bet a sixpence you don't know how to do a blessed thing beyond playing the fine lady, and then to talk of earning your own living! You intended to work roses on canvas, I suppose, and get a farthing for a week's labor; or knit worsted thing-em-bobs, and sell a guinea's worth of materials for tuppence ha'penny. A thriving girl you'd be at the end of a month! My dear young friend, you are much too sensible to have ever thought seriously of such a thing. You perhaps thought to turn governess or school-mistress, or go on the stage, and live by the labor of your brains and not of your hands. Was n't that it?"

"No, I meant what I said. To live by hard, honest labor, as my parents did before me, was and still is my intention."

Tufnell looked at her for a minute in silence, with a laugh in his blue eyes: he seldom laughed aloud.

"If you are so very proud of your parents' honest toil, why don't you go to your father and be his pupil as well as his daughter?"

"Oh, Mr. Tufnell, I could'nt. It was partly from him I fled. How could I change a home of refinement and luxury for the constant companionship of a man I had never known, never loved, who had deserted me, put me voluntarily away from him when I was young and helpless; who had—oh, horrible!—killed his wife, my mother? I am heartless, unnatural, what you please; for I have no feeling of filial tenderness for the man, nothing but dread, aversion, horror. Yet, though no tie of kindred binds me to Sir Griffith or Lady Egerton, as I think of *them*, the alien blood in my veins throbs with love and gratitude. Oh, with what shame do I remember how bitterly I felt toward them at first! for in the frenzy of the moment I accused them of being the cause of all my pain; but now that feeling has passed away, and nothing but unbounded love remains."

"I must confess that I become more and more puzzled every minute;" and in his excitement, Tufnell pushed up the glasses from his eyes, revealing them dim with a moisture drawn forth by the girl's words. "Don't you know that that man Silliman, Sullivan—what's his name? has no—can have no legal control over you—that he willingly gave you up to adoption, and that anyhow you are of age, and allowed by law to choose for yourself where and with whom you shall live?"

"I know that very well, Mr. Tufnell, but"—

"Then why the—hem!" All in a blaze of wonder and impatience he caught himself just in time, and taking out a huge red silk pocket-handkerchief, proceeded to mop his face in silence, and let his excitement cool. Then putting his hands on his knees, in his favorite attitude, he went on, with partially regained composure: "Why, let me ask, if you feel toward the Egertons as you profess, did you not remain as you have been for the past seventeen years? You have not suffered hitherto from your position, and why should you now?"

"Ah, that is just it," sighing deeply. "So long as I was ignorant of the truth, I was happy, but once I knew it there was no more peace for me. I grew up with a pride of pedigree, and this is perhaps a just punishment for my pride. Am I in any way different now from what I was as Lucy Egerton? People liked and petted me then; but when it became known to them that I was another man's child—of humbler origin and lower station—yet the same in myself as ever, my bringing up, which alone makes or mars man or woman, was cast aside, forgotten; and simply because less worthy **parents had brought me into the** world, no longer was I a fit companion for young ladies. You do not know all I have heard said of myself, Mr. Tufnell, that was unspeakably galling; you would scarce credit it were I to tell you. But I am humble now, very humble; for **what have I of which to be proud? Well may the pauper sons of** earth sneer at pride of birth and ancient pedigree! What name, **what** fame have they to shield and keep from dishonor? But elevate **them to** a high station, give them **wealth and power, and** will not the sense of pride grow and increase with their ascent? ay, as would mine this moment were I raised once more to all I have so lately lost. And I dared call myself humble! No more humble than he is Christian, who, good when nothing tempts, is weak when evil tries him. What virtue in humility when there is naught to make one proud? A name I have, but not Name with its attendants of honor, power, position, friends, wealth, fame. *Name* that in itself alone oftener deters great men from crime than any sense of moral rectitude within. 'What's in **a name?'** In my case, not these things, but dishonor, low birth, enemies, poverty, shame, weakness. These are the surroundings of Lucy Sullivan!"

She fell into silent thought, while Tufnell looked with pity at the bowed head beside him. How sad it was, he thought, to hear the young philosophize; they to whom all the world should be bright, and fair, and pure; and Lucy was very young to be learning **by sad experience the** weaknesses of **human nature.** He had himself passed through the furnace of contumely **and** sorrow, and knowing what it **was** to suffer in its fire, pitied her with all his heart. He let **her** muse awhile, and then spoke:

"Young friend"—she started—"we have wandered from the point of '**why did you leave home?'** Suppose we go back to it."

"Well, Mr. Tufnell, when I first hid myself in the old house I simply felt that I wanted to **get away from all who** knew me, at **once and forever.** On mature deliberation, I would have acted in the same way—not on impulse, but for these reasons: Although the law would permit me to choose between two homes, my conscience would not. My father had forfeited all claims upon my affection, it is true, but he was still my father, and, if he called me to him, moral law would force me to obey. I ran away, for one thing, to be out of hearing of that call. But putting him out of the question,

8

there were other reasons quite as powerful, perhaps even more so, which were strengthened each day by what I overheard. I could never hold up my head under the weight of unkind words and looks that would be heaped upon me by the outside world, once my true origin became known to others than the townsfolk and neighbors to whom it had been an old familiar story well-nigh forgotten. Even from them might I expect little mercy now that the story had been revived. But if in time I came to endure it all patiently and some one should ask me to be his wife—he is" faltering, "I mean, he might be, sensitive—a callous nature could never win me—and then, don't you see, if he ever became ashamed of me, if he felt the sneers of society, if he grew unkind—oh, it would kill me!" Then forgetting her companion, everything but the sorrow weighing most heavily on her heart, now that it had found words, she burst wildly forth: "To drag him down in the eyes of the world; to know that he winced at the sound of my name and lost all ambition, as he would have done—avoidance, neglect, mutual recriminations perhaps—oh, horrible! horrible!" with a convulsive shudder. "If I had stayed, had yielded to temptation beyond my strength to resist, kept my secret from him and married him, all my fears would have been fulfilled to the uttermost, for, oh, he is false, false to the core; not sensitive, but weak—weak and unmanly! 'I could not marry her under existing circumstances, considering her position and mine' —those were his words. If I had not found him out until too late! If I had told him the truth and he, fancying himself strong, had persisted in marrying me, what an end—what an end would have come to all my dreams! And yet, did I say he was weak? No, no, it is I, wretched girl, I, who am weak! for false though he be, I— I—"

Her head sank upon her hands, and she burst into passionate sobs which shook her whole frame with their violence.

They were kind and gentle, albeit awkward hands, that forced hers from her face, loosened her bonnet-strings, and opened the window to admit the refreshing air.

"Come, young lady, don't be ridiculous. What a foolish child it is, to cry so. Now, don't, please, my dear. No man is worth such tears. Dear, dear, what shall I do with the girl! She'll have hysterics, and I have no idea what to do for a woman in hysterics, except to give 'em salts. Have you any salts, my dear? She's too far gone to heed me, poor thing; and what can I do for her! No salts, no cold water, no nothing! She'll get worse! she'll faint! perhaps die, and I be tried for murder! A pretty scrape for a respectable old bachelor to be caught in! Hush, hush, don't cry, my dear child, if you don't want me to take you home again. How would you like to turn about and go back in the next train to that man Sullivan? No effect, no effect; she does n't even hear me. I'm afraid I'll have to—yes, I must, I *will* summon the guard!" and he made a frantic plunge at the alarm.

But Lucy had heard him; his excited words and movements had helped to bring her to herself, and she strove for mastery over her feelings. She caught his arm before he touched the alarm.

"I a–am all ri–ri–right, Mr. Tufnell," she sobbed; "d–don't, please d–don't mi–mind me." And then she buried her face in the cushions, and with all her strength kept back the swelling sobs; and it was only occasionally that one overpowered her and made itself heard. She suffered doubly now, for had she not told her secret to this man? The hot blood surged with shame and throbbed in her temples as she imagined what he must think of her. How could she ever again meet his eyes with hers that had never before shrunk from mortal gaze? She wished, for the moment, that something would happen, some accident, a collision, a broken rail, anything that would separate them. Why had he interposed in her affairs, with his meddling curiosity? Why had he come with his ill-judged kindness to unsettle her mind and undo the work of all these days; to break down the bulwark of pride and scorn she had raised around her aching heart? By what right did he take upon himself to thwart her wishes, to argue, to threaten, to betray her into acknowledging her secret? Oh, to think that he knew that secret! All else she could forgive, but that. To have the most sacred feelings of her soul brought under the observation of another; to be laughed at, sneered at and held in derision! Then she tried to remember what she had said. She could not. All was vague beyond the cautious beginning; and here came a ray of light. If she had begun cautiously, why, perhaps, she had ended in the same manner, and had been carried away by thoughts she had not expressed in words. Perhaps, after all, he had not understood what she had said, and thought her the more foolish for crying about an imaginary personage. Ah, she would not mind that in the least, if only he did not know the truth. Balm of Gilead in the idea! and she raised her head to look at him. Quietly he sat, and innocent he looked of the knowledge she feared he possessed, as he tranquilly read his newspaper. He looked up and met her tearful eyes full of a pathetic meaning he could not understand; but a kindly smile lit his face, and then as her head sank once more he broke the long silence.

"These things are becoming much too common. Let me read you about this fearful colliery explosion."

As he read she heard of death coming in its most frightful form,
unexpectedly and painfully, to young and old, the happy and the
miserable alike; of others maimed for life; of, the most to be pitied
of all, those whose loved ones perished, or were crippled and thus
became a constant source of sorrow to themselves and all around
them. She forgot her own troubles, as he intended she should,
while she listened to this tale of suffering, alas! but of too frequent
occurrence; yet like the old, old tale of love, ever soul-stirring,
rousing our best feelings, and making us better for the time. When
he had finished, they sat in silence until the train began to approach Folkestone. Then he told her to put on her bonnet, and she
sat up meekly and did as he wished; and when presently the train
stopped at its journey's end, he stepped from the carriage, helped
her out, and together they walked away; he chatting pleasantly, she,
silent and thoughtful, her hand resting trustingly on his arm, much
the better, more humble, and less sore at heart for her recent out-
burst of emotion.

CHAPTER VIII.

My voice shall sound as you do prompt mine ear; '
And I will stoop and humble my intents
To your well-practiced, wise directions.

— II Henry IV: Act V, Scene 2.

"I HAVE not yet decided the important question as to your
being in the right or in the wrong," said Jolliffe Tufnell, as
he and his companion walked on through the principal streets
of Folkestone.

He had been telling an amusing anecdote for her diversion, but at
its conclusion turned abruptly to the "much-vexed question."

"I must sleep on it," he continued, "and in the meantime your
incognito must, I suppose, be preserved. This dress you wear is
too remarkable. Give me your promise to make no attempt to escape from me, and I will do all that is necessary and right, and
proper for you, as regards your concealment.

"You are kinder to me than I deserve," she returned, with tears
in her voice, "and I will not leave you without your knowledge."

"And permission," he added; "remember that I have your promise to abide by my decision."

"Yes; and I yours to judge impartially. You have failed to convince me that I am in the wrong; and if I have failed to convince
you that I am in the right, why, our compact is at an end, and we
part."

"We will not talk about that until to-morrow," he replied. "I must have time to think it over, and I asked for your promise not to run away, in order that I need not act as your keeper. What I want you to do is to change your appearance without further delay. Go into that hairdresser's there and buy yourself a black wig, for your own hair is too remarkably pretty and uncommon to escape attention; I will go into the shop beyond, and when you have made your purchase, walk slowly up the street until I catch up with you. Do you—ahem—need money?"

"No, thanks," she answered a trifle haughtily, and entered the hairdresser's shop.

A few minutes later they were again walking on together. Tufnell had bought a shepherd's grey plaid shawl, and folding it around Lucy, created a marked change for the better in her antiquated appearance.

"Now, there remains but one other thing to decide upon," he said, "except the momentous question which I have reserved. You must pass for somebody or other at the hotel. It would never do to acknowledge you as a young lady. You must call yourself Mrs. —something or other—a widow—would not Mrs.—Mrs. Whym do?"

"Very well, indeed, except as regards its aptitude."

"Therein lies its only merit, child. But let us settle on a line of conduct to pursue. We must not appear too intimate—Mrs. Whym. If you want me to take tea or breakfast, luncheon or dinner with you, you must send me a request for the pleasure of my company, by a waiter. Do you understand?"

"Perfectly."

"And do you think you can play your part until we come to some other arrangement?"

"Quite sure, Mr. Tufnell; and I am deeply grateful for the trouble you are taking on my account."

"Trouble ceases to be trouble and becomes pleasure in gratifying a Whym," he said, bowing.

They had reached the Pavilion Hotel now, and were registered as "Mrs. Whym, Liverpool," and "Jolliffe Tufnell, Esquire, Knocklofty Hall, ——shire."

As they went up the stairs together, he whispered, "Say that your trunks have been sent on to Lyons, Paris—anywhere;" and then they separated, and went to their rooms.

The hotel was not full, and Lucy having her choice of some of the best rooms, selected a sitting-room with bed-room adjoining that looked out on the pier, and harbor, and the blue water of the channel beyond.

When she had succeeded with no little difficulty in washing the tear-streaked paint marks from her face, had put on a plain black dress from her traveling-bag, and covered her bright head with the black wig, she wrote on a card:

"Mrs. Whym's compliments to Mr. Tufnell, and hopes he will give her the pleasure of his company at dinner this evening at 6."

But before she rang the bell, she returned again and again to the looking-glass to take one last look, and make sure that no golden hair peeped out under the black wig; no vestige of a wrinkle remained. It was a startlingly changed face—one she herself could scarcely recognize, that looked at her from the glass; finally, gaining a little confidence, she summoned the waiter, and nervously awaited the result of his coming. Would he notice any difference in her appearance? No. With a careless, though respectful glance he took the card, and after receiving her orders for dinner, left the room. She wondered at herself for having been so foolishly nervous, as she stood at the window looking out at the water with the vessels gently swaying on its surface. There was not much that was pleasing to the eye in the masts and coils of rope, lobster baskets, and nets, oars, sails, spars, and luggage strewn about on the pier, nor in the tarpaulin-hatted boatmen loitering about the docks. Perhaps her thoughts were following the smoky track of the fast receding Boulogne steamer, the one she would have taken had she kept on her way as she had at first intended, and thinking how much better off she was under the protection of this man whom she began to like, and whom she felt intuitively would help her in her purpose, than if she were now approaching the French town, alone, friendless, without an idea of self-maintenance, beyond the wish for work of some unknown kind.

Whatever were her thoughts, here it was that Jolliffe Tufnell found her when he opened the door after a thrice-repeated and unheard knock. As his foot struck against a chair, she turned with a start, and came towards him.

"What's the matter, young friend, turned suddenly deaf like Miss Pross? Phœbus!" with a step backwards and both hands raised, a huge bulwark of defense. "Is this the fair-haired angel I knew at Bratton—this witch, this black-haired, black-eyed sorceress? Avaunt, dark spirit! thou makest me feel as Duncan might at the approach of Macbeth, or he at sight of moving Birnam wood. By Jove!" as he retreated laughing, and sank into a chair, "mother nature knew what she was about when she provided that golden fluffy stuff to soften the outlines of your face. With your dark eyebrows and lashes it made a pleasing sunshine and shadow;

but now you are positively all shade. Grand and wicked-looking; decidedly handsome when your color deepens as it does now; but for all that, were such beauty natural, I would consider my life safer in the keeping of a Sicilian bandit than in your hands, should your ebon locks wave in anger. What a change a mere wig has wrought in you! I wonder if it could do as much for me?" as he rose quickly and strode to the looking-glass. " I'm awfully ugly, and no mistake! And yet I would hardly change in appearance with the handsomest man in England," spreading his coat-tails before the fire. " There is much comfort in feeling that one has some slight defense against the machinations of obedient daughters whom my repulsive looks make almost rebellious, for once in their lives, to the wishes of designing mammas. It is an enormously pleasant sensation to be run after, even if money be the magnet; but when it comes to matrimony, if a man has plenty of the golden loadstone, he wishes it at the top of Mount Blanc—for a time, if only until after the ceremony. Moderate wealth, although by no means the synonym of happiness, believe me child, is nevertheless one of its necessary concommitants and—Hark! I hear the clatter of dishes in the hall—premonitory signs of dinner, so be on your guard, Mrs. Whym."

In the presence of the waiter and during the progress of dinner, the conversation turned upon topics of the day—Lord So-and-so's speech—the last motion in the House—the recent indisposition of the Queen and probable consequences of her death—Tennyson's new poem—the failure of Cheat, Steal & Co.—the success of young Thalberg's "Aphrodite"—advancing civilization of the Japanese—the coming Centennial celebration in the United States, and so forth and so on. Tufnell, either from motives of kindness to his vis-a-vis, or from a mere love of exercising his conversational powers—perhaps it might have been from a combination of both—kept the talk very much to himself. Narcissus was not more enamoured of his own beauty than this man appeared to be with the sound of his own voice, as Proteus-like he changed with marvelous and never flagging rapidity from subject to subject. But when they had left the table and drawn their chairs before the fire, and there was no apathetic but open-eared waiter in the way, it was silence and not confidential talk that fell upon the two. Long they sat and watched the coals drop through the bars into the ashes beneath, and perchance to one or other of them came the thought that in like manner would they one day drop from the noisy active world, where genius blazes forth for a time, giving light to those around, sometimes igniting with its fire other and more sluggish souls, oftener seeing those around shine with the reflected lustre of its own unnoticed flame—drop from this bright world, worn out by the inward blaze which takes its flight into eternity, leaving naught but ashes behind. At length, with a sigh which roused Lucy and made her look up, Tufnell brought his mind back from the land of dreams, rolled his chair back a few inches, placed his arms at the favorite angle and spoke:

"Mrs. Whym—by-the-bye altogether too appropriate a name in a world where every one is playing at odds—Mrs. Whym, I suppose you have heard the popular saying, 'turn about's fair play'? All popular sayings are true, and this one is particularly applicable to the subject of my thoughts. Young lady, you have told me a great deal to day, of which it must have been most painful to speak." A vivid flush crimsoned Lucy's face at the remembrance of that last unwittingly acknowledged secret. "I had no right to your confidence and I am most grateful for your trust in me—it was not misplaced. Now, although you may not care a farthing for the affairs of an old fellow like me——"

"Oh, Mr. Tufnell," deprecatingly.

"It is not natural that you should, my dear."

"Then mine must be a very bad nature," she said, softly.

"Well, well, so much the better if you can feel interested; for what I wish to tell you of my own life may be of service to you in proving that you are not the only one in the world who has met with sorrow. I have never before spoken on the subject and it is rather painful to probe the wound."

"Oh pray, pray, do not speak about it now, Mr. Tufnell, if it will cause you pain."

"Nonsense, child! It will do me good in the long run. The human heart needs sympathy, but I have always shunned it, because until now I never met one whom I thought likely to give the genuine article. You have suffered recently, are suffering now, poor child, and will know how to pity. Besides, I have another and stronger reason for speaking, which I will not tell you until to-morrow morning. It is early yet;" looking at his watch, "and I will make my story short."

CHAPTER IX.

"Beneath an exterior **which** seems, and may be,
Worldly, frivolous, careless, my heart hides in me,"
He continued, "a sorrow which draws me to side
With all things that suffer—nay laugh not," he cried,
"At so strange an avowal."

—*"Lucile."*

OLDING his arms and **leaning back in his** big arm-chair, Jolliffe Tufnell told the **story of his life, as though in the** fire, which lent its reflection to his glistening spectacles, his attentive eyes saw the whole **in panorama.**

"I was always ugly," he began; "that fact was the first idea grasped by my infant mind, and, therefore, I use it as a starting point in my narrative. It was forever dinned into my **ears by my good** humored, not very handsome father; by my cold, proud, beautiful **mother; by my brother Ralph, six years my senior, and who from an early age gave** promise of great manly beauty. Even the **servants ventured to** jest upon the subject, for I was not a pet, scarcely like **a son of the** house, but a neglected little monster of ugliness. **Two sisters younger** than Ralph, had died in infancy, and **my mother hoped for a girl in me. I,** the last child, was a sore disappointment to her; she had set her heart upon a daughter and from **me, a** hideous urchin, it turned with repugnance. The estate, not a large one, for my **father was a younger son, was,** of course, settled upon Ralph; yet notwithstanding he would have **it all, I was regarded by him with** undisguised disfavor, **as** something that necessarily increased our father's expenses, and, consequently, decreased the sum total he would be able to leave at his death. My brother wanted no one to share his pottage. And so I came into the **world an incumbrance,** a hindrance, a bore to every one, a load of misery and unhappiness to myself. All superfluous cash went upon Ralph's education, and then to give me one, for without it I could not be expected to make my way in the world, my father was obliged **to scrimp and save.** It was hard upon him, but he made me feel it, **not with** the intention of **being unkind, but because** he did not **understand, did** not take the trouble to understand, my unfortunately sensitive disposition. Unconsciously he would wound me with unthinking **remarks, and** send me off to cry my heart out with childish misery in some out of the way corner.

"Sometimes Ralph, who looked down upon me with contempt from his own height of happiness, would find me in my hiding place, and jeer and laugh at the 'great big girl.' Ah, how often have I wished

I was a girl! For many a long day I believed that the little girls
who occasionally came with their mammas to the house, were, when
at home, kept upon pedestals like statues to protect them from
harm. Whenever they chanced to come, I was always brought into
the room for their amusement; not to play—oh, no, but to be
laughed at by them and their mammas for my uncouth appearance.
My name, even, sent people into convulsions. Jolliffe—Jolliffe!
Oh, Phœbus! what a name! and taken in conjunction with Tufnell
—it was diabolical. My father's choice, it was; and little thanks to
him, for a man too fond of fun at another's expense. His favorite
amusement was to have me brought in after dinner, place me on the
table, and, while I stood there in an agony of shame, tell the laughing company how I had but one natural gift—my beauty; and that
my one hope in life was to marry some beautiful heiress who would
take me for my charms alone. My mother sometimes pitied me, and
saved me from these scenes, but oftener she was too much occupied
with my handsome brother who was her idol now, to have thoughts
to spare for me. Ah! it was cruel—cruel—to torture a child so.
And yet they were good people as the world goes: charitable, hos-
pitable. In sickness, no one could be kinder than my mother so
far as my bodily needs were concerned; but beyond the tips of her
fingers on my pulse, her hand never touched mine in caress. No
kisses, no loving words were for me. To minister to my soul she
knew not how. My father would say: 'Feel better, Jolliffe? Hurry
up and get well, for I have a large dinner party next week and want
to exhibit my curiosity.' They never sought my love, but they had
it—they have it now, for they knew not what they did.

They sent me to Eton, where I was the butt of my form, of course, but
at this school I found my first—my only friend—Louis Dunraven, a
boy in the sixth form. I was his fag; or rather, he called me such to
protect me from the cuffs and blows that would have been unsparingly
bestowed upon me had I fallen into other hands. He had passed
through that wretched period of boy life at a public school, in the
service of a tyrant; but when it came to be his turn to exercise
power, instead of revenging upon another what he had suffered himself, he saved me, the weakest in spirit of the whole school, from
many a thrashing. We lodged in the same house, and, despite the
disparity in our ages, formed a strong and lasting friendship. Of
course mine was the advantage, for I had nothing to give but my
whole heart—a very worthless and scanty return for all his goodness
to me. He helped me in my studies, corrected my Latin verses for
me, turning my spondees into dactyls or dactyls into spondees as
occasion required, taught me to bowl slow twisters and keep wicket,

for he was captain of the eleven; in fact I may thank him for all that
I know, for I had no talent, no genius, nothing but perseverance
brought into play by gratitude for his kindness, and the wish to
please him. He was a good boy, a good man, and when I think of
the way in which his life, which from a human point of view should
have been filled with happiness, was brought to a conclusion, I dare
not murmur at my own hard luck. Ah, Louis! noble-hearted, high-
minded, generous Louis! to him I owe the little that I have, and his
life I nearly ruined. When he left Eton and went up to Cambridge,
I had risen in the school and was able to hold my own. Even then,
his kind interest in me did not cease. He wrote me encouraging
letters full of advice and hopes for my future. He was reading for
holy orders, and I determined to follow in his footsteps. When I
timidly broached the subject at home, my father laughed, Ralph
sneered, but my mother said, 'let him have his own way.' So it
was settled and in due time I went up to Cambridge. Dunraven
was still there and expected to take his degree in a year. Formerly
we had been like elder and younger brothers; now we were more on
an equality, for I had grown older in mind more rapidly than in years.
He was greatly liked and respected, not only by all the fellows of
his own college, but of the others who knew him, and was an immense favorite with the authorities. Again he was of service to me,
for as his friend I was spared much that a shy, unsociable, ugly fellow like myself was likely to encounter. I was just nineteen and in
two more years would have taken my degree, when my father died.
Ralph came into possession of the property, and his first act was to
marry a vain flaunting woman of shady antecedents. Broken-
hearted at her son's misalliance, my mother left the house without
a word of reproach or farewell to the idol who had so illy repaid her
motherly love. I traced her out, and found that she was living
comfortably but plainly and in great retirement on her small jointure.
Of course I did not wish to pain her by my presence, and she never
knew of my having discovered her place of abode.

"Ralph's wife was extravagant, and spent more than his income.
One day he wrote me a heartless letter saying that I had had quite
enough education; that it was humbug my going into the church,
as he knew of no patron from whom a living was to come, and that
I must give up the idea unless I chose to starve. He would buy
me a commission in the line, and then I might go my own road to
ruin as fast as I pleased; but anything else to assist me he would
not do. My choice then lay between the army and the poor-house.
What was I to do? All my worldly wealth was the meagre legacy
left me by my father—too little to enable me to remain at college

until I was prepared to take orders. He knew well his advantage, and he took it. I was naturally submissive, and I yielded to necessity. Reading for the church, I entered the army, and you may guess the result. With no taste for dissipation, poor, unprepossessing and diffident, I soon became a target for the heartless chaff of the barrack-room and mess-table. Those who tormented me now, brothers in arms, but brothers in naught else, held my heart with no ties of kindred, and my blood often rose in anger. I could not afford to quarrel with them, however, and bore their jibes as best I could.

"Dunraven was ordained now, and about to be married. And in his brotherly letters of sympathy and advice, his feelings occasionally carried him away, and he would write in glowing terms of his *fiancée*. She was radiantly beautiful, he said, sweet tempered as an angel and as good, and—all lovers talk alike, I suppose—and in six months they were to be married. Poor Louis! his bright dreams of happiness were never to be fulfilled. His betrothed is an old maid now—Miss Julia Lifford." Not noticing Lucy's start of surprise, he went on, quiet and motionless, his voice alone expressing varied feeling as the scenes of his life passed in review. "Now was the wedge inserted which eventually shivered his happiness and my peace of mind. He lost his father and the marriage was postponed. My father's elder and only surviving brother, an old bachelor, was taken down with a sudden attack of gout in the stomach, and went the way of all flesh. The Knocklofty estates being strictly entailed in the male line, fell to Ralph; but not long did he live to enjoy them. He was thrown from his horse while hunting during the following winter, and broke his neck. He died childless, and I thus, suddenly and unexpectedly, came into ten or twelve thousand a year, and a place of my own. Would he had lived and saved me from what I became! Hitherto I had suffered only through others; now, came a time when I myself was to be the tormenting demon and destroyer of my own peace. Of course, I could not have that woman, Ralph's wife, in my house; my house! think of it! and do not blame me if my sudden fortune nearly turned my brain. I, who never before had, or expected to have, a superfluous shilling. Well, when she was comfortably settled elsewhere, much against her will, too, for she couldn't comprehend that I was master now, I obtained leave and sought out my mother, and offered her a home under my roof. She accepted it. All her old hopes buried in the grave, she gave what remained of her affections to me. The human heart must have something to love, and when all else was gone, she turned to me. Oh, it was exquisite pleasure to feel that a mother's love was mine! and I was as a happy child for the first time. It would have been cruel to thwart any wish of hers, and perhaps have lost me the new-found treasure. To her every desire I yielded. I would have left the army now, and followed out my cherished plan; but no, she would not have it. 'The head of the Tufnells enter the church like any beggar? Never! My duty was to my tenants, my mother, society, to my country; I should go to Parliament; I must leave the army, of course, but not yet; it was her wish, her command that I remain in it another year; I could exchange if there was any talk of foreign service, and for that matter I could go into the Guards or some swell cavalry regiment, or the Rifle Brigade—any crack corps, now that I was rich enough to go the pace with any of them; but stay in the army I must, and learn something of life. Intimate association with polished, well-bred men of the world, and entrance into fashionable London society, to which my possession of a handsome income now enabled me to have access, would cure my morbid sensitiveness, rub off the queer corners of my character, and polish me down into something like a gentleman. See how much improved I was already.' That was salve to the wounds she gave me. I was improved then? ay, but not by the means she supposed. It was the knowledge that I had become of consequence to some one in the world, that made me a happier man; and assured of my power to give pleasure, I was consequently more self-possessed and perhaps a little less *gauche* in manner. I am naturally weak, and I yielded to importunities which, while they took much of pleasure from life, yet enhanced the value of it by proving that it was a subject of interest to another. I joined my regiment at Maidstone, a different being from the one but recently snubbed and mercilessly chaffed in the mess-room. My brother officers were now kinder, more friendly, and all at once seemed to take an immense interest in me. Some, even, fastened on me like leeches. It was easy to see that my new position in life was the cause of this sudden change, and I might have shaken them off and returned to my old existence. No; it was too lonely; the new life was too enchanting. It was delicious to find myself run after, and made much of, and to hear my sayings laughed at and repeated as *bon mots*. It was all so new, and strange, and delightful, that I forgot cause in effect, and was completely carried away by the tide of endless dissipation. Unconsciously I was led deeper and deeper, by light-headed thoughtless companions into all kinds of folly until I was almost afraid to look back. At last, it seemed impossible that I could ever retrace my steps. I played more heavily and drank deeper to deaden thought.

"The London season opened. My mother had come up to town and taken a house for the season in Bruton street, and I, as much to be near her, and in for all the gaities of London, as to cut away from the wild set I had been in, exchanged into the ——th Lancers, then quartered in Hounslow and Kensington. My mother being in mourning went out but little, and at first, I managed to devote much of my time, when not on duty, to her; and for a time I fondly imagined that I had succeeded in altering my former mode of life, and away from the old influences and temptations, hoped to accomplish a complete reformation. If my mother had aided me in my good resolves, perhaps all would have been well. On the contrary, she insisted that I should go out as much as I could; she wouldn't for the world be a tie upon me, and what was London in the season without London life? Of course, I gave way again, and weak as I was, I needed slight persuasion. I was soon drawn into the giddy whirl of pleasure, and what with dinners, and balls, and parties, and opera suppers, by night; and dejeuners and garden parties, and—I was going to say kettledrums, but they hadn't come into fashion yet—by day, I soon had time for little else, and sometimes I didn't see her for weeks together. Besides, I quickly discovered that I had made a sad mistake in another matter. I had thought my comrades in the old regiment reckless and dissipated; but they weren't a tithe to my new brother officers. The ——th was a 'fashion famous' corps, and regarded as the fastest set of men in the service. Meeting them only at mess and on duty, I might have held myself aloof from their rapid style of life, but mixing in society with them it was impossible. All my hopes of altering for the better vanished with the temptations that now beset me; all my good resolves went to the winds, and the old story of brainless dissipation repeated itself with me, only to a tenfold degree.

"Rich and unmarried, my ugliness was forgotten, and I had my pick and choice of the prettiest girls—the prettiest were generally the poorest—at the balls; and I might have had the same in matrimony. For one alone I felt anything beyond a mere liking. For the first time in my life I was in love, and all things now become tinted with rainbow hues. *She* was not poor, she had a snug little fortune of her own, so that I felt sure she would not marry for money. Little as I cared what brought the butterflies of society about me, so long as they came, I could not bear that this nature's butterfly should be attracted by the same light. Her mother and mine were old friends, and I was intimately received at their house, where Mildred showed to even greater advantage than in the ball-room. A year before, I would not have had courage to fall in love, and now I actually asked a good, pretty girl to marry a fellow who was ugly, weak minded, utterly devoid of strength of character, and without a single redeeming trait. And she loved me—*me!* the worthless scapegrace. From her own lips I heard the confession, and it lifted my mind above the life I was leading. With shame and remorse I determined on a new course. The demon that possessed me was strong, but love was yet more powerful. Fatally for me love had to do its work alone, unaided by moral courage, a virtue that was not mine.

"Nothing to do but to cast off wild associates, you will say, an easy task. Not so. Once intimate with young men of fashion, 'twas no easy matter to break away from them, and the company they led me into. With moral courage, the thread of intimacy might have been snapped at once, but without that all important essential of a man's character, one loiters upon the road of good intentions, never entering the city of good acts; fortunate, if at last, one does not stray into the region of crime.

"Each day with increasing repugnance I resolved to leave these companions, but not just now, I would say; 'tis hard to lose all I have gained, and again be looked upon as a milksop, and a 'Miss Molly.' Wait; it will be easier by-and-bye, to slip stealthily out of this net. Once I am married none will wonder at the sudden change in me. What possessed me I know not unless it was the fiend himself.

"At length my mother began to look grave at my delinquencies whenever we met. She, who had urged me to the edge of the precipice! Was it my fault that I had fallen over? I worked guilty conscience into anger and the belief that all were to blame but myself; and yet the burden that I placed upon other shoulders made mine feel none the lighter for its division."

He paused an instant, and then in a lower voice, deep and hoarse, continued:

"At last the day was set for my wedding, and I decided as the first step in the right direction to retire from the army, and sent in my papers to sell out. Feeling already half a reformed man, I went to see my mother. She met me with reproaches, which in my then frame of mind seemed so unjust that they annoyed me and I angrily left the house. I went at once to Mildred, thinking in her society to forget all trouble. She had evidently heard rumors, perhaps exaggerated reports of my doings, for she was constrained, even cold in her manner. In no mood for asking an explanation, I fled from her to men who received me with open arms.

"I dined at mess that night for the last time. My retirement I knew would appear in the morrow's *Gazette*, so, as it was to be my last appearance there as one of the cloth, it was made a sort of farewell affair to me. After dinner some of us went to the opera. Almost the first person I saw was Mildred in one of the boxes, and a man whom she knew I hated paying her marked attention. The sight maddened me, and leaving the house with one of my companions we wandered into a gambling house, a low sort of a place, where I am ashamed to say I had been before. With repugnance and yet with less reluctance than usual I sat down to play. My opponent was a semi-gentleman of notedly bad character. At first he let me win, the usual tactics of course, and then as the stakes increased the tide turned and I began to lose. This angered me. Mad, mad, mad I was that night; goaded to insane fury by my mother and Mildred—the more mad, the more furious that I knew they were not altogether wrong and that I was far from altogether right. I drank deeper than any there, for had I not more harrowing thoughts to drown? Play ran high, and luck, as ever, was against me. I lost heavily—heavily. Madder still with drink and excitement, half my fortune was about to be staked, when a hand was laid on my shoulder, and a familiar voice sounded in my ear. I looked up and beside me stood Louis Dunraven.

"A hush fell on the assemblage. A sense of shame almost sobered me; and when he whispered to come away I rose quickly to obey. Then the silence was broken by the clamor of the low habitués of the place who had been waiting patiently for the time to arrive when they might fleece me of my all. ' The stake was up,' they said. ' No, it was not yet put up,' answered Louis. They knew it was not, but still persisting that it was as good as done, and my honor in peril—ah, I think it was!—they added taunts to me and him. To him, a clergyman for coming to such a place; to me for being weak, unmanly and dishonorable, to be thus controlled by the will of another. With Dunraven at my side their sneers were pointless shafts, and more by the insults heaped upon him than by their language to me, the good angel within me was roused, and stood forth to help me in this hour of need, conquering the demon that had ruled so long. One man, one of the worst characters in the room, a sort of professional gambler grasped me by the arm as if to force me into my seat again. I wrenched it from his grasp, and with all my soul up in arms aimed a blow that laid him sprawling at my feet. In another moment he was up and upon me, and we were struggling together in the midst of overturned tables and chairs, to the sound of crashing glass and excited human voices. I heard the click of a pistol, and was hardly conscious that a third had joined us before I found myself separated by the width of the room from my antagonist, and beheld Dunraven standing between us, the rescued pistol in his hand.

"'Gentlemen,' he said, 'this commotion may bring the police. It will be worse for you than for us, if it does.' Completely cowed they slunk away, and the crowd thinned perceptibly. Unmolested we left the place. Kind brotherly words, free from reproach, I listened to that night. I asked him how he had known of my whereabouts. Passing through London, he said, he had called in Bruton street. Into his ear my mother had poured all her fears for me and my future, beseeching his help in reclaiming me. At once he had set out in search of me, no procrastination in his character, and had succeeded in tracing me from place to place."

CHAPTER X.

Then black despair,
The shadow of a starless night, was thrown
Over the world in which I moved alone.
— The Revolt of Islam.

"DUNRAVEN was obliged to leave town the next morning; but assuring me that he would return in a few days, he made me promise to keep away from temptation in the meantime. Gladly and gratefully I gave the pledge. Parting from him at the railway station, I returned to my rooms in Curzon street, it being too early to go, as he had advised, to see my mother; and there I found a man waiting for me with a challenge from the fellow I had floored the night before at the gambling-house. I had no intention of accepting it and told him so. He then coolly informed me that if I refused satisfaction to his friend, reports, exaggerated and highly colored, would be set flying of Dunraven's exploits in a gambling-house. Seeing that such reports, if once set afloat, would have sufficient foundation of truth to blast his character forever, I began to waver. Here were two inevitable results of my folly, and between them I must choose. Greater disgrace to myself, or immense injury, perhaps ruin to my friend. There is nothing in friendship, in life, or in charity, without sacrifice. Could I allow him to be the one to offer up the sacrifice to friendship? No! if I was ever again to hold up my head I must keep it free from a weight of selfishness. My brain confused, and unable to think clearly, the thought never occurred to me that even my fighting this duel might not save Dunraven's name, but would be the most likely thing to bring the whole affair before the public.

9

Idiot that I was I accepted the challenge. The following morning at dawn we met; and would it had pleased Heaven that I might have been the one to fall! But no, it was intended that by living I should expiate my faults. My adversary was dangerously, perhaps fatally wounded at the first fire, and I fled at once to the Continent. Then followed days and nights of sleepless misery while his life hung in the balance, for I had now fully awakened to the realization of what I had been—what I might be guilty of. Dunraven, my true friend still, came over to me there, and soothed and comforted me as a father might. He owned that stories of his connection with the affair had begun to be whispered about, and his character assailed, but consoled me with the assurance that in my power it would be to set him right before the world. Oh! those days and nights of suspense, remorse and penitence—days and nights never to be forgotten! Long, long they were, but not without end; for just when it seemed as if I could endure them no longer, the clouds began to lift; news came that the wounded man was out of danger; then he was recovering and the clouds rolled higher—farther still they rolled, for he was almost well. Then I thought it safe to return, and coming back to England, lived in retirement for a short time longer.

"One night before the man was completely recovered, I went with Dunraven to see him, and—but never mind about that now. At last he was well; and then I came out from my seclusion, and did all that lay in my power to clear Dunraven, writing a true account of his connection with the gambling-house fracas to the newspapers, and giving my personal assurance of his innocence to such of my friends as did not shun me. His previous character for honor and integrity stood him in good stead, and he stepped forth unscathed by the furnace of scandal.

"In all these days I had not seen nor heard from Mildred. How I longed to go to her! but I durst not. I asked my mother's advice on the subject. 'It was her place to make the advance, not mine,' she said; 'I had better wait.' I did wait, day after day, week after week, with heartsick yearning, but nothing came of it. During this time I noticed that my mother seemed naturally to turn against the woman, who, if she truly loved me, could not have deserted me now. Slowly and warily, though I guessed it not at the time, knew it not till long afterward, she tried to undermine my love, but she only succeeded in sapping all my love for life.

"At last, one afternoon in the park, I met Mildred face to face. We were in the Row. With a joyous bounding of the heart at being in her presence once more, I urged my horse to her side. Her eyes flashed angrily upon me, and giving a cut with her whip upon her horse's flank, she dashed ahead without a word. I could not have been more surprised, more stunned had her whip come down upon my head. In a sort of daze, I passed the hours until a note came to me from her. I tore it open eagerly, hoping against hope. 'As your ungentlemanlike behavior of to-day,' she wrote, ' proves that your feelings are not fine enough to enable you to understand a tacit breaking off of our engagement, I write to inform you beyond your power to misconstrue, that I consider myself freed by your conduct from all promises of an alliance with you. In the future we will meet, if meeting be inevitable, not as friends, but as strangers.'

"All that night I lay upon the floor where I had fallen, not less crushed than the crumpled note in my clenched fingers. With the morning light my sense of manhood asserted itself. Outwardly calm, I sat down and wrote to Mildred, saying that for her I could have no reproaches; she had acted, no doubt, wisely; I forgave her freely for the pain she had given me, and in order that her dreaded meeting with me might not be inevitable, I was going away to the wildest parts of the world to seek—I knew not what. Then a few words of farewell to my mother. I could not trust myself to bid her good-bye, for her prayers might have had force to keep me against my will. Then alone I left home and civilization, and went forth into voluntary exile. For months I wandered in the wilds of Africa, endeavoring by danger and bodily fatigue to still the pangs of memory. Partial success was all I achieved. Of my adventures I could tell you to-night and to-morrow night, and the next, and yet again the next, night after night, for perhaps weeks; but for that style of narrative I am not in the mood.

" Let us pass them over in silence, and come to the time when entering Cairo I was obliged to apply to my bankers for money For weeks I lingered in Egypt, impelled by some unreasoning motive to wander through the country of the Nile. Perhaps the verdure-giving river reminded me of the love which had at one time flooded my barren life with promise of a rich harvest of bliss, yet had left it more sterile than before, but unlike this faithful stream never to return. There I wandered and there came to me a letter from my mother. It commenced with reproaches to the cruel, cruel boy who had left her so long in anxious suspense, without even a line to say he was alive, and whose whereabouts she only by an accident learned from his bankers. Then came entreaties for my return, followed by prayers for forgiveness for something yet unmentioned, that she had done. It had been all for my good, she said, and with the

best intentions for my welfare, that she had acted as she had, and I
could not refuse pardon for the fault which had sprung alone from
her love for me. Long drawn out was her letter, as though to ward
off, as it were, till the last possible minute, the confession begun
upon the fourth page; a confession of a wicked plot against my
happiness, interspersed with innumerable excuses for the double
part she had played. Condensed I will tell it to you. My marriage
with Mildred had never found favor in her eyes, for her ambition
had led her to believe that I could make a more eligible match—
one that would add greater consequence to the Tufnells, by giving
me powerful connections. There was such an alliance to be made.
Lady Jane Montague was one of thirteen daughters—poor, or she
would not accept me—but she was of one of the oldest and most in-
fluential families in England. My mother was well aware of the
futility of trying to reason with me, and with the patience of a wily
woman, waited her opportunity to cause a breach between Mildred
and me. After the duel she had felt that the reasons that I should
marry into this family were stronger than ever, and it was this time
she chose to carry out her scheme. She pretended to make a confidant of Mildred, and into her ear the mother poured complaints
against the son. By inuendos and half-finished sentences, sighs
and tears, she conveyed far more than she could have done in a
straightforward tale; and effected her purpose far better than by
the latter mode of action. Poison administered drop by drop
found its way insidiously to Mildred's heart; whereas from one large
potion she would have turned with distrust, doubting what it shocked
her to believe. When the man I had wounded was well, she sent
me word by my mother to come to her that I might have the chance
to set myself right if I could. Failure loomed before my mother if
she allowed us to meet, so she never delivered the message. To
Mildred she affected to make excuses for me, yet in such a manner
as to leave the inference that I would not come. During these days
she talked to me of the virtues of this other woman. I thought that
in the kindness of her heart she was but seeking to fill the void in
my affections, and received her words in the same spirit. Ah! if I
had only had firmness then to crush the thought in her mind! She
might have relented and rejoined the broken thread of my love.
But sufficient of this scheming. It is painful to tell such things of
one's mother; but bear it in mind, as I do, that her motive was my
welfare. Enough to say that she succeeded in her purpose, and we
were enstranged, as you already know. Hardly had she begun to
see, as she thought, clearly to the end, when I was gone. As time
passed and she heard no word from me, the fear seized upon her

that some evil, she knew not what, had befallen me. Filled with guilty remorse, she confessed the truth to Mildred, beseeching forgiveness; and that angel of goodness forgave her. They mingled their tears, each comforting the other with the hope, which neither felt, that I would soon be heard from, and that all would yet be well. It was when news arrived that an adventurous party of Englishmen and Americans — one of them of the name of Tolfree, which was at once construed into Tufnell—penetrating into the Arabian deserts had been murdered and robbed by Arabs, that they gave up all hope of ever seeing me again. My Mildred, my flower, began to droop and fade, slowly, painlessly, yet surely, and oh! bitterest drop in my life-long draughts of sorrow, this letter of my mother came too late! She—she was dead."

Overpowered by emotion Tufnell bowed his head and covered his face with his hands. When he again spoke, his eyes were still shaded, his voice husky.

"Again my unfortunate mother cried for merciful forgiveness; but no, my heart was hardened against her, I could not forgive. With a cruelty greater than hers, so great that it is with shame I confess it, I wrote but two lines to say that she had killed one, and would soon have another death upon her conscience. I went once more upon my travels. Purposelessly I wandered over the world to America, China, Japan, the Indies, a great weight upon me, a great void in life. Years went by and I was still an aimless wanderer upon the face of the earth; but do not think that in all this time I went about hanging my head and sighing. True sorrow does not parade its woe. There were times when I even laughed, when I seemed to others a pleasant companion—this without egotism—and there were moments when mere trifles pleased me. Yet, through it all remained the sense of something wanting, something lost. Thoughts of my mother had constantly risen in my mind, and at first I strove to put them aside, but as time passed I thought of her less hardly, and one day I wrote to her, not kindly, I grieve to say, but still dutifully and with no harshness. The expected answer did not come. I wrote again in vague alarm. This brought a response from one who called herself my mother's companion, saying I must return home at once if I wished to see my mother alive. I went where home might have been, but was not; a place so full of happy meaning to him who has one, conveying such painful thoughts of impossible bliss to the wretch who knows no hearthstone. What a terrible change in my once beautiful mother! A single glance and the face, lined by remorse and sorrow even more than by age, was pillowed on my bosom, the shrunken form clasped in my arms, and she was forgiven, thoroughly—heartily. How peaceful to me, as I know they were to her, might have been these last days of her life, had it not been for something which had happened in the past, that I now learned for the first time. My truest friend, he to whom I owed so much, Louis Dunraven, had been foully murdered in the woods near Bratton, it was supposed by Guy Egerton. I had written to him frequently while away, but at length became offended at his strange silence, and discontinued my unanswered letters. The murder had been committed so long before, that with difficulty I obtained any information on the subject, and my mother who at the time had been in trouble about me and oblivious to all else, could give me but few particulars. I had doubts of that poor boy being guilty, and with the hope of solving the mystery of the murder and the boy's disappearance arose a new interest in life. A work was before me at last, and to it I determined to devote all my energies. While my mother lived, which was longer than had been expected, my presence was too precious to her to allow me to do much else than to give my time to her; and in those last days by her bedside reading and talking on religious subjects, my lost faith came back to me, and before she died she had my promise to try to live a Christian life. Still young, yet utterly estranged from the world, I was very lonely, but I had purposes now in life, and the resolve to do some good to others before I too quitted this earth. What would I not have given to leave the busy world and spend the rest of my days in retirement! But I felt that there were duties before me which I must not shirk; that where I could do most good, there I must be; and putting aside inclination I mingled once more in society. In these last few years I have been enabled to save many young men from my own fate, or perhaps, a worse one; and in one way and another to do more good, very little it is true, yet far more than I had ever hoped to accomplish.

"I am not unhappy now, and when the one great purpose of my existence is achieved, I dream of a quiet, peaceful old age in retirement at Knocklofty Hall—a battered worthless old ship coming into harbor after a long and tempestuous voyage, to drop slowly to pieces till the place thereof shall know it no more.

"Do you know that I never see a steamer sailing over the water with a great cloud of smoke in her wake, that I do not think of human sorrow. As the dark and heavy mass leaves the funnel, at first it spreads above the vessel like a great black pall, darkening all beneath by its shadow; but by degrees, as the ship speeds onward, it forms into a train, and hangs behind as more springs forth to take its place, thinning slowly, melting into air, that which is farthest fading first. And at last when a tranquil haven is reached, the smoke no longer issues forth, and of what has before darkened the air, soon nothing remains but specks of soot upon the water.

"Does not sorrow come ever fresh and new, the griefs of to-day thrusting aside the woes of yesterday, until, as we advance in life, those that have come first fade into insignificance? Peaceful harbors there are, where, if we have not foundered in the tempest of affliction, or been wrecked upon the rocks of despair, we may find rest while present trouble sinks into the past, and we gain strength to renew our voyage into the troubled waters of the future; where, at last, worn out with buffeting the billows of adversity, we may drop anchor and slowly fall to pieces.

"It is my one hope that in some quiet harbor I may find my rest, and, when the last timber crumbles and falls away, that all my worldly wealth may go to freight a better craft than I myself have ever been."

CHAPTER XI.

This narrow isthmus twixt two boundless seas,
The past, the future, two eternities.
— Veiled Prophet.

KNOCK—knock—knock at the door of one of the private sitting-rooms in the Pavilion Hotel, Folkestone. It was breakfast hour, and according to appointment, Jolliffe Tufnell had come to share the morning meal with his friend Mrs. Whym. The breakfast table, with its snowy cloth and hissing urn, was laid when, in response to a gentle "Come in" from within, he entered; and Lucy was reading over the advertisements in the supplement of yesterday's *Times*, while she awaited his coming

"Good morning, Mr. Tufnell," she said, as she laid down the newspaper, and came forward to meet him with a smile; "I am glad to see you so punctual; see, the clock on the chimney-piece has only just struck."

"Punctuality, my dear, in keeping one's engagements, I regard as a virtue; quite as much of a virtue indeed as patience, if we may judge, I am sorry to say, by the infrequency of its practice among mortals. You slept well, I need not ask, for you are looking remarkably well this morning. I was right, you see, in thinking a breath of sea air would do you good."

It was true; there was a vast change for the better in Lucy's looks, since they had last met. Her face had lost much of the expression of settled gloom it had worn the day before, and the first faint rays of the sunshine of hope and a contented heart seemed to be peeping forth in her smiles. But the recital she had listened to the night before, had, perhaps, more to do with the improvement than the saline tonic of the atmosphere.

"Yes, I do feel wonderfully light-hearted this bright, beautiful morning; wonderfully light-hearted, I'm ashamed to say;" and she hung her head.

"Nonsense, child! why shouldn't you? But come," changing the subject as he saw the old shadow creeping back; "suppose— though you are the hostess, and it's manners in a guest to wait to be asked—suppose we go to breakfast. I'm awfully hungry."

"Oh, dear! I forgot," the shadow gone again, as she ran over to the table; "I waited to make tea till you came. I did't think—"

"You didn't think, my dear, that like the ghost in Hamlet, I'd come so carefully upon my hour; that was it, wasn't it? Well, so much the better, for if there is one thing more than another I like to see, it is a young lady engaged in the domestic occupation of making tea;" and he followed her over to the table, to superintend the operation. "One spoonful for each person, is the formula, I believe. But that won't be enough when there are only two people, will it? I hate weak tea."

"And one for the pot, you know;" said Lucy, taking a third spoonful from the tea-caddy. "There, that will do famously; besides, strong tea is bad for one's nerves, they say."

"Oh, yes, I know they say so; but it's just like everything else they say, you'll find; all rubbish. Do you know, my dear young friend, that I've observed, as a fact, that the old women, who are regarded as the proverbial tea-drinkers of the world, bar the Chinese of course, are, some of them, the coolest, most deliberate, nerveless old hands going. Let me give you a bit of this broiled ham, Mrs. Whym? I can recommend these rolls, too, they're really very fair for a sea-side hostelry. Thanks; yes, its quite strong enough, I confess; a trifle more sugar, please. By the bye, talking of tea and the Chinese, reminds me of a yarn I heard when I was in Hong Kong." And so, while Lucy did the honors gracefully, and listened, Tufnell rattled on, feeling strangely happy in his present frame of mind, this man of moods, and determined that the talk should not lag, so far as he was concerned. He put off the consideration of serious matters until the waiter had taken his final departure; for he had a fixed belief that all servants of the "male persuasion"—as A. Ward puts it—were cast in the yellow-plush mold. But at length, when he had finished his second cup of tea, and the waiter with his Tower of Pisa-like tray of crockery and Britanniaware had descended to the regions below, he drew two chairs, for himself and Lucy, before the window, intent upon the discussion of the business of the day.

"I want to have a little talk, now, about your affairs," he said; "and in the first place I must tell you, that after a night's reflection on all that you said to me yesterday, I have determined to assist you in your project. You are of age, your own mistress, and though frankness compels me to say, that I cannot but censure your conduct in leaving those who have been all in all to you, yet, feeling as you do at present, I cannot advise you to return to them. Try your plan of life: I have no doubt that in time, when your mind becomes more tranquil, and you have thought over the matter seriously, you will see it all in a far different light, and feel better able to endure what now appears to you to be unbearable. I would be sanguine of a happy future for you, if it were not for one thing. It troubles me. Misunderstandings, springing from some slight cause, so often lead to life-enduring sorrow and regret, that I cannot feel quite satisfied about—Is it not possible that you misjudge Mr. Ingolsby? that you did not rightly interpret his words? His conduct during the search for you was not what one would expect from a man who spoke as you suppose. Would it not be wise to seek an explanation?"

"Mr. Tufnell," and as Lucy answered, her flushed face was turned aside, and her fingers closed tightly upon each other, "this is the last time that that man must figure in our conversation. He should not do so now, but that I feel it my duty to speak without reserve to one who has won my perfect trust, by his disinterested kindness and confidence in me. The expression used in reference to me, to which you refer, was explained, if explanation it needed, by Sir Griffith's response. I remember it perfectly, and it convinces me of his meaning. To you I can never cease to be thankful for all your goodness, and willingly will I take your advice; but on this one subject—Oh, forgive me! forgive me! if I seem ungrateful," and her eyes sought his in supplication; "for I cannot allow any one to dictate to me modes of conduct, which my woman's nature will not sanction; on this subject my own heart must be guide and mentor."

"I beg your pardon, child. 'Tis I who should apologize for my apparent intrusiveness; but believe me I only wish to assist you, as I would have liked some one to have aided me when I was young in adversity. As you wish it, then, we will not again refer to the matter. And now to decide on a future course of action. Have you any idea in what manner you can support yourself?"

"What I want, Mr. Tufnell, is a position which can be obtained without having to furnish recommendations or references; where I will be seen by few, and those few unlikely to discover my identity, with work that I am capable of performing, not too hard, yet remunerative, and where I will be so situated that I can remain disguised."

"And where on the face of this earth, where the right niche for the right person is seldom, if ever, found, do you expect to find such a place?"

"There is not only such a niche in this world for me, but I also intend to enter it," she said, smiling.

"Where?"

"In the service of a lady of rank."

"How?"

"As a lady's maid."

"Well!" and after this third monosyllable, a final ejaculation of wonderment, conveying a meaning the very reverse of what the word itself expressed, Tufnell rose abruptly from his seat, and thrusting his hands deep into his pockets, paced the room. "Young woman, young woman, this will never do. Be your birth what it may, you are a lady by education and refinement, and you must not take the situation of a menial. Be what you will, but not that. It goes against me to consent."

"It is not your consent I ask, but your assistance," she said, quickly; then fearing she had wounded him, for she thought she saw him wince at the brusqueness of her words: "What else can I do? For a governess I would require recommendations—references; and even if I succeeded in obtaining such a situation without them, I would live in hourly dread of detection. I have been told that my voice could make my fortune; but even supposing such an assertion to have been more than mere flattery, what concealment on the public stage? There is much work to be done in the world, but none other than what I suggest, that I am in a position to seek or accept, or am competent to perform. There is no alternative, and I must accept the only mode of living that is open to me."

"My dear child, there is *one* alternative—you can marry."

"Marry!" she exclaimed in utter amazement; "and whom, pray?"

He had paused in his walk directly before her, and stood looking over her head into the waters of the English Channel, far beyond.

"I told you the story of my life with a purpose. I thought that it was not right that a young girl should be cast adrift upon the world, and when once you knew me as I was, I determined to offer you a home. I cannot say that I love you; but I do like you—like you very much; and if in a few months time you are still of the same mind in regard to the Egertons, and are devoid of feelings of repugnance toward me, a home is open to you, and I ask you to be my wife;" then lowering his eyes for the first time to her face, where varied emotions were so rapidly changing its expression that he tried in vain to detect which held the strongest place, he went on without waiting for a reply: "You no doubt think me a very queer fellow, to be making such a proposal at such a time, and on our short acquaintance; but one must use extraordinary measures in an extreme case. I have little doubt that in time this affair of yours will come all right; but if by any chance it should not, and you remain dependent upon your own exertions, the best possible thing you can do is to accept a home from me. I have no one to care for in the world, and I will spend my life in trying to make you happy; and in doing so will find happiness myself. I do not want you to answer me now, for you may not at present see clearly the merits and demerits of my proposition, as I wish you to do; but a few months hence, leaving sufficient time for everything to take place that is likely to happen, you can tell me 'yea' or 'nay.' And now, will you allow me to inquire into the state of your finances?"

"Fifty pounds, minus my traveling expenses up to the present time," she answered, grateful that he did not ask her to speak on the other subject he had just left. She could not have done so then—she knew not how.

"And will you not permit me to assist——"

"No, no," she interrupted; "it is enough to support me until I can earn more."

"But if you should by any chance require help in this way, you will allow me the pleasure of being useful?"

"I hope and trust the necessity may never arise; but if it should, I promise to apply to you."

"Thank you," he said as heartily as though she had granted him some great boon. "Had you not better cross over to Boulogne to-day?" he added: "I will join you in Paris, for I must run home to show the servants that I have not been kidnapped or otherwise made away with, as my sudden and unaccountable disappearance might lead them to suppose; and more important still—I want to get a change of clothes. I might telegraph to have them sent to me, it is true, and that would show that I was alive besides, but I really think it best that you should continue your journey alone. Should all come right again, it will be better for you, believe me, than if it were known that I was with you all the time. I will see you off, of course, but we must first find out when the boat leaves," and he started for the bell-rope. "Oh, the very thing! here's a Bradshaw on the chimney-piece. This is a wonderfully well-appointed place of entainment for man and beast, I must say: two capital chimney ornaments, a clock—a clock that strikes, and a Bradshaw. Now, let's see. South Eastern Railway, page 326; here it is: 'London and Paris in 10 hours, Thursday, October 4th, Tidal Express leaves Charing Cross and Cannon street, 1:25 p. m. Folkestone, 3:50'—we have abundance of time—'arrive in Paris 11:30.' That's rather late, I'm afraid; but you can drive directly to the Magnifique in the Italiens —the best hotel is the safest. Are you afraid to travel alone?"

"If I were, I should not be so far on my way already. Have no anxiety, pray, in that respect."

"I am glad you have so much confidence in yourself," he said, closing the book and putting it back in its place beside the clock; "for I confess to having felt decidedly nervous myself at letting you cross the Channel and go on to Paris alone. I must remain here till to-morrow."

"Why?"

"A very good reason, my friend. When I went out shooting yesterday morning, as a matter of course, I had not the faintest idea that I was starting on a journey to Folkestone, and had but a small sum of money in my pocket; luckily, enough to carry me as far as this, for I traveled third-class when I found the farmers in your carriage. I can't very well leave here, you know, without paying my bill; for they don't know me, and my style of dress, you will confess, is not exactly the thing to inspire confidence in a landlord's breast. I would telegraph to my bankers in London for a small draft, but for the very same reason—I don't know a soul in the place who would or could identify me. If it was known that I was here, it would, of course, be all right; but in transactions of a monetary character the British banker is a very careful animal. So the only thing I can do is to write, for happily they know my signature, and wait for the return post. I'm blessed," and he emptied the contents of his waistcoat pockets on the table, "if eighteen pence three farthings is not the sum total of my present cash on hand!".

"This is most unkind, Mr. Tufnell," Lucy said in a hurt tone; "you shower kindnesses upon me, and yet will not give me the pleasure of making even a poor return. You will not condescend to borrow from me to whom you would offer your bounty."

As she spoke, she drew forth her purse and placed it in his hand. Silently he took a sovereign, and returned the rest, his man's heart, no doubt rebelling at receiving assistance of such a kind from a woman, yet his gentleman's nature forbidding him to pain her by a refusal.

"I will meet you in Paris in two days at latest," he said, as a few hours later they stood together on the deck of the Boulogne steamer, amid the throng of passengers just come down by the "Tidal" from London. "In the meantime you can be on the lookout for your 'lady of rank;' but if you do not succeed in finding one desirous of your services, I must once more come to the rescue; that is, if you will still accept my humble assistance. There goes the last bell, and they are drawing in the gangway bridges, so I must go ashore. I won't say good-bye, but *au revoir.*"

And, as the mooring-lines were being cast off, and the paddles were beginning to turn, he gained the pier, leaving Lucy looking wistfully over the rail—the old sense of loneliness gathering about her heart and dimming her eyes, now that she was again alone, and the one true, honest-hearted friend who had shed the only ray of sunshine upon her past week of sorrow, and lifted so much of the weight from her heart, gone from her side.

Tufnell stood on the end of the pier and watched the steamer till it was but a speck in the offing, and its black smoke a mere blur against the distant sky; and then, after wiping away with his red silk pocket-handkerchief a haze which had gathered upon his spectacles, he lighted his short clay pipe, stuck his hands into his pockets, and walked slowly back to the hotel.

CHAPTER XII.

Honest labor bears a lovely face.
—"Patient Grissel": Act I, Scene 1.

LUCY, registered as "Mrs. Whym, England," had arrived at the Hotel Magnifique, Boulevard des Italiens, Paris.

The coming of a plainly-dressed English "Mrs." thus unescorted, unattended, and luggageless to the fashionable French hotel, happily for her, did not excite the remark or attract the attention it would have done in conventional, straightlaced old England; for so long as her manners and address appeared to be those of a lady, and she gave other and more tangible and satisfactory evidence of the possession of means wherewith to meet whatever expenses she might incur while she remained under his roof, the voluble and volatile landlord troubled not his head, if she had chosen to leave her husband or her maid at home, or had seen fit to travel abroad with no articles of raiment or personal adornment, beside those she wore, than what might be contained within the narrow limits of a small black leather traveling-bag. As for the people stopping at the hotel, nothing surprises a Frenchman; the English guests regarded a thing that might have surprised or even shocked their ideas of propriety at home, as unworthy of note in Paris; and the Americans "minded their own business."

The rough passage across the channel; the reaction from the excitement of traveling for the first time in a strange country unattended; the depressing influence of the feeling that she was alone in a strange city, where even the blind beggar in the street had a companion in his dog, and every one of the throng filling its gay thoroughfares, appeared to act in concert with somebody else, while she remained solitary among them all, made her feel miserable and sick at heart. To one who had always been an object of solicitude, this sensation of being "one apart" was inexpressibly painful. For what more utterly dispiriting to any one, than the enforced consciousness that with those one is thrown amongst one has nothing in common, except it be the belief that from henceforth and forever it is to be thus.

Are there not times when there seems to fall upon all nature a dark, disfiguring pall; when all things lose their charm; when there appears to be nothing worth living for, nothing to keep one plodding on through this dreary, dreary world? The mind grows weary, and the soul asserts itself and calls for something nobler, more satisfying—far, far beyond this monotonous every-day life. A mere trifle, a word, a glance unkind, the book we have been reading, the first view of some grand scene—any of these, trivial in themselves, may on a sudden cast a spell upon what before had given greatest delight, till in a moment it dwindles into nothingness, and dark dissatisfaction, with all that was, or is, or may be, usurps the place of light. We feel that—

"It is not all of life to live, nor all of death to die."

We cannot resist, we cannot conquer the shade that falls upon our heart; strive as we may, the spell still holds us slaves, until relaxing of itself, the human instincts spring into place once more.

Lucy was under this strange influence, and her courage sank; and though blame her we must for the unacknowledged pride which had brought her to this pass, yet pity her we can for the pain that she suffered.

Bright, therefore, was the sunshine that Jolliffe Tufnall brought with him, when, resplendent in a blue frock coat, pearl gray trousers, and a tall hat, he came at last; for it dispelled the gloom which oppressed her.

It was only his good-humored smile, his cheery words and odd ways, but sunshine it was to her, and once more she took heart, and looked forward with firmness and courage. Was she already unfaithful to her first love? She put the question to herself, and the answer came back: "Not so. I fear I value the mere human presence more than the man, good and kind though he has been to me."

When no pleasing visions come to beguile our hours of loneliness, but crowding thoughts of unhappiness harass the mind, a human presence then seems all in all; unless it be that we have reached that morbid state, when brooding on our sorrows gives us something akin to pleasure. Lucy, fortunately, had not reached the latter state; hers was a nature which though it could of necessity stand alone, yet craved human sympathy and protection.

Almost his first question was about the "lady of rank."

She had been too far from well both in body and in mind, Lucy told him, to make any inquiries as yet, but at once she would set about doing so.

"You, a lady, stopping at this swell hotel," he said, "cannot step directly from such a position into the character of a lady's maid. The fact, too, that you were staying here, if known to those from whom you might seek employment, would be apt, at least, to excite suspicion as to your true character, and be almost certain to prevent the very result you wish to accomplish. I thought it safer for you to come here at first when you were alone and unprotected, but I only intended that you should remain until I could join you again. What you must do now, is to take lodgings, change your name again, and prepare some suitable clothing. The lodgings, you yourself must find, for, of course, I must not be seen or known in the matter. A young woman in the station you are to occupy, has, or should have, no gentlemen friends. The sooner you can get away from here the better, for, if there was no other reason, it is confoundedly expensive."

He watched her narrowly as he spoke, with the hope that now it had come to the final point of really sacrificing her position, that her courage and determination would forsake her.

"And am I no longer to have the benefit of your advice?" she asked anxiously, but with no sign that could be construed into wavering from her purpose.

"We can write," he answered, laconically.

So it was settled, and Lucy with little difficulty found humble lodgings in the neighborhood of the Faubourg Montmartre. There she remained five days without seeing or hearing from Tufnell; and the sense of loneliness that had again come upon her, was less painfully felt, as her mind was occupied by work which kept her inexperienced fingers busy. Not quite new to such work however, they were also ready, supple fingers, guided by an ingenious brain, and at the end of these five days her maid's slender wardrobe was completed. The other lodgers whom she met on the stairs as she went to and from her meals, knew she was English, in spite of her perfect accent; and having apparently had some experience of the coldness and reserve of her nation, from other Britishers with whom they had come in contact, beyond a "*bon jour, madame,*" or "*après vous, mamselle,*" left her to herself. She was not sorry, for it freed her from the annoyance of idle questions, idly asked. In busy solitude, therefore, she passed the time away, only going out for her modest dinner, and simple breakfast, to a quiet little restaurant in the next street. On the morning of the fifth day, as she was returning from the latter meal, the *concièrge* put into her hand a letter addressed to "Miss Sullivan." She opened it quickly, and read:

"MY DEAR CHILD:

"I was thinking of the advisability of advertising for a place for you in a French family, when by the luckiest chance, I found what I doubted—with reason—if you would ever find; viz: just the place you want. The Amtenhursts (Earl, Countess and niece) are here, arrived yesterday, *en route* for Italy, and last night while passing through the hall I met Lord A. who took me to their rooms. We were talking together when Miss Courtenay (the niece) came into the room, and informed her ladyship that 'Jones was no better and refused to go with them any farther, considering her illness a bad omen.' No more was said on the subject, but my head running on ladies' maids, I began to wonder if this Jones could be one, and then an idea struck me. I questioned a chambermaid, who no doubt puts me down as infatuated with Miss Courtenay—misguided creature! (that is, the chambermaid) and this is the result of my inquiries. Jones *is* a lady's maid—Lady Amtenhurst's own; has been taken suddenly sick, and refuses to go a step farther. They are traveling with no other servants but a French courier, so I would advise you to apply for the place, its advantages being that traveling will do your mind good; in an English family you will feel more at home than in a French one; they do not know the Egertons; Lady A. is a kind good woman; and you will not have to mix with servants. Come as soon as you get this—say you heard she wanted a maid, and refer her to me for a character or any necessary recommendations. A man does not generally know much about it I suppose (I'm blessed if I do) but never mind, I'll manage to make it all right for you, if you will trust.

"Yours sincerely,

"JOLLIFFE TUFNELL."

One hour later Lady Amtenhurst was sitting alone in one of their *appartement au premier* at the Hotel Magnifique, when a plainly-dressed woman was ushered into the room.

"What is it you would speak to me about, my good woman?" her ladyship asked as the other stood silent and embarrassed.

"I heard, my Lady, that you were looking for a maid," and the voice trembled slightly.

"Not exactly that. My present maid is sick and I fear will be unable to remain with me; still I had not yet thought of filling her place. But sit down: you will be tired standing."

There was something in the tone of her voice that gave a kindliness to the words, in themselves but commonplace, and caused Lucy—for it was she—to put aside her veil, as she sat down."

"I have even thought seriously," her ladyship went on, "of continuing our journey without one." An unmistakable shade of disappointment crossed the face she was scrutinizing, and she asked: "Is it for yourself you want the situation?"

"Yes, my lady."

"You are young to have much experience, and you seem above the position."

The color rose painfully in that sad young face as Lady Amtenhurst waited for an answer to her half interrogatory, half assertion.

"I was educated above my station, it is true, and with no thought that I should ever work for my daily bread, but—but I assure you, my lady, that I was born of very humble parents."

The look of wistfulness and truth in the soft black eyes, changed the other's glance of keen scrutiny into one of compassion.

"Poor girl; and after your mind having been elevated and given a taste beyond your sphere, you are now compelled to earn your bread. I was right, then, in supposing you had little experience; and much as I like your appearance, I am afraid you would not suit me. I want a woman thoroughly competent to take all trouble off my hands in traveling."

"I am not so ignorant as you think, my lady."

"Were you ever in service before? I thought this was your first trial."

A moment Lucy paused before she answered, to ask herself if it were wrong, in speaking the truth to imply what was false? Her intention was not to injure or defraud any one; she felt herself capable of performing all that would be required of her; if she let this place slip through her fingers, would not the same question be asked by others? and she knew of no other way in which to earn her bread. It was one of the necessary evils of the course she had

10

chosen, and adopting for the time being the doctrine that "the end justifies the means," though it went sorely against her conscience, she answered:

"I lived in one family several years."

"Their name?"

"Egerton, my lady."

"Egerton—Egerton. Have I not heard that name lately?" mused Lady Amtenhurst. "What was it I heard in connection with the name? Oh, yes; I remember now: a daughter eloped or ran away with somebody. Are these the same people?"

"Yes, my lady," and the tell-tale blood bathed her cheeks.

"Unnatural girl to run away from her father and mother. Were you with them at the time?"

"Yes, my lady."

"Why did you leave them?" and her ladyship's eyes were once more keen and watchful.

It was evident that she was imperfectly acquainted with the story of Lucy's disappearance, and it was not likely that she would suspect this applicant for a situation as her maid, to be the runaway daughter of the Egertons; but to remove any doubts that might by chance have entered her mind, Lucy determined to make a bold stroke, and still adhering to the dubious maxim she had resolved to be governed by, tell what was true, yet so word it that a very different conclusion from the actual fact would be drawn.

"I left them when the young lady did; and because, my lady, it was with my assistance that Miss Egerton escaped. Without my help she could not have done it."

"Oh, indeed! You are a frank young woman, to tell me this."

"I tell you because I feel convinced that, had you been in my position, your ladyship would have acted in the same way. Oh, my lady! if you could have known the poor thing's sufferings, being in my place, you would have done as I did." She paused abruptly, conscious that her feelings were carrying her away from her assumed character.

"But are you not sorry for it now? Would you not undo your work?"

"No, my lady," she answered, looking up steadily. "I acted truly by her who was my mistress. She was the one to decide for herself between right and wrong—not a poor servant."

"But you are not an ignorant menial to serve as a tool in other people's hands. Your appearance, your language, everything is above your position, and you should have used the discretion given you by Providence."

" Perhaps so, my lady, but," with a sigh, " I acted according to my lights."

"And you expect me to take you into my service after this confession?"

" My lady, if I have been true to one, does it not follow that I can be true to another? If you take me into your service I will be true to you till death."

She did not know what a powerful pleader was the sad sweet look which met the searching gaze fixed upon her.

Lady Amtenhurst rose quickly, and took a few steps to the centre-table, and resting her hand upon it, stood in thought. As quickly she turned again, and came back to Lucy, who had risen.

" I know not what possesses me," she said with a puzzled look. " Had another woman spoken as you have done, I should have rung and had her turned from the room. Were you discharged when your young mistress was missed, or did you leave with her?"

" I left with her, my lady."

" Where, then, is she now?"

" I cannot tell your ladyship."

"And why did the silly girl leave her home?"

" That is her secret, my lady. Were it in my possession, I am sure your ladyship would not have me tell it."

" Will you not try to induce her to return?"

"It is not my place to advise, but to serve, my lady. I have done that which I thought right, and I must go through with it to the end;" and sad was her voice, as with something of disquiet, she thought of the path which once chosen, she must now follow.

" Edith!" called Lady Amtenhurst.

A minute's silence, while she and Lucy stood with looks bent upon the floor. Then the door of an adjoining room which had been ajar, opened wide, and a small, fair-haired woman entered.

" Did you call me, aunt?"

" Yes, Edith, come here."

As she came forward, staring somewhat rudely at the stranger, Lady Amtenhurst drew her arm within her own, and led her to the window. Her ladyship spoke in a low voice, and then her companion left her side, and going to the table for a photograph album, her eyes rested upon Lucy, as she passed back with it to the window.

"A remarkable face!" she audibly whispered; " not by any means remarkable, auntie. A very ordinary face, I call it; if not positively ugly. I would strongly advise you to take her. Jones positively refuses to go on, and where else shall we find another? and I want so much to leave here to-morrow."

Her aunt said something about "going without one," at which Edith pouted and jerked her shoulders.

"Impossible, auntie!" she exclaimed, leaving the window. "I could never manage to get on without a maid, whatever you might do. Do you know how to dress hair, young woman?" to Lucy.

It was something she had always had a fancy for, and now she could honestly answer:

"Yes, Miss."

"And you know all about dressing one for parties, and altering dresses, and packing, and all that sort of thing?"

Not quite pleased with her new interlocutor, Lucy replied:

"I can do all that may be required of a lady's maid, Miss."

"We want to leave Paris to-morrow, so this afternoon would be the best time for you—"

"Come, come, Edith, not so fast, my dear," interrupted Lady Amtenhurst, coming forward and laying her hand upon her niece's arm. "I cannot at present make up my mind whether or not to take this young person. I will think about it, and let you know to-night," to Lucy. "Do not form any hopes that I will engage you, for it is very doubtful. But if I should, can you be ready to leave with us the day after to-morrow?"

"No, no; to-morrow, auntie.' '

"We leave Paris the day after to-morrow," said her ladyship, quietly but firmly; and Edith, evidently but too well acquainted with her aunt's quiet firmness, turned away with a gesture of ill-concealed impatience.

"I can go any day, my lady," said Lucy.

"Your address?"

"27 Rue Jacqueline."

"And name?"

Promptly came the word "Sullivan;" although prudence was whispering, "She may know more of this story some day, and suspect the truth." But conscience answering, "You have imposed upon this kind woman enough—mislead her no further," conquered prudence, and she repeated:

"Sullivan, my lady."

She left the hotel, and walking rapidly along the gay Boulevard with its crowd of fashionable promenaders, brilliant shops, and handsome equipages, turned into the Rue Laffitte, and passing on through the quieter and humbler streets of the Faubourg Montmartre, reached her lodgings, wondering as she went at the liking for Lady Amtenhurst that had sprung up in her heart, and surprised, now that the dreaded interview was over, at the courage which had come to her so quickly when once she found herself in the room she had entered with such nervous anxiety, scarcely knowing what she should say. But the conviction that in the new life there would be hardly less deception than had she retained a position that was not rightfully hers, forced itself upon her, and did not fail to alloy with fresh misgivings, the hopes she had been indulging of peace and rest come at last.

CHAPTER XIII.

The leaves of memory seemed to make
A mournful rustling in the dark.
— " Fire of Drift-Wood."

IT was that hour between day and dark when the world slowly resigns itself to night, parting reluctantly with the last lingering rays of light which break the fall of sudden darkness. That twilight hour, sad, yet not melancholy, when, the present all forgotten, past moments of bliss are lived again, and the future rises bright and beautiful; when thoughts chime in of joys long passed that are now but sweet and lingering memories— thoughts of tranquil happiness—thoughts of what we are and might be—of what we are not—of what we would be—thoughts of loved and lost ones—thoughts of loved ones not yet ours—of what might be, of what can never be; thoughts of an ideal perfect world as we would have it, but can never know except in dreams; so that when the hour is passed and gone, and we realize that life and dreams are not as one, life by contrast loses half its charm. Exquisitely happy and doubly precious because so rare, are some moments in life, but in their reality worth far more than those we dream. If thou wouldst find them, oh, reader, and feel their true value, beware of thoughts which crowd into that little hour, when day departing, in gentleness gives way to coming night.

When twilight fell upon Paris that early October evening, little of its beauty found its way to the humble room where Lucy sat. But though the tall surrounding houses shut out the gorgeous sight of richly-tinted clouds in fantastic groupings, above where the God of day had sunk to rest, the influence of the hour stole softly in, and fell upon her half closed eyelids.

No view from the window, no fire in the grate, no beauty in the room; nothing for the eyes to rest upon with pleasure, she closed them upon the outer world, and looked upon the inner. Shadows of by-gone happy times gathered round her, and began their tale of

" Days that are no more,"

while the stars came out one by one, and the night, gradually closing in, filled the room with its darkness. Then in interruption
came a step upon the stairs; slowly and heavily it ascended while she
waited to hear it pause at her floor and go to one of the other rooms,
or keep on to the story above, that she might resume her musing in
silence. The step paused when it reached the top of her flight, and
then she heard it approaching her room. Wondering who it could
be, she was half tempted to jump up and lock the door, when a tap-
tap-tap was given on the panel outside.

"Oh, it is the *concièrge* with the letter from Lady Amtenhurst,"
she said, reassured by the thought, as she hastily struck a match
and lighted her lamp. "Entrez!"

The door was thrown open wide, revealing—not the slovenly old
concièrge—but a strange, dark figure in the shadow without.

"Who can it be?" she thought; "a messenger from her ladyship,
perhaps."

Taking up the lamp in order to discover from a closer inspection
who her unknown and hesitating visitor might be, she moved toward the doorway, and the light fell upon a middle-sized man,
dressed in that peculiar loudness of style which always betokens the
absence of taste, if not of gentility. A short cutaway coat, buttoned
so as to show an expanse of yellow waistcoat below, and a gaudy
crimson scarf in which was stuck a huge horse-shoe pin, above;
trousers of the most gigantic check; an eye-glass screwed into one
eye; a small cane twirled lightly under one arm; and, to crown all,
a tall white hat with a wide black band, tilted knowingly over one
ear, and displaying on the uncovered side of the head, a staring crop
of bright red hair.

Lucy looked a moment at the remarkable figure, in inquiring
doubt, and then started back in surprise.

"Mr. Tufnell!" she exclaimed.

"The same," he answered.

"You here! Did you not say—"

"That you were not made for this life," he interrupted. "But
'season your admiration for a while,' as Sir Griffith would say, and
I will explain. Put on your things, child," he added, as he entered
and shut the door after him, "and come out for a walk. Whew!
what an atmosphere! They evidently do their own cooking somewhere on this floor—essence of garlic predominant."

"Have you anything very important to tell me, that you come
here to-night, in this guise?" she asked, smiling in spite of herself.

"Nothing; except that I gained you the place you so nearly lost;
that's all. I am glad my elaborate toilet amuses you. I did it to

prevent the people below, and those I might meet on the stairs, from taking me for a gentleman. I am not a very elegant specimen at best, and I tried to dress myself as much like a swell-mob gent as I could. These yellow gloves and flaming scarf, to say nothing of this Palais Royal watch-chain, which I purchased with the cane, ' for this occasion only,' are about the correct things in that line; and as I spoke the very worst French I could manage to utter—not a very difficult task for me, by-the-bye—to the *concièrge*, I have n't a doubt but that he put me down for a cad of the first water, or whatever the French for that animal is. Do you know it's been awfully hard lines getting this beastly glass to stick in its place—but spectacles would have spoiled all, and I had to have something of the kind to keep me from breaking my neck, or being run over at every street-crossing. This brute of a cane, too, I mean to throw away after to-night. I never carried a walking-stick in my life, and I'm too old to begin, or rather, more properly speaking, not old enough, I hope. But get on your bonnet, or hat, or whatever you call it, this moment; for I will not tell you another thing till we get out of this hole into the street."

Lucy straightway obeyed, and ten minutes after they were walking arm-in-arm in the quiet streets of the neighborhood—some of the quietest in the gay metropolis.

"I would take you along the Boulevards," Tufnell had said, as they left the street door, " but they are too bright and full of people, and as there are no end of people, I find, in Paris just now, whom I happen to know, some one would be certain to turn up who would recognize me, for all my caddish get-up. We must only hope for a promenade there together at some future day under happier auspices, and content ourselves for the present with—as they say in America—' a walk around the block.' I came to bid you good-bye," he continued, as they walked along, and looking at her through the inevitable spectacles, which had now replaced the discarded eyeglass. " There is no knowing when we shall meet again; for who can tell what will be the next freak you will take into your head."

"Are you going away?" Lucy asked.

" It is you who are going away, not I, child."

" I?" she exclaimed. " Why, nothing is settled with Lady Amtenhurst."

"I beg your pardon," he replied; "everything is settled in that quarter, and you leave with them the day after to-morrow."

" You know more about my affairs, it seems, than I do myself," she said, smiling. " How does it happen?"

" Why, the truth is, I was anxious to know how you had succeeded, so this afternoon I ran in to see Lady Amtenhurst and her niece. I suppose you know I have the reputation of being very odd, and therefore I can say or do almost anything, and people only shake their heads and laugh. Without danger of exciting suspicion, I asked directly who was the woman in black I had seen leaving their rooms this morning. 'It struck me I had seen her face,' I said, 'somewhere before, but my memory for faces was truly wretched.'"

"How could you?"

"By-the-bye, that is a question I want to ask *you* presently. But let me go on, please. Miss Courtenay at once informed me that it was impossible that I could know the woman, for she was only a servant." A flush overspread Lucy's face. "I asked her if she thought I had never seen a servant whose face I might remember? 'Isn't that strange,' she said, 'Auntie insists that it is a remarkable face, and you seem taken with it, while for my part, I saw nothing but very ordinary flesh and blood.' Thus it is that different people regard the same object. Then she went on to tell me in her usual confidential manner—her aunt interrupting ineffectually to say I could take no interest in their domestic concerns—that they could not leave until they had secured a maid in place of the sick one, and they would miss some people they wished to join somewhere if they delayed any longer. Here had this English woman turned up in the most providential manner, and 'Auntie' did not want to engage her because she had assisted some girl to run away from home. 'Just as though I was likely to take pattern by a scatter-brained damsel,' she added, 'and leave my comfortable home with the assistance and at the instigation of this woman; it's too absurd!'

"My astonishment at this information must have been visible in my face; and to give a reason for it, I exclaimed, 'Why, the face now vaguely connects itself with a story I have heard! What was the name of the girl who absconded?' 'You know her, I have heard you speak of her;' replied Miss Courtenay, 'Lucy Egerton. By-the-bye, what sort of looking girl was she?' 'Quite pretty,' I answered; 'a blonde;' and I knew that a vision arose before them both, quite at war with black eyes, even should the idea of a black wig come into their heads. Then she went on, with a profusion of strongly emphasized words: 'How *could* she do anything that would cause public talk about her! Anything like publicity would kill *me*, I *know*; for *I* have one of those sadly *sensitive* natures that *shrink* at the *least thought* of notoriety.' 'As the spider at a touch on his web,' thought I, mentally supplying a simile. While she was dilating on the beauties of her own nature, my thoughts were busy upon the nature of your communications to these people, and too much occupied to take an interest in this extremely sensitive young creature. 'Oh, I remember it all now!' I exclaimed, 'this woman was —' I paused, quite certain that Miss Courtenay would supply me with the clue I wanted; and she did. She finished my sentence for me—'Was Miss Egerton's maid,' she said.

"And now while I think of it, let me ask you, with a few of Miss Courtenay's emphases, that question: *How could you tell such a story?*"

"I told no story," cried Lucy, dropping his arm with an indignant flush, as she halted abruptly. "I said I lived with the Egertons several years, which was true; and called Miss Egerton my mistress. Her ladyship found her own meaning in my words, and I did not take the trouble to explain that I was my own mistress. My only fault was in speaking of Miss Egerton, when no such person exists."

"And you call it no fault to mislead without an absolute lie?" he asked.

"We will not argue that point," she answered, with a sigh, "for I have doubts myself that might lose me the argument."

"You were honest, at least, in giving the name Sullivan; as for the mistress question, it strikes me that the events of the past fortnight have pretty clearly demonstrated that—if you will excuse the slang for the sake of its expressiveness—the boot is on the other leg. Miss Sullivan has, I think, fairly proven herself the mistress of Miss Egerton. But come; don't let us stand here any longer. I have not half finished what I wanted to say; at all events, we can select a more secluded spot, not so near a gas lamp, if you insist. We are attracting attention; at least, I am."

She silently took his arm again, and they walked on.

"Where was I? Oh, yes. I went on to say," continued Tufnell, "that this woman, this maid, was greatly prized by Lady Egerton; even Sir Griffith thought her a treasure; that they were not at all surprised at her having served their daughter so faithfully. Lady Amtenhurst then asked me what induced the girl to leave her home. I began to answer, 'She made the discovery that —' when by the most fortunate chance, Miss Courtenay interrupted, saying: 'Just think! Sullivan must know where she is, and won't tell.' At the name Sullivan I started, and asked, 'Who?' 'The woman, the maid, her name is Sullivan,' replied Lady Amtenhurst. 'Ah,' I said, not knowing exactly what else to say, and cutting my remark as short as possible, for I now saw that the wisest thing I could do was to give them no information whatever on the subject, not knowing how it might tally with what you had said. I eluded all further questioning about you, the young lady; but the praises which belonged to that personage, I lavished upon you, the waiting-maid. My grand *coup* was this little sentence—the last on the subject before I took my leave. 'I am sure your ladyship, in fact I am positively certain, that were this Sullivan to return to the Egertons, they would receive her gladly for her own sake, with no reproaches, and freely forgive the past.' You see the spirit of your prevarications had entered me, and this last *equivoque* was effective. 'I think I will engage her,' said Lady Amtenhurst; 'and in that case we leave here the day after to-morrow; so will you give us the pleasure of dining with us to-morrow, Mr. Tufnell?' I accepted, went to a theatrical costumer in the Rue Lepelletier, picked out this dress, arrayed myself in it in a room off the shop, and stole out in the dusk to bid you farewell."

"Are you not surprised," asked Lucy, "that they had no suspicion whatever of the truth?"

"I should have been more surprised if they had. When a woman hears of a girl running away from home, she does not look for her in every pretty waiting-maid who may thereafter chance to be in her service, though she will expect to see her in every beggar she meets in the street. If one were reading a novel in which the kitchen scullery-maid was a tolerably good-looking girl, one would set her down at once as the heroine; but when in real life, a lady dismisses a maid, she is not likely to suspect every one who applies for the place, of being a princess in disguise. Oh, no; it is not the fear of discovery that troubles me; but the thought of what you may have to endure; not from Lady Amtenhurst, for she is too true a lady to hurt the feelings of any one; but of that affected little piece of goods, Miss Courtenay, I have my doubts."

"Who is this Miss Courtenay?" asked Lucy.

"The orphan child of a younger brother of the present Earl, who married beneath him. Having lost their only daughter when an infant, the Amtenhursts have made one of her, and she affects the airs of a young duchess, without the graces, I am sorry to say. Now that all is arranged," he continued, "my conscience begins to prick. If I had left you to yourself, you would have been obliged to return in the long run. But you are like a horse that has got the bit between his teeth; you are your own mistress, and nothing can stop you. Nothing was to be done but to guide you clear of the pitfalls."

"Without your aid, I don't know what I should have done," she answered gratefully. "Do not regret your generosity. What you have done was for the best, and believe me, you will find it so. You do not know all I have suffered, and how you have lessened the pain. I felt so hardened toward all mankind, judging all by a few poor examples, when you came to prove that there is kindness and goodness in the world. I do not even now think there are many like you. You have done me good in many ways, and I thank you sincerely."

"Don't say any more, child," he interrupted. "You make me happier than I deserve to be. May the event prove that I have done right. Will you not allow me to relieve the anxiety of your friends by telling them that you are alive and well?"

"Friends?" she said, with a sudden expression of pain; "I have none. Every one, even those I loved best, turned from me in the hour of trial. What anxiety can they feel who care not for me? No, no, Mr. Tufnell, not a word to them, I com—I beg!"

"Command" came easiest, but she chose the milder word.

"Well, well," he said, with a sigh; "be it so; though it is not as I would wish. Is there nothing more that I can do for you before you go?"

"Nothing, thanks."

"You will join the Amtenhurst's to-morrow morning, so we are not likely to meet again before you leave Paris."

They were approaching the lodging-house now.

"Will you keep me acquainted with your movements?"

"If you wish it—yes," she said.

"And promise me one thing, child," he added. "Do nothing rash; go off on no tangents, at least, without letting me know your purpose."

"This is the last romantic act of my life," she answered, giving him her hand as they reached the doorstep; "all the future is to be the quiet, uneventful life of a lady's maid."

"Not with one of your disposition; and remember, you have Miss Courtenay to please as well as her aunt, and I pity you, and doubt your success. But keep your temper, child, whatever you do. Just one thing more let me say before we part." He took both her hands now, and held them as he spoke. "You remember the offer I made you? Think of it, and three months hence give me your answer. Fate may frown, life may prove difficult; whatever happens, do not forget that at any moment you can end it all by one word to me. Good-bye, child; God bless and prosper you."

Before she could speak, he had dropped her hands, and his dark figure was striding down the street.

A moment hesitating she stood; the next, a hand was on his arm, a breathless voice in his ear:

"Mr. Tufnell—I—I—give you leave—to tell one—*only one*—Sir Griffith—that I am safe—I can trust you to tell no other. Make him promise to keep it a secret from every one—even his wife—she does not love me much."

Then Tufnell in his turn watched a figure disappear in the darkness, and went on his way, saying to himself, "There is genuine goodness in her, though she tries her best to hide it."

And she, as she paused on the threshhold, and glanced up at the sky, fancied that the stars in twinkling expressed a gladness for the softening of her heart.

"He lost a son—he has lost a daughter," she thought. "Is not his loss even greater than mine? To lose one's children is a great trial, but—O, Alva! Alva!"

CHAPTER XIV.

There is a letter for you, sir.
　　　　　　　　—**Hamlet**: Act IV, Scene 6.

The letter, as I live, with all the business—
　　　　　　　　— Henry VIII: Act III, Scene 2.

JOLLIFFE Tufnell sat over his toast and coffee in the breakfast-room at Knocklofty Hall. The mail-bag was late that December morning for the first time in the history of the London and Bratton railway line, and he sat *minus* an expected letter from his London solicitors who had the investigation of an important matter for him in their hands—*minus* his *Times*, *minus* his *Field*, for it was Saturday; and while he munched his toast and sipped his coffee, he looked out at the white, snow-covered ground, and bare leafless trees beneath the leaden sky, and mused:

"Two months and not a line, but a couple of brief notes, which might as well have been telegrams, from their remarkable brevity. Can it be possible that I have been mistaken in her? that she is— no, I'll not think it. She promised to write, it's true; but, poor child, who can tell how her every moment may be taken up? I must not forget that she really has two mistresses to serve, and one of them—that Courtenay minx—would alone be enough to employ the time of two maids with her die-away airs, or I am no judge; besides she must have her own needs to attend to, as well as her own troubles to occupy her thoughts. I am too exacting; I'm a despicable old brute, that's what I am. The poor child has had a sufficient share of misery to endure, without expecting her to add to it by having to write to a hideous old scare-crow like me. After all she only promised to keep me posted as to their whereabouts, and so she has, poor thing; quite enough to satisfy any one but a grasping extortionate old duffer. What right have I to expect a pretty young girl to be writing to me, and giving up what little time she may have to look about her in strange lands? to compel her to draw upon her slender means for postage? It's scandalous, outrageous of me, and I ought to be ashamed of myself for having written her the complaining letter I did. But what else could be hoped for, from an inconsiderate selfish old beggar!

"Heigho! There it goes snowing again: no hunting for days to come—that's very evident. How many poor creatures may there be at this moment, perishing from cold and hunger, and here am I, comfortably housed, clothed and fed, and growling, and whining because, forsooth, a nice, sweet, pretty girl, doesn't happen to write me a long letter. Bah! Jolliffe Tufnell, I am positively ashamed of you, you ought to be well kicked, that's what——"

"Mail, sir," interrupted the old butler, as he entered with the leather bag in his hand. "Train was stopped by a snow-drift at Sawbridge Cutting, sir," he added, handing the bag to his master; "stopped a hour and a 'arf, sir, and that——"

"Accounts for the delay, I have no doubt," said Tufnell. "Leave the bag on the chair, Boffins: I shall open it shortly. That will do."

"Yes, sir;" and Boffins, cut short in his narrative, and impeded in his observation of the bag's contents, took his departure with dignified pomposity.

Tufnell gave him time to reach his pantry, lighting a cigar to fill up the interim, and then took out his bunch of keys and unlocked the bag. Besides the newspapers there were two letters: one addressed in a round business-like hand, and with a London postmark; the other in the angular caligraphy of a woman, and covered with foreign postage stamps. The latter he picked up eagerly with a gratified smile about his lips, paused a moment to knock the ash off the end of his cigar and mutter, "what a brute I was!" and then opened it and read:

"Rome, December 12, 18—.

"Dear Mr. Tufnell:

"Your reproachful letter lies beside me. No, it was not negligence, my failing to write to you as I had promised.

"My time is not my own, as you are aware, and when we are not passing from one place to another, and between the intervals that I am allowed for sight-seeing, Miss Courtenay manages to keep me constantly busy with one thing or another: brushing her hair while she reads, or reading to her myself as she seems to have discovered that I have a talent that way; packing and unpacking, etc., etc., etc.

" Truth to tell, I have had a *few* leisure moments; but when I had time to think, what is called ' homesickness' came upon me, and I was not capable of the exertion of writing.

" Do not think that I am unhappy; but at times, the ' blues' get possession of me, and do battle with the spirit of contentment that would otherwise reign supreme; and then I can but sit and think till they tire of me and take their flight. But sometimes they are so persistent that it is only when some duty calls that they will be-gone.

" On the whole I think you are fortunate to have got the two short notes from Cologne and Frankfort telling where and how I was. Now, however, I am going to make you sorry for your im-portunity, by boring you with an account of our travels, and the discoveries I have made in this new sphere of action.

" Although I am longing to pour forth a descriptive torrent of enthusiasm regarding all the wonders of this Eternal City, mercy for you, who have seen all and much more, bids me refrain. I will give but a bare account of our course, with whatever digressions it will be impossible to restrain.

" We have been nearly two months in coming from Paris to Rome, stopping of course *en route* for days and even weeks at different places of interest; and as this is my first trip abroad of any length, my enjoyment is in proportion to the space we traverse. Under other circumstances I could be perfectly happy roaming over the world, but although Lady Amtenhurst always allows me time to see everything of interest, yet, as a serving-woman, there are many places that I cannot enter. Whenever I accompany them, it is as a servant, allowed a position in the rear, and of what I do see, I am not able to converse. Interchange of ideas is half the pleasure of life, particularly when viewing new and historical scenes, and here where so many are to be gleaned, mine have to be held in close confinement. Lady A. is kind beyond expression, but it is the kind-ness of a superior to an inferior, of course, and all the time there exists a barrier between us with the words in great glaring letters of admonition: ' Thus far shalt thou go and no farther!' But what right have I to complain? If cultivation of the mind gives one a fund of peaceful enjoyment, by furnishing a stock of thoughts and ideas from which to draw mental employment in moments of bodily idleness, I should be grateful for past and present advantages. I feel that I could be happy in perfect ignorance, with those around me I love; but if that be impossible, this other source of happiness is left me, and I try to be thankful, and pray daily for a contented spirit. It will come in time, but until it does, bear with my change-ful moods—you, the only friend I have.

" I was about to tell you of our journey, when I (nothing uncom-mon, you will say,) ' went off on a tangent' to thoughts and feelings —the natural consequence of traveling, I suppose; but I have re-versed the order of things by placing effects before their cause. To begin at the beginning—let me tell you what you know already: We left Paris on the seventh of October. Miss Courtenay, for whose benefit this trip is taken, chose the route along the Rhine in preference to the more direct one through France, and we reached

Brussels that evening. I was sorry to be obliged to pass the pretty town of Valenciennes, with its avenues of tall trees intersecting the fields, an improvement, I think, on our low hedges, fragrant hawthorn though they be. At first I wished to see everything, and pass nothing by unnoticed; but now I have learned to be satisfied with a sight of the more important objects of interest in our course, feeling it beyond the power of human mind to grasp every detail of even a part of this great world.

"The next day we drove to the battle-field of Waterloo (by the goodness of Lady A., I being of the party), along the road by which Wellington marched. It was with mingled awe and repugnance that I looked upon the scene—awe for the arena where nations had struggled for power—repugnance for the ground where had been sprinkled human blood, shed by human ambition. We remained in Brussels over Sunday, and I was surprised to see all the shops open and street-hawkers as busy as the tradespeople. On Monday, they went to Antwerp, leaving me to await their return; and I took advantage of their absence to explore the town, visiting the church of St. Gudule, the cathedral of Notre Dame de Chapelle, and a lace-manufactory, where I could not but pity the poor women who destroy their eyesight in dark rooms with but one ray of light to fall upon their work. From Brussels we went to quaint, antiquated Mechlin, with its grotesque-looking houses, and on to Liege—famous in history, thence to Viviers, Aix la Chapelle and Cologne. I was never so glad to leave any place as Cologne, after three tedious days; it is so dark and dismal at night when the shops are all shut, and one feels such continual need of *eau de Cologne*, which is not prevalent in the atmosphere.

"However, one glimpse of the Rhine, which we came upon here, repaid us for wandering through dirty streets to see the unfinished Dom Kirche and its relics; the churches of St. Ursula and of the Eleven Thousand Virgins, and St. Peters, which contains the famous altar piece of Rubens; a Roman ruin, a botanical garden, etc. We went by rail to Bonn, the birthplace of Beethoven, where the beauty of the river really begins, and there were delayed two weeks at the Hotel Bellevue by the indisposition of Lady A. I stayed with her, while the earl and his niece drove out to see the sights every day; not many they said. Our best way to Mayence and the quickest, would have been by steamboat, but Miss C. preferred the land, and so we went, resting in different towns along the line. How abundant and weird are the legends of the Rhine! Our guide had them at his fingers' ends, and they were called forth by every crumbling tower and castle; and love, murder, ghosts or demons seemed to be connected with every beetling crag. From the fortified city of Mayence we passed on to Frankfort, where I took greater pleasure in exploring the old town, with its narrow streets and gabled houses with lofty peaked roofs, than in the modern part where streets are broad and well paved, and the houses almost palaces. I was vastly amused by the custom of raising the hat to all classes, and it seemed so strange to see persons of rank, bowing politely to shopkeepers. We stopped at Heidelberg to see its famous castelated ruin, and the celebrated Heidelberg tun, which they tell me used to be filled with eight hundred hogsheads of wine when the Electors held their court there; and also visited the church divided into two sections for Protestant and Catholic worship; and then passed rapidly through Carlsruhe and Baden-Baden (where we are to make a stay on our return; so Miss C. says) to Strasburg, where we remained ten days at the Hotel de Ville, waiting for some people who failed to come, why, I know not, nor who they were, but it was apparently a great disappointment to Miss Courtenay. Our next stopping place was Basle, a larger place than I expected to find, and some of the scenery picturesque and beautiful. It was provoking in the extreme, resting here upon the verge of Switzerland, the land of mountains, glaciers, cliffs, cataracts, lakes, rivers and forests—what a vast combination of the beautiful in nature!—to feel that it would all have to be passed so close and left unexplored. Next summer, I believe, we are to go through the Tyrol, but it was too late in the season now, and, indeed, the cold during our ascent to Berne was intense, and warned us to hurry on. Parting with little reluctance from the bears in stone, and bears in flesh, that met us at every turn in this town of bears, we moved on to Geneva, passed through the twelve miles of tunnel under Mont Cenis, into Piedmont, made a stay of two days at Turin, and on by rail to Genoa-*La Superba*. We remained there a week for the sake of seeing the palaces and villas of its Doge and noblemen; the cathedrals, churches, colleges and universities; academies of arts and sciences; manufactories, statuary, paintings and monuments. Being in the birthplace of Christopher Columbus inspired me with the wish to visit America, and see, if in their homes, Americans are as kindhearted, generous and chivalrous as I have been led to believe from the few specimens I have met with.

" By steamer on to Leghorn, whence we went by rail in less than an hour to Pisa—again Lady A. taking me when I could have been left behind—and our heads were thoroughly upset by one glance down from the top of the Leaning Tower. The belief that the pile was falling made us make a hasty descent, and Miss Courtenay actually screamed with nervous dread, although her courage is her greatest boast. Returning the same afternoon to Leghorn, we started on our way once more, and spending a few days in Civita Vecchia, reached Rome last week. Here we are, and here we remain until after the Christmas Holidays, the programme then being that we are to go to Naples for a glimpse of Vesuvius, come back to Rome for a few days, and then on to Florence, Venice, Vienna, the Tyrol and home. And all this is for the benefit of Miss C.—Lord and Lady A. having been over this ground many times before. And, do you know that I sometimes fancy that her ladyship dislikes Italy, and she certainly avoids one portion of it—Florence. I have often observed an expression of pain at the mere mention of its name, probably attributable to unpleasant associations; but she is so thoroughly unselfish, that as her niece insists upon visiting the place, she has consented to go with her at, I really believe, great cost to her feelings. Hers is a beautiful character, and each day I feel more drawn toward her; and a wild fancy sometimes seizes me to tell her all about myself, and ask her pity, her sympathy, and her help. She would give them, I think, and from her it would be welcome; but I dread to make the test, for so many illusions have been dispelled, that if this be one, I would have it last, and look up to her as long as I may, as the most perfect type of womanhood I have ever met with. Here, at least, is a well-matched couple. Lord A., with his genial warmth of manner, thaws even the coldest, and yet, withal, there is a certain air of refinement about him which marks the line between the manly *bonhommie* which puts all classes at their ease, and the demonstrative *camaraderie* which jars upon gentle nerves, and invites the 'hail-fellow-well-met' portion of society to rough familiarity. He is innately proud, and the existence of the feeling is proved by its very suppression. Too proud of the characteristic to acknowledge pride—as it were—no trace of it is to be found in his manner; yet there is nothing of carelessness for his own fair name and fame to prove its absence, and it is as surely in his nature as in mine.

"In him, it is a virtue, a shield; in me, I fear, a vice, a peace-destroying power; but with him before me for an example, why may I not bring it under subjection, and free it as completely from its outward visible form and inward pricking points as is his, and make it a guard, an armor, against 'the slings and arrows of outrageous fortune,' rather than a secret tormenting magnifier of the wounding powers of every-day trifles?

"Had I remained with the Egertons, it should have protected me from feeling the sneers and slights of the world, and braced me against unkindness by the consciousness of good in myself, and superiority to the rank from which I was taken. But instead, listening to all that was said against me, it urged me to the course I pursued. Without the help of humility to bear meekly, even if painfully, my lot in life, it was impossible to remain, although, too, I discovered before I left, that my principal motive for leaving was without foundation. I still say *impossible*, and so silence the doubts which torment me. Do you understand me? I hope so, but doubt it.

"My chief amusement is studying Miss Courtenay's character; and yet, be as studious as I may, I cannot fathom it. She is decidedly of an open disposition; ever ready to tell her most secret thoughts to any one who asks them, and as she appears perfectly well acquainted with all her own traits of character, and frequently makes them a subject of conversation, it is all the more strange that I cannot make her out. Profiting by your advice to keep my temper, we get on capitally together; and though she is something of a task-mistress, I feel grateful to her for taking my thoughts from myself. I fear I do not show much gratitude by my words, but my excuse is your knowledge of her failings; and you don't know what a relief it is to think and write of anything but the subject that now troubles me, that of my having left the Egertons. Yet, see what a loadstone it is, for I am getting back to it again. I cannot write without expressing the thoughts uppermost in my mind, and as I have no wish to punish you, I will bring to a conclusion this test of your powers of endurance. Your letters are always welcome, and for the next month will reach me here.

11

"Many thanks for informing me of the movements of the Egertons. I am almost sorry now that you wrote to tell Sir Griffith of my existence. I only hope (as you are kind enough to do), that they will not extend their tour to Italy.

"Believe me,
"Yours, very sincerely,
"LUCY SULLIVAN."

"P. S. The name is not yet familiar to me, though losing much of its first strangeness. You cannot subscribe to the popular fallacy that the pith of a woman's letter lies in the postscript, after this."

Tufnell thought he could, as he laid the letter down with a smile, and opened the other, which ran as follows:

"8 GRAY'S INN, LONDON, W. C.
"December, 14, 18—.

"JOLLIFFE TUFNELL, ESQ., Sir:

"We are this day in receipt of a communication from the Chief of the Police Department at San Francisco, California, in reply to ours of the twentieth ult., informing us that a man named Martin Silliman, and answering in every particular to the description you furnished us with, even to the scar under the eye, was living in that city, and following, as was suspected by the police authorities, the business of a professional gambler.

"We are now in a position to submit the evidence you have accumulated of the man's guilt to the law officers of the Crown, so that the whole matter may be laid before the Foreign Office, and the requisite steps taken for his apprehension, under the treaty of extradition between Great Britain and the United States.

"Awaiting your reply,
"We are, sir,
"Your obedient servants,
"BLUEBAGGE & PARCHMENTE.

CHAPTER XV.

The dawn is overcast, the morning lowers
And heavily in clouds brings on the day,
The great, the important, day.
— "Cato:" Act I, Scene 1.

RAINY day in Rome. Something one seldom thinks of in connection with the proverbially blue and sunny vault of an Italian sky; yet the clouds hung as dark and heavy, the wind moaned as drearily, and the rain was as persistingly monotonous in its drip, drip, drip, and certainly quite as wetting and dispiriting in its effects as on any day in less favored old England, two-thirds of the year through. Dismal and dreary beyond measure were the deserted streets, and seeming doubly so by contrast with the pageantry that had made the city gay during the so recent Christmas holidays. The peculiar-looking Calabrian minstrels, the *Pifferari*, in their wild and striking dresses and huge zampogne and high-peaked caps, decked with sprigs of heather and ribbons gay, lounge and sleep no longer on the steps of the Piazza di Spagna; the Trasteverini, in picturesque costumes, who boast of being the only true descendants of the ancient Romans; the fierce bandit-like men; the peasants from the deserted tombs of the Campagna, are no longer seen—none of the gay throng that at the firing of the cannon from the massive castle of St. Angelo on Christmas Eve, flocked to the Basilicas for vespers; that assembled on Christmas morning in St. Peter's to hear the beautiful Pastorella sung by the whole choir, and at a later hour crowded in gorgeous array to High Mass, and to see the Pope in his flowing scarlet robes, sparkling with jewels, borne above their heads in his chair of State, preceded by his guard of sixty Roman nobles, surrounded by cardinals in scarlet, bishops of Eastern churches, priests in purple and white, swinging golden censors as they moved, and carrying lighted tapers, and the Great Cross. The splendid ornaments removed from the altars, images of the Virgin stripped of their gayest dresses, the papal banners taken in, the shops despoiled of their floral decorations.

The Amtenhursts had left Rome for Naples when all was over, but now, returned once more to the Eternal City, were moping through this rainy day at the Hotel d'Angleterre, waiting for a glimpse of sunshine to light them on their way again.

Lady Amtenhurst, with " Coningsby" in her hand, sat interrupted in her reading; Edith Courtenay reclined on a sofa, with her eyes half closed, dreaming away the hours, and sighed and grumbled at the weather; the Earl was busy over some important correspondence at his writing-desk, and Lucy, the paleness of her face increased by the contrast of her black hair, stood just within the threshhold.

"You have a strange fancy for these art galleries, Sullivan," said Lady Amtenhurst. "You may go, of course; but don't be late, as we dine out this evening. It is very wet," she added, glancing at the window, "and you had better wrap up well, and not catch cold."

"Rain never hurts me, my lady," answered Lucy, bravely.

"What on earth can *you* know about paintings, Sullivan?" asked Miss Courtenay from her sofa, without opening her eyes. "Are you going to write a book on art, for the benefit of persons in your sphere of usefulness?"

"Edith, take a book and read," quietly remarked the Earl, still busy with his letters, and with the nearest approach to sternness his kindly voice could ever reach.

"You may go, then, Sullivan," said Lady Amtenhurst, "and I hope you will enjoy yourself."

"Thank you, my lady;" and Lucy's flushed face left the doorway.

With an umbrella over her head, and her dress lifted above her stout boots, Lucy tripped along the Via della Fontanella to the Palazzo Borghese, heedless of the down-pour, her mind filled with thoughts of the treasures of art she was hastening to look upon for the last time, and wishing that to her had been given genius like these masters, whose master-pieces she had learned to love.

Almost all her spare moments in Rome had been passed at the rooms of the Palazzo Borghese, and this was to be her farewell visit.

A couple of hours went swiftly by as she wandered from picture to picture, gazing with wonder and admiration at the gems which adorned the walls of the Palazzo's thirteen rooms.

At length it was time for her to go, and with a last lingering look at her especial favorites: Albano's Four Seasons, Backhuysen's magnificent sea-piece, and Raphael's entombment, she passed reluctantly from this wonderful world of man's creation to the cold and dreariness without.

It was still raining when she reached the Piazza and the wind freshening into a gale. But it was not far to the hotel, and opening her umbrella she stepped bravely out. She had not taken many steps when one of those heavy showers which come in the midst of a rain storm, came upon her with all its violence. The rain poured down in torrents, and, blown into sheets of water by the fierce gusts of wind, drove her pitilessly before it, along the deluged pavement.

Her umbrella a mass of tangled whalebone and torn gingham, the result of an attempt to retain its possession at a more boisterous street-crossing; her cloak and hat dripping and her boots soaked through, she sought the shelter of a shop's awning until the force of the shower had spent itself. With a gasp of relief and a reproachful glace at her demolished umbrella, she was about to retreat farther back from the driving wind, to the alcove between the door and window, but she found it already occupied. Another person, a young girl, had like herself taken refuge there from the storm. A slight girlish figure in a dark sealskin jacket—a pretty, anxious face with large sad eyes peering wistfully from beneath a little fur cap at the streaming torrent without: by far too delicately pretty an object to be out of doors on such a day.

As Lucy stood regarding this little flower in the midst of such bleak surroundings, the wistful look gave way to one of quickly-coming brightness, the lips parted, and the girl's whole face lighted up as she eagerly bent forward. Turning to see the cause of this sudden change, Lucy's eyes fell upon the figure of a man enveloped in an Ulster, his face half hidden behind his umbrella, as, battling with the wind, he struggled along the Via de Condotti and on toward where they stood. Her heart gave one bound into her throat, while the rushing blood went surging and throbbing up into her brain, and then ebbed quickly back, leaving her cold, white and frigid. Would he pass on? Shrinking farther back to the wall she looked again. No; he was close at hand and coming directly towards them. Did he see her—recognize her? He was looking over and beyond her, and now, in passing, brushed against her skirts and went straight to the girl in the alcove with outstretched hand and smiling face.

"Florence!"

"Alva!"

Strange heart of woman! When Lucy thought it was she he sought, all her mind was on avoidance; but as he failed to recognize one with veil-covered face so different in appearance to the Lucy Egerton of old, her feeling was one of mingled anguish and anger. Anywhere and under any circumstances would she have known him, and now he had passed her so closely as one never seen before.

"What on earth brings you out of doors this fearful day?" Ingolsby asked.

"I was on my way to get this prescription made up for papa: I did not like to trust any one else," the little voice answered. "But when did you arrive?"

"I only arrived in Rome half an hour ago, and was just on my way to your hotel. You must have wondered at my delay in coming, but I started immediately on receipt of your letter. I was with some friends in Basle, and by the luckiest chance returning to London about some business matters, found your summons lying at my club. I did not wait an hour after I got it, and traveled post-haste in terrible anxiety, lest I should find little Florence alone in this strange place. Is there really no hope?" he asked, sorrowfully.

"None, the doctors say," she answered with a sob. "Poor, dear Papa! it is so hard to lose him, and we so far away from home too; and I have no one else in all the wide, wide world."

"You forget, Florence," Ingolsby said, in a gentle tone, bending down; and as his companion caught his whispered words, a blush spread over her fair face, and a smile shone through her tears.

The gesture—the whisper—the mute rejoinder—were too much for Lucy. From where she stood, she had seen all, heard all, and giving her own interpretation to it—the one she most dreaded was the surest to suggest itself—staggering as from a blow, she turned and left the friendly shelter, and regardless of the pelting rain and driving wind, fled through the narrow streets, pursued by thoughts that almost maddened her.

Now in one street, now in another, heedless of where her steps turned, the one haunting vision bewildering her brain, on, on she dashed. When there were such in the world as this gentle, lovable little beauty to ensnare men's affections, who could care for *her?* Pitiless was the picture she drew of herself as she fled through the dark and cheerless streets—hardly less to be pitied in her suffering than the maidens of old, who had marched, footsore, weary, and degraded, through this very city, to grace while they shamed the triumphs of their tyrant conquerors. Not less powerful a tyrant had conquered her—Love; and vain had been her struggle for freedom. Its golden chains still upon her, crushing her down with their mighty weight, on, on she went, and it was not until chance led her back into the Via del Corso, that she awakened to a consciousness of surrounding objects. Dripping, saturated, heavy-hearted and foot-sore, she reached the door of the hotel.

To go quickly to her room, lock the door, and fall upon her knees by the bedside was the impulse that she followed. Beyond that, what her thoughts, what her actions during the time she remained there, she herself could never tell, and none else could ever know—

"That anguish which is to sorrow what ecstasy is to joy,"

must have been hers. Let it rest in oblivion.

The early January night had come and darkened all about her, when some one knocked at her door.

"Sullivan! Sullivan! Are you asleep or dead? Sullivan! Sullivan! Will you answer?"

Lucy stirred and **shivered,** wondering vaguely what it could mean. The wind moaned dismally without, and the rain pattered and splashed against the window panes; again came the voice, as the door handle **was** violently shaken:

"Sullivan, I say! Open the door **or answer** this minute!"

All at once a **sense of** her forgotten duties dawned upon her, and she started up to open the door; then remembering that her wet clothes **were still upon her, she** answered hastily but with difficulty, for the words seemed to **stick in** her throat:

"I will come in one **moment,** miss."

"So you have returned **from** your gadding, have **you? But I** wouldn't hurry, if I were **you,"** replied Edith Courtenay's voice, in its most sarcastic tones. "Ladies' maids of elegant leisure, with tastes for the fine arts, should not be disturbed from their before-dinner **naps,** by any manner **of means! But come at once, and** don't keep us waiting any longer—do you hear?"

"Yes, miss," hoarsely, but meekly.

"Don't wait to **finish the chapter, if you've** been reading," Miss Courtenay added **as a finisher, and then rustled** and swept from the door.

Lucy, with all **the** dispatch that stiff, cold fingers, aching bones, and a swimming head would permit, and with nervous dread of another commanding summons from without, changed her wet and sodden garments, and hastened to Lady Amtenhurst's apartments.

Lady Amtenhurst was alone, sitting before **the** glass in **her** dressing-room waiting to have her hair **dressed.**

"You are **a** little late, Sullivan," she said kindly, as Lucy entered. "I **suppose** you forgot that **we dine** out to-night. Did you see everything you wished?" she asked, **as** Lucy's nervous fingers began their work upon the soft white hair.

"No, my lady," Lucy answered, striving hard **to** steady her voice at recollection **of the** scene she *had* witnessed.

"Were you **not then** pleased with the paintings? As Miss Courtenay says, it **requires a** highly cultivated taste to appreciate the full beauties of the master-pieces, and you have had so few opportunities of seeing fine paintings—"

"Yes, my lady," Lucy replied at random, her thoughts far away.

"That **whatever** taste you have, must be natural to you rather **than acquired?"**

Mechanically filling the pause, Lucy answered:

"Yes, **my** lady."

"To which gallery did you go to-day?"

Slowly and dreamily:

"Yes; my lady?"

"The Borghese, the Collona, or the Badin—which one?" sharply.

"No, my lady!"

"What—to none of them? Then where did you go? What paintings did you see?"

"Yes, my——"

"Don't 'my Lady' me so much, Sullivan, but answer my question."

"I—I—beg your pardon, my Lady, I did not quite catch what your Ladyship said?"

"I asked you to which gallery you went to-day, and what you saw."

"Went to-day?" repeated Lucy slowly and absently. "I don't quite know. It was all among strange streets, and I think I wandered about and lost my way."

"Where are your wits, Sullivan? You don't seem to know what you are saying," said Lady Amtenhurst, and looking up she caught sight of Lucy's face reflected in the glass, and noticed for the first time, her extreme pallor, heavy eyes, and drooping mouth. "Good heavens! what a pale face! Are you ill?"

"Oh, no, my Lady: only a headache," pressing her cold hands on her hot, throbbing temples. "I cannot think, it aches so badly, that is all, my Lady; and please excuse me if I am a little stupid."

"Poor thing. You really look ill. There, that will do—no, I can do everything else myself very well. Miss Courtenay will be waiting for you, and then you had better get to bed as fast as you can. I am afraid you have taken cold."

Miss Courtenay was, on this evening, as Lucy had already had some evidence, in one of her disagreeable and unamiable moods. Her temper, at best, was not the most angelic, although in her own estimation she needed but wings to complete her fitness for a celestial habitation. Character she had none—imaginations many. Constant novel reading, acting upon a mind naturally imaginative and a trifle weak, had led her to draw comparisons between herself and every heroine of romance from Bulwer to "Ouida,"—comparisons which ended in a firm conviction, that she was formed for one, and that each and all of their good qualities—with none of their bad— were embodied and exemplified in herself. But certainly, her practice was not in accordance with her manifold precepts, imagination not being quite strong enough to carry her beyond the verge of mere assertion into actual proof by action of the truth and sincerity of her professions; yet strangely enough she never seemed conscious of failure in performance, but still remained firmly convinced of her own perfection.

She was reading before the fire in her room when Lucy made her appearance.

"So you have come at last," she snapped out, throwing her book into a corner, and seating herself at the dressing-table. "Of course Lady Amtenhurst had to keep you to put in the last pin for her, and will still expect me to be ready in time. Gracious! you needn't pull my hair out by the roots. I want puffs and curls. Here, pick up that book first, and give it to me. Now, go on."

A long pause, while Miss **Courtenay** read, and Lucy's fingers worked slowly and painfully.

"Those puffs are frightful, Sullivan!" she cried at last, looking up suddenly. "Take them all down this minute, and make a braided coronel."

Then she read once more while Lucy with aching head and breaking heart worked on. Another glance in the glass.

"The braid is too rough, I tell you; do it over again."

Lucy silently obeyed, and while her *difficile* young mistress read on, finished the task.

Miss Courtenay raised her eyes again from her book and contemplated herself with every imaginable pose of the head for five minutes at least. Then in a pettish whimper:

"It is not becoming, after all, so I will have the puffs and curls."

The puffs and curls were just completed, when Lady Amtenhurst came in, preventing, no doubt, by her presence another change in her niece's coiffure.

"Now, my dear aunt, don't hurry me, please. It is all Sullivan's fault if I am late. I never saw any one so awkward as she is to-night; her fingers are all thumbs. Sit down there before the fire, and while she dresses me, I'll tell you a bit of news. The waist before the skirt, always, Sullivan. What do you mean?" with a stamp of the foot.

"Don't be cross, Edith; the poor girl is not well," said Lady Amtenhurst.

"It's her own fault for going out in the rain and mud—to look at pictures, forsooth. I never feel any sympathy for fools. You know that old humbug, what's-his-name, in the next passage, who has been dying ever since we came back? Well, as I was passing this afternoon I stopped a minute to inquire how he was. He's not dead yet, and his daughter, would you believe it—Oh! good gracious, Sullivan, do you want to pull my hair all down again with those hooks?"

"I am glad to hear the poor old man is better, for his daughter's sake, if not for his own."

"I didn't say he was **better**. I simply said he wasn't dead. As for his daughter, I wouldn't waste any compassion on her. She seems wonderfully **cheerful**. Would you believe it, she positively smiled, while I stood there with as long a face as I could manage, thinking it the correct thing on such an occasion. If it were Flossy, my poodle, that was sick, *I* should be *quite* overcome with grief, but I suppose it's the way with these Americans; they have no feeling. Perhaps it would be better for me if I was not so sensitive. Unfortunately, on the contrary, I **am** *all* heart, *all* feeling and—Good heavens! Sullivan, do you take me for a pin-cushion?"

"But what is your bit of news, my dear?" asked Lady Amtenhurst.

"I will tell you, if you will allow me. She came to the door grinning and grimacing, as I told you, and hardly giving herself time to say, ' her father was in less pain, thanks', when she blurted out with even a broader grin—almost a giggle, in fact—that Mr. Ingolsby——Oh! do you want to murder me, Sullivan? It's lucky that pin had a head—or something to stop it. I wish you would be more careful. Where was I? This awkward, clumsy thing keeps putting me out so. Oh, yes. She blurted out that Mr. Ingolsby had come at last, and she was so happy—*so* happy. Did you ever hear such a thing!"

"Who is Mr. Ingolsby, my dear?"

"Oh, you **know**. I met him at the Ogilvie's last year. A handsome, manly-looking fellow, with the loveliest violet eyes. But of course *you* **never notice those things**. The man whom they all said was engaged to that runaway Egerton girl—you remember. I never believed it though—never. Betwixt **you and me**, aunty dear, I think he was awfully spoons **on me**—and I never gave him the least **encouragement**. But that's always the way with men: the more you snub them, the more **they like you**. They do say some girls are **the same way**, though I can scarcely credit it. Were any man—no matter how I loved him—to offer *me* a slight, that would be the last of it between *us*, *I* can tell you—my necklace, Sullivan—I hate a spaniel's nature in a girl. Did I say necklace or bracelets? Be good enough to give me my necklace, will you, and don't stand there looking vacantly into empty air? And now he's engaged to this American girl—father's rich, of course—at least she told me before we went to Naples that she was engaged—confiding little idiot—and I suppose it must be to this Ingolsby, she went into such ecstasies about his coming, as I told you. What on earth *is* the matter with you, Sullivan? Can't you stand without clutching the bed-post like that? *Now*, my bracelets. **Isn't it romantic?** father dying in a strange land—consent given—absent lover called **to take his** bride, and **the old man's** dollars—a marriage by his death-bed—bless you, my children—et cetera, et cetera, **et cetera.** Bracelets, I told you—*not* slippers. My gloves too. Ingolsby is a fortunate **fellow, I think,** for besides the father's money, the girl is rather pretty, though I confess to admiring blondes far more, myself," with a side-glance at the looking-glass. "Are those my gloves? If you are not enough to try the patience of Job! Give me my fan, and don't look for *it* among my boots. I am thankful to get from under your awkward hands at last, and I feel as though my clothes had been thrown at me, as indeed they have been. If I was not naturally good-tempered, I do believe you would have made me cross. Put away all those things, and you had better pack my trunks, for we may have to leave here to-morrow, if the weather changes. Come auntie, I'm ready." And Miss Courtenay swept from the room, without a thought of kindness for poor suffering Lucy, to play the angel amongst strangers.

Lady Amtenhurst staid a moment behind.

"Never mind those trunks till to-morrow," she said kindly. "You look dreadfully sick, poor girl. Button this glove for me, please. How hot and feverish your hands are, and they were so cold a short time ago," she added, with real concern. "You've caught a bad cold, child, and must take some gruel; ring and order some made, and go directly to bed."

"Do come, auntie!" sounded from the hall.

"Do as I tell you," said Lady Amtenhurst, stopping in the door-way for a parting admonition. "Do not pack a thing to-night." Then she followed her niece, and Lucy was left alone with her confused thoughts.

At once she set to work packing.

"It is better to have it over and done, for to-morrow I may not be able," she thought. "I feel so strange—as though reason were going from me." And as she bent over her work, while the objects about her whirled and danced, and a cord seemed to be tightening across her forehead, she wondered vaguely to herself, why it was that she placed such faith in the truth of what Edith Courtenay had said. It might all be but an idle exaggeration of hastily assumed facts. Ah, but had not she herself, seen and heard with her own eyes and ears? There was corroboration.

On any other subject she would have doubted; but on this one that concerned her so nearly—so dearly—she accepted every trifle as a proof of what it brought untold agony to believe.

CHAPTER XVI.

Peace hath her victories
No less renowned than war.
— " Samson Agonistes."

ISPOSITION is inborn, unchangeable this side the grave. Character, on the contrary, formed alike by every trivial circumstance and great event, at first a diamond in the rough, is dependent mainly on those who shape it for its lustre.

Wrought upon in a bungling fashion 'tis ruined; formed by a master hand its beauty is assured; and the sharper the instruments lent by Providence—sorrow—privation—sickness—loss—the clearer are its hidden beauties brought to light, and the nearer it approaches to perfection. Yet there are those, the exceptional provers of the rule, totally devoid of stamina, upon whom nothing has a lasting effect; not that they are adamant, but so impressionless, as it were, from the very excess of their ductility, that the occurrences of every passing moment sway them by their influence, and wounds which seem to penetrate to the core, are quickly healed, and no effort of fortune can form a scar upon the surface. Wavering and uncertain as a flickering light, they are the sport of circumstances, be their disposition what it may. Character and disposition are without doubt strongly combined, yet art can separate the two, and mold the one while it has no direct power over the other.

Take a little child born of fiercely-passioned parents—teach it, train it; the character formed, will, in a manner, control the disposition it no doubt inherits, by the knowledge of right and wrong, though the instincts of passion are still there, powerful to break all bounds when temptation comes. Ingratitude and the world's baseness harden a truly benevolent man but in appearance. Within the fence of distrust, the generous heart still lives, and impulses of good are as strong as ever, though restrained by the belief gained by a sad experience, that they will meet with no response.

Who has not met with gentle kindness in those renowned for hardihood and strength of will, as in the timid and shrinking and infirm of purpose; and are not the weak and vacilating often as cruel as those of sterner make? Though each is, in a degree, under the influence of the other, character and disposition are, therefore, not inseparable. Each distinct in itself, they go rather hand-in-hand together; character, when rightly formed and molded, holding in check, guiding by its intellectual vigor—if not indeed keeping subservient to its dominion—the animal propensities, the natural bent of disposition, be they good or bad.

Of a naturally good disposition, anxious to find the right course, but apt to be led astray by an over-sensitiveness, Lucy's character, forming almost completely of itself, could not be perfect. With strength in herself to change it to a certain extent, she had mastered passionate outbreaks of temper. But something more was required to make her what she should be, and sorrow and trouble had prepared the way for the greatest of all reformers, sickness; and the chances were that with courage to persist in the changes wrought by this messenger of Providence, lasting benefit to her character would be the result. All unknown to herself she had been struggling between life and death; and now when she had returned to consciousness, and her eyes rested, at first vacantly, but with growing perception, upon all the inevitable appurtenances and untidiness of a sick room, her great weakness was no longer a marvel to her. Where she was—with whom—what had ailed her—she knew not. Everything about her was strange and unfamiliar. That she had been sick and well cared for was evident, and with so much knowledge she was satisfied to close her eyes once more, and with no thought in her mind but of present passive comfort, perfectly content to rest quietly, almost unconsciously in the coolness and silence of the darkened room.

Gently as an infant she breathed; sometimes she slept, sometimes stirred—not in pain, but to relieve the tedium of perfect comfort, by a change from one restful position to another, revelling, as it were, in the very abundance of ease.

Presently her hand passed into a strong grasp; fingers pressed her pulse. It was too great an effort to raise her eyelids. A murmur of voices fell softly upon her ear, and then footsteps passed from the room. Another hand was upon hers, but this time soft and cool, and a light kiss fell upon her brow. In an instant her black eyes, now languid and weary, were opened and gazing up on the face bent over her.

"Dear child," murmured Lady Amtenhurst's gentle voice, "I am so thankful you have been spared. Do not fret and worry yourself with idle thoughts, for I will tell you everything when you are strong enough to listen. Go to sleep now, darling, and you will be well all the sooner."

The days went by in quick succession, and as Lucy gained in strength, crowding thoughts came pressing on her mind. When the first apathy was over, she found that her black wig was gone! The discovery of that fact brought to her the recollection of her disguise, and then all the forgotten past flashed quickly up before her. The vision of the stormy day in Rome came too; but to her wonder, it brought no pang. She was still too weak to feel intensely; but as strength grew, an aching pain that she could not master came gnawing at her heart, and she lay and thought, and showed no wish to speak. The doctor, a French physician resident in Florence, was surprised—annoyed. Her recovery was slower than he wished for—had expected. It was strange; he could not account for it. Would the "young mees" tell him how she felt? Was there anything that troubled her mind? She would be well in time, she said, and turned away her head.

Such a state of things could not last. Dr. Latour insisted that she should leave her bed. In obedience to his mandate, and assisted by an old nurse, she rose, and day after day, lay upon the sofa, propped up by pillows, to outward appearance still weak and faint. Lady Amtenhurst with anxious solicitude proposed a drive—a walk even, across the room, leaning upon her arm? No; she preferred perfect rest and quiet. Would she not like to talk, to be told how she came where she was, to have the blank in the past filled up?

"Not now, please," she would answer with a beseeching look. "By-and-bye I should like to talk and give some explanation of myself, as well as hear all about my sickness. But not now: I am not able."

Then she would lapse into dreamy silence and Lady Amtenhurst would go away in despair. Dr. Latour was a nervous, irritable man, albeit a clever practitioner, and the tardy recovery of a patient always put him out of the little patience he possessed, especially when the delay was unaccountable. "Dis is absurd, young Mees," he said to Lucy once. "Uzzer people have had ze brain fevaire, and got well—so—while I snap my fingaires. You are young—you have one good constitution. Why then is it zat you fail to find strong hels? *Sacre tonnérre!* because you have not what ze Engleese call ze 'vim.' Quite sure, it is in yourself to say, 'I will be seek or I will be well.' You say, 'I will be seek,' and lie here. *Parbleu!* young Mees, you are one grand absurdity: you have nosing to ail you, and you play to be ze invalide. Stand up—dance—seeng—laugh—play on ze piano—go out to drive and walk—talk and be gay—zat is ze way to get well. You mope yourself here all ze day, and quite sure, you always be no bettaire."

Lucy raised her drooping head.

"Have patience with me, doctor, and I will do all you wish. Not now, for I cannot, but by-and-bye."

"Ah, dis 'by-and-bye'—dis 'have patience!' You take all I have, and *sacre tonnèrre!* you cry for more. You have one grand insanity! *Bon jour*, young Mees; when ze doctaire's advice is refused, ze doctaire is in ze way," and indignantly the old fellow rushed from the room. How little he understood the workings of her mind!

The next day he returned, thoroughly determined that extreme measures should be taken to rouse her from her apparent lethargy. But what was his surprise—his "grand satisfaction"—to find a light in her eyes and a faint color in her cheeks. She laughed, she chatted, she jested with the light-heartedness of a merry school girl, and the sense of returning happiness within seemed to lend a strange beauty to her face, and brought back all its lost dimples. She gave a promise to drive out the next day, and the doctor went away enchanted.

Something had prevented Lady Amtenhurst from paying her usual early visit to Lucy's room; but the doctor had scarcely gone when she came hurrying in. Lucy sprang up to greet her with a smile, and so delighted was her Ladyship at the marvelous change in her sad face, that she threw her arms around her and kissed her. "My dear, dear child, how much better you look this morning. It was so good of you to try and rouse yourself. We shall have you well now, in a few days. I am so glad I prevailed upon the doctor to spare this," she said, smoothing back Lucy's hair from her forehead. "He had ordered it all to be cut off. It would have been a sin."

Tears were in Lucy's eyes as Lady Amtenhurst sat down beside her on the sofa.

"You have been so good to me," she said. "I don't deserve your kindness, indeed I don't, for I have been such a wicked, wicked girl."

"Oh, no, my dear, I cannot believe that, although I do not think, in regard to one matter, that you have done wisely."

"You know who I am then?" asked Lucy.

"Yes—that is, I think I do," said Lady Amtenhurst smiling. "When you were delirious you raved about different people, your own hard fate and fear of discovery; and when I found your black hair was a wig, and knowing that Lucy Egerton was a blonde, I guessed how it was. You are she, are you not, dear?"

"I was once, but am not now," Lucy replied, looking down.

"Nonsense, Lucy—I may call you Lucy? I had hoped that all those delusions had vanished—that you no longer harbored those foolish ideas."

"You do not understand me, dear Lady Amtenhurst, and you cannot until I have told you all my story, and who, and what I am."

"You are excited, my dear child, and it is perhaps not well for you to talk. Lie down and rest, and don't think any more of this unpleasant subject."

"You think my mind is wandering," said Lucy, meeting Lady Amtenhurst's anxious look with a smile. "Put your hand on my forehead and feel how cool it is. It will be a great relief to me to tell you all."

"Very well, Lucy, as you please. But let me arrange these pillows more comfortably for you." And Lady Amtenhurst sat down to listen with a rather dubious air, not doubting that the fever had returned to the convalescent.

As briefly as possible Lucy told her of the discovery she had made on the night of the masquerade—of her hiding in the house, and overhearing conversations—of her subsequent flight and meeting with Jolliffe Tufnell in the railway train, and of all his kindness to her.

"These are the bare facts," she went on, "but my motives in leaving Bratton—oh, Lady Amtenhurst, I feel as though I could tell them to you, if you have patience to listen. My leaving home as I did, must seem such a foolish act to one who does not know the workings of my heart."

"Tell me all, Lucy; I would gladly hear it. And, my dear, there was one name very often on your lips when you were ill—what had he to do with all this?"

"That is just what I would tell you," Lucy answered, as her head rested, oh, so naturally! upon the other's shoulder, and an arm was passed affectionately around her waist. "Can you not guess how it was? He stole away my heart, and then cast it from him, and it came back to me all seared and scarred and bruised. He was first in my thoughts when I learned who I was, and I thought how wicked it would be to marry him under a false position and a false name, or to tax his honor by telling him the truth; and I, in my pride, could not bear that he should be ashamed of me.

"In the madness of the moment I determined to run away and hide—where, I knew not, but I trusted to my wits. Then I overheard what strengthened instead of weakened me—as it should have done—in this resolve. I heard—oh, it was cruel—I heard, what came as the last great blow. He told Sir Griffith in my hearing that he could never marry me! It was, perhaps, better, I fancied, that I should thus know what would prevent me from ever returning; and then I fled—fled from shame of my birth, in anger at all around me, and for lack of strength to meet him again. I felt as if I should never wish to return and renew the old life, never again see the scenes of so much unhappiness, and in my selfishness I forgot the sorrow I might be inflicting upon others who had made themselves dear to me. I told myself that no one cared for me or would feel my loss. I forgot right and wrong and the duty I owed to those who had made me what I was, and had tried to make me happy. I forgot all but my own trouble and sorrow and fear of the world's tongue, and kept down the whisperings of conscience. I was my own mistress, I said; my father had cast me off; I had a right to do what I pleased and was accountable to no one for my actions, if I earned my bread honestly and injured no one. So I argued—so I have argued with myself since—but I have not been happy. 'Twas an argument that while it convinced the head, failed to reach the heart. I had thought, too, that I had conquered my love for one who had shown himself unworthy of it. That fearful day in Rome, I met him, and when I knew that he had given his heart to another, I found to my cost how great a place he still held in mine. I have been very ill, but I know not how I came to be so. That I have been near to death I feel instinctively, and I have been roused to earnest, serious thought.

"All these days that I have lain here, I have been thinking and repenting and forming a great resolve. I see my error now, and I would atone for it. I am going back, humbly to ask forgiveness for my fault, and to let those to whom the right in its truest sense belongs, decide what I am to do in the future. If they will take me back, gratefully will I go. If they send me to my father, I am resigned, and determined to accept the decree. If they tell me to work I will do it gladly; and if, as I richly deserve, they cast me off entirely, then—oh, Lady Amtenhurst—"

"Then come to me, child, if anything so unlikely ever happens," said Lady Amtenhurst, kindly, as Lucy faltered. "In my house you will always find a home. Poor child, how you must have suffered! And this is a noble victory over your own wrong impulses. It has been a hard trial, but I have no doubt a wise one, sent by Providence to chasten and subdue. Do not lose hope, Lucy; there may be a bright and beautiful future before you," she added; "a future that you dream not of now."

"Ah, no; quietly, peacefully happy it may be, but more I do not —I cannot expect. From the relief I feel, now that I have decided to give up my own will to others, I know that I will be far more contented than I have been. Now that I have made up my mind to do what is right, and that I feel a consciousness of some little good in myself, I am much stronger and abler to bear and to suffer.

12

You cannot conceive the relief of renouncing a project, that your conscience was forever condemning."

"Ah, Lucy, 'tis the error of young people to believe that none have experienced such suffering as their first trial brings them! I can understand your feelings but too well, and give you my fullest sympathy, for my own has not been a happy lot. But my chief sympathy is with those who must have loved you as a daughter, and mourned for you as one. May you never know the sorrow, darling, of losing a child!"

"Dear, dear Lady Amtenhurst, have I given you pain?" cried Lucy, throwing her arms around the other's neck, as she saw the tears well up into the soft, dark eyes: "am I forever to give pain to those I love best? Oh, Lady Amtenhurst, I do love you so dearly, and I would bring smiles to your lips rather than tears to your eyes!"

"Then, behold them, Lucy," she said smiling, "and invoked by your own words. Do you know I was drawn toward you from the first, and although I could not imagine why it was, I have ever felt a certain unwillingness to ask you to perform menial duties. Your disguise was excellent, but you could not conceal your refinement. That is something that clings to one. I never yet saw a person who could assume it, nor one who, having it, could cast it aside at will. You cannot imagine Edith's surprise and consternation when she heard of your sudden change from a chrysalis into a butterfly. She is very anxious to see you."

"Is she?" said Lucy, laughing. "Let her come and satisfy her curiosity to-morrow, for I am beginning to feel tired now. I hope she bears me no malice for having detained her here so long—we are in Florence, are we not?"

"Yes. Would you like to hear how it all happened—how you were taken ill?"

"I should, indeed," Lucy answered eagerly. "I remember nothing since that rainy night at the hotel in Rome. All is a blank since then until I found myself here."

"I tried to tell you all, before now, dear, but you would not hear," said Lady Amtenhurst. "That wet day in Rome which you speak of, you caught a violent cold. I noticed you were feverish and ill that night. The next day was bright and pleasant, and we left for this place. You, poor child, insisted upon attending to your duties, though I could see from your wild manner, that the fever had already begun its work.

"Before we arrived here your mind began to wander, and you had to be lifted from the carriage into the hotel. I, myself, nursed you, with the assistance of a woman whom the doctor sent, and every one has been so kind in their inquiries after the young English lady; for they all think you are traveling under my charge. It is, perhaps, as well that they should have this idea, for it would not be pleasant for you to have your wild freak noised about. Do you intend to write to your friends in England?"

"Oh, no; I want to go to them and take them by surprise. It will be harder for me, I know, than if I prepared the way by letters; but it is only right that I should feel the weight of their displeasure when I so richly merit it."

"Very well, my dear; it shall be as you please. But you have talked too much, I fear. We must not forget that you are still far from strong; and that flushed face reminds me that I am not to allow you to become excited. Lie down, child; I will darken the room, and get a book and read you to sleep."

With a great weight lifted from her heart, Lucy lay and watched, with loving eyes, the kind and gentle face of Lady Amtenhurst, and listened to the words she read until they became a distant murmur in her ears, as her eyelids slowly closed, and she passed off gently into dreamland.

CHAPTER XVII.

Happy those beloved of Heaven,
To whom the mingled cup is given,
Whose lenient sorrows find relief,
Whose joys are chasten'd by their grief.

— "*Marmion.*"

HAT a world of truth is expressed in that little French phrase "*L'homme propose mais Dieu dispose!*" Never yet did an event occur as planned or pictured by man; and still he schemes and toils and makes his programme for the future, his mind ever busy with visions of what is to be, learning only by repeated experience, the fallaciousness of his hopes; but never is the lesson so well learned, that he has not still some slight lingering faith in the complete fulfillment, eventually, of his designs.

Lucy was young and inexperienced, and the difference in her present position from the one she had expected to occupy when her flight was planned, left her with no doubt as to the result of her resolution to return. The Egertons would take her back, and she would go to them in meekness of spirit, and lead a quiet useful life. Such would be the future, she felt convinced, as she fell asleep that bright and beautiful day in Florence. Would her slumber have been as tranquil had she known what thoughts were in the mind of one, who, with impatient longings to see her eyelids unclose, bent lovingly over her as she lay? Ah! who can doubt the goodness which allows the mind such rest, when great and unexpected changes come in life, that it may gather strength to bear the sudden tidings of good or ill!

For many hours Lucy slept, while through the closed blinds of the open windows came the subdued hum of voices from the Lung Arno, oftentimes lost in the louder sound of passing vehicles; and upon the hot window panes, the buzzing of flies told of the warmth without and enhanced the pleasant coolness of the rooms by their noisy revel in the intense heat beyond the boundary of the Venetian blinds. Beside the sofa where she lay, her senses unaffected by the drowsy, slumber-inviting surroundings, patiently watching and waiting, sat Lady Amtenhurst. At last Lucy stirred, and opened her eyes; and as they rested upon the gentle face bending down so near her own, she fancied for the moment that her illness was once more upon her. Then consciousness returning, remembrance came, and she answered the look of tenderness with a smile. With a cry of joy, Lady Amtenhurst threw her arms about the half-risen figure, and as her cheek rested against the soft flushed one of the girl, her tears fell on Lucy's face.

"Lady Amtenhurst, what is the matter?" was all Lucy could say, in her great surprise.

"They are tears of happiness, darling, not of sorrow. Try to join me in my gladness, if you can, for great joy has come to me to-day. Oh, my darling—my darling! 'tis a joy I have never in my wildest moments dared to hope for."

"And may I not ask what that great joy is, dear Lady Amtenhurst?" asked Lucy, as tears of sympathy stood in her eyes.

"I was admonished not to excite you, my child, but what can I do? Oh, Lucy, I must tell you! While you were asleep, my husband called me from the room—look up at me, darling—and imparted to me the tidings which have brought me this happiness. When I was younger than you, Lucy, I had a child—and I lost it. To-day I know that it is alive, and once more to be my own! What greater blessing could I wish?"

A thrill of wonder and undefined pleasure, and a feeling she could not quite understand—half of jealousy, half of a wild intangible wish—passed over Lucy as she looked into the flushed, excited face above her.

As she lay there she felt a keen sense of shame for her apparent coldness and want of sympathy with her friend's new-found happiness; but it was an utter impossibility for her to express in words all that she felt, and in silence she waited till Lady Amtenhurst found voice to speak.

"Yes, Lucy, I will tell you everything," she said; "everything from the very first, and then you can judge how great must be my happiness. I will tell you of a time when I was as young, and pretty, and lovable as yourself. I had a father, then, Lucy; we were alone together in the world, and all in all to each other. To others he was cold and stern, but not to me. He was a man of strong passions, but he kept them so thoroughly under control by the power of his will, that few ever guessed with what intensity he could love or hate. For some reason that I never learned, the bitterest enmity existed between him and my husband's father, the old Earl of Amtenhurst, and therefore it seemed a strange freak of fate that caused him, while he went over to Ireland on business one autumn, to leave me with some friends—the Duncumbes of Lieceistershire. It was the first time we had been separated, and there at Bletchleigh Manor I met Arthur Courtenay, Lord Amtenhurst's second son, a handsome young lieutenant in a fashionable Hussar regiment, and who, among others, was down for the shooting. Knowing my father's prejudice I tried to avoid him; but people are thrown so much together at a country house, and he sought me out so persistently that I found it impossible to succeed. It was one of the tricks that Cupid often plays. In spite of duty and wishes and fears, my unwilling heart opened to receive him. When he asked me to marry him I told him of my father's dislike to his family. He said he knew of it, but we loved each other, he was independent in fortune under an uncle's will, and no one had a right to keep us apart. It would be easy to obtain my father's forgiveness, once the knot was tied.

At eighteen one seldom doubts the likelihood of success. We were married in secret, and I trusted to my powers of persuasion to reconcile my father to the match. I did not know him as well as I thought. His first passionate outbreak when I acknowledged my act, was fearful. He cast me from him, bidding me go to my husband. He refused to listen to my entreaties, and our intercourse was severed, for he would not see me or speak to me again. The barrier that thus arose between us destroyed much of my happiness, for love cannot completely absorb the pain of breaking old ties. Nor did I have my husband long. We had been married but four months when his regiment was ordered to India. My physician would not allow me to accompany him, as I was unfit to bear the

climate of Bengal at that season, and I was well nigh broken-
hearted at the separation. How painful was our parting you can
imagine; but he was scarcely gone when my father came and offered
to take me **abroad.** I was surprised and delighted at the idea of a
reconciliation. I went with him, and our old life was renewed. It
would have seemed as though the past few months were a dream,
had it not been for the memory of Arthur, my husband, and the
birth here in Florence of my child.''

" **Here in Florence!**" cried Lucy, as the recollection of Lady Amtenhurst's antipathy toward the place flashed across her mind.

" Yes, dear; it is an extraordinary coincidence, is it not, that in
its birthplace, the place where it was lost to me, after nineteen long
years I find my child again? It was a sacrifice of my feelings to
come here now, for the town has always seemed hateful to me ever
since; but I came to please Edith, and for the sacrifice I made I
have, indeed, received a blessed reward. Well, dear, when I was
nearly recovered from my illness, I was told that both my baby and
my husband were dead. My baby had lived but two days after its
birth, and my husband had been mortally wounded, in an engagement
in which a portion of his regiment had taken part shortly after its arrival in India. To be thus bereft of husband and child at one fell
swoop, as it seemed, was more than one in my comparatively weak
condition could bear up under, and for days I wavered between life
and death. Health and strength slowly came back to me, and as
soon as I was able to travel we left Florence for Rome.

" It was then the unhealthy season of the year, but I never thought
of that, until my poor dear father was stricken down with the Roman
fever. It seemed as though fate was never to be satisfied with my
losses. On his deathbed he said something to me that I could not
then understand, but which has since been made plain to me. 'All
connection between you and the Amtenhursts is severed,' he said;
'and I can die happy thinking that my daughter is not as one of
them. You will never know what I have done for you, child, and
what care and anxiety I have saved you. You are very young, and
should marry again; but make a better match and be happy.' I returned to England, mourning for a father, a husband, and a child,
believing it to be a punishment for my undutiful conduct; and I lost
all interest in life. But what was the astounding news that greeted
my return! The report from India had been incorrect: I was not
a widow, for my husband was alive! The announcement of his
death had been premature. He had been dangerously wounded it
was true, and had been at death's door for weeks, he wrote me, but
he was now fast recovering, and had applied to be invalided and

sent home. The next steamer from Bombay brought him to me, looking thin and pale; but I had my Arthur again, and was happy. If my child could only be returned to me in the same manner, I thought, then nothing would be wanting to make my happiness complete. But it was not to be then; that joy was reserved by Providence to gladden my heart in later years, as it has this day. The months slipped quickly by while Arthur gradually regained his strength, and the day approached for him to leave England again to rejoin his regiment. 'Twas a day that never came. Two weeks before the Transport in which we were going out, (for I had determined to accompany him this time) was to sail from Plymouth, his elder brother, the Earl, was thrown from his horse in attempting to force the animal over an impossible jump in a steeple-chase he was riding, and received injuries from which he died in a few hours; and Arthur thus became the Earl of Amtenhurst. Then followed years of happiness, unalloyed save by the remembrance of my child—happiness as perfect as can be known in this world. But I tire you darling, so I will be brief. One day when going about among the tenantry, I noticed a strange woman whose face yet seemed familiar to me. She had come to visit her sister, the wife of one of Arthur's tenants, and I fancied it was but the resemblance between the two sisters that had struck me. But the next day she came up to the house asking to see me, and said that she had once been my maid.

" I remembered her then, as the woman whom I had taken to the Continent when I went with my father, and who had been with me here when my child was born. She said she had a secret to disclose that had weighed heavily upon her conscience for many years. She had long tried to find me, but only knowing me by the name of Courtenay, had never succeeded. 'Twas a secret she had promised my father to keep from me, but she could not rest contented until she told me. Imagine my surprise, darling, when she informed me that at that moment my child might be alive! I don't know whether it gave me, at the time, most pleasure or pain, but now I can never cease to be grateful. She told me a long story of how the very day my child was born, the intelligence of my husband's death arrived, and that my father came to her and said that some people in the place who had recently lost their child were going to adopt mine. She brought it to them that evening and the very next morning she was sent home to England by my father, with a large sum of money in payment for her promise never to reveal the circumstance to me. The woman tried to excuse herself for the part she had taken in the proceeding, by saying that she had a large family to support, the money was something she could not resist, and that she thought at the time my father knew what was best for me, and it was not her place to question his acts. Ah, Lucy, it was hard to forgive her! I told my husband all, and in trying to appease his indignation I forgot my own. We got all the information we could from the woman. The name of the people to whom she gave the child was Silliman; that was all she knew of them except that they were English. My father had had the child christened before parting with it, calling it Florence, after the town where it was born. What a strangely complicated character was his! He thought of the welfare of the child's soul, while giving no heed to what its future earthly life might be. To this day I can but guess from his last words what were his reasons for doing as he did, for he never told them to human being. Thinking Arthur was dead, I suppose he wished to break off all connection with the family of Amtenhurst at once and forever, and perhaps thought it best that I should have nothing to remind me of the past or to recall the hated name. Whatever his reasons were, and however he erred in judgment, I am sure he had solely my good at heart.

" With these slender facts, my husband immediately started for Florence. The Sillimans had gone away. With great difficulty, he succeeded in tracing them from place to place, to London, where the clue was broken. We advertised and employed detectives, and at last discovered that Silliman had sailed for America about two years after receiving the child. The information was given by a man who had made the passage with him in the steamer to New York, and who, on his return to England, had seen our advertisements. This man knew no more, and could not even tell us whether he had a wife and child with him or not. They had formed a slight acquaintance on the ship, and had never met again after parting on the dock in New York. It was encouraging, however, to have learned so much, and my husband's solicitor wrote over at once to institute inquiries. Arthur even crossed the ocean himself, but was obliged to return unsuccessful, leaving the matter in the hands of a lawyer. Years passed and we lost hope; it faded away by degrees, and at last passed entirely from our hearts. Until to-day, I knew no more than what I have told you, and the rest of my story I learned from my husband but an hour ago, for he told me nothing of what was coming to light in America, fearing to raise hopes that might never be fulfilled. The lawyer with whom the matter had been left, and who had exhausted every means of tracing out Silliman, without success, went to reside and practice his profession in San Francisco. One day in a trial in which he defended some man who was being tried for the murder of a gambler, one of the witnesses was an Englishman named Silliman. Remembering the name, he sought the man out, and questioned him. At first he answered with reluctance, but at last, after a promise of being well paid for any information he might give, made a full statement, which he swore to, and which was sent over by the lawyer to my husband. His statement was to this effect:

"In September, 18—, the month and year I was here with my father, he and his wife were also in Florence. Their only child, an infant, died while they were here, and shortly after its death, he received an anonymous letter, asking him if he and his wife would take a child, and adopt it as their own. If so, they must take it at once to England, and five thousand pounds would be given them.

"They accepted; the child—a golden-haired little girl two days old—and five thousand pounds in Bank of England notes in a packet, were brought to them by a woman who would not answer any questions. He and his wife returned to England taking the child with them, but knowing nothing of its parentage, and rented a place near Bratton, the owner of which was obliged to retrench by living on the continent for a few years. Here they established themselves, slowly winning recognition from the neighbors roundabout. They had lived thus over a year, when Mrs. Silliman died of a rapid decline, and her husband's funds running low, he determined to try his fortune in America. The child was his sole encumbrance. How you tremble, my dear! listen quietly, I am near the end now. Sir Griffith Egerton, who was one of his neighbors, and whom he knew slightly, was reputed to be a benevolent and eccentric man. He had recently lost his only son. Silliman went to him, told him how he was situated, of his lack of money, and his intention of going to America—a child of eighteen months was a thing it would be impossible for him to take with him, and what to do with it he knew not, unless Sir Griffith would consent to adopt it in the place of his own lost son. Sir Griffith consented; he adopted the child, changing its name from Florence to his own favorite one of Lucy. And so it was that Florence Courtenay, called Florence Silliman—not Sullivan—became Lucy Egerton! My daughter—oh, my daughter!"

Long before the last words were spoken, mother and daughter had been clinging to each other, their tears mingling, as Lucy murmured through her sobs: "My mother—my mother."

Oh, the unspeakable love, and peace, and joy that filled Lucy's heart, soothing all the wounds of past sorrow! To be wrapped in a mother's arms, to feel warm loving kisses pressed upon her tearful eyes, to see a manly form enter the room and know that a father stood before her, and, turning toward him with a strange sense of shyness, feel herself clasped in that father's embrace! A dream—surely, a dream! and she trembled at thought of the sad awakening.

But 'tis no dream, Lucy. Guided through mysterious ways to your own rightful home, a haven far happier than any in your wildest dreams, what more can you wish for? The joyful heart, with a little pang answers quickly: "One more to love me—only one!"

CHAPTER XVIII.

Why did she love him? Curious fool, be still,
Is human love the growth of human will?

—"Lara."

AVINGTON COURT is a grand old place, with its miles and miles of undulating park-land studded with oaks, larches, elms and beeches, stretching away on one side to the dim blue-gray hills, and on the other to the cliff-bound sea. At the head of its mile of winding beech-bordered avenue stands the house, a great red brick pile of the time of Elizabeth, that nobly bears its weight of years, and is just sufficiently modernized by plate-glass windows and internal improvements to give it an air of the comfort and luxury of advancing civilization without detracting in the least from its antique beauty. Here, in the most perfect harmony, taking example by the lives of the master and mistress, reign the *Lares* and *Penates;* and not a spot is to be found in this great mansion to which exquisite taste in the arrangement of its belongings does not lend a charm. It is the chief feature of this house—the blending of minor details into a pleasingly harmonious unity.

Look into the dainty breakfast-room, where the morning sun creeps warmly in through the half-closed blinds, casting bright gold upon the carpet, and dancing merrily in reflected rings upon the ceiling, lending an extra whiteness to the snowy table-cloth, extracting a delicious perfume from the roses which cling around the casement, and peep slyly in at the open sash, breathing an incense through the room—look, and if the sunlight playing among the curling, golden hair, dazzle not your eyes, you will see, there by the window, bending over a full-blown rose, a girlish figure, robed in softly-falling folds of white, with a gentle face, of strength and sweetness, contentment and peace contending with a certain sadness of expression, and when you are told that it is the Amtenhurst's newly-found daughter, Lady Florence Courtenay, you can scarcely doubt that here stands the one object long needed to complete the beauty of the *entourage.*

When news of the Amtenhursts' good fortune spread through the county, Avington Court was the scene of liveliest rejoicing, and all day long, for many days, crowds of people had come streaming to the house to offer congratulations, and gratify their curiosity by a glimpse of this daughter. All went away more or less pleased, to discuss manners, appearance, and family likeness, and each and all agreed as to the facts that she was unmistakably like her father, a lady, and evidently well educated.

On the whole, Florence's advent was a great success, although there were those who, of course, found unkind things to say; and she herself was intensely amused, and not a little pleased, at becoming such a *lionne*. As soon after her illness as possible, the Amtenhursts had returned to England, changing all their plans for the ensuing spring. They had remained but two days in London, and it was on one of these days that Florence, driving with her mother, from whom she could not bear to be parted, even for an hour, lost from her finger the ring that I had given her.

Jolliffe Tufnell knew nothing of their arrival till he met Lord Amtenhurst at the Club, and when the Earl thanked him for his kindness to his daughter, the man's astonishment was unbounded. His lordship asked him to dine in Eaton-square, that he might hear the whole story, and in delighted surprise he listened that evening to the tale. When it was over, he drew Florence aside to tell her, in his own odd way, that though his hand was still at her disposal, he gave up all hope of her accepting it now; and notwithstanding that he should like to have so nice a little wife, his happiness, he candidly avowed, was not dependent upon her answer.

Laughingly, she thanked him for his kindness, and then, with an unfeigned solemnity, assured him of her determination never to marry. And so it came about that they made a compact for a lasting friendship.

From him she learned that the Egertons were still away from home, but were expected back very soon.

"Miss Lifford," he said, "has, I think, gone to meet them; at any rate she has left Bratton, and I do not know where she is to be found."

Florence never dreamed that the house in town would be prepared for their reception, as she was aware of Sir Griffith's distaste for London life. Therefore, it happened that I learned nothing of her presence in town; and in two days the Amtenhursts left for Avington Court.

Thinking of her old friends, and all their kindness to her, Florence stood caressing the rose, and it was not till her father came close beside her, that she was aware of his having entered the room.

Lord Amtenhurst was a tall, soldierly-looking man, of a commanding air, with one of those closely-shaven, peculiar faces, which in youth make a man seem older than he is, and in riper years delude one into taking much from his real age; without coldness of expression, but having great command of feature; with nothing of sternness, but much of dignity, in his manner; without guile himself, but a keen observer of humanity; a man not given to deception, but never to be deceived—few men disliked him, for though he sustained the dignity of his position, it was with a manner free from arrogance, and all trusted him, for all knew his worth.

As he took his daughter's hands in his and smiled down into her upturned face, the sunlight shining upon his auburn hair, wonderfully increased the likeness between father and daughter. " What were the thoughts that seemed to be troubling my little one ? " he asked her.

As she looked up at him, she longed to throw her arms about his neck, and tell him how much she loved and revered him; but it was not as though she had known him all her life, she still felt a little timidity in manifesting her filial affection. So she simply drew him to his chair and brought him his letters and the morning papers, chatting away the while.

" Troublesome [thoughts are not proper guests for an exquisite morning like this, are they, papa? They really remind me of some people who come into the midst of a pleasant group with long lists of grievances, and unpleasant remarks, and unkind little speeches, casting a shade where all before was bright; and they are quite as difficult to exclude, for they come pushing and forcing their way in spite of one. Let me read you the news, before mamma and Edith come down," she added, unfolding the *Times* and seating herself on a stool at his feet.

" I would far sooner hear what your thoughts were about."

" What! You would have me play the part of those I have condemned, and parade imaginary troubles in the midst of so much brightness ? "

" You cannot dim the sunshine, Florence, and I can be no duller."

" Can I not? See ! see ! " she cried; " a cloud passes over the sun in anticipation, even."

" It is being eclipsed by your brilliancy, little one," he retorted, pleasantly.

"It hides its diminished head, lest it be further insulted by such comparisons. But won't you be good now, and let me read to you?"

"No! the papers can wait, but my pleasure cannot;" and he jestingly puckered his pleasant brow into a portentious frown. "Confess now, to disloyal thoughts."

She clasped her hands across his knee, resting her head upon them as she sat at his feet; and all her gayety gone, replied:

"I was thinking of the Egertons. I wish so much that they knew of my good fortune."

"They do know, in a measure," he said. "As I told you, I was sick when news of you came to me from Silliman, and I instructed my solicitor to go down to Bratton in my place. I always understood that he had done so, but arrived too late. When I took Edith up to town the day before yesterday I had a long talk with him, and as we are on the subject now I will tell you what I learned. Parkins had urgent business on hand which would not allow of his absence, and therefore he wrote to a friend of his, whom he knew was staying at Bratton Hall, to break the news to Sir Griffith. His letter did not arrive in time to prevent your flight, but this person (I suppose it must have been the Mr. Strutt I have heard you mention —I didn't ask his name) nevertheless informed Sir Griffith of the fact that you were my daughter. So you see that they know who you are, and have given up all hope of ever again claiming you as a daughter. Tufnell relieved their minds of anxiety, a long time ago, by writing to Sir Griffith that you were safe, well and happy. What more can you wish?"

Perhaps it may be as well for me to say here, what was not known to me for some time yet, that though Sir Griffith was possessed of these facts, for some private reason, or it may have been from a mere freak of his odd nature, he did not impart his knowledge to either his wife or me. Had he but told what he knew even to Jolliffe Tufnell, Florence might long before have found her parents; but all things seemed to conspire so that it might not be until she saw the error of her chosen way, that she should regain what she herself had unwittingly cast aside and fled from.

Florence was thinking while her father spoke, of that conversation, so well remembered, heard in the corridor at Bratton Hall. This letter from Parkins could not then have reached them. Ingolsby, who had so soon after learned what was her birth, must before long know of her reinstatement, and she wondered bitterly if he would still sneer at love and lowliness, and if her father's coronet would make it at last possible for him to extend his hand to the girl whom he had once thought too far beneath him for that honor. She

wanted to see him and test him; yet she felt that whatever way
the trial ended, it could bring no happiness to her. If he resumed
his old manner and tried to assert pretensions to her favor, he
would be far too despicable any longer to occupy her thoughts;
but if he loved this other girl and was true to her, all hope for herself was equally at an end. To one of her nature, however, the
knowledge that her love was not misplaced, even though hopeless,
would at least bring a strange sort of proud pleasure, and merely
thinking of the chance of its possibility brightened the expression
of her face. Glancing around the cheerful room, and up in her
father's face, she felt ashamed that she could not feel perfectly
happy for all her good fortune; and determined to appear so at
least, that she might not pain those who loved her, she said, smiling:

"How strangely everything has come about! I promise you not
to fret any more, papa, but to wait patiently for all things to come
right of themselves, as my efforts in the past seem to have altered
the face of things, and but increased a confusion that I tried to
lessen." As she rose and walked to the window, humming the
light, sparkling music of "La belle Helene," her father's thoughtful eyes followed her across the room. He was trying to understand his only child and found it no easy task, sunshine and shadow
followed each other so quickly in her moods. Just then Lady Amtenhurst came down, her presence bringing additional warmth and
brightness to the pleasant room.

"I overslept myself this morning," she said, returning Florence's
caress. "I find it so very nice to be once more in my own happy
home, that I am becoming dreadfully lazy. What news, Arthur?
You have not yet opened your letters!"

"I had quite forgotten them," he replied laughing, and as they
sat down to breakfast, he began to look them over. Two begging
letters, three on business, one from a friend put aside for future
reading, and then came one which brought a smile to his lips.

"Good news for you, Florence! Parkins writes me word that he
hears the Egertons are in town, and that they are going to remain
in Park Lane.

Florence answered nothing, but her face expressed all her pleasure.

"Then had we not better go up to town at once, Arthur?" asked
Lady Amtenhurst; "Florence is of course anxious to see them."

"Yes, mamma," she said, "but I don't like to give you the
trouble of going; papa could take me."

"It is best that I should go, darling, and call upon Lady Egerton. Edith," as that young person hurried into the room, "what
do you say, to our all spending a week or two in town?"

" Oh it is not for me to choose, dear aunt; my pleasure is a secondary consideration now that we have Florence to please," she replied, and even before she spoke, her manner of seating herself at the table, proved to discerning eyes that she had given great offense this morning to her right foot, by allowing the left one precedence in rising. " Besides," she added with an air of martyrdom, " it is my nature to make sacrifices, even though they are not appreciated."

" It is not absolutely necessary for you to go with us, Edith," remarked her uncle; " you can remain here alone if you like."

"I was not aware that I had the credit of an unsociable disposition, and a fondness for a deserted house. But of course it shall be as you wish; oh, certainly, I'll remain here, and associate with the rats;" and she tossed her head, as her voice was checked by a lump in her throat.

" You misunderstand, my dear," said her aunt. " We wish you to do only what will be most agreeable to yourself. Come to town with us by all means."

" I'm sure I'd do anything to please your ladyship. If I must go, I will strive to do it with a good grace," and a second lump displaced the first one in her throat.

An expression of despair passed over Lady Amtenhurst's face. The Earl put down his knife and fork, and very quietly said to his niece: " Edith, will you be kind enough to tell me in plain terms what it is you wish to do, and we will arrange our plans accordingly. Will that convince you of the strength of our regard?"

" Thank you, uncle, but I have no ambition to be made the bear in the cellar. I know my place, and my duty now is to obey; not to propose what may prove disagreeable to others," and a third lump struggled fiercely for place, as she cast a glance of injured innocence at her cousin.

Florence had taken up the *Avington News* as the discussion began, and now as her father's color rose, hers rose too, but not from the same cause.

" Oh, papa!" she exclaimed, almost piteously: " they have me in the paper!" It was a fortunate turn to the conversation, for the question was immediately asked what she meant, and with many blushes she read aloud that piece, copied into the *Morning Post* the next day, which so startled Sir Griffith, although unintelligible to his wife and to me.

What a laugh they had! Not so much at the article as at Florence's consternation on finding herself famous. Even Edith joined in, though her laugh had not the ring of true merriment.

" They took enough time to discover your perfections," she said rather spitefully, " or else they failed until now in forming a eulogy worthy of the subject. Were it about me, I know I would never have courage to show my face again in public. Poor child, what an object of ridicule you will be! "

"Do you really think so, Edith?" asked Florence, in dismay.

" Never mind, Florence," said her father, rising, " you will have the benefit of your cousin's experience in the art of enduring ridicule; and you will find her a very competent teacher for the knack of sharpening your weapons of defense."

" Good, gracious me—" began Miss Courtenay, in indignation.

" Your pardon, Edith," interrupted the Earl; " but really I do not like to hear terms misapplied. You seem far from good this morning, and anything but gracious," and he calmly lighted a cigar.

As Edith appeared to be upon the verge of taking refuge in tears, Florence, goodnaturedly, tried to change the topic by asking:

" Well, papa, dear, which of us then go up to town?"

" Your mother, you, and I. Edith must decide for herself. We will start to-morrow morning."

He left the room puffing at his cigar, apparently unruffled, although he often confessed that these brushes with his niece were most trying to the temper. The only visible effect that they ever had upon him was to loose his sarcastic powers upon the world for an hour or two afterwards. Lady Amtenhurst followed him, saying:

" Get your hats, girls, and come."

In a few moments the three passed out on to the terrace, Edith stalking ahead majestically. A pretty little grey-hound came running to meet and fawn upon them. Edith gave it an angry poke with her parasol.

"Nasty little brute!" she cried.

Florence, out of compassion for the whining dog, began to play with it. They chased each other up and down the broad terrace, the animal spirits of both raised to the highest pitch. The graceful little creature capered and barked. The hardly less graceful girl clapped her hands, and laughing, ran nimbly over the gravel. They reached the edge of the terrace, where stone steps led to the lawn beneath. She turned to go down them, tempted by the green grass below; the dog leaped against her, she stumbled, fell forward, and caught at a stone urn; but missing her grasp, came down upon her bent ankle. Lady Amtenhurst ran to her daughter's assistance, for she sat unable to rise, her lips quivering with pain.

" I cannot stand, mamma. Please call papa." Her father came and carried her into the house, and it was many days before she could rise without his aid from the couch where he placed her. He would have delayed his trip to town, and the proposed explanation with the Egertons, on account of her accident, but she begged him to go alone.

"Go to-morrow as you intended, please papa," she said, "but come back to me soon. You won't stay more than a day, will you?

"No, darling; I will return as soon as possible; it may be, to-morrow evening."

He wrote at once to Sir Griffith saying that he would like to see him on a matter of interest and importance; and that, as he would be but a few hours in town, and as the chances of finding him at home were slight, he took the liberty of asking him to meet him at his solicitor Parkin's office, in Lincoln's Inn Field, at any hour from eleven till two on the following day. The next morning he went up alone to London, and Sir Griffith receiving his letter at the breakfast-table, they met in Parkin's office at eleven o'clock.

With no doubt as to what was to be the subject of the conference, Sir Griffith went to the *rendezvous*. Long was the talk of the two men about the girl who was almost equally a daughter to both of them; and they parted mutually pleased with each other, and regretting that the Earl's promise to Florence forbade his remaining to dine with the Baronet in Park Lane.

"I wish you could stay and tell the women-folk," said Sir Griffith, "I can't. They would deluge me with unanswerable questions, so that I should lose all patience before my story was half finished. I know what I'll do!" slapping his knee. "I'll go directly to Strutt, and tell him, which will be easy enough, and he can retail it all at home. It was only yesterday I gave him permission to tell that double-distilled essence of curiosity, Miss Lifford, to whom Lucy really belonged, and he need but add a word or two more. The furies protect me when it is discovered that I have kept a secret from my wife and cousin all this time! I must take a run into the country till their anger cools."

"Run in my direction, Egerton. The ladies will be only too delighted to see you."

"Without my wife and Julia? That would be fanning a blaze with a vengeance, and destroying all chance of my ever again being taken into favor. Wait a few days, and we will come down *en famille*. Eh, my lord?"

"By all means, my dear fellow. You could not do anything that would give us all more pleasure. I only beg of you not to defer your visit too long."

13

"Very well; we'll come," Sir Griffith said. "Tell Lucy—Florence, I mean—that I have forgiven the offense, and am prepared to hug the offender."

CHAPTER XIX.

They stood aloof, the scars remaining—
Like cliffs which had been rent asunder;
A dreary sea now flows between.
—"Christobel."

THE sun had gone down behind the tree-tops where they stretched far away to the west, and was sinking to rest in the distant sea; but his beams which had but a moment before lighted up the tall, red brick chimneys, and glistened on the upper window panes of Avington Court, glancing and gleaming upon turret and gable, and throwing long, straggling shadows athwart the walls, still lingered in a flame of blazing colors in the sky above—lingered, and then faded slowly and reluctantly into the sombre gray of neutral-tinted twilight. The cawing rooks were whirling through their last aerial quadrille before taking up their quarters for the night among the beech-tops; the flowers were folding their delicate leaves about them, unconscious of the coming dewdrops—

"Those tears of the sky for the loss of the sun,"

which were soon to fall gently and tenderly upon the darkening earth. The occasional hoarse note of a bull-frog sounded from the grass, night birds began to wake and plume their feathers, the air grew still and soft, saddened by the death of day, and the stars one by one peeped forth dimly in the deepening blue above.

At an open window of her own room, her eyes not wandering over the landscape, but with a steady gaze fixed upon one particular opening in the trees where the view stretched far, far away, sat Florence. There was a strange longing and unrest within, for all her outward quiet. Her ankle was painful, and she was feverish and unreasoningly desirous of something—anything—she knew not what; but with a vague, though abiding sense of certainty that the evening would bring it to her. All the afternoon she had sat and watched that opening in the trees, and now, as the hour approached when the London train was due at Avington station, she looked out into the gathering gloom, and strained her eyes more and more to catch the first glimpse of smoke that would tell of the coming of the toiling iron monster.

"The train must be late, mamma," she said, without turning her head. "What time is it now?"

Lady Amtenhurst, who sat reading by her side, glanced for the half dozenth time, at least, in fifteen minutes at the ormolu clock on the chimney-piece.

"It still wants five minutes, my dear, of the time. But I really doubt, Florence, if your father will return to-night."

"Yes, he will, mamma. I know he will," Florence answered with the simple assurance of a child. "Hark!"

Her face brightened as she bent forward, and a faint distant whistle echoed through the still air: then a quickly-passing dark line crossed the opening, with a wreath of white smoke floating upward, and the long-looked-for train had reached the little station down there behind the trees. In silence Florence and her mother waited while the ticking of the clock on the chimney piece told of the tediously passing minutes. Five—ten—fifteen minutes: what an age! and then upon the gravel the faint sound of coming wheels, came to them through the window, and Florence held her handkerchief ready for waving. Then, in a turn of the drive out from behind a row of beeches, appeared the carriage, and Florence's handkerchief fluttered from the casement. In a moment an answering flutter came from the carriage window; another moment and a second flag of truce was seen waving beside the first.

"Papa has brought some one with him!" she cried, and her face flushed and her heart beat as she thought, "who is it?" Then as the carriage whirled up the drive, and passed round the house and out of sight, she sank quietly back. Lady Amtenhurst had gone to meet the new comers.

Presently there were footsteps in the corridor without and Lord Amtenhurst came hurrying into the room.

"And how is my Florence, now?" he asked, bending over her and kissing her tenderly.

"Immensely anxious to hear the news, papa, dear. Who did you see? Were they glad or sorry? What did they say? Were they not awfully angry with me? and oh, I forgot!—who was that you brought with you—Sir Griffith?"

"Question upon question, after the manner of your sex. And pray, how do you happen to know that I brought any one down with me?"

"I saw two handkerchiefs."

"*Ergo—et cetera, et cetera.* And your logical brain refused to acknowledge the possibility that one man might carry two handkerchiefs?"

"He wouldn't wave them both together, if he did, I'm sure—would he?"

"Hardly, my dear; you're right," her father answered, laughingly; "that is, your deductions are. Well, little one, I shan't keep you in suspense any longer. I saw only Sir Griffith in town. He asked me to dine with him; but I thought of you waiting here for my return, and I declined. My news, however, was no news to him, for he had seen the whole thing in the *Morning Post*, and though he tried to make his congratulations warm, I could see that, poor old fellow, he felt your loss very keenly."

"And how are Miss Lifford and Lady Egerton?"

"Both quite well, I imagine. I did not see them; but Sir Griffith promised me to bring them both down here very soon, for a long visit; so you must make haste and mend this troublesome ankle. But there was another old friend of yours whom I met. He came up to me in the street with a face all aglow with wonder and excitement, and poured forth a torrent of questions equal to yours. He, too, had been reading the *Morning Post* at his Club, and as a matter of course, had chanced upon that oft-recurring article on my and your mother's happiness, and your virtues."

"*He*, papa; who?" Florence asked in a low voice. "Who?"

"Why Ingolsby, of course, who else?"

"Alva Ingolsby?" The tone of her voice as the name left Florence's lips, was, to the ear of her father, one of utter indifference; yet a sudden pallor, unseen by him in the gathering darkness, overspread her face, and though its expression was one of surprise and contempt, there was yet a strangely mingled look of pleasure in her eyes.

"Alva Ingolsby?" she repeated, dreamily.

"Yes; Alva Ingolsby. And a charming young fellow he is, too. I positively never saw a man so anxious as he was to hear of one not related to him, nor about to be. Well, my dear, I must run off now and dress for dinner. One musn't be late in one's own house, you know.

"Oh, but you haven't told me yet who it is you brought with you!"

"So I haven't. Well, child, it is—But why not come down and see for yourself?"

"I'm almost afraid to venture. The poor ankle is very weak yet, and I do so hate to go hobbling about with a stick. Oh, I'll tell you what, papa," and a happy thought seemed to strike her; "if you could only manage to carry me down stairs, I think I might venture. Do you really think you are strong enough, papa? I'm an awfully heavy girl, small as I look, I can tell you; do you really think you could manage it?" and she looked up hopefully.

"Without the slightest difficulty, I'm sure, my child. Very well, then," looking at his watch; "I'll give Putnam just twenty minutes to get you ready, and then I'll come back for you. There— I have rung for her. And you might tell her to put on some of your most becoming ribbons, child. Twenty minutes, remember, not a second longer," and the Earl was gone.

Florence had enough of the feminine desire to please, not to require any hint as to the toilette she should select; and, thanks to the agile fingers of Putnam, the last pin was inserted, and the last lace tied, when Lord Amtenhurst came back.

It was, indeed, a most enchanting vision of blue and white loveliness that his strong arms bore in them down the broad staircase, and into the drawing-room below.

How her heart beat as they approached the door! and how it sank when she saw only her mother in the room. But she was scarcely settled on a sofa, and the cushions arranged by loving hands, in the most luxurious manner possible, when some one else entered the room. Yes, she was right! It was as she had thought, nay, hoped, from the first moment that she had seen the second handkerchief waving on the evening air, but had not dared express to her father—it was Alva Ingolsby; and looking just as she had seen him so many, many times in the old days, save that there was an unusual flush upon his face.

As he approached, her eyelids fell, and she put forth her hand without looking up. He took it, murmuring some almost indistinct words about "pleasure," and "congratulations," and "being deeply grieved at her accident," and a more constrained greeting on both sides it would be difficult to imagine. Both greatly embarrassed and striving to command their feelings, each felt the coldness of the other's manner, and neither doubted but that they alone were assuming indifference; and each, nettled by the other's coldness, lost in consequence something of their embarrassment, if not of their frigidity.

Florence's womanly pride came to the rescue. In her eyes Ingolsby's manner expressed a fear that she felt more for him than he could return; for ever-present in her mind was the vision of that scene in Rome under the shop-awning, its shadow falling upon all things. She would not play the part of the forsaken damsel, but would prove to him beyond the peradventure of a doubt, that his egotistical fears were groundless, his compassionate solicitude without cause. No one should ever guess the truth until she had conquered this wild fancy; and, looking up, she caught her mother's eye, and felt with keen pleasure that she and no other could understand her feelings, and sympathize with them, and aid her in her task.

"Papa did not tell me you were here, Mr. Ingolsby. This is an unexpected pleasure," she said, with the cold civility of a hostess to a stranger-guest.

"Did I not see you, or rather your signal, at the window as we drove up? It was you, was it not?"

"Yes, I suppose it must have been, if you refer to seeing a handkerchief waved. No one else would be so silly—but then, you see, I have a way of doing foolish things." She stopped short, fearing he might take some meaning from the remark she had no intention of conveying when the words were uttered, and added quickly: "I did not see you, though. Were you with papa? Oh, was it Mr. Ingolsby you brought with you, papa?" turning to her father, with just a shade of disappointment in her voice—a tone Ingolsby did not fail to detect. "You wouldn't tell me who it was, you remember—you naughty papa."

"I thought the pleasure of meeting as old a friend as Mr. Ingolsby would be so greatly enhanced by the surprise of seeing him, that I hadn't the heart to forewarn you, my dear," replied the Earl, playfully.

There was an awkward pause as Florence hid a very red and annoyed face behind her fan, and Ingolsby bit his mustache in silence.

"You are very old friends, are you not?" continued Lord Amtenhurst, looking from one to the other. "Sir Griffith told me you were."

"I have known your daughter, Lord Amtenhurst, since she was scarcely more than a child," Ingolsby answered quietly, with a reproachful glance at Florence.

"Ah, so I thought. So I understood from Sir Griffith," returned the Earl, whatever momentary doubts he may have had, at rest.

"And as one scarcely more than a child, papa, your daughter has, I assure you, been the recipient of much sage advice from Mr. Ingolsby," said Florence. "Do you remember, Mr. Ingolsby, that day when our acquaintance was hardly more than begun, that you so generously told me of all my faults and imperfections?" she asked, for the moment wishing to pain him, but the next instant regretting the words, for her heart was full of gratitude.

Ingolsby's face reddened painfully as he answered with an embarrassed little laugh: "I fear that you have on more than one occasion thought my presumption great, Lady Florence; but, I assure you, repentance has always followed after—always;" and as he repeated the word with peculiar emphasis, their eyes met for a moment.

Florence thought she understood him, and with rising anger replied quickly, laughing as she spoke: "I'm afraid it would be impossible for me to ease your conscience, Mr. Ingolsby, without wounding your pride; therefore I will leave you to repent at leisure."

"How late Edith is," interposed Lady Amtenhurst, anxious to stop this by-play which was very clear to her. "I think you know my niece, Mr. Ingolsby?"

"I had the pleasure of meeting her at the Ogilvies' place in Devonshire, last year; but I scarcely think she can remember me," said Ingolsby.

"On the contrary, she speaks of you quite often. The Ogilvies' is one of the very few places I allow her to visit without me."

"Speaking of the Ogilvies, reminds me that I met Sir Philip at Parkins' to-day," said the Earl, "and he told me they thought of spending the summer in Switzerland. By-the-bye, Ingolsby, what an immense favorite you are with my crusty old lawyer Parkins. He was saying all kinds of nice things about you."

"He is very kind, I'm sure," said Ingolsby. "I brought him a letter of introduction from a brother lawyer of his in America when I came over, and he has been of great service to me in some legal matters I had to look into, and we have seen a great deal of each other. He has been, I must say, far from crusty with me, your lordship."

"You are not a client of his," said the Earl, drily.

"You are an American, Mr. Ingolsby, are you not?" asked Lady Amtenhurst.

"I have lived in America many years, your ladyship, but I am an Englishman by birth. I am afraid, though, that I must confess to an equally divided allegiance," Ingolsby replied, laughing.

"Are not the Americans a very odd sort of people—half civilized, with queer manners and customs?" asked Florence, with the most provoking innocence.

"According to Dickens, I am sorry to say, yes; in reality, no," answered Ingolsby, warmly. "He has drawn individuals who, though their prototypes might in rare instances have been met with by him in his travels, are not by any means representative Americans. That there are a multitude of quaint characters to be found across the ocean, peculiarly American—I can think of no better way to express it—it would be absurd for me to deny; no people on earth, perhaps, afford a more extensive field to the honest humorist; but I do contend that not from the pages of Dickens should the world gather its ideas of them. As a people, they combine the traits of every nationality, and, with the strong good sense of an Englishman possess an off-hand generosity that is not ours. They are luxurious in their homes, though everything has a newness about it that would be distasteful to you, Lady Florence; their refinement is equal to ours; in many respects, their education far superior; their business talent is immense, and fortunes are sometimes made and lost twice and thrice in a lifetime. They are truly a wonderful people, even for the age in which we live."

"A Daniel come to judgment!" cried Florence. "Were I qualified to judge I should feel tempted to confess your 'exposition hath been most sound.' As it is, I can only say, 'American Notes' I have always thought one of Dickens's most amusing books. The people he writes about all seem natural enough to me."

"Seem—yes; and the book is amusing, I'll grant you. That's just where it is. I have laughed again and again over the book myself, but precisely as I have laughed at the lisping absurdities of 'Lord Dundreary,' who *seems* to most untraveled Americans I've met, a very fair to-the-life picture of an Englishman—his one fault in their eyes, perhaps, being that he doesn't drop his h's—yet I question if there is a man on earth, not even excepting Sothern himself, who ever came across such a creature in England."

"I spent a few weeks in New York several years ago," observed Lord Amtenhurst, "and as a bountiful recipient of American hospitality, I can bear witness to that one phase, at least, of what you so aptly term their off-hand generosity, Ingolsby. I went there well accredited, of course; but I found that the most potent credential I bore, and one that I believe insured me the most genuine kindness at their hands, was the simple fact that I was a stranger; a recommendation which I am ashamed to say would do very little for a man in England had he no other to offer. Whatever angels are entertained unawares in the world, receive not, I am afraid, their entertainment from Englishmen."

"How severe you are on your countrymen, papa," said Florence, with a surprised look at her conservative father, for expressing such liberal views. "I thought English hospitality was proverbial the world over."

"Proverbial, my child? Yes, so it is; but proverbial for the rules and regulations which tie it up and hamper it. My stay in America showed me that. Do you know, Ingolsby, that I never hear the phrase, 'English hospitality,' that I do not think of the man who refused to save the young woman from drowning because he had not been introduced to her!"

Ere the laugh that followed the Earl's remarks had subsided, Miss Courtenay, arrayed *en grande tenue,* with a great rustling of silk and ribbons, and redolent of much perfume of *patchouly*, came sweeping into the room. She welcomed Ingolsby with *empressement*, and then stooped to imprint a kiss on Florence's brow.

"Are you coming in to dinner with us, Florence, dear? Indeed, I would not advise you to do so until your poor, dear ankle is quite strong again. Would you, Mr. Ingolsby? Don't you wonder how she could have been so awkward as to sprain it in the way she did? Now, if it had been *me*, who could feel astonished?" and she paused, in vain, for a compliment on her grace, as dinner was announced.

"Will you come in with us, Florence, dear, or have your dinner brought to you here?" asked Lady Amtenhurst.

Florence hesitated.

"Pray don't think me selfish, Lady Florence, but sooner than that we should be deprived of your society, might not the 'poor, dear ankle' be induced, with a trifle of assistance, to bear you that far?" suggested Ingolsby.

Florence decided then. "Thanks. I will remain here, mamma, please."

Ingolsby in silence offered his arm to Lady Amtenhurst; Miss Courtenay took her uncle's, and so they left the room, Florence assuring them her solitude was by no means a punishment.

It is doubtful which enjoyed their dinner less: Ingolsby under fire of Edith Courtenay's charming little speeches, and airs, and graces; or Florence between the cross-fires in her own mind, of pleasure at Ingolsby's proving to be less despicable than she had feared, and pain at the thought of having to give him up to another. And then the evening was no improvement on the quarter-hour before dinner, Florence continuing her covert attacks, and Ingolsby parrying them as gracefully as his solely-tried patience and his bewilderment at her strangely-altered manner would permit. At last a random shaft fairly drove him from her side. Speaking about some public man, one of the heroes of the hour, Lord Amtenhurst remarked. "He is one of those men who have a secret in their lives, and yet the people place great confidence in him."

"And after the manner of such persons, he will turn out utterly unworthy of it," she said, looking at Ingolsby as she spoke, and wondering if he had, as she had often fancied, a secret in *his* life.

A glance of reproachful surprise flashed from Ingolsby's eyes as he turned toward Miss Courtenay.

"Will you not give us some music, Miss Courtenay?" he asked. "A song, please."

"With the *greatest* pleasure. I make it a *rule* not to be one of those dreadfully tiresome people who require so *much* urging that one grows weary of asking," and Miss Courtenay seated herself at the piano. "What style do you like; gay or sad?"

"Sing me ' Looking Back,' " Ingolsby replied, as he searched for it in a book of ballads that lay on top of the piano. "Here it is."

"Never mind turning over the leaves for me. It makes me nervous to have any one standing beside me when I sing. Besides, I don't need the music—*really*. I always make it a *rule* to know *all* the accompaniments of my songs without. If there's one thing I *hate* it's to hear a person refuse to play ' because they haven't their notes.' "

So Ingolsby went over and leaned his arm upon the chimney-piece just across the corner of the room from where Florence's sofa stood, and with his back to her, looked down upon the rug at his feet.

Edith Courtenay's voice was a good one—a *mezzo-soprano*, sweet, and well trained; and as she sang the words of that pathetic song of Arthur Sullivan's, Florence studied the profile reflected in the mirror above the chimney-piece. As she watched the well-known, handsome features, the face saddened more than she had ever seen it, her own softened unconsciously; and her heart spoke through her eyes when Edith reached the words:

> "Oh! my love, I loved her so,
> My love that loved me years ago."

As the words rang out in all the beauty of the most affecting strains of the melody, Ingolsby looked up and their eyes met through the medium of the mirror. His lighted instantly, and with a smile he turned toward her; hers quickly fell and she caught nervously at her fan. Had he come to her side she could not then have feigned; but when she glanced up again, he was leaning over the piano, and her heart beat in anger at him and at her own weakness. The song ended, she whispered to her father:

"I am very tired, papa; please take me up stairs."

And so the evening ended with a cold "good-night" from her compressed lips.

The next morning Ingolsby left without seeing her, and came directly to me, in ignorance of the fact that I knew less than himself. And then came our quarrel, interrupted by Mr. Strutt who brought with him a budget of news.

And now, kind reader, can not you guess from what sources I have gathered the strands with which I have woven this little history of Florence's—I should rather say, perhaps, more fittingly—Lucy's adventures, after her disappearance on the night of the fatal masquerade?

Apart from Florence's own diary, think of all those from whom information was derivable, and who were not only able but willing to impart it freely. Sir Griffith, Ingolsby, Lord and Lady Amtenhurst, Miss Courtenay, and last, though not least, Jolliffe Tufnell; and yet, determined to rely as little as possible upon my imagination, the work of selecting and dovetailing, and filling in the bare outline furnished me by Mr. Strutt's narrative has been no easy task; but, as Sir Griffith would say,

> "What I have writ, I have writ,
> And would it were worthier."

BOOK THIRD.

CHAPTER I.

—— That drama of passions as old as the hills,
Which the moral of all men in each man fulfills,
Is only revealed now and then to our eyes
In the newspaper files and the courts of assize.
                                        — "Lucile."

BRATTON Hall is thrown open once more, and a goodly party of us is assembled at the old place. The Amtenhursts have come down with Florence, who, to me, scarcely yet seems as one of them, and my particular and pet aversion Edith Courtenay. Ingolsby is here, happy and mysterious in his manner, and utterly oblivious to Florence's pointed avoidance. Jolliffe Tufnell has deserted his own ancestral halls for ours, and Mr. Jedediah Strutt, as pugnacious as ever, has left his dingy office and manifold clients to the tender and watchful care of his wizened clerk, and joined our party for a day or two. With Sir Griffith, Lady Egerton and myself, our circle is complete. For what purpose are we gathered together? In pursuit of pleasure? Ah, no. After many years slumbering sorrow is to be awakened, old wounds are to be probed, deadened pain is to be aroused once more, that justice may be done. Even the knowledge that poor, lost Guy Egerton's name is at last to be cleared of the horrible suspicion resting upon it, cannot lessen the pain of remembrance or overcome my pity for the man whom retributive justice has overtaken.

Martin Silliman, he who was once supposed to be our Lucy's father, was arrested in California some months ago under a requisition from Her Majesty's government, based upon evidence accumulated through the untiring efforts of Jolliffe Tufnell, brought over to England in charge of two special emissaries from Scotland-yard, and to-day, here at the Bratton assizes, is to be tried for the murder of Louis Dunraven, committed eighteen years ago.

Our entire party, save Edith Courtenay, whose nerves are too delicate to undergo the excitement of a murder trial, is assembled in the Assize Court at the Bratton town-hall. The place is crowded by all classes of people. The spectator's gallery, where we sit, is crammed, the aisles and passage-ways choked, the barristers' pale invaded. Men line the walls, stand on the backs of forms, on the window-sills, and in the doorways—human heads pop up in the most impossible and unexpected spots, and the constables, under-sheriffs, ushers, and crier are taxed to their uttermost to preserve order and silence; for to-day a buried mystery of the past is to be unraveled, the true sequel to the story that has slumbered almost forgotten in the minds of the old, and been held as a sort of dim tradition by the young, is to be made manifest; and high and low, young and old, look on and listen with eager curiosity as the trial proceeds.

Mr. Justice Gush, of the Queen's Bench (who this year goes the Midland Circuit), has taken his seat upon the bench, the jury has been impanneled, and the indictment read to the prisoner—a tall, pale man, with a face deeply marked with the lines of riot and dissipation, and dark hair and beard thickly sprinkled with gray; and who stands up in the dock with the same look of stolid indifference upon his countenance that it wore when he pleaded "not guilty" upon his arraignment.

Sergeant Headstrong, with Mr. Dawkins, Q. C., appears for the Crown; Mr. Toddy, Q. C., for the prisoner.

Mr. Dawkins opens the case for the Crown, briefly stating the facts which the prosecution expects to prove against the prisoner, the evidence being all circumstantial in its character, and then the examination of witnesses is commenced.

After some preliminary proof as to the finding of the body, the date, and the cause of death, the latter being internal hemorrhage from a gunshot wound, Michael Jennings, an old man, is called and steps into the witness-box with much difficulty, and is sworn. He is examined by Mr. Dawkins:

"What is your occupation, my good man?"

"Gamekeeper at Bratton Hall, sir."

"How long have you been in that situation?"

"Twenty-one year, three months, and (counting on his fingers) nine days."

"That's near enough. Did you know the deceased, Louis Dunraven, in his lifetime?"

"I did, sir; an' a better piece o' manhood never trod the earth."

"Just answer my questions—no more."

"Very good, sir; but—"

"That will do. When did you see him alive for the last time?"

"On the mornin' o' the murder, sir. An' oh, but he was gay and happy, as was young master Guy for the matter o' that."

"Go on and state all that occurred on that occasion, but recollect —nothing irrelevant."

"Irreverent, is it, sir? An' do you think I could be that a—no, no, you don't know your man, sir."

"Irrelevant is not irreverent, my friend. I mean: say nothing that does not pertain,—has no connection, with the matter in hand. Go on now, and state all you know?"

"Well, sir; I'll tell all I know, an' that isn't much, an' if I go a bit too far, or irrelephant as ye call it, ye can just stop me up. I remember well the last day I saw Mr. Dunraven an' young master Guy. It was a beautiful clear mornin' about eleven o'clock or half past, maybe. I was standin' at the door o' my cottage, when I spied 'em a coming briskly across the meadows between me an' the park hedge, wi' their guns under their arms, a laughin' and talkin' as they walked. They walks straight over to me, an' Mr. Dunraven, he says, 'Jennings, my man,' sez he, 'have you got such a thing as a nipple wrench?' 'I have sir,' sez I. 'Fetch it out then,' sez he, 'for the nipple o' my right barrel is foul.' I asked 'em to walk inside while I got the wrench, but they said as 'ow they'd got a permit to shoot on the Tufnell place and was in a hurry. Well, sir, I gets the wrench, an' Mr. Dunraven 'ands me his gun, an' I unscrews the nipple o' the right barrel, an' there sure enough was a bit of an old cap a stickin' in it; so I gets a bit o'——"

"Never mind about that. What sort of a gun was it?"

"A double-barrel shot-gun, sir, by Purdy o' London."

"Was there anything else about the gun that you noticed?"

"Yes, sir. There was a little plate on the top o' the stock wi' Mr. Dunraven's name on it."

"Did you see the guns that were produced at the inquest?"

"No, sir. I was laid up wi' the lumbago."

"Would you recognize Mr. Dunraven's gun now, do you think?"

"Certain I would, sir."

A gun is handed up to the witness. Dawkins continues:

"Examine that carefully, and tell me if it is the gun Mr. Dunraven had on the occasion you speak of?"

The witness makes a long and careful examination of the gun; cocks it, draws out the ramrod, blows into the muzzle, takes the barrels out of the stock, and puts them back again, puts it up to his shoulder and takes a long aim with one eye shut, at a couple of old ladies in the far end of the gallery, much to their evident terror, lowers it, lifts the hammers and blows into the barrels again and says, decisively:

"No, sir. That be not the gun."

" What maker's name has it ?"

" ' Greaner, Liverpool,' sir."

The gun is handed back, and another is shown to the witness.

Mr. Dawkins. " How about that one ?"

Jennings takes the gun, gives a quick glance at the top of the stock, raises the hammer of the right barrel, looks a moment with a gratified smile at the nipple, and exclaims:

" That be it sir, sure enough! and there be the name on the plate: ' *Louis Dunraven, July* 3, 18—.' "

" Can you identify it in any other way ?"

" I can, sir," knowingly.

" How ?"

" By this crack in the nipple. I was afeered I had done it, I remember, wi' the wrench, an' spoke to Mr. Dunraven about it. But he said as 'ow it was there before, an' no harm done. I took particular notice of it then. It's a peculiar sort o' crack, sir, shaped like a S, as ye can see for yourself. There's be no mistake about the gun, sir—maker's name be the same, too."

The old man is now cross-examined by Mr. Toddy for the prisoner. His memory is tested, and his patience worried; but he remains firm in his statements, nothing new is discovered, there are no contradictions, and he leaves the box with a well-satisfied air.

The next witness is John Crawsly, an honest, intelligent-looking young man.

" Did you ever see the deceased during his lifetime ?" asks Mr. Dawkins, after a few preliminary questions.

" Not that I remember, sir. I was very young at the time the murder was committed; but I saw him after he was dead. I remember that, because he was the first dead man I ever saw, and my father took me up to Bratton Hall where the body lay."

" How old were you at the time ?"

" Nine, sir."

" Did you testify at the inquest ?"

" I did not, sir."

The gun identified by Michael Jennings as the one in the possession of Louis Dunraven on the morning of the murder, is here shown to the witness.

Mr. Dawkins. " Did you ever see that gun before ?"

Witness. " Yes, sir.

" Was it ever in your possession ?"

" Yes, sir."

" How came it there ?"

The witness hesitates, turns very red, then pale, looks up at the ceiling, down at the floor, and fidgets with his hat.

" Come, answer my questions," says Mr. Dawkins, impatiently.

" I—I—s-st-stole it," stammers the young man, turning red again, and looking very much frightened.

" But please, sir, I was a very little chap then, and I didn't know, sir—"

"Never mind about that, now," Dawkins interrupts unfeelingly, "but tell us how and where you got it."

" I found it in an old barn belonging to Mr. Silliman, the prisoner, sir; leastways, it was a barn on the place he rented—the old Delamayn place. My father rented a farm near by, from Squire Delamayn, and I used, when I was a slip of a boy, to be up at the house, where Mr. Silliman, the prisoner, sir, lived, and I was a great favorite with the servants. About two weeks after the murder I was up at the house, and the cook, she kept me to dinner; but afterwards I played some prank or other—gave a bit o'meat with mustard on it to the cat, or summat o' that sort that she didn't like, for I was full of tricks, like all young boys, sir—and she turned me out, and told me to go home. The servants had all been talking about the murder, and I was that frightened that I didn't dare to go home alone, as I'd have to pass by where the body was found; so I crawled off to the stables, thinking to sleep among the horses, but they were locked, and I couldn't get in. There was an old barn, though, just back o' the stables a bit, and I crept in through a little window, and curled myself up on a bundle o' straw, tremblin' with fear all the time of ghosts and goblins. But I soon fell asleep, and I must have slept a long time, for when I woke up, all of a sudden like, with a shiver, the moon was well up in the sky, and it hadn't risen when I lay down, for I remember groping my way in the dark to the barn, and now it was almost light as day."

" Cut your story short, young man, and come to the point," says the judge, sharply, looking up from his notes with a scowl.

" I will, sir. I was waked by the sound of voices. I opened my eyes, and there, by the open door, stood two men, or leastways a man and a boy about my own size. I was awful scared, and couldn't catch what they said at first, but after a bit, when my heart stopped a thumpin', I heard the man say: ' You understand me, boy? Get as far on the road as you can, and to-morrow I'll pick you up as I pass, and take you on up to'—I didn't catch the name o' the place. Then the little 'un, he thanked the man for summat. All on a sudden the man, he swore a terrible oath, and snatchin' summat away from the boy, he says: ' D—n! what are you doing with that gun?' ' I was going to throw it away on the road, somewhere,' said the boy. ' Give it to me, and I'll sink it in the ditch,' said the man;

and then he came over to near where I was lying, and as he passed the window the moonlight fell full on his face, and I saw it was Mr. Silliman, the prisoner, sir, and he had a gun in his hand. Well, sir, he walked straight past me; I could almost have touched the **gun-stock with my** foot, and he stooped down and stuffed the gun carefully away under the straw, and sayin' to himself, 'It 'll be safe enough there for the present.' And then they both went away together, and presently Mr. Silliman, the prisoner, sir, he **came** back alone, and goes and stands where he'd hid the gun, and I heard him say: 'Would to heaven, I'd had the nerve to kill the **boy**, too: dead men tell no tales.' **I was worse** frightened **than ever** then, thinking as maybe he saw me, and **meant me.** Well, he stood a minute or so mutterin' to himself, and then he went out and **shut** the door and locked **it.** I didn't **sleep** much more that night, **but** when the daylight came, the fear left me, and I searched among **the** straw for the gun and found it. **It was a fine gun, I** thought, **and** a cryin' sin and a shame to see it sank in the ditch and ruined, and if no one was to have it, it would be no loss to anybody; so sir, to be honest about it, I just stole the gun and ran away home with it as fast as ever I could. But it was no use to me, for I couldn't use it myself, and when I saw Mr. Dunraven's name on it, I didn't dare to show it, or speak of it to a soul, so I just hid it away, and tried to forget all about it. But that only made me think all the more about it, and that's why I got the whole thing and everything connected with it fixed so clear in my mind. At last one day I told my father about the gun, and he sent me off with it to Sir Griffith Egerton, sir, and I told him the whole story, and he took the **gun**, and has kept it ever since, and if you please, sir, that's all I have **to say** about how I got the gun."

The cross-examination by the prisoner's counsel develops nothing **new,** being mainly devoted to memory tests, and the usual effort **to** betray into contradictions, neither of **which modes of attack are** successful; for, as the witness has sensibly accounted for the **remark**able clearness of his recollection through eighteen years of the particular facts he has testified to, by the indelible impression made on his mind by the effort to forget them, it can matter not if he cannot remember the cook's surname, or whether the Bratton Railway line was open at the time; and for the same reason is he able to repeat his evidence, piece by piece, without material variation.

Mr. Toddy shakes his wig well forward on to his forehead with a twitch, draws his gown up by a nervous convulsion of the shoulders, (a peculiar trick he has when vexed, Mr. Tufnell tells me,) and sits down.

14

There is a moment's pause as the young man Crawsly leaves the box and makes his way back to his seat. Dawkins consults his notes and looks at Headstrong, while the judge looks up as if impatient at the delay, **and the** silence of expectation as to who will be **the next witness, and what** the testimony, **falls upon the entire assemblage.**

CHAPTER II.

Great contest follows and much learned dust.
— "The Garden."

"JOLLIFFE TUFNELL! Jolliffe Tufnell! Come into court! Come into court!" shouts the crier.

"By Jove, that's me!" says Tufnell, rising hurriedly from his seat next me and leaving the gallery.

A minute later he shoulders his way through the throng below, **and steps** eagerly into the witness-box, his face glowing with excitement. He stumbles as he enters, and barely saves himself from coming down on all fours by a timely clutch at the railing. **The** titter which flew around the room at his appearance, breaks into a well defined guffaw at this exhibition of awkwardness, **and the crier calls:**

"Si–lence!"

Tufnell turns even redder than before, and takes out a red pocket-**handkerchief;** and the judge, looking up fiercely over his spectacles, **admonishes the crowd** that upon a repetition of their breach of decorum **he will order the** Court to be cleared.

This has a most salutary effect; an instantaneous hush falls upon **the assemblage, and** Tufnell, apparently much soothed in nerve by the restored quiet, as well as by the vigorous mopping his face has undergone, thrusts his handkerchief into his coat-tail pocket, and smiles good-naturedly around. **He** is one of those strange creatures who with the very best intentions, seem by their very presence **to take away from the solemnity of** any occasion, and he very **nearly** provokes another titter. But he is supposed to be one of the most important witnesses for the prosecution, and the anxiety to hear his evidence overcomes the risible propensities of the audience even more than the judge's previous warning, and checks the laugh. Tufnell is sworn, the usual introductory and stereotyped questions answered satisfactorily, and in reply to **the** inevitable—"Did you know the deceased in his lifetime?" **he answers:**

"I did. We were friends from early boyhood. He was, in fact, the dearest friend I **ever had; and** this trial, I **may** say, without claiming too much, is the result of my efforts to bring his murderer to justice. Of the prisoner I have long had my suspi——"

"One moment!" exclaims Mr. Toddy, jumping to his feet. "That is improper. Your suspicions are not evidence. I object, my lud."

"We do not contend for a moment that they are," says Dawkins, quietly. "The answer was not responsive to any question of mine. Never mind your suspicions, Mr. Tufnell," he adds, as Toddy subsides into his seat, "but state what were the circumstances, if any, that aroused them?"

"He was always getting me out of scrapes," commences Tufnell, rather vaguely.

"Who? The prisoner?" asks Toddy, with a grunt.

Tufnell looks at him savagely.

"No; Louis Dunraven, the man he murdered."

Toddy jumps to his feet again.

"Now, I ask your lordship if that is proper?"

"Certainly not," says his lordship, very sternly, and thereupon delivers to Tufnell a lengthy lecture upon the impropriety and danger of a witness usurping the province of the jury, a dissertation much too learned, and far too tedious, for me to repeat here. The end of it is, that Toddy sits down again and Tufnell proceeds.

"Louis Dunraven — as I before stated —" he says with a look at Toddy, "was always getting me out of scrapes. Once he came to take me away from a low gambling den, where, I'm ashamed to say I was, and there in his presence I got into a row with the pris—"

"One moment," interrupts Toddy, again rising. "I object to all this, my lud. We are here, may it please your lordship, to try a man for his life, and not to listen to a confession of youthful follies, which may be all very proper and praiseworthy, and commendable, in its proper place."

His lordship looks as though he would like to hear from the other side, and Dawkins is about to respond, when a sign from his associate checks him, and for the first time in the progress of the trial, Sergeant Headstrong gets upon his feet.

It has hitherto doubtless been a puzzle to many, what in the world such a personage as Sergeant Headstrong was in the case for at all; for apparently, so far, not a word has he uttered, not a move has he made, but has sat there in his seat like a bewigged statue, and for all that he has appeared to have done, he might as well have been in his chambers in Lincoln's Inn. Such had been my impression, until Mr. Tufnell enlightened me.

"Done nothing!" he exclaimed, in answer to my question. "He has done everything. To all appearances he lets Dawkins manage the case; for Dawkins is a Q. C., and Q. C.s don't like coaching in public, as a rule, even from sergeants-at-law, but it's safe to say, there hasn't been a question of importance asked to-day that old Headstrong hasn't either dictated or made some timely suggestion about, though you or I couldn't see it with his back to us. He does it all by a sort of pantomime; a wink here, a half frown there; an elevation of the eyebrows, or a smoothing down of his bands with the feather of his pen. Dawkins knows all his signs like a book, and sees them all with the side of his eye, for before he got his silk gown, he used to be junior to Headstrong in no end of cases and learned all the old fellow's ways; and now whenever they happen to hold briefs on the same side—which is often, they pull together so well—Dawkins, though now a Q. C., is willing, for old times sake, as it were, to play junior to his old leader without appearing to do so. This, at least, is what my solicitors tell me, and they consider us very fortunate in having secured such a team as Headstrong and Dawkins on the Crown side to-day."

But I have left the worthy Sergeant upon his feet. That he is a tall, broad-shouldered man, with tufts of grey hair sticking out under his wig, and grizzled whiskers that stand out on either side of his face like open window-shutters, is all that I can see over the intervening heads, for his back remains as it has been, towards me.

"May it please your lordship," he begins, in a cléar resonant voice that echoes through the court. "My learned brother," with a motion of the thumb toward Toddy, "should not forget that the evidence on the part of the prosecution is, as was stated in the opening, of necessity, circumstantial in its character. Such being the case, it is a difficult matter to determine what facts are not admissible in evidence that would in any manner even tend to point to the prisoner's guilt, or in any way illumine the path of the jury in their search for the truth. The facts which the witness was about to testify to transpired many years ago, some time indeed before the commission of the murder, and, I think, it is not improper for me to say, will disclose in the recital of them, much that is proper for the jury to hear, in order to enable them to arrive at a just verdict. In the recital of these facts, there may, of course, be many things spoken of and alluded to, which, of themselves, are immaterial and inadmissible, but which when viewed in connection with other circumstances become important. I therefore ask that the witness be allowed to go on without captious interruption, and relate in his own way all the facts and circumstances in his own knowledge that aroused his suspicions of the prisoner's guilt, and if necessary, the wheat of his evidence can be separated from the chaff when your lordship sums up. The witness, I may add, is an intelligent witness, and I feel confident will furnish us with more of the former than the latter. In support of these views, if indeed support they need, I will cite, if your lordship pleases, Starkie on Evidence (pages 20–21 and 78–79), and the case of *Rex* v. *Chuddleigh* (2 Russell & Ryan's Reports, page 642), a case very similar to the one at bar, in which Lord Chief Justice Abbott lays **down the rule** in a very elaborate opinion."

This is in a measure all Greek to **me, and as I catch Tufnell's eye** as he stands in the witness-box, he grins at me. But the long and the short of it is that Toddy's objection is overruled by the judge, and Sergeant Headstrong seats himself with, as a young gentleman behind me, evidently a cricketer, expresses it "the air of a slogger who has just made **a swipe to square leg for six."**

Tufnell goes on where he left off.

"I got into a row with the prisoner, as I was saying, at the gambling house. We afterwards fought a duel, and I wounded him. One day, when he was recovering from the wound, Dunraven and I were——"

Toddy: "**One moment.** Can't you fix the date? How long before the homicide was this?"

Tufnell: "Three months perhaps—not more. Dunraven and I were out walking in London one evening. We stopped at a house in Finsbury Circus and Dunraven said, 'Do you mind coming in a moment, Tufnell? **I want to see** Silliman, and you can wait in another room.' I consented. We were shown into a front room, and Dunraven passed into the one beyond, leaving me alone. He left the door between the rooms ajar and as I felt a sort of grim curiosity to see the man I had wounded, for I hadn't seen him since the duel, before I knew what I was about I was looking through the aperture at the prisoner lying upon his bed. **He** did not see me for I stood far back and the light was dim. A lamp upon a table beside his bed shone full in his face however, and I saw it plainly as he turned **his head and looked at Dunraven.** He half rose in the bed and with a diabolical look upon his face, swore a great oath. 'If I ever have **an opportunity,** and be sure I will make one,' he said, 'I'll be even with **you yet for this,** you white-livered, lying, hypocritical, psalm-singing parson! But for your interference with that unlicked cub, **I would not be** here now. I owe it all to you, d——n you! and so sure as **there is** a Heaven above us I will be revenged.'

Dunraven very quietly answered: 'Leave Bratton at once, give up the house you have **rented** there, and **remove** from the neighborhood **at once** and forever, and I will spare your reputation, but I cannot conscientiously **permit a man of** your **character to live among** my friends and impose himself upon them as a man of honor and a gentleman, when I know him to be the **reverse.** Never return there, but as soon as you are able to attend to it, give up your lease—it will **be accepted I'll promise** you—and have your traps sent up to **you here; but never show your face** there again. That is all I ask.' I **suddenly remembered that I had no** right to listen and turned away. I **still heard their voices for some time,** as if in argument—then the prisoner's **grew loud and angry.** Believing him to be a desperate man, especially after the threat he had uttered, I had fears for Dun- **raven's safety, even though I knew the** prisoner to be weak, for it wouldn't require much strength to pull a trigger, I thought, and those sort of fellows always keep pistols under their pillows. So I **walked over to the door** again and glanced in. Dunraven was com- ing **towards the doorway with** his back to the bed, and there I be- **held the prisoner in the act of cocking a** pistol, with a look of in- tense **hatred fixed** upon my friend. He tried to level the weapon at **Dunraven, steadying one** hand with the other while he took deliber- ate **aim. I was about to spring** forward and shout to **Dunraven,** when a **sudden** twinge of pain seemed to seize the prisoner, **he grew** deathly pale, his features twitched convulsively, and letting the pis- tol fall on the counterpane, **he** sank back with a groan. All had **passed in an** instant, **and** the next moment Dunraven and I found ourselves **in the** street. I told Dunraven what I had seen, but he only laughed and made light of it. These are the facts on which my suspicions have been based."

Toddy **believes that Tufnell** is the most important **witness the** prosecution will be able to produce; without him the one great evi- dentiary fact—the previous threat—could not be proven against his client; but to attempt to shake him in his present confident mood would be useless. Yet he thinks from his manner of entering the box, he can be easily excited and thrown off his balance. To that **end, with the** help of a little gentle badgering, Mr. Toddy, Q. C., applies **himself** without **delay.**

Toddy. "Why didn't you give your evidence at the inquest?"

Tufnell. "I didn't happen to be in England at the time. I sup- pose that was the reason."

Toddy (with a sneer). "And you couldn't make it your business to return to see justice **done on** behalf of your best friend on earth—I believe that's what you called the deceased?"

Tufnell. "I was somewhere in the wilds **of South** Africa at the time, rather beyond the reach of either mails or telegraphs, and knew nothing of the murder. The first I knew of it was three years ago."

Toddy. "Three years ago! Come now, that's too good. A man ignorant of the death of his 'best friend on earth' for fifteen years after it takes place! Where, in the name of common sense, have you been ever since? In the moon?"

Tufnell. "Not exactly."

Toddy. "Up in a balloon?"

Tufnell. "No."

Toddy. "Where then?"

Tufnell. "On earth." (Laughter.) The judge looks up with a scowl.

Toddy. "On earth, eh? And heard nothing of your friend for fifteen years! You spent the intervening period after the fashion of Rip Van Winkle, I suppose?"

Tufnell. "No."

Toddy. "How then?"

Tufnell (with a grin). "Traveling."

Toddy. "Ah! Been to Egypt?"

Tufnell. "Yes."

Toddy. "And seen the Pyramids, of course?"

Tufnell. "Oh, yes."

Toddy. "Sure you're not one of the chaps out of Cheops?"

Tufnell (good humoredly). "Quite sure."

Toddy. "Where else have you been?"

Tufnell. "It would be far easier for me to tell you where I haven't been."

Toddy. "Well, where haven't you been, then?"

Tufnell. "To the best of my recollection: the Polar Sea, the Antarctic Continent, and a place called Payta, in South America."

Toddy. "And what made you leave them out?"

Tufnell. "The last place I avoided through the advice of an English naval officer; the others, I couldn't get to, unfortunately."

Toddy. "And you've been everywhere else?"

Tufnell. "Yes."

Toddy. "And what pray sent you traveling over the world for fifteen years like that?"

Tufnell. "Money—I haven't a doubt."

Toddy (warmly). "Come, answer my question. You know perfectly well what I mean. What motive had you in keeping away from England all that time?"

As Tufnell answers I can almost fancy I see his eyes flash through his spectacles.

"What my motive was, sir, I deem it **totally** unnecessary for you to know, or for me to inform this jury. It has nothing whatever to do with the issue in this case, and you are lawyer enough, I take it, to know that your question is not cross-examination. What you want to get **at, however, I** will tell you without giving you the trouble of asking **so many** questions. I left England eighteen years ago, **unknown to a** soul but my bankers. They even didn't know what became of me **after I** left Egypt. I traveled—for reasons which it is my desire and privilege to keep secret—under an assumed name, and **from the day I** left Liverpool until my return fifteen years **later, I corresponded** with no one, never saw an English newspaper, or if I did, studiously avoided reading it. Thus it is that I only heard of my friend **Louis Dunraven's** death for the first time upon my return."

Beyond a slight hunching up of his shoulders, and the merest **trifle of a nod** with his wig, Toddy takes no note of Tufnell's retort; but he sees it is a waste of time to go on as he began, so he stops his bantering and asks: "You are sure the man you saw on the bed that evening eighteen years ago," drawing the words out with a significant grimace for the benefit of the jury, "and who pointed the pistol **at** your friend, was the prisoner at the bar?"

Tufnell: (Confidently.) "I am. And I'll tell you why if **you** like."

Mr. Toddy does not appear at all anxious to know "why." He believes the identification will be damaging to his cause, and, sorry he asked the question at all, is about to lead off on another tack when the judge growls out:—

"**Go on.**"

Tufnell: "I saw under his right eye, in precisely the spot where **that scar** now appears, a barely-healed cut and a recent discolora**tion of** the skin that was caused by a blow I struck him when I knocked him down **in** the gambling-house the night we had the row. I hit him with my left hand, and this ring, which I wore at the time, it was that gave the cut. It is a singularly-shaped scar you will observe, and if you will apply the ring to it **you will** see that, strange as it may appear, the edges will correspond."

This is done, and Tufnell's statement so far corroborated.

A few more questions Toddy asks, wishing evidently at each reply that he had left Tufnell severely alone; but vexed alike at his own ill success, and the other's firmness, he cannot refrain from giving him one parting shot. Shaking his wig and convulsing his gown, he asks:—

"Did you, or do you know to whom the prisoner referred by the expression, 'that unlicked cub?'"

Tufnell: (Smiling.) "Me, of course."

Toddy: (With an expression of mock surprise that would have made his fortune on the boards.) "You! *You* an unlicked *cub?* Oh, I see. (Light seeming to dawn on him.) You were eighteen years younger then. That is all."

If it had been a theatre, a round of applause would have greeted Toddy as he sits down with a gratified air at the slap he thinks he has given Tufnell. As it is, a laugh which at the judge's frown and crier's "si-lence!" dwindles into an inaudible smile, shows the audience's appreciation of his parting shot. But it is a shot that Tufnell with tact deprives of much, if not all of its force, by the sensible way he receives it. Instead of appearing annoyed, as ninety-nine out of a hundred would, he turns it aside with the shield of his good humor, and leaves the box with a smile which tells that he enjoys the joke, though it be at his own expense, quite as keenly as any one.

The court now adjourns for refreshments; the judge toddles off for his chop and glass of dry sherry, glad, doubtless, to doff that ponderous wig, if even but for a half hour; and we, to avoid the crush and scramble of exit and re-entrance, prefer to remain comfortably ensconced where we are till the end.

"It will be but laying down our appetites upon the altars of comfort and curiosity," says Sir Griffith; "a sacrifice which I have no doubt you ladies will find no difficulty in making, if you but select the latter altar for your offering. Eh, Strutt? For my part, were it not that comfort is involved, and the question were but one of appetite or curiosity, I confess I should far sooner gratify the one than the other."

"From the way I look at the question, I think I should have to agree with you, Sir Griffith," says Mr. Strutt.

Our sacrifice, however, is one that Mr. Tufnell will not allow to be complete, for soon he appears, followed by a waiter from the coffee-room of the hotel across the way, bearing aloft upon a tray a goodly supply of ham sandwiches, glasses, and two quart bottles of "the charming widow." We are at first doubtful as to the propriety of the proceeding, and hesitate lest so glaring a contempt of the sacredness of its tribunal bring upon us the punitive thunders of the outraged majesty of the law.

"Perfectly proper," Tufnell says, reading our looks; "the court is not sitting now, and you might smoke if you liked. I'll leave it to Mr. Strutt."

Mr. Strutt, with a longing eye at the sandwiches, concurs without a murmur, and Mr. Strutt is an authority on such matters. In no way disposed to question the disinterestedness of his concurrence on the present occasion, and fortified with a legal opinion on the subject, our misgivings are banished, and regardless of the envious glances of our less fortunate neighbors, we discuss the repast that **has been so thoughtfully** provided for us, and the evidence that has **been given, at the same time.**

CHAPTER III.

Not yet thou knowest me, and seeing me, dost not
Think me for the man I am, necessity
Commands me name myself.

—Coriolanus: Act IV, Scene 5.

THE recess for luncheon is over, our sandwiches and champagne disposed of, **those of** the audience who had left their places for a breath of fresh air, or something more substantial, come back to find them occupied by others who **refuse to deliver up** possession; the jury return and take their **seats with a** recuperated expression about their mouths; the counsel **on both** sides are in their places, the crier yells: " Si-lence!" again, **making far more** noise himself than anybody else, whereupon the judge re-enters, seats himself with much dignity, blows his nose, takes out his spectacles and wipes them slowly and carefully before putting them on, gives a sort of nod over the top of his desk at nobody in particular, **and says:** " Proceed;" and the case of Regina v. Silliman goes on again.

Sergeant Headstrong rises and says:

" Call Alva Ingolsby."

" What can he possibly know?" think **I, aloud, as** in response to the usual summons, Ingolsby makes his way to the witness-box and **is sworn.**

" Something important, you may be sure," whispers Tufnell, who has resumed his place at my side, with a queer look, " or old Headstrong wouldn't be ' up and doing.' **Listen."**

" What is your name?" asks the sergeant.

Ingolsby smiles up at our party, and keeps his eyes upon us as he gives his name on oath. Distinctly it rings through the courtroom, and there follows a hum of excitement as many start up in wonder. Toddy nearly draws his gown over his head so great is the convulsion of his shoulders at the announcement; while the prisoner starts perceptibly, gives a quick and searching look at Ingolsby, turns a shade paler, as he studies each feature, then compressing his lips hard, he nods his head slightly as if some sudden determination had taken possession of him, and resumes his former attitude and expression of stony indifference. For my part, I sit as one dazed, scarce believing that I heard aright, when Ingolsby answered so quietly but impressively:

" Guy Egerton."

Can it be true? he, Alva Ingolsby, the long-lost Guy Egerton? Hurriedly I glance around at our party, seeking some explanation. Sir Griffith with a tearful smile motions us to be quiet, for not to me alone is this unexpected. Lady Egerton has risen wildly to her feet, Lady Amtenhurst striving to soothe her emotion; while Florence, who sits next to me, pale and trembling, grasps my arm convulsively. Of us all, Sir Griffith, Tufnell and Strutt alone prove their previous knowledge by present calmness; and as it suddenly occurs to me that I can best solve the mystery by turning my attention to the witness himself, I place my hand upon Florence's to keep her still, and listen to the testimony with the strangest feeling at my heart I have ever experienced, as Sergeant Headstrong continues the examination.

" Who are you?"

" I am the son of Sir Griffith Egerton of Bratton Hall."

" Did you know the deceased?"

" I did. I was with him on the day he was killed."

" Please state all the circumstances that transpired on that day, that you remember, so far as they relate to the death of Louis Dunraven."

There is almost absolute silence as Guy—for such he must be henceforth—goes on and relates the story of that eventful day, now for the first time given to the world by him in whose keeping it has lain hid for so many years, and so intent are all to catch each word as it falls from his lips—such a breathless hush is there, that the crier's services are unneeded, and the scratching of the pens as the evidence is taken down in the pauses, would alone prevent our hearing the proverbial pin should the dropping thereof by any chance occur.

" On the morning of the twenty-second of September, 18—, Louis Dunraven and I left Bratton Hall for the purpose of shooting over Mr. Tufnell's property at Knocklofty. It was about ten o'clock when we left the house, and we walked down the avenue for about a quarter of a mile, and then took a short cut across the park and through the fields. I remember distinctly, stopping at the gamekeeper Jennings' on the way, to have the gun fixed. Dunraven had, in snapping a cap to clear the barrel before loading, by some means got the nipple stopped up with a fragment of the cap, and I recollect being very impatient at the delay we had to make there, as I was anxious to be among the birds.

"We reached the dividing-hedge between our place and Mr. Tufnell's, and walked along till we saw a keeper on the other side. We hailed him, and Dunraven showed him the permit. He let us in through a gate some distance away, and showed us where to go. We soon got among the birds and commenced shooting. After keeping together some time, we separated, Dunraven striking off to some outlying covers, leaving me to pick off the birds that would be driven in by him. I soon lost sight of him among the bushes, and he seemed to be having good sport, for every time he shot, both barrels followed one another in quick succession. Presently I heard a single shot. I was loading my gun at the time, and my ear having got accustomed, as it were, to the double report, I paused a moment and listened for the second shot. None came, however, and though I supposed, of course, it was because he had had but one bird to shoot at, I don't know why, but it seemed to strike me all of a sudden as strange. The sound of the report, too, didn't seem like Dunraven's gun. It was sharper, as if the charge had been heavier. It then occurred to me that some one else might be out shooting over the place, whom we hadn't seen as the bushes were very thick and high. Then I thought that couldn't be, for Mr. Tufnell himself had gone abroad, and no one else had the right to shoot there. I waited and listened, but no more shots were fired. Then I supposed Dunraven was returning, and sat down on a stone to wait for him. Half an hour passed and he did not come. I began to wonder what could be the matter. It couldn't be that he had got out of earshot, for he couldn't have gone much farther without getting off Mr. Tufnell's land and on to the Delamayn place, which was let to the prisoner at the time.

"At last I felt alarmed at my friend's long silence, and set off in search of him in the direction he had taken, shouting to him as I walked on. I received no answer to my calls and kept on with a strange sense of dread coming over me. I had made my way through the bushes for perhaps a hundred yards or so, when I heard a rustling among the leaves as if some one was coming toward me. I stopped, thinking it was Dunraven. The sound continued and presently I saw the figure of a man emerging from the thicket. I was just upon the point of calling out, when I saw it was not Dunraven. It was the prisoner at the bar. He had a double-barreled gun under his arm, and his face was pale and wore an anxious expression. He stood still a moment and looked around him cautiously, then back, as if at some object behind him, with a queerly-mingled expression of gratification and repugnance. He then struck off to the right in the direction of his own place, and disappeared among the trees. He had evidently not seen me, and as soon as he was well out of sight, I started on again. I had not gone far when I espied a dark form stretched on the ground under a tree. Greatly frightened, I ran up to it and found it was Louis Dunraven. He lay upon his back, his gun by his side. He was quite dead, and the ground beneath him seemed to be saturated with blood, and blood oozed from between his lips. I was stupified with horror, my gun dropped from my hands, and I knelt down beside the body, and covering my face with my hands to keep out the terrible sight, I burst into tears. How long I remained thus I cannot tell, but suddenly I felt a hand upon my shoulder. I looked up quickly, and there stood the prisoner. He caught me by the arm and accused me of murdering my friend. I sprang to my feet incensed at the horrible accusation, but my anger rendered me speechless. This he pretended to construe into an evidence of my guilt. Grasping me tightly by the arm, he said it would be useless for me to deny it—of course I would do that, it was but natural; but that he had heard the shot fired, and shortly after had found me bending over the body, and his evidence with all the corroborating circumstances would hang me, young as I was. At a glance I saw the position I was in. In my unnerved condition I exaggerated it of course. But I was very young—not yet twelve—and knew nothing of law. I had heard and read stories of how men had been convicted on circumstantial evidence of murders and robberies that they had never committed, and as these stories all came back to my mind, my fears so worked upon my imagination that I already felt the rope around my neck. The prisoner affected to pity me. He said he knew my father well and that the disgrace would kill him. The shooting of my friend might have been an accident; he hoped for his part, it was. But who could prove it? I couldn't testify, and the circumstances all looked the other way. It would be a pity to see so young a boy hanged, and to save me from such an ignominious death, and my people from the terrible disgrace, he would help me to evade justice and escape.

"In the state of mind to which my exaggerated fears and his words had brought me, I was only too willing to accept his aid; my gratitude to him was unbounded, and I poured forth a torrent of thanks. He led me off by an unfrequented path, helped me over the wall into his place, and bid me crawl under a hedge. 'Stay there,' he said, 'and as you value your life, don't let a soul see you. I will come for you after dark to-night, and bring you to a place where you will be safe. And here, take this gun,' he added, giving me the gun be had been carrying; 'you have your neck to save, recollect, at any cost, and may need it to keep too curious people at a proper distance.' I took the gun, having in my haste forgotten my own where it had fallen by Dunraven's body. **The** prisoner then left me. **After** he had gone I discovered that the gun he had left with me as his own was Dunraven's. How it had come into his possession was a puzzle to me, and I began to think he had done it purposely to fix the murder upon me, and had gone off to inform on me and deliver me up. Not knowing what to do with the gun, and fearing to stir lest I should betray my hiding-place, and expecting every moment to hear the officers of the law coming to apprehend me, I lay under the hedge all day in an agony **of fear.** When it was quite dark the prisoner came back. He told me to get up, and warning me to keep silent, and step as noiselessly as I could, brought me across one or two fields to an old barn, behind his stables, and there, securely locked in a small upper room, he kept me concealed for a week, bringing me food morning and evening. When I had had time to reflect, and my excitement had cooled down, I began to think I had acted very foolishly, and had almost made up my mind to go home, tell the truth, and brave the worst. **I was at a loss,** beside, to account for Silliman's anxiety for my escape. He was not a friend of my father's—that I knew; barely an acquaintance, in fact, as he was a comparative stranger in the neighborhood, and I couldn't imagine what motive he could have in thus befriending me. I told him one night that I feared I was acting unwisely in hiding myself in this way, and that I thought I would go **to** my father at once and tell him all, as no one could possibly suspect me. ' You are a little fool!' he exclaimed, with an oath. He took a newspaper out of his pocket and **threw it to me.** ' **Read that,'** he said, 'and see whether anybody **could possibly sus-pect you.'** I took up the paper **and** the first thing I saw was the **account of the inquest on** Dunraven's body, and that the verdict of **the coroner's jury had accused me** of the murder. ' I made my testimony, you'll see, as strong against you as I could,' he added. ' I knew it would really make no difference in the verdict, as the facts were all so dead against you, how my evidence went, so I thought the bitterer **I was,** the less likely would they be of suspect-ing me of aiding and abetting your escape. By Jove!' said he, ' do you know I'm positively making myself an accessory after the fact in doing so ! **It isn't** everybody **would do that** for a friend, is it, my boy ?'

"When I found that I was thus publicly and formally accused of the crime, I was overwhelmed. All my fears returned with redoubled force, and I no longer hesitated to fly. That night Silliman brought me an old jacket and trousers, and a battered-slouched hat as a disguise. I left my own clothes hid away in the loft, and then he let me out. The gun which he had given me—Dunraven's—I had kept, and wanted to take with me, but he took it from me. He told me what road to take, and said for me to walk steadily on along the high road toward Hull, and he would follow me in his gig before sunrise next morning, and pick me up. I gained the high road and walked all night in the direction he had named. It was a bright moonlight night, I remember, and early next morning Silliman caught up with me in his gig about fifteen miles from Bratton. We reached Hull about noon, and there he got me a position as cabin-boy on the American bark "Hiawatha." There he left me, after buying me an outfit and giving me £10 to keep my pocket. In two days the bark sailed for New York, and I did not see the prisoner again until three weeks ago, when I went to the jail to identify him upon his arrival from America in charge of the officers. I had no difficulty whatever in recognizing him. He is older, of course, and wears a beard, but his face, I don't think I shall ever forget. In any event I should know him by that scar under his eye. It is a most peculiar one."

"During the days you were under the prisoner's care, did he speak to you of the deceased?" asks Headstrong.

"Once he said that the world was well rid of the hypocritical parson, and I, in boyish fashion, fired up, and defended my friend. He then became furious, and I thought he would strike me; but he controlled himself and went away."

"Are you the Guy Egerton, you say, whom the verdict of the coroner's jury accused of the murder?" asks Toddy, in cross-examination.

"I am."

"You sailed for America, you say; how long ago was that?"

"Eighteen years."

"And where have *you* been ever since? Traveling too?"

"I remained in America over fifteen years. For the past two years and a half I have been in England."

"What name have you borne?"

"Alva Ingolsby—a name I assumed in the United States."

"And why did you not come forward and acknowledge yourself before now?"

"I waited for an opportunity to clear myself from the accusation made against me."

"Don't you know you could have done that at any time by delivering yourself up and standing your trial like a man—if you were innocent?"

"**Yes.** But I desired more than simply to clear myself. I desired to bring the real murderer to justice."

"And failing to secure the indictment of some other person for the crime, you would have lived and died as Alva Ingolsby, I suppose."

"Not by any means. I returned to England for the purpose of claiming my own name. I came to Bratton and made myself known to my father. I told him the whole story as I have told it here to-day. Mr. Tufnell had previously been to him for his assistance in getting together evidence against the prisoner whom he said he suspected. We three consulted together and it was determined to keep my existence a secret until the whole case was completed and Silliman in the hands of the law."

The deposition of Captain Waterman of the bark "Hiawatha," now a large ship-owner in Boston, taken under a commission, is now read in evidence. It corroborates Guy in every fact relating to his shipping as cabin-boy at Hull, and gives a description of the man who accompanied him and procured him the berth, that tallies with the appearance of Silliman as he is remembered by old Brattonites, in every particular. Sir Griffith is also about to enter the box for the purpose of testifying to the identity of his son; but Mr. Toddy, who manifestly thinks he will make a point with the jury thereby, says he will make no question as to that, and Sir Griffith quietly withdraws. This closes the case for the crown, and Mr. Toddy, Q. C., rises to address the jury for the prisoner.

CHAPTER IV.

Guilty, my lord, guilty; I confess, I confess.
    — *Love's Labor Lost:* Act IV, Scene 3.

MR. Toddy begins by saying that the prisoner at the bar stands in the truly unfortunate position of being without one human being to bear testimony for him. "The very nature of the case, the very character of the evidence adduced by the prosecution precludes the possibility of his being able to produce any witnesses on his behalf. Eighteen long years have been allowed to pass since the crime with which he is charged was committed, and during that time the prosecution, or rather the tool of the prosecution, this man Jolliffe Tufnell, has been busy gathering together the threads of the fabric which they have sought to weave about the prisoner to-day. There is no direct proof of his guilt offered in the case. It is all inference from facts, which, of themselves, taken by themselves, fairly and without prejudice, are perfectly consistent with the prisoner's innocence. After an eighteen-year's long sleep this charge is raked up against this man, when death and time have silenced and scattered those who might to-day have spoken for him. His wife is dead, his servants gone, no one knows whither, not a soul living who could prove for him the one great and powerful fact in cases of circumstantial evidence, an *alibi*. Of all his household who could speak of his whereabouts on that unhappy day, he himself alone remains; but, gentlemen of the jury, so far from his being able to tell you aught of the occurrences of that day, he too might as well be dead and gone, for by the inexorable laws of his country, his lips are sealed. They have chosen well their time, gentlemen of the jury; they have exhibited rare strategy." He warns the jury against relying on the testimony of witnesses who have remained silent for so long a time without a better excuse for their silence than has been given, and pays his respect to each witness in turn, showing up the weak points of their evidence, and slurring over the strong.

"Take the two chief witnesses for the crown," he goes on; "the only witnesses, I might say, for the others are mere puppets ready to answer any pull of the string their masters may choose to give; let us take these two, and see who they are. One yet remains accused by a sworn jury of the very crime of which the prisoner at the bar now stands indicted. What such a witness's interest in securing a conviction must be, it is unnecessary, I am confident, for me to even hint to you; for I take it, gentlemen of the jury, that you are men endowed with at least ordinary human reason, and can see that for yourselves. Why, by his own confession, he admits his prime motive to be to clear his own name. Of course, his desire, as he tells you, to bring the murderer of his friend Louis Dunraven to justice, is all very well, and very praiseworthy, and very proper; but, gentlemen of the jury, a desire that has been kept under control, such wonderfully perfect control, that it never gave sign of its existence for a period of fifteen years, and then only when its possessor desired to return to his native land, and claim his ancestral name, cannot be, cannot ever have been, a very consuming one, and is about on a par with this man Tufnell's indifference as to the welfare, condition or fate of his dearest friend on earth, for about the same period of time. If Louis Dunraven could speak to-day, he

15

might well exclaim: 'Save me from my friends!' As for this man Tufnell, the other of this wonderful pair, I hardly deem it necessary for me to speak of him, or the marvelous story he has related here to-day."

He nevertheless does at considerable length and with much asperity. "But, gentlemen of the jury," he continues, "why need I say more? It is for the prosecution to prove the prisoner guilty, not for the prisoner to prove himself innocent. Have they done so? That is for you to say by your verdict. I assure you, gentlemen of the jury, that never in my professional career, and I flatter myself," he adds with a consequential simper, "it has been one of *rather* varied experience—never have I seen a weaker case made out on behalf of the Crown." He then goes on to admonish them of the dangers and pitfalls of circumstantial evidence. "Circumstantial evidence, eighteen years old," he reiterates. "The only consideration it should receive at your hands, gentlemen of the jury, is a respect for **its age.**" He impresses upon them the fact that it is their duty **to acquit if** there be one link, even the smallest, weakest link, missing **in the** chain, for the strength of the whole chain is that of its **weakest** link—no greater—and every reasonable doubt must be **thrown in favor** of acquittal. He reminds them of the immense, **the grave, the awful** responsibility that rests upon them—the life of **a fellow** creature swings in the balance, dependent upon their word **as to its** fate; a human life is in their hands. But let them remember their duty and their oaths, and he will have no fear **as** to the result. And then, with a mingled appeal to their sympathy for the man who stands before them comparatively friendless and alone, and a last admonition to remember the tremendous responsibility resting upon their shoulders,—"a responsibility from which strong men might well shrink, or at which brave men might well shudder," Mr. Toddy concludes his hour and a half's speech.

"The usual stereotyped 'speech for the prisoner,'" says Tufnell **with a** spice of animosity in his voice as Toddy sits down. "I've **heard** a good many of them in my life, and they're all alike. The **facts** of each case differ vastly of course, but the 'speech for the **prisoner,'** is the same from beginning to end the world over. It's **the identical** terrible responsibility—reasonable doubt—sworn duty **—life** at stake—fellow creature—every-man-innocent-till-proved- **guilty,** harangue in all of them."

Sergeant Headstrong follows in a speech an hour long. He meets all of Toddy's objections at every point; shows the great difficulty the witnesses for the prosecution have labored under; that their long silence, so far from being suspicious, has been owing to the ignorance of what each other knew, and a consequent impossibility of concerted action while that ignorance continued; pays a glowing tribute to the zeal and untiring industry of Jolliffe Tufnell; takes Toddy severely to task for his unmerited strictures both on him and Guy, and administers something more than a mild rebuke in return; goes carefully over the evidence and reweaves before the jury, thread by thread and piece by piece, the net that surrounds the wretch at the bar; demonstrates in the most convincing manner the presence of every necessary link in the "strongest chain of circumstantial evidence that has ever been wrought in any case, and *he* flatters *himself* that his experience has been somewhat extensive, though probably not quite so *varied* as that of his brother Toddy;" and after explaining the difference between direct and indirect or circumstantial evidence, and claiming for the latter a superiority in proving power, as "men may lie, but circumstances can't," finishes by asking the jury as men of common sense to look at all the circumstances of the case "and *he* will have no fear of the result."

The judge now sums up the case to the jury, and in his unprejudiced exposition of the law and facts, steers a middle course between Toddy and Headstrong, that comes like oil upon the troubled waters of the jury mind.

At 6:45 the jury retire to, deliberate on their verdict. At 7:33 they return into court. There is death-like silence as the foreman announces, in a shaky voice:

"We find the prisoner at the bar guilty of willful murder."

Silliman hears the verdict without flinching. Then the judge tells him, in a solemn voice, to stand up, and asks him if he has anything to say why sentence of death should not be passed upon him. Silliman remains silent for a moment, his lips set tight; but notwithstanding the compression, the corners of the mouth twitch nervously, and his eyes wander wistfully about. Murderer of my poor Louis, as I firmly believe him to be, I cannot help pitying the wretch, as friendless and alone he stands there, striving to appear self-possessed and indifferent, in the face of the most terrible doom that can come upon man on earth. At length his lips move, his fingers clutch at the dock-railing in front of him, and he says hoarsely:

"No; I have nothing to say. That is, I have no reason to advance why the law should not now take its course. On the contrary, I acknowledge the justice of the verdict. But I do not wish any one who hears me now, to imagine that I am impelled to make this admission by any such maudlin stuff and nonsense as qualms of conscience. I have been playing a desperate game, with all the odds against me; yet, while there remained the ghost of a chance for me, I didn't give up hope. But a **card** was played against me to-day that I was unprepared for—a card that I didn't think was out—that I didn't believe was in the pack, even, and then I knew the game was up. That card was Guy Egerton. Still I had one trump left, my counsel's speech. I played that, and good as it was, it couldn't overcome the odds against me. And now I wish to say here to my friend Mr. Toddy, for a friend he has indeed proved himself to me, that I thank him sincerely for the very able defense he has made to-day in my behalf, and that I hope he will not think too hardly of me for deceiving him as I have from the beginning. My only excuse for doing so must be, my fear that he would throw up my case if I told him the truth; at all events, I thought he would make a stronger defense if he believed me to be **innocent.** I couldn't afford, with my life at stake, you see, to take the chances on such a vital point. But now, finding myself as I do, without a **trump** left in my hand, what can I do but throw down my cards and give up the game like a man? I did kill Louis Dunraven. I confess it. **What** my motive was, has been but partially indicated by the evidence. I had deeper and greater reasons for hating him **than** any one living knows. What those reasons were, I do not choose to state, nor is it necessary. Suffice it to say, that I hated him with a deadly, insatiable hatred.

"That day, eighteen years ago, I knew that he and young Guy Egerton were going to shoot over the Tufnell place. I lay in wait for them, and watched their movements. When they separated, I followed Dunraven stealthily. Three or four times before then I was on the point of shooting him from behind a tree, but each time something prevented. At length, as I said, they separated. I dogged him, and creeping noiselessly upon him from behind to within three or four yards, just as he was stooping to pick up a bird he had shot, I took deliberate aim under his right shoulder-blade, and fired. He straightened up, and then throwing up his arms, with a sharp cry fell backward among the tangled grass. I stood ready to give him the second barrel, if he showed any decided signs of life; but he only gave a sort of spasmodic quiver, and then straightened out and lay quite still. I stood watching him for nearly half an hour, and then ventured up and felt for his heart. It had ceased to beat: he was dead. I didn't stay long there after that, but started to go home. I had got some distance away when I discovered that I had left my gun beside the body and had picked up the other one in place of it when I came away. I hurried back to remedy my blunder, but what was my chagrin to find the boy Guy bending over his friend's body. My first impulse was to kill him, too. I wish to heaven now that I had! My gun was up to my shoulder and my finger pressing the trigger, when the thought of accusing him of the crime suggested itself to me, like a flash. Like a fool—as to-day has been proved—I acted on the second thought and let the boy live. All that took place after that has been truth-fully detailed by Guy Egerton. I will not waste time in repeating it.

I will state, however, that in the excitement of finding the boy there and getting him away in accordance with my plan, I forgot the object of my return, and carried away Dunraven's gun a second time. So I gave it to the boy, knowing that if by any chance he should be found hiding away under the hedge with it in his posses-sion, it would be almost proof positive of his guilt. My great mis-take—next to not shooting him when I found him at the body—was not to have informed on him while he lay under the hedge. While I live—not very long that will be now, by-the-bye—those mistakes will be a constant source of unavailing regret. My own gun I was forced to sacrifice. I couldn't go back a second time for it—fearing to be seen about there so much; but, as it luckily hadn't my name on it, its presence there wouldn't implicate me, I thought. In any event I could have coined some story about its being stolen, now that I had provided myself with a scapegoat. But I never felt quite secure till the boy was gone, and sailing safely away on the high seas. Shortly after this I lost my wife, and then I determined to act on the advice Dunraven had given me, and leave Bratton. The people in the neighborhood, had begun—thanks to his tattling tongue—to give me the cold shoulder. Not that they had ever been much the other way to me—the good people of Bratton are not given to opening their arms very wide to strangers, as a rule—still there was a difference, slight though it was. That didn't trouble me much, however, but I had got tired of the pokey, drowsy place, which I had only consented to come to and live in to please my wife. So, once she was gone, I decided to throw up my lease, sell everything, and cut the place for good. Where I went, or my doings afterwards, has, of course, nothing to do with the present matter; nor have I any desire to inflict upon any one a history of my life. This, I believe, is about all I have to say—not why sen-tence should not—but why it *should* be passed upon me. I am ready."

It has grown quite dark whilst the wretched man has been speak-ing, and there is a pause after he gets through while the lights are lit. Nothing now remains to be done but the passing of the death sentence. This scene we are none of us anxious to witness, and as the judge is putting on the awful black cap, our party rises and leaves the gallery. Guy, who has been waiting below since he left the witness-box, makes his way to his mother's side, and leaning upon his arm she goes out. Lady Amtenhurst with Sir Griffith, Lord Amtenhurst with me, and Florence with Mr. Tufnell follow after, Mr. Strutt, in solitary state, bringing up the rear.

At the door our carriages are waiting, and in a few minutes we are whirling toward home; the Amtenhursts and Strutt in one carriage, the Egertons and myself in the other, and Tufnell in his dog-cart. The carriage-door is scarcely shut when Lady Egerton turns to her son who sits beside her, and putting her arms about his neck—she, the cold and stately—falls sobbing on his shoulder. Who can guess the depths of feeling in every human heart, till the hand of fate unseals their fountains! Her maternal affections have been touched and she is no longer the self-possessed, self-contained woman, but the loving, happy mother; and feelings long dormant are aroused and spring into renewed life and strength, as she clasps her only child to her heart. Guy puts his strong arm around her and bends his manly head to murmur caressing words of filial love. It is a touching sight, and Sir Griffith, folding his arms and throwing back his head, whistles a bar or two of "The Fine Old English Gentleman," very *allegro* and *pianissimo*, to hide his emotion. I have not yet exchanged a word with Guy, but this is no time for it. He smiles at me and that is enough.

We drive rapidly and soon reach home. We have all alighted when the other carriage drives up. Lord Amtenhurst helps out his wife and Guy goes forward to Florence's assistance. She does not take his outstretched hand, and avoiding his eye, springs out. But her dress catches on the step and she falls forward into his arms. Quickly she recovers her balance, and without a word, her face white, and lips compressed, rushes up the steps into the house, and on to her own room. Guy looks after her with a puzzled expression, and we slowly mount the steps, enter the grand old hall, and almost immediately separate to make some slight preparation for our late dinner.

CHAPTER V.

"And will ye pardon then (replied the youth)
Your Waldegrave's feigned name and false attire?
I durst not in the neighborhood, in truth,
The very fortunes of your house inquire;
Lest one that knew me might some tidings dire
Impart."

— "Gertrude of Wyoming."

IN the west drawing-room at Bratton Hall we are enjoying a quiet hour after the fatigue and wonder of the day. The gentlemen having lingered but a short time over their wine and cigars from kind consideration for our desire to have Guy amongst us, Sir Griffith now sits there by the centre-table making out a list of guests for the grand dinner to be given next week in honor of his son's return, and discussing with Jolliffe Tufnell the advisability of omitting this one as "stupid" and asking that one as "good company," in order that there may be an element of hilarity, yet none be left out who may resent the indignity. Poor man! he finds the task a Herculean labor, and bites his pencil in disturbance of mind, while Tufnell vainly tries to lessen the difficulty by proposing all sort of impossible people. With the exception of Miss Courtenay, who sits apart listlessly turning over the leaves of a book to show her utter want of interest in the conversation, the rest of us form a group with Guy the centre of attraction. He sits by his mother who reclines upon a sofa; Florence in silence plies her crochet needle, the only industrious one of us all, except as regards the asking of questions; and we demand from Guy a more satisfactory account of his life and adventures than we were able to glean from his recital at the trial to-day.

"You must tell us all about your life in America," says Lady Egerton; "and how you lived and made your way in the world."

"I will," Guy answers; "but I'm afraid you'll be disappointed to find my story very commonplace after the one great event of my life. You know already how Silliman got me the place on the ship, as cabin-boy. The vessel carried one passenger, an elderly American gentleman named Clinton, who was making the return voyage to New York by long sea for the benefit of his health. In the position I occupied I was enabled to render him some trifling services which pleased him, and for want of better employment he would talk to me, and ask me questions, and we grew to be great friends. He called me a very gentlemanlike little cabin-boy and asked many questions about myself. My mind revolted at the thought of telling him untruths, so I said to him frankly that I could answer no questions, that all I was at liberty to tell him was, that I had been sent away from home by a kind friend who had found me my situation on board, and that I was going to seek my fortune in America."

"Did you really think you would be hanged?" interrupts Lady Egerton.

"I did, mother mine; I was only eleven, remember, and not very learned in the law. Mr. Clinton did not at first seem quite pleased at my reticence, but he afterwards told me he had taken a strange fancy to me, and when we were approaching New York he asked me if I would like to be an errand-boy in his office. I was only too delighted, as you may imagine, and jumped at his kind offer."

"Where did you find the name you adopted?" asks Lady Amtenhurst.

"Alva Ingoldsby? I found it in the London directory," Guy answers, laughing. "I came across it when I was a very small boy and it hit my fancy, so when I was at a loss for a name it was the first I thought of, and I adopted it."

There is a general laugh at this, and Sir Griffith calls out:

"Telling them where you got your name, Guy? Take care how you spread the report, or you may have a law suit on your hands with a thousand pounds damages. I say, Tufnell, old Meredith won't do," referring to his list; "deaf as a post."

Tufnell's answer is unheard, as Guy continues:

"Mr. Clinton was a lawyer, and I was soon installed in his office in New York. When he had proved my trustworthiness, and I had grown old enough, he advanced me to the position of clerk. My life was very happy, for he treated me as a son. He had no children—was an old bachelor, in fact, and as I showed a taste for law as I grew older, he allowed me a good deal of time to study, advising me to adopt the bar as a profession."

"But why did you never write home in all this time?" I inquire.

"I did. I wrote to my father, telling him everything, and inclosed my letter to Silliman asking him to give it to him. I might have known, of course, if I hadn't been so young, and had reflected a moment, that he would never deliver it, fearing it might implicate him in some way with my escape. But the worst of it was the fellow deceived me by writing me back word that my father was incensed at me beyond any hope of forgiveness; that he had now a daughter in place of me whom he disowned, and fully believed to be guilty; and he advised me if I wished to keep my neck out of a halter, to keep quiet, and by no means to tell my secret to any one."

"The wretch!" cries Lady Egerton.

"I never for a moment suspected then that Silliman was deceiving me, and kept silent for a year. Then I determined to write to my father direct, but in order not to implicate Silliman, I avoided all mention of his name, merely saying that a friend had assisted me in getting away. But fate seemed against me. This letter miscarried, for my father never received it, as I afterwards found, and I then thought that his silence meant everything that Silliman had said, beyond a doubt, and I abandoned all hope of a reconciliation."

"But did you not very soon discover that, even if guilty, you were too young to be hanged?" asks Lord Amtenhurst. "From your law reading, I mean."

"I am not so sure as to that, your lordship," Guy answers, with a smile. "I remember coming across some cases in Blackstone one day where children under twelve were executed for murder, and that rather gave me a cold chill. As you may imagine, I read everything that bore upon the subject with immense interest, and I found that the law conclusively presumes children under seven to be incapable of crime, but between that age and fourteen they are only *prima facie* incapable, and evidence will be received to show a discretion to discern between good and evil. Thus in one of the cases I have mentioned, a boy of ten hid himself after the murder—my case, you see—and that was deemed to show a guilty knowledge, and he was hanged."

"That is the case of *Rex* v. *Hodges*," says Mr. Strutt, grasping eagerly at this semblance of "shop" in the conversation, to break his long silence. "It's an extreme case, a very extreme case; and Blackstone only cites it to show to what lengths courts will sometimes go. If I didn't know that the case was reported in Plowden a century before his time, I would think it had been tried before Jefferies, from its barbarity."

'Good gracious me!' cried Miss Courtenay from her distant seat, stopping the leaf-turning process a moment to smother a yawn, "Haven't you people had enough of law and murders and hangings to-day, without wanting a repetition?"

"As I grew older, I began to suspect Silliman," Guy continued, going back to his story and silencing Strutt, who, with a deprecating glance at Miss Courtenay for her cruel remonstrance, returns to the twirling of his thumbs over one another, as he silently contemplates the fire. "I began to suspect his motives in aiding my escape, and as I came to weigh all the circumstances of his connection with the affair, as my mind matured and was aided by the books I read, I had no doubt that he was the real murderer. How I longed to return and confront him with the accusation! but I had not the means. My kind friend, Mr. Clinton, who was very well off, at first gave me a home and clothed and fed me for my services. After a year or two he paid me a small salary, increasing it each year; and I saved my money with the intention of coming to England and asserting my innocence. Unfortunately I was tempted to speculate—everybody speculates in America—hoping to double my small fund, I risked my savings upon some fluctuating bubble of Wall street, and, as a matter of course, lost every penny. My patron, on the contrary, by investing largely in California mining stocks, made a fabulous fortune, as did also his only brother."

"Why didn't you tell your patron your secret?" I ask, "and borrow money from him to take you home?"

"Why do you always anticipate my actions?" Guy replies, laughing: "I told him the whole story. He said at once that Silliman was the guilty party, and the only way to clear myself was by his conviction. It would never do, he said, for me to accuse him openly, till I had conclusive proof of his guilt; and his advice was, for me to go home quietly, under an assumed name, and see what evidence could be got together against him; for if I were at once to acknowledge myself, he would take alarm and get beyond the reach of justice. We little knew he had left England and was in America, but where, thanks to the treaty of extradition, he was still within reach. My good friend furnished me with all the money I needed, and I was to have sailed in the next Cunard steamer for Liverpool; but he was taken suddenly ill, and I could not leave him. His illness was a long and serious one, and it left him a weak, aged man, liable to go off at any moment. One day he called me to him and said: 'Do you know that you have grown into my heart, boy? A son could not be more dear to me. You are very young, and have many years before you. I am going fast. Will you not delay a little longer vindicating yourself, and remain with me the short time I have to live?' I could not refuse: I loved the old man who had done so much for me. I postponed my return and stayed with him, doing all I could to make his last days happy. I think I succeeded, and it gives me pleasure to remember his satisfaction in having me near him. Three years and a half ago he died, and I then learned for the first time that I was his heir. He had added one more to the innumerable benefits he had heaped upon me; and I could accept his bounty without compunction, for his only relatives, a brother and a niece, were as wealthy as himself. Do you know, I felt his loss as keenly as though he had been a blood relation." Guy pauses, and the hiatus is filled up by Sir Griffith:

"Must ask such a prominent man? But think what it entails! A sour old maid of a daughter, a grumpy sister-in-law, and a wife like a — like —"

"Beer-vat," suggests Tufnell.

"A wife like a beer-vat," repeats Sir Griffith. "'I thank thee, Jew, for teaching me that word.' 'So much for Buckingham!'" and he draws the pencil through the inelegible name.

Glancing with a smile over his shoulder at his father, Guy goes on:—

"When all my affairs were settled up, I bid good-by to old friends, James Clinton and his daughter Florence among the oldest and best, sailed for England—'The home of my boyhood, my own native land!' and here I am—cleared and reinstated."

"Florence—Florence Clinton—where have I heard that name?" Miss Courtenay questions herself in an undertone, as she closes her book, and looks back dreamily into illimitable space. "Oh, Mr. Egerton!" she exclaims, starting up and coming forward with a suddenly-acquired interest in her tone—an interest I am uncharitable enough to believe to be coexistent with her knowledge of the manner of disposition of Mr. Clinton's fabulous fortune.

"Oh, Mr. Egerton! Don't you remember that you arrived in Rome the day before we left; that terribly stormy day? We met you in the evening, and you said that some friends of yours were staying at the hotel, whom you had come to see all the way from England. They were the same people whom you met in America, were they not? Their name was Clinton."

"Yes. They were the same," Guy answered. "James Clinton, and his daughter Florence."

"And do you know what has become of them? I felt so terribly for the poor, dear girl. I hope her poor father has recovered; he was so very ill, you remember."

"He died there—in Rome—a few days after you left."

"And Florence, the poor child," with a look of breathless agonized interest, "left all alone!"

"Not quite alone," Guy says quietly. "Some American friends, who chanced to be passing through Rome on their way home, took charge of her, and she returned to New York with them."

Miss Courtenay, with a host of reserve questions, makes a mistake in pausing to wipe away a tear; before she can ask another, Lady Egerton, who has been waiting for an opportunity to speak, says:

"Do you remember, Guy, how slyly your father introduced you to me as a young lawyer from America? The wretch dared to introduce my own son to me as a stranger!"

"'Excellent wretch,' madame," calls out Sir Griffith. "Omit not the all-important prefix."

"Did you tell Sir Griffith everything at once?" I ask Guy.

"Yes. And he received me as the good father that he is. He also, as you heard at the trial to-day, had had his suspicions of Silliman awakened by Mr. Tufnell, who, at the time, was busily employed in hunting up witnesses, and seeking a clue to the whereabouts of Silliman, of whom they had lost track. I had brought, among others, a letter of introduction from Mr. Clinton to a friend of his, a Mr. Parkins, a London solicitor. This Mr. Parkins was Lord Amtenhurst's lawyer, and—strange coincidence—had been engaged in tracing this very Silliman for his lordship, though from other motives than ours. From him we learned four months ago, that Silliman was in California. Mr. Tufnell's solicitors at once wrote out to the police authorities at San Francisco, and ascertained that he was still there, and from the description, was the identical man we were after. We immediately had proceedings taken under the extradition treaty; or—the rest you know."

"When you found that Silliman was no longer in England," I remark, "and had got together such a strong case against him, why on earth didn't you come forward at once and acknowledge yourself to the world, instead of keeping us so much longer in ignorance?"

"You must blame Sir Griffith for that," Guy answers, with a sly look over at his father. "I was only too anxious to throw off my disguise, but he wanted to give you all a great surprise, in regular dramatic fashion."

"You might at least have trusted your own mother," Lady Egerton says, in a tone of reproach.

"Yes; but not his own mother's tongue," shouts Sir Griffith across the room—

> "'Trust not a woman, not e'en a mother,
>   With aught in your heart you hold secret.
> Men, if you must trust, trust one another,
>   And the act you will never regret.'"

"Heretic!" laughs Lady Amtenhurst. "Don't you think a mother's anxiety for the welfare of her child—"

"Would have spoiled everything?" interrupts Sir Griffith. "Of course it would. A woman's love rules her judgment; and if that wife of mine had chanced to think she saw a quicker way out of our snarl, woe to our schemes. I'll invite young Caryll, Tufnell, instead of that nonentity Maitland," and he becomes once more absorbed in his list.

There is a pause in the conversation, and Guy, turning to Florence, asks her:

"Why so silent, Lady Florence?"

Without raising her eyes from her work, she answers:

"My attention has been occupied by my work—seven, eight," counting her stitches.

"That remark is not very complimentary to Mr. Egerton, Florence," says Miss Courtenay, looming up again in full force. "He has been telling us of his life in America."

"Yes? Three, four."

"Oh, you are enough to provoke a saint! You're as bad as a child learning the piano, with your ' one, two, three, four—one, two, three, four.' Come, Mr. Egerton," putting her arm through his, " let us leave this tiresome creature to her loops and chains. Come and talk to me. You'll find *me* an appreciative listener. I want you to tell me what sort of girls the American girls are, and if they are not shocking flirts," and she leads Guy away, an unwilling victim, his face cannot conceal, to a sofa in a distant bay window. As they move away, Guy glances round at Florence, and from her eyes flashes back at him a look strangely scornful. The reason for it he appears as much at a loss to understand as am I.

"What is the matter with you, child?" asks Lady Egerton. "You and Guy seem to be far less friends than of old, and you should be now like brother and sister. You were once my daughter, he is now my son."

Florence does not answer, but bends over her work.

I feel inclined for the moment to quote Betsy Trotwood, and exclaim:

"Blind, blind, blind!"

CHAPTER VI.

Last scene of all,
That ends this strange eventful history.
— As You Like It: Act II, Scene 7.

'TIS Florence Courtenay's last day at Bratton Hall. To-morrow, the only tie which still seems to bind her to us—her presence at her old home—will be broken, and after a brief fortnight's reunion, she is to leave us for good and all. She and Guy are still at odds, obstinately, inexplicably, and all hope seems over of the wedding which I had thought would have prevented, for some time, if not for aye, the settling back of the old

Hall into its wonted state of humdrum quietude. Mr. Strutt left
us the day after the trial to rescue his clients from the wizened
clutches of his clerk Wiggins. Mr. Tufnell, too, has returned to
his ancestral halls, despite our efforts to detain him longer; but we
see him every day, and this morning he is to join a riding party we
have planned to some Druidical ruins recently unearthed by some
wandering members of the archæological society, in our neighborhood.

The appointed hour for starting has come and gone ten minutes
ago, and we stand on the terrace awaiting the arrival of, as Guy remarks—" the late Mr. Tufnell."

"Oh, Tufnell, Tufnell! Wherefore art thou Tufnell?" says Sir
Griffith, in a mock sentimental tone. "I told him we should start
at eleven. I suppose we shall only have to give him another ten
minutes' grace," and he walks off with Lord Amtenhurst to the
horses which stand, impatiently pawing the gravel, under the shade
of a large oak.

"How I detest people who always require grace," cries Miss
Courtenay, pettishly, as habited and hatted she stands drawing on
her riding-gloves. "Why on earth can't people be punctual? *I*
make it a *rule* always to be so."

"Perhaps he misunderstood, and will join us at the ruins, instead
of here," says Lady Amtenhurst.

"I hardly think that possible," remarks Lady Egerton, "for I
heard Sir Griffith impressing it upon him that we were to leave here
together."

At this moment Guy, who has been having a look—as is his custom—at the saddle-girths of his own horse, and at those of one of
the side-saddles as well, comes leisurely back, just in time to pick
up Miss Courtenay's whip, which, by-the-bye, she seems to have
managed to drop at a very opportune moment.

"You must be my cavalier to-day, Mr. Egerton," she says, as he
hands the whip to her. "Sir Griffith I'm afraid of; Mr. Tufnell's
afraid of me, at least he acts as though he were—at all events he's
not here; and riding with one's uncle is just the merest trifle too
slow for even me; so, recollect, you belong to me to-day."

Good breeding forbids the direct refusal I know must be hover-
ing on his lips.

"I feel highly flattered, Miss Courtenay, especially as from your
own confession, your choice appears to partake much of the quality
of Hobson's; but I'm afraid I'm half engaged already," and he
glances toward the house from which Florence has not yet come
forth, with an evident desire in his eye to move on.

"Oh, my cousin don't want you;" Edith cries, laughingly. "She's such a queer, rum sort of a girl, as you men say; goes about with the old fogies, and avoids nice people like us—you and me. Button this, please," and she holds up her gloved hand to him. There are two things which some girls always seem to want: a glass of water, and to have their gloves buttoned, and I wonder to myself, as Guy, with flushed face, bends over the glove, seeming for the moment to find the button-hole too small or the button the reverse, if the fact has ever come under his observation.

"I'll get you out a hairpin, in a second," Miss Courtenay adds, with the very slightest upward movement of her free hand. "No? Oh, thanks, you have managed it at last. Why there's Florence, now, and without her habit."

Guy walks away, evidently annoyed at being caught at the glove-buttoning operation, and goes down the steps in quest of a flower for his button-hole, as he hurriedly informs Miss Courtenay.

"Where's your habit, dear?" Lady Amtenhurst asks, as Florence joins us.

"I've changed my mind; that is, I've determined, after a slight struggle, to sacrifice pleasure upon the altar of duty," Florence answers with a constrained smile. "If I go with you, Lady Egerton's tidy will not be finished before we leave to-morrow; if I stay, it will be done to-night, and I shall have the pleasure of pinning it, myself, upon her chair. So you see that self has a little, the least bit to do with it."

"What nonsense, child!" exclaims Lady Egerton. "You can take it home with you, and send it to me when its done."

"Or I'll help you with the finishing touches this afternoon when we return," suggests her mother. "Will not that do?"

"Thank you mamma, dear, but I would really prefer doing it all myself."

"Oh, let the little oddity have her own way, if she will," snaps out Edith Courtenay. "She'll only be a spoil sport, with her long face, if she comes. She enjoys solitude, and I sometimes think she's trying to get up a character for eccentricity. Next to sick people, odd ones are so interesting, you know."

Drawing Florence aside, I look into her face and say:

"Child, it's not the tidy; it's Guy."

Wistfully returning my gaze, she replies:

"Yes, Julia. He must not have a chance of speaking to me alone. I shall be happier, safer, here by myself, than with him. Don't *you* urge me to go," and to avoid further persuasion, she turns to meet her father who is approaching with Sir Griffith.

"Time's up!" shouts the baronet. "To horse! to horse! 'and witch the world with noble horsemanship.'"

The horses are led forward, but strange to say, I seem to have lost all interest in the excursion; so, when Lady Amtenhurst and **Lady Egerton have entered** their phæton, and the Earl comes forward to put me on my horse, I propose waiting for Mr. Tufnell and **riding after** them with him when he arrives. There is some demur to this proposition at first, but as I will be no great loss to the party, **it is at** last decided that I shall remain, and follow them in an hour with Mr. Tufnell, if he comes, but if he fails, alone, as I know the **road so well.**

Guy, who has been mounting Edith Courtenay, comes forward.

"**It** is unfortunate that **our small** party should be lessened by three. How can you be so cruel, Lady Florence, when you must know that each one taken **from** our number decreases our chances of enjoyment?"

"You will find my cousin Edith **a** host in herself, I haven't **a doubt**," she replies coldly, **and turns away to** rub the nose of her **father's horse.**

"Perhaps our good friend Tufnell is even now impersonating James's 'solitary horseman,' and groping his way among the ruins in search of us," remarks the Earl.

"**In** which case the sooner we go to his relief the better for him," says Sir Griffith, shaking his bridle-rein and leading the way down the avenue. The Earl, Edith, **and** Guy, follow at a brisk canter, Lady Egerton's ponies bringing up the rear, and Florence and I are left alone upon the terrace. When they are quite out of sight and hearing, I turn to her as she stands gazing after them, with her fingers tightly laced.

"Why do you wish to avoid Guy, Florence? Why do you treat **him so** coldly, and snub him so persistently?"

She flushes, and answers hotly:

"Because he deserves it. Don't tease me with questions, Julia, **for I** cannot answer them. You may be assured of one thing, I **never act without a reason.**"

Away she trips up the broad stone steps into the house, and on **up the stairs.** I turn to follow her, but as I do so, the sound of a **horse's hoofs on the gravel** reaches my ear. Thinking it is one of **the party** returning, I look back and see Jolliffe Tufnell riding up **the avenue at** a stretching gallop.

"Late, by Jove!" he exclaims as he draws up at the foot of the steps, and looks around. "Just my luck—I knew it," and out comes the red silk pocket-handkerchief to wipe his streaming face.

"Hello!" he shouts suddenly, springing off his horse, and, throwing the rein to one of the grooms, he strides over to me. "Miss Lifford—as I live! Why, I thought they had gone?"

"So they have," I answer, quietly. "I don't see how you could have avoided meeting them."

"I took a short cut across the fields, is the reason, I suppose. But how comes it you are not with them?"

"I waited for you—to show you the way," I say, laughing. "Just as if you didn't know every inch of the roads for miles around."

"Did I know this particular road never so well, I should run a greater chance of losing my way with Miss Lifford by my side, than were I alone," and a grin—nay more—a diabolical grin overspreads his features.

"Will you take the chances? Shall I order my horse?"

"Not just yet at all events. To tell you the truth, Miss Lifford, I am not very keen about investigating the ancient relics. I confess myself utterly indifferent as to what precise style or order of architecture the Druids regarded as the correct thing. I never did have a fancy for poking about ruins, and it's always been a sort of puzzle to me how any one could. At any rate we can go another day. So, with your kind permission, instead of your ordering your horse I will tell Robert to take 'Bluebeard' to the stable. The fact is, Miss Lifford," he continues, after giving directions to the groom about "sponging 'Bluebeard's' mouth out, and loosening the girths;" "I've been wanting to have a bit of confidential talk with you for some time past, and," with another grin of evident pleasure, "I'm uncommonly glad of this opportunity. Come, let us sit down here," dusting a stone seat near the balustrade with his pocket-handkerchief. "I've been looking for this, and hoping for it a long time," he begins, with another grin, as we seat ourselves. Then there is a pause, while he looks straight before him, and mops his face. Then he takes off his hat, and turning to me, puts both hands on his knees and says abruptly: "Miss Lifford, the fact is—I'm lonely —I want a wife." He stares at me through his spectacles, and my thoughts fly to Florence. He loves her, and wants my assistance, think I. He goes on: "Dunraven was a very dear friend of mine. I don't think it would be his wish that you should live a lonely life."

Me? Oh, I suppose he wants me to come and live with them after the wedding—a bait to catch my good will, ah, ha, Mr. Tufnell! You seem wonderfully sure of success, upon my word.

"We are too old for romantic ideas, you and I; and yet, I'd not make half a bad husband. I'm sure you'd make a capital wife."

16

Me, again? Puzzled, I sit silent, **and** as the truth begins to faintly dawn upon me, he says in a strangely husky voice:

"Will you marry me, Miss Lifford—Julia, I mean?"

I am amazed, confused; I can't speak. And yet, now that it has come, it does not **seem** so strange—so unexpected. What shall I say? I really believe I like the man more than I thought, with all his odd ways. He waits patiently for my answer, seeming quite confident as to what it will be. That nettles me; but when he gently takes my hand the feeling of irritation quickly melts away, and I let him keep it. At last he murmurs something about "silence" and "consent." I blush like a girl, and the impudent creature takes advantage of my confusion and—and—kisses me.

As I sit here in the soft summer **air, in** this familiar spot, with an accepted lover by my side—the **place** which once **was** Louis Dunraven's—and gaze off over the old gray balustrade of the terrace into the long and beautiful vistas of park and woodland extending as far as the eye can reach, I can imagine that the dead past has come back again—that the days of my girlhood are returned.

As Louis' friend, the man beside me is more to me than any other man can ever be. I tell him so, and he is delighted.

Again the tramp of horses' feet sound on the gravel below, and a horseman appears through the trees coming slowly up the avenue.

"By Jove! It's Egerton—Guy, I mean," Jolliffe says, **jumping up.**

"Can anything have happened?" I ask, anxiously.

"Nothing worse than that his horse is dead lame, my dear. Must have picked up a nail or something. What awfully hard lines on the poor fellow! to have to leave her that way."

My mind at rest as to Guy's return, which I, who know the situation, do not regard as such "awfully hard lines" on the poor fellow, and without waiting to enlighten my companion as to the true state of affairs, I beat a hasty retreat into the house before Guy can see me, and take refuge in Lady Egerton's boudoir. Instinctively I move towards a mirror and survey my reflected face and form, it must be confessed, with something of complacency. I am not so very old, only six-and-thirty, and the face I see there might easily be plainer. 'Tis not so fresh a face, perhaps, as it has been, but it bears the stamp of serene, self-controlling, mature womanhood, which is, after all, more to be prized than the wavering lights of unformed, pink and white girlhood. This arrangement of my hair is decidedly becoming, and how wonderfully a well made, well fitting habit sets off one's figure. A woman always—if she looks at all—looks her best in a riding-habit, so I've been told; and I really believe it's true. I shouldn't be surprised if Mr. Tufnell—Jolliffe, I mean—thought so too. Men are such strange creatures. Or, perhaps, it was my voice that won him. I don't sing badly; that is *very* badly; as well as most English women, at all events. But that's not saying much, I'm afraid. It can't be my fortune that he's after. He's too well off himself to think of that, and too honest as well, I'm sure. Oh, no, it's only for myself that he likes me; and really, I'm not such a bad bargain for Mr. Jolliffe Tufnell, after all. Nor is he for me, for that matter. He's not so awfully ugly, and one doesn't notice his awkwardness half so much when one gets accustomed to it. It will make a vast improvement in his appearance when I persuade him to discard those horrid spectacles. I must get him to give up red silk pocket-handkerchiefs, too. He'll do it for me, I know; he's such a kind-hearted fellow. Knocklofty Hall is a nice cosy old place, and we shall get on famously together, I haven't a doubt. Knocklofty Hall—what a name! It's such a pity that both master and home should have such dreadful names. Mrs. Jolliffe Tufnell, Knocklofty Hall. Not so utterly bad—a trifle odd, no more. Julia Tufnell! How strangely it sounds. Heigho! Poor Florence; I wish she would make it up with Guy—for he loves her, I know—and be happy; as happy as I am. We might then have a double wedding, and cheer up the old place in good earnest. Hark! There are voices in the next room and I mustn't be caught before the glass.

The heavy damask curtains that divide Lady Egerton's boudoir from the room adjoining are down. I peep between them and see Florence and Guy, he with his hand on the back of a chair from which she has evidently just risen.

"We had got but a short distance beyond the avenue gates," he is saying, "when my horse stepped on a loose stone or something, stumbled and strained a tendon of a fore leg. He was too lame to think of going on, so there was nothing to do but return for another horse, and I've been ever since getting back."

"I should advise you, then, not to waste any more time, if you hope to rejoin your companions."

"I am in no hurry to get back to them, I assure you. The truth is, I was only too glad of the excuse to get away and return here, because—"

"Dear me, I've left all my rose-colored worsted up-stairs. Excuse me, Mr. Egerton."

She is passing him to leave the room, when he steps before her.

"Will you not allow me a few minutes' conversation, Lady Florence? Will you not tell me what it is that I have done to make you treat me as you do?"

"I shall never have this tidy done in time if you insist on delaying me," she answers evasively. "You must really excuse me, Mr. Egerton. Allow me to pass, please."

As she attempts to pass him, Guy puts his hand lightly on her arm, but she shakes it off, angrily. Then he raises his head proudly, and placing his hand on the door-handle, says with determination: "Then I demand as a right what you refuse as a favor. I love you, Florence," and his voice softens; "I love you, and your cruel treatment of me pains me deeply."

She turns from him with a gesture of impatience, and crosses the room. He follows her.

"Nay, turn not from me so, for the time has come when I must speak, and you must listen."

"*Must*, sir?"

"Yes, Florence, must. I must know from your own lips, now—here in this room, what your real feelings towards me are. If you dislike me, tell me so honestly in words. Your actions ought to tell me that, perhaps you'll think. They ought indeed, heaven knows. But actions, even the most severe and cruel, one who loves and hopes is but too apt—too prone to misconstrue. If you hate me, despise me, as your manner of late would seem to imply, tell me so, that I deceive myself no longer; that I may strive to learn to love you less; that I may give up all hope of you at once and forever. If you like me, Florence—dare I use the stronger word?"

Save an angry flush that mounts to her temples, and then dies away leaving her as white as marble, and a haughty curling of the lip as her breath comes and goes fitfully, no answer comes to poor, pleading Guy.

"No? Then, if you even merely like, do not actually dislike me, let this misunderstanding be explained, and—"

Florence turns towards him quickly, but though her eyes still flash, there are tears in them, and the scornful lip trembles as she speaks:

"This is not a question of likes and dislikes, but one which involves your honor—your claim to the title of gentleman. You force from me terms which I never intended should pass my lips, but which are justified by actions of yours in the past that are indelibly stamped upon my mind. Guy Egerton, you are unmanly, dishonorable, disloyal. You have done that which I never believed it possible for you to do— which I would not, could not have believed if I had not heard from your own lips the words which proved it to me. If what I say is not sufficiently plain, your own conscience can supply you with a clue. My visit here, my stay under the same

roof with you, has been made, believe me, much against **my** wish.
In obedience to duty **I yielded** to the wishes of others and consented to come. But in doing so I trusted, nay, I had the right to
expect that while I remained, good **taste—a** common regard for the
simple proprieties of life—would forbid your thrusting your presence
upon me, would shield **me** from annoyance **from** you by word or
look. In this, I regret, I was mistaken. **You do** not even try to
throw the cloak of **a gentleman** over your imperfections. **I** will not
be detained longer in this room. Let me pass!"

Guy has stood looking at her **in** utter bewilderment **while she has**
gradually been working herself into a passion, but **now he folds** his
arms, and still standing between her **and** the door, says resolutely:

"**My manhood will not permit me to rest quietly under such ac-**
cusations. I feel in my heart, where you would have me seek for a
clue, that I am guiltless of these **charges you make** against me; **and**
I demand as a right that you give them **some** definite shape, that **I**
may at least have the chance of disproving them."

Through all her indignation, something of admiration for the man
before her shows plainly in Florence's face; but trying to hide it
she turns **her face** aside.

"**You** are thrice unmanly **to** ask me this, knowing, as you must
in any event, how difficult is the **task** you would thus put upon me."

"I am sorry," he says, kindly but firmly. "But so it must be.
Your **own** sense of right must see the justice **of** what I ask."

She hesitates, her color comes and goes, there is a tremulous bit-
ing **of the lower** lip, and a rapid tapping **of** one foot upon the floor
as she seems struggling with herself.

"Then be it as you **say**," she says in more subdued tones, though
the hoarseness of passion still lingers in her voice; "though I **can-**
not, unless the evidence of my senses **is not** to be relied upon, but
believe that you are now fully cognizant **of** everything of which you
plead ignorance. **However disagreable the** recital may be, recollect
you have forced **me** to it. **When you first came to Bratton you** saw
me as the adopted **daughter of Sir Griffith (you must of** course
have known that I **was not your sister),** but when you learned how
low was my birth, when you thought me the child of a murderer,
you found it impossible to marry me. Love was insufficient to
smooth the obstacles in our path—what was love, indeed, when
weighed **in the** balance with wealth and pedigree? A chimera! the
delusion of some poor half-starved wretch in a garret! I quote your
very words, Mr. Egerton, the words I heard you address to Sir
Griffith, my faith in man fading away as I listened."

Guy's expression of face shows that **he** recollects them, but there

is no sign or semblance of shame in his looks **as he attempts to**
speak. Florence holds up her hand. "**Let me finish.** Don't
think that I blame **you** for giving utterance **to** these sentiments.
You were perfectly right not to wish to lower yourself in the world's
estimation. It is for your conduct since then, and now, that I feel
resentment, not for what you said **then.** I am another being **now.**
I am no longer of obscure birth and parentage—there are **no** longer
any obstacles for impotent love **to** overcome, and love steps **man-**
fully forward and tries to win an Earl's daughter. You will pardon
me, Mr. Egerton, if **I** justly feel **no better** suited to you now, **not**
having changed in myself, even though placed upon a loftier social
pedestal. You must judge me by your own standard if you think I
could have altered so quickly."

As she finishes speaking, she stands for a moment regarding him
with eyes that look the scorn and contempt her sarcastic **words**
have but partially veiled. Then, with a sudden revulsion, **a** sad,
half-relenting expression comes into them, and reaching backward
for a chair, she sinks into it and covers her face with her hands.

Guy moves slowly to her side with arms still folded.

"**This is a grave** offense, Florence, that you charge me with," he
says, and though his tone is serious, if Florence would but look up
she might detect, as I think **I can,** a smile lurking about the corners of his mouth: "a very grave offense. But I hardly think I ought
to blame you for forming so poor an opinion of me; for after the
words you say you heard me utter, my conduct, I will confess, must
have seemed to you most reprehensible, and **I** no longer wonder
at the treatment you have bestowed upon me. Still, I think
you might have afforded me the opportunity of righting myself in
your eyes—unsusceptible of explanation as my words may have
seemed. To this, at least, was I entitled at your hands. Thanks,
however, to my own persistence, which you are pleased to regard
as ungentlemanly intrusiveness, I am now at last afforded that opportunity, and happily I can explain everything; and, I am satisfied
can convince you of my sincerity from first **to last. The** words
you have quoted as mine were used by me in a conversation I had
with Sir Griffith, as we walked together in one of the upper corridors, one night, **a few** days after you took your flight, or rather
secreted yourself in the house. I remember them perfectly. At
the time they were spoken, Sir Griffith and I were both aware—
mark me—*both* aware of the fact that you were the daughter of the
Earl of Amtenhurst."

Florence starts perceptibly; her hands fall from her face into her
lap, and her fingers play nervously with her worsted, as she sits
with eyes bent upon the floor.

" Your father's solicitor, Mr. Parkins," Guy continues, "whom I knew, and who knew me to be Guy Egerton, wrote to me to break the news of your being Lord Amtenhurst's child to Sir Griffith— knowing the unwelcome tidings would be a severe blow to the old gentleman, and believing me the fittest person upon whom that duty should devolve. Parkins's letter arrived the very morning you were first missed, and it was after I had broken to my father in the library what to him was the sad intelligence of your real parentage that we sent for you to inform you of it, and discovered then, for the first time, that you had gone. All of this, if you doubt me, Sir Griffith can corroborate. Until then I had thought you the child of the man we had been hunting to his death, and as such—" He pauses and Florence murmurs:

" As such, you in charity asked me to be your wife."

" Not so, Florence, I loved you then, as I do now. You are unjust. I was going to say, that as such was the case, it had long been a matter of serious doubt with us, whether we ought to take measures for the man's apprehension when his whereabouts should be ascertained. And need I tell you that rather than you should suffer for the crime of your supposed father, I had determined to let the foul stain that had rested so long upon the name of Guy Egerton, rest there forever; I would have given up my inheritance, and remained Alva Ingolsby for all time. This sacrifice I was prepared to make for your sake, Florence, and would have made, had your true birth not been discovered. It was because I saw you carried beyond my reach that I spoke as I did that night, and used the words you have repeated. I was hurt, disappointed. Though the necessity for any sacrifice on my part no longer existed, and I was now free to regain my true position in society, I knew that until that position was regained with an unsullied, untarnished name, a result it seemed then doubtful when I should succeed in accomplishing, I must banish all thoughts of you from my heart. As Alva Ingolsby, I could never hope to win the hand of an earl's only daughter."

There is silence for a moment, and then Florence rises slowly from her chair, and without looking at Guy, holds out her trembling hands to him.

" Forgive me. I have wronged you, wronged you deeply, and I am sorry."

" Forgive you?" and with a happy smile, he is putting his arms about her, when she steps quickly back.

" Mr. Egerton! You forget yourself. There is another Florence—Florence Clinton."

Guy looks puzzled for an instant, and then the truth seems to flash upon him.

" I beg your pardon," he says coolly; "there is no such person as Florence Clinton, that I am aware of."

Florence raises her eyes for the first time and looks at him in mute wonder.

" There was, once upon a time," he continues, with a quizzical smile, " but she is Florence Arnold now. I have the letter here," touching his breast-pocket, " telling me of her marriage."

" From her?" suspiciously.

"No; from her husband."

"And you never loved her?"

" Never. Were you jealous?"

With downcast eyes and blushing face she murmurs, softly, " Yes."

Guy stands motionless, enjoying her embarrassment, for she knows not what to say —what to do. She looks up shyly, at last, with a pretty, tremulous smile of mingled consciousness and joy, and then he takes her in his arms, and all past misunderstandings are forgiven and forgotten as he presses her to his heart.

Presently he leads her to a sofa and drawing her to his side they talk with lowered voices.

" My own darling, mine at last; mine whom I have loved and waited for so long," he says, imprisoning one little hand. " You don't know how many times your cold and cutting manner has hurt me of late, darling. I could not make out what it was that I had done, and I would have thought you had learned to love another had it not been for one little thing. You won't think me very conceited if I tell you, will you? Quite sure? Do you remember that night at Avington when you had sprained your ankle? You were dreadfully unkind to me that night."

" Yes? And were you not cold and distant too?"

" If I was, it was because I had made a vow to myself not to betray my feelings till I had regained my own name and station, and become more your equal in the eyes of the world; and I found it no easy task to hide what I felt. Your conduct was inexplicable to me, and it pained me more than I can express. I asked your cousin to sing the words dearest to my heart, and as I listened and was carried back to the long-ago, I chanced to catch *somebody* looking at me with an expression which my vanity construed as favorable to my wishes. That look has kept me ever since from despairing."

Florence blushes and looks down.

"I was thinking of Florence Clinton that night," she says. Oh, Guy, you do not know—you can never know all that I felt as I too listened to the words of Edith's song. You are a man, and cannot understand the workings of a woman's mind, or all the ins and outs of her character—they often puzzle even herself."

"I doubt if it would give a woman as much happiness to be understood as it affords her pleasure to think that no else can understand her."

"And I doubt," Florence replies archly, "if a man's perfect knowledge of his own character gives him half so much gratification as it gives a woman to puzzle over hers."

"And I again doubt," laughs Guy, "if even a man's just appreciation of his own virtues is half so gratifying as when he vainly supposes a woman's character is clear to his comprehension. But tell me, dearest; how did you hear about this other young woman—Florence Clinton? From your cousin Edith?"

"That rainy day, when you met her in the Via Condotti, in Rome, I was seeking refuge under the same shelter. It was when I was playing lady's maid, you know."

"What! were you the woman whom we thought must have been taken with a sudden fit of madness, to go forth from her snug retreat without apparent reason, into the driving storm?"

"I suppose so. I heard you whisper something, and I fled."

"Whisper something?" he repeats meditatively. "Ah, I remember, now. The poor girl was in low spirits, at the thought of losing her father, and I reminded her that she still had Philip Arnold, even though he was far away in New York. She had written to me when her father grew worse, as the only friend near at hand to come to her aid, that she should not be left alone in a strange place. After her father's death we found some American friends of her's, on their way home, and in their charge I placed her. That was three months ago, and yesterday I received Arnold's letter telling me they were married. To think that the whisper which brought comfort to her, should so nearly have been fatal to my own happiness!"

Florence's response is a blush of shame at having ever doubted him.

"And do you remember," he continues, "now that we are on the subject of reminiscences, at dinner that day, the day Sir Griffith made you draw your fate, as you called it, from the cup, and which turned out to be the masquerade—do you remember expressing your horror at the thought of being united to a man with the stain of blood on his soul?   Ah, how your remark sunk like lead into my heart."

"Did you think I could not love you if others thought you guilty? Love is a powerful teacher, Guy, and it has taught me the force of this:

"The ruling passion, be it what it will,
.The ruling passion conquers reason still."

Had you really spilled blood, even by accident, and had we met afterward for the first time, I knowing it, could not have loved you; I would not have allowed myself to do so.   But once you had found your way to my heart, you might have committed any crime, and if you were but true to me, I fear you would still have been my own, own love."

Guy's only answer is a passionate embrace.

"You really love me then—now and for all time?" he asks.

"It has always made me sad to hear people say that affection dies after marriage.   I don't believe that it does.   Do you, Guy?" and she looks up at him with serious eyes.

Earnestly, he answers:

"No, darling; I do not.   An unhappy wedded life is the result of a hasty marriage between those who are utterly uncongenial in tastes and sentiments, and who make the discovery of their unfitness for each other only when the honeymoon is passed.   You and I know all of each other's faults and good qualities, and there are no unpleasant awakenings to look forward to, as to peculiarities of disposition and character, in the future.   I have no fear, Florence, that my love will ever grow cold.   May I hope for the same endurance from yours?"

She does not answer him in words, but nestling closer within his protecting arm, bows her head over the strong hand, which clasping hers, yields gently to her touch as she presses it fondly to her lips.

"That is the seal of obedience," he says, laughing softly. "Where now must you place those of love and honor?"   Shyly she puts up her arms, and drawing down his head to a level with her own, imprints a kiss upon his brow.

"Honor!" he exclaims.   "You are reversing the order of your vows."

As she hesitates to give the last token, he bends his head, and murmuring, "Love," takes it with his lips from hers.

"By Jove! found at last; I've been looking for you everywhere. What on earth are you doing, my dear?" says Jolliffe's voice behind me.

With a sudden consciousness of the unworthy part I have been playing, and eager that he shall **not** discover what has kept me so long absent from his side, I turn quickly to meet him. As I take his arm and lead him away, to the awakened **sense of** shame for what I have been doing is joined the thought which flashes through my mind: Would this scene ever have been enacted; would past events have followed in succession as they have; in short—would this tale ever have been told, had no unseen observer stood and listened thus—

BEHIND THE ARRAS?